W9-AVK-428

THE STRANGER INSIDE

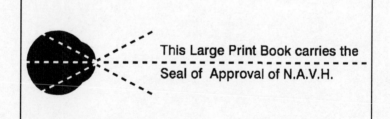

This Large Print Book carries the
Seal of Approval of N.A.V.H.

THE STRANGER INSIDE

LISA UNGER

WHEELER PUBLISHING
A part of Gale, a Cengage Company

Farmington Hills, Mich • San Francisco • New York • Waterville, Maine
Meriden, Conn • Mason, Ohio • Chicago

GALE
A Cengage Company

Wheeler Publishing Large Print Hardcover.
The text of this Large Print edition is unabridged.
Other aspects of the book may vary from the original edition.
Set in 16 pt. Plantin.

LIBRARY OF CONGRESS CIP DATA ON FILE.
CATALOGUING IN PUBLICATION FOR THIS BOOK
IS AVAILABLE FROM THE LIBRARY OF CONGRESS

ISBN-13: 978-1-4328-7052-2 (hardcover alk. paper)

Published in 2019 by arrangement with Harlequin Books S.A.

Printed in Mexico
1 2 3 4 5 6 7 23 22 21 20 19

In loving memory of
my wonderful grandmother
Millie Miscione
and my magnificent,
dear agent and friend
Elaine Markson

For what is evil but good tortured by its own hunger and thirst?

Kahlil Gibran, *The Prophet*

LAST NIGHT

I wait because I have nothing but time.

From the quiet, dim interior of my car, I watch the quiet neighborhood, settle into the upholstery. Autumn. Leaves lofting on cool air. Tacky, ghoulish Halloween decorations adorning stoops and lawns, hanging from trees — skeletons, and jack-o'-lanterns, witches on brooms. It's a school night, so no kids playing flashlight tag, no pickup soccer match in the street. Maybe kids don't even do that anymore. That's what I understand, anyway. That they're all iPad-addicted couch potatoes now. It's the new frontier of parenting. But you'll know better about this than I'm likely to.

Younger families live on this block. SUVs are hastily parked. Basketball hoops tilt in driveways; bikes twist on the lawn. Recycling cans wait patiently at the curb on Wednesday, garbage on Friday. Tonight, there's a game on. I see it playing on big screen televisions in three different open-plan living rooms.

But the house I'm watching is dark. A beautiful silver Benz that's about to be repossessed sits in the driveway. It's one of those cars — the kind that people dream about, an aspirational car, the kind you get *when* . . . But it certainly hasn't brought its owner any happiness. The guy I'm watching — he's depressed. I can see it in his slouch as he comes and goes, in the haunted circles that have settled around his eyes.

I can't muster any compassion for him. And I know that *you* aren't shedding any tears. In fact, I'm willing to bet that you've spent at least as much time thinking about him as I have — even though, of course, you have other things on your mind now.

An older man walks his dog, a white puff of a thing on a slender leash. Not a dog at all really, more like an extra-large guinea pig. I sink a little deeper in my seat, then stay stone-still. I haven't seen this man on this street before, and I've been here most nights for a while. He's out of his routine, I guess, maybe decided to take a new route tonight. I'm not too worried, though. My car — a beige Toyota Corolla — is utterly forgettable, practically invisible in its commonness; the windows tinted (but not too dark). If he doesn't see me, a lone person slouched in the driver's seat and clearly up to no good, he won't even notice it.

I'm in luck. He's squinting at the screen on his smartphone. He's older, not fluent with it. So it takes all of his concentration. That device is the best thing that ever happened to people who want to be invisible. He walks right by, oblivious to the car, to me, to his surroundings. Even his dog is distracted, incurious, nose to the pavement. Sniff, sniff, sniff. Finally, they're gone and I'm alone again.

Time passes. I breathe into the night.

One by one, windows go dark except for the odd light here and there. There's an insomniac in 704, a nurse who comes home after 3 a.m. on Wednesdays and Fridays to 708.

Just after 2 a.m., I slip from the car, close the door silently and shoulder my pack. I am a shadow shifting through the shadows of the trees, drifting, silent, up the edge of the house. I easily pick the lock on the side entrance — you can learn how to do anything on YouTube these days — and enter the house through the unlocked interior door. From the garage into the laundry room. From the laundry room into the kitchen — a typical suburban layout. I stand

11

inside for a moment, listening.

I can still hear it, you know, the sound of her father's voice.

I am willing to bet that you hear it, too. Maybe in those quiet moments, when you lie in bed at night, the wail of total despair comes back like a haunting. I imagine that your mind drifts back to that courtroom. Your face pulled tight with that helpless mingle of anger and sorrow, nostrils flaring just slightly. I was right there with you even though you didn't know it. Or maybe you did. Sometimes I wonder if you know how close I am. If you sense me.

When the verdict was delivered, there was a moment, remember? A tiny sliver of time where the information moved through synapses and neurons, a heartbeat. In that breath, I watched her mother drain of what little energy and color remained in her too-thin body. I watched her father buckle over, her brother dip his head into his hands. The unforgiving light of the courtroom grew brighter somehow, an ugly white sizzle. And then the room exploded in a wave of sound that contained all the notes of despair, disbelief, rage. I'd been there before, in the presence of injustice, as have you. You know how it wafts like smoke from the black spaces beneath tables and chairs. It rises up, tall and menacing. *I was always here,* it seems to say as it looms over you, towering, victorious. It brings you to your knees. In the presence of nothing else do you feel smaller or more powerless.

When we're young, we're naive enough to believe. We're raised on the comic-book ideal of good vanquishing evil. We believe that white magic is stronger than black. That criminals are punished, and justice is always served. Even when it seems that evil might triumph — no. In the final moment, a cosmic force does the reckoning for good, one way or another. We want to believe that.

But it's not so. Not always. Sometimes justice needs a little push.

I make a quick loop through the house to assure myself that everything is as it was the last time I was here. The decor is Target, IKEA chic, white and dove gray, with bold accent patterns. There are lots of those picture collages with words like LOVE and DREAM and FAMILY: her parents — smiling and benevolent; her wedding photos — gauzy, a fairy-tale dream; a gaggle of gap-toothed nieces and nephews; girls' night out, toasting with pink drinks in martini glasses. Throw pillows and soft blankets, knickknacks, decorative pieces of driftwood are artfully arranged. She was house-proud, the woman who lived here once. She liked things pretty and comfortable. Now, surfaces are covered with dust. Her home, it smells like garbage.

As I finish my tour, I feel a twist of sadness for her. Here's someone who did everything right. She followed all the rules, went to college, worked in public relations, got married, got pregnant. Pretty, and, by all accounts, sweet and kind. And look. Her cute house, her little dreams, her innocent life, empty, rotting. She deserved better.

Nothing I can do about that. But this is the next best thing.

I know what you're thinking. What anyone might think. Who am I to say that a man found innocent by a jury of his peers is guilty as sin? And even if he is, *who am I* to deliver justice?

It's true. I am no one. But this is how I *knew.*

When Laney Markham went missing, I immediately suspected that it was her oh-so-handsome husband. Because let's get real: the incident of stranger crime is a statistical anomaly. (We both have a thing or two to add to that conversation, don't we? But I'm sure you'd agree that statistically it's true.) The idea of the *other,* the stranger, the destroyer who breaks into your home and kills your family, or takes your child? It does happen. But not as often as a man kills his wife. Or a father rapes his daughter. Or an uncle molests his niece. Those things don't always make the news. Why? Because it's *not* news; that's the everyday horror show of normal life.

So there's that. The it's-always-the-husband thing. But what sealed it for me was those national morning show appearances. He did the circuit, ostensibly to plead for the lovely Laney's safe return. Tall, with movie-star good looks, he was a natural. And those morning show hosts, they lapped it up. Laney? She was a beauty, too. One of those luscious pregnant girls — even prettier with her little baby belly, glowing skin and silky, hormone-rich hair. If the Markhams had been less good-looking, this would have been less of a story. You know it's true.

Anyway, he gets on camera and starts to weep, and I mean *blubber.* Steve Markham stares right at the camera, tears streaming down his face and he begs for whoever took his wife and unborn child to just bring them home. Quite a performance.

Except.

Men don't cry like that. Men, when they are overcome by emotion to the degree that they lose control and start to weep, they cover their faces. Crying is a disobeying of every cultural message a man ever receives. To weep like a woman? It fills him with shame. So he covers his face. That's how I knew he killed his wife. Steve Markham was a sociopath. Those tears were as fake as they come.

You remember. I know you were thinking the same thing.

You might say that's not enough. I know you; you follow the rules — or, anyway, you have a kind of code. But we all know there was enough physical evidence to send the bastard to the electric chair. It was those lawyers with all their tricks — cast doubt on this, get that thrown out, confuse and mislead the slack-jawed jury with complicated cell phone evidence. This satellite says he was there at this time, couldn't have done it.

Still, I generally wait a year. Just to be sure. I watch and wait, do my research. At least a year, sometimes much, much longer, as you know. I choose very carefully. I think about it long and hard. Because it would suck to be wrong. I wouldn't, couldn't, justify that. It's a line I can't step over. Really. Because then — what am I?

Anyway, my old friend, I'm gratified to

report that the year since he was acquitted of his wife's murder has been very bad for Steve Markham. He lost his job. All his friends. His lover-slash-alibi Tami — you remember her, right? The whole case hung on that mousy blonde from Hoboken. Well, she broke up with him. I'm sure you know all this. If I know you, you're keeping tabs, too.

You probably didn't know that for a while he hung around Tami's place, stalking. I thought we were going to have a problem, that I'd have to act before I was ready. But Steve is nothing else if not a smart guy. Probably figured it wouldn't look *great* if his girlfriend turned up dead less than a year after his wife's body was found in a shallow grave, just miles from her own home, she and her unborn child killed by multiple stab wounds with a six-inch serrated blade (from her own kitchen). He finally stopped following Tami, the one that got away.

He's about to lose the house. Last month, the lights went out. The pool where they think he killed his wife has turned green, water thick now with algae. Sure, he had his book deal. He did the talk show circuit, this time playing the innocent man, wrongly accused, on a tireless hunt for his wife's killer.

He'd been unfaithful, he admitted, grim and remorseful. He was sorry. So sorry. More crocodile tears.

He burned through the advance money fast. It wasn't *that* much. Between agent commission, taxes, it was no windfall. He might have made it last. But people don't get it. Money, if you don't protect it, is flammable. It goes up in flames and floats away like ash. The IRS is after him now. The system. Maybe it does have its ways of getting you, even if you slip through its cracks at first.

I make no attempt to be quiet as I unpack my bag. I drape a plastic tarp over the couch, lay another one in front of the door where he will enter the room when he hears me. I lay things out. The duct tape. The hunting knife. There's a gun I carry in a shoulder holster, the sleek, light Beretta PX4 Compact Carry with a handy Ameri-Glo night sight and Talon grip. It's only meant to inspire cooperation. To have to use it will represent a failure of planning on my part. But there are always variables for which you can't account.

By the time he rouses from sleep and moves cautiously into the front room, I am sitting in one of the cheap wingback chairs by the window. He is not armed. I know

18

there is no weapon in this house. There was a baseball bat under the bed. Maybe he thought that someday Laney's brother or her father would come for him. But the baseball bat is gone now. In the trunk of my very forgettable car, in fact.

"Hello, Steve," I say quietly and watch him jump back. "Have a seat."

"Who are you?"

I work the Cerakote slide that puts a bullet into the chamber and watch him freeze. It's a sound a man recognizes even if he's never had a gun pulled on him before.

"On the couch."

The plastic tarp crinkles beneath his weight and he starts to cry again. This time? It's real.

"Please." His voice is small with fear and regret.

But do I also hear relief?

We all believe that story, that cheaters never win, and justice will be done. Even the bad guys believe it.

Isn't that right, my old friend?

ONE

It was just a peep, the tiniest little chirp. But Rain's eyes flew open and she lay there in the dim morning, listening. She could tell by the light outside the window, by the bubbling of nausea in her stomach that it was *way* too early. Hours before the alarm would go off.

Now a groan, just a light one.

Go back to sleep, she pleaded silently. She pushed her head deeper into the pillows, tugged at the covers. *Please, baby.*

Now a hiccup, almost a cry.

"Leave her." Greg, groggy, draped a heavy arm over her middle, pulled her in. "She'll go back."

No. She wouldn't go back. Rain could already tell. Outside her window, the manic chirping of birds. They'd nested in the oak on their lawn, two starlings that chattered all day, starting at dawn. It was cute, a lovely detail of their domestic life. Until it wasn't.

Now two quick little sounds from the baby monitor on the bedside table. "Eh — Eh."

She pushed herself up, head full of cotton, stomach churning. She'd been up with the baby just two hours earlier, feeding. Growth spurt.

Greg stirred. "I'll get her."

"No." She put a hand on his shoulder. "Get some more sleep before work."

Greg sighed, pulled those blissfully soft covers tight around him.

Over the monitor, she heard the baby sigh, too. Then the soft, even sound of Lily's breath like ocean waves. Rain reached for the monitor and turned on the screen. A perfect cherub floated on a cloud next to a white stuffed bear. A little burrito in her loose fleece swaddle. A wild head of red hair. But no, it wasn't red — it was white and gold, auburn lowlights and orange highlights. It was fairy princess hair. And her eyes weren't blue, they were facets of sapphire and sky, sea green.

Her baby was an angel, wasn't she? Beautiful and sweet beyond expression. *Get ready for the biggest love of your life,* Andrew, her executive producer, had gushed when she'd announced her pregnancy. He'd teared up a little, gazing at the picture of his twin boys, then ten. And he was right, of course. That love, it changed her — just like everyone said it would. In myriad ways.

But it was also obvious to Rain that her child was trying to kill her. Slowly. With an adorable, gurgling, two-tooth smile.

Death by sleep deprivation. No mercy.

She sank back into bed, closed her eyes. But her brain — as manic and chirpy as her starling neighbors — would not stop chattering.

Finally, she put on her robe and moved quietly down the stairs. Might as well use the time and mill some organic baby food and store it in those perfect little blue-lidded glass jars. Apples. Sweet potatoes. Broccoli. Five a.m., and she had pots boiling on the stove.

She watched them bubble as she drank her coffee. Caffeine. Thank god. She would not have survived the last thirteen months without it. She'd given it up when she was pregnant, but as soon as Lilian Rae made her entrance, Rain was back on the sauce.

She let the aroma wake her, let the magic elixir work its way through her body. The body that was just starting to feel like hers again, now that she was trying to wean the baby — at the not-so-subtle behest of her husband. Greg had walked in while she was nursing Lily to sleep earlier that week.

(Yeah, yeah. She knew you weren't supposed to nurse your baby to sleep. But come *on*. What other benefit was there in being a human Binky?)

He'd tenderly touched Lily's silky hair, then gazed at Rain with an odd smile.

"How much longer?" he'd whispered. It was date night. He'd brought home dinner, a bottle of wine.

"Five minutes?"

"No," he said. "I mean how much longer are you going to nurse her?"

She'd tried not to let her body tense with annoyance, measured her breathing. Mommy gets upset, baby gets upset. That simple.

"I don't know," she'd said tightly.

It was one of those loaded moments, air simmering with all the things each of them wanted to say but didn't. Instead, he'd pressed his mouth into a line — *he* claimed that expression meant frustration, *she* read it as disapproval — gave a quick nod, left the room. After some time seething, she'd unlatched the baby, placed her gently in the crib.

How much longer? she'd thought. *What kind of question is that?*

"I want you back," he'd said at the table, gentle. He touched her hand. He wasn't a

24

jerk, was he? One of those clueless men who thought her body existed for his pleasure only. "We said six months."

"I want me back, too," she admitted.

She wanted to nurse Lily, loved the closeness of it, those soothing quiet moments with her baby. She wanted her body back, wanted to feel sexy again. It seemed everything about motherhood was this complicated twist of emotion, a delicate balance of holding on and letting go.

And, seriously, those nursing bras? Some of them were cute, but for the most part they looked like pieces of equipment rather than lingerie. She hadn't felt sexy in ages. How could you be sexy, hot, erotic when you didn't even own yourself?

"So," he'd said at dinner that night. "Can we get on a plan?"

Thanks to a Google search — how to wean your baby! — she was on a plan. The morning and midday feedings were solid food now. Which meant she could have a glass of wine at night and not have to "pump and dump" (another sexy bit of breastfeeding terminology). The pediatrician said so. Anyway, she'd vowed never to put that pump back on her breast again. God, how much more like a cow could a thing make you feel?

She could already feel that she was producing less milk. Her breasts were smaller, more familiar. She'd bought some new lingerie, lacy, pretty, no cup clasps in sight. Sexy? She wasn't feeling it yet. But she was getting there.

She drained the vegetables, milled them into mush, then filled the little jars.

Very sexy.

She liked the way they looked with their cheerful blue tops lined up in the fridge, which was stocked and tidy. Everything in order, everything sorted. There was a satisfaction in it. She ran the house with a frugal, high-end, minimalist zeal. She did the grocery shopping, cooking and day-to-day cleaning. The cleaning lady came once every other week to do the big stuff. She did a load of laundry every day. The dry cleaning, mainly Greg's work clothes, got picked up on Tuesdays and Thursdays. She ran the house the way she used to do her job — with accuracy and efficiency.

She was only half listening to the news broadcasting from her phone as she wiped down the quartz countertop, though it was already clean. The news was bad, as usual. She tried not to get hooked in as she managed the fresh tulips that dipped from their glass vase, pulling a wilting one, adding more water. On the distressed gray cabinet, she spied a sticky handprint. She wiped it clean. The sun was streaming through the big windows now. She put some of Lily's toys in the wicker basket, rearranged the fluffy white throw on the cozy sectional where she and Greg spent most of their time now that they were parents — who knew you could watch so much television.

"— Markham, tried and acquitted for the violent murder of his pregnant wife, Laney Markham, was found dead in his home early this morning."

The words stopped her cold, a board book clutched in her hand. She moved over to her phone, turned up the volume, something other than caffeine pulsing through her system.

The voice was familiar, and not just because Rain listened to this National News Radio broadcast every day, but because the woman speaking was her closest friend and former colleague. And the news show was the one Rain used to write, edit and produce.

"Markham was found not guilty last year in the stabbing death of his wife. His defense leaned heavily on cell phone records that confirmed his alibi that at the time of his wife's murder, he was out of state with a woman who turned out to be his lover.

"Police are investigating. This is Gillian Murray reporting, National News Radio."

She could almost hear the lick of glee in her friend's voice. The two of them had covered the story together for over a year, were both crushed when Markham had been acquitted. No one else had ever been charged with Laney Markham's murder, and the murder of her unborn child.

It had stayed with them both, the terrible injustice of it nagging at them. They looked on with impotent rage as the machine took over — Markham's inevitable book release, the talk show circuit where he pretended to be tirelessly looking for his wife's killer. They had to see his face nearly every day, the mask of the wrongly accused man so fake, so painted on, Rain couldn't see how anyone might believe it.

I used to believe in justice, Gillian said one night over too many drinks. *I don't anymore. Bad people win. They win all the time.*

Rain had tried to cheer her up, but how could she? Her friend was right.

She snapped off the broadcast, stared at the jars of baby food. The room swirled around her the way it used to, when a story got its teeth in her.

Someone killed Steve Markham. He got

away with murder, until he didn't. A million questions started to take form. Who, what, when, where? Why? It touched another nerve, too.

Greg came down the stairs, dressed in his workout clothes, holding a garment bag. He was watching her. From the lines of worry etched in his forehead, she could tell he already knew.

"You heard about Steve Markham?" she asked.

"Just got the news update on my phone," he said, rubbing at the crown of his head. He put the garment bag on the couch, tried for a smile. "You and Gillian should get together and have a toast. Markham finally got what he deserved."

"Who do you think did it?" she asked.

"You would know better than I do," he said. His voice was gravelly, soft. She'd never heard him raise it, in all their years together. "The brother. The father. The guy had no shortage of enemies."

"Lots of people make threats," she said. "It's another thing altogether to take someone's life. Even someone who deserves it."

She poured him a cup of coffee from the French press, handed him an apple. This was his preworkout breakfast. He'd put on weight during her pregnancy. But he'd lost it all. In fact, he was in better shape now than he had been when they were first dating, the muscles on his arms strong and defined, his body lean. She could not say the same for herself. She tried to squeeze herself into her old jeans the other day and wound up lying on the bed, crying. Had she *ever* fit into them? It seemed impossible.

"What are you thinking?" he asked. He wrapped her up, kissed her on the forehead. "What's going on in that big brain of yours?"

"It's just — odd," she said. "A year later. Someone kills him."

He moved away, took a bite of his apple, a sip of his coffee.

"It's a good day when people get what they deserve. Isn't it?" he said, moving toward the door. "One less psycho in the world."

Why didn't it feel like that? She was aware of a hollow pit in her stomach.

"I'm going to get a workout before I head in," he said.

Oh, how nice for you, she thought but kept it to herself.

"Okay," she said instead. "Do you think you'll be back in time for me to work out tonight?"

There was a bit of an edge to all of it. Who

stayed home? Who worked? Who had time to be with friends and indulge in hobbies? They both worked at giving each other time.

"I'll try, honey," he said. "But you know how it is, right? You can't always just leave."

Greg was the producer for the local television news program. Local news.

"Right," she said. "There might be some breaking story about the sheep-shearing festival this weekend."

He gave her a look. "Don't be a news snob, babe. We can't all cover major cases for the National News Radio, can we?"

He came back to where she stood in the kitchen, pulled her in again, this time for a kiss on the mouth.

She felt herself smile, light up a little. That's one of the things she first loved about him, that he didn't have the huge, hyper-inflated ego of the other men she met in news. She could tease him, and he didn't sulk. It didn't always work in reverse, she'd be the first to admit.

"That was nice last night," he said. "You look good, Rain. You *feel* good."

"So do you," she said. His lips on her neck, his hand on her back.

"I'll get home," he whispered. "I promise."

He downed his coffee, then moved toward the door.

31

She followed him out to the car. Autumn crisp and cool on the air. A stiff wind bent the branches; she pulled her robe tight around her. Yes, she was the woman who went out into the driveway in her pajamas. So what?

Greg put his bag in the back, walked over to her and rested his hands on her shoulders. The shine of his deep brown eyes, the small scar on his chin, the wild brown hair that he couldn't quite tame unless he cropped it short. She saw worry in the lines on his forehead, in the wiggle of his eyebrows.

"Don't let this pull you under again, okay?"

She didn't have to ask him what he meant. The Markham case. It had shaken her, rattled them. That person she was when a story was under her skin — she wasn't a good wife, a good friend. In fact, she wasn't good for anything except the story she wanted to tell.

That was then — another life, another woman. She had Lily now; she was a mother. There wasn't room for both parts of herself. She was smart enough to know it.

Another kiss — soft and familiar, the scent of him so comforting — then he climbed into their sensible hybrid SUV and drove off. She watched him, his words echoing in her head.

Got what he deserved.

Her pulse raced a little, that early-morning nausea came back. She wanted to call Gillian but knew she wouldn't be able to talk for a while yet.

As she stepped back into the foyer, Lily started crying. Game on.

But while Lily ate her oatmeal, secure in her high chair, Rain retrieved her laptop. She half expected the lid to groan like the door on an abandoned house, maybe find some cobwebs covering the keyboard. It had been a long time since she thought about work.

She opened the files she'd kept from the Markham case, and started rereading her old notes, sifting through the digital images, the saved internet links.

She used to dream about Steve Markham, and in her dreams, he had the cold yellow eyes of a wolf. They often, in her dreams, shared a meal across a long table, lined with plates of rotting food — overripe fruit split open, red, spilling innards and seeds on the white cloth, decomposing meat buzzing with flies, wilting greens turning to slime.

He'd be laughing, teeth sharp. And though she wanted to run, she'd be lashed to her seat, staring, mesmerized by his hideous grin.

When he'd been acquitted, she fantasized about killing him herself.

But the rage passed, left a kind of emptiness in its wake. A terrible fatigue of the mind and the spirit.

She was remembering all of this when Lily tossed her sippy cup onto the table in front of the laptop.

"Ma! Ma!" Lily yelled happily, looking very pleased with herself.

Rain gazed over the computer at her daughter, apple cheeks and tangle of hair, face and bib painted with oatmeal.

"You're right, bunny," she said, snapping the lid on her laptop closed and lifting the pink cup. "Let it go."

Two

But she couldn't let it go.

That was always her problem.

She could never just let things go.

That's what made her a good reporter, and kind of shitty at everything else. A dog with a bone, in fact, according to her husband. She held grudges, which every shrink and life coach would tell you was bad for your marriage, your life. She did not meditate. She was not Zen, by any means. She did not go with the flow. She held on. Dug in deep.

Rain strapped Lily into the jogging stroller — because there was no way Greg was going to get home in time for her to go to the gym, however pure his intentions. Her fatigue from the too-early morning wake-up had lifted a little (thank you, three cups of coffee). Lily kicked her legs and waved her chubby arms with joy, cooing happily, resplendent in rainbow leggings and pink fleece.

At the end of the driveway, Rain surveyed the tree-lined street, as was her habit.

She looked for unfamiliar parked cars, strange lone figures loitering. Even here — where the sidewalk was always empty of strangers, where precious clapboard houses painted in muted grays and blues, eggshell or soft maroon, nestled in perfectly manicured lawns, where it seemed not even weeds were allowed to grow — she watched for him.

But no. Today there was just the neighbor's mottled tabby delicately licking her paw on the stoop. Tasteful Halloween decorations hung on doors, a cornucopia, a smiley witch with glittery yarn for hair. Collections of painted jack-o'-lanterns on wooden porch steps. Nothing too creepy or scary, of course. Peaceful. Safe. Their street was a picture postcard of suburban bliss, the place where nothing bad ever happened. Until it did.

Then she was doing that thing she did where she took a peaceful scene and imagined it descending into chaos — a gang of thugs loping up the street smashing the windows of expensive cars, an earthquake splitting the street, a raging wildfire turning homes into ashy ruin. Or, her personal go-to, a hulking form moving from the dappled shadows under the oak. A shadow, waiting to destroy the pretty life she'd built with Greg. Yes, around every corner could be your worst nightmare. She knew that, better than most.

"Stop it," she said to herself.

"Op it!" echoed Lily, giggling.

"Mommy's a little crazy," she told her daughter, who would no doubt figure it out for herself soon enough.

She put one earbud in, leaving the other to dangle so that she could hear the street noise and Lily. Listening to the news, she pushed them onto the sidewalk and started a light jog toward the running path. Dulcet voices droned about trade wars escalating, a rocket headed for Mars, fires burning out of control in California, the suicide of a beloved celebrity chef. Was the world really so dark? Shouldn't there be a channel just for good news?

She tuned out a bit, listening instead to the sound of her own breath, eyes vigilant to their surroundings. She was hoping for more news on the Markham case when Gillian called.

"You heard," said her old friend by way of greeting. That tone, taut with excitement, it stoked the fire in Rain.

"I heard *you* this morning," she said. "What happened?"

"I don't have all the details, but I called Chris."

Christopher Wright, lead detective on the Markham case — and Gillian's ex. Hot, hot, hot. But distant, too into the work. Fuckable, but not datable. Which, you know, could be okay. But it wasn't okay for Gillian. She wanted the whole thing — the wedding, the baby, the house. Chris — he wasn't that guy.

"He said — off the record — that it was *bizarre.*" Gillian leaned on the word.

"Oh?" Rain stopped at the light, kept jogging in place.

One of her neighbors drove by. Mitzi, the older lady from across the street, waved and smiled. Rain waved back. Mitzi had offered to do some babysitting. Now that Lily was older, Rain was considering it. Just an hour or two every other day so that she could get back into a real workout routine, think about maybe doing some freelancing. Money was tight-ish. But the real truth was, she missed working. She hadn't admitted this to anyone yet.

"Something like this?" Gillian said. "You've gotta assume it's Laney's brother or her dad, finally making good on the threats they delivered in the courtroom. That's the first thing you think. You expect a big mess. Overkill. Right?"

"Right."

There it was. That tingle, that tension. In the business, they call it the belly of fire. That overwhelming urge to know, to get the story, to find the truth. She crossed the street, moved onto the path that circled the park. Of course, it was more than that for Rain.

"Wrong," said Gillian. "Chris wouldn't tell me much — very tight-lipped. He just said that the scene was 'organized.' He said, and I quote, 'It was obviously planned and executed cleanly.'"

"What does that mean?"

"That's all he'd tell me. Police are holding a press conference later today."

Frustration. Nothing worse than the delay of information.

"Keep me in the loop." But she wasn't in the loop. She was so far out of it that she didn't even exist anymore. Which, a year ago, was what she wanted. Wasn't it?

"Of course," Gillian said. Then a sigh. "Wish you were here."

"Me, too," she said. She meant it. And she didn't. Complicated. Everything was so goddamn complicated.

"How's our girl?" Gillian asked.

Gillian was the date-night sitter. Once a month or so, she came in from the city, stayed with Lily while Greg and Rain went out. Gillian slept in the guest room, and spent the next day with Rain and Lily, while Greg slept in or played golf or whatever, or vegged out in front of a game on television. It was the rare win-win-win scenario.

"She's missing her auntie Gillian," said Rain.

There was that pause. The pause Rain was guilty of herself, when you're doing something else — checking your email, texting, surfing the web, whatever — and talking on the phone.

"Saturday, right?" Gillian said, plugging back in.

"Still good for you?"

"Wouldn't miss it."

"Bring details."

"Deal."

Rain circled the park a couple of times, thinking about what Gillian had said. The scene was organized. *Obviously planned and cleanly executed.* That *was* weird. Murder is a mess, especially a revenge killing. Rage usually isn't careful; it doesn't plan. It doesn't clean up after itself. Usually.

Something niggled at the back of her brain, like she should be remembering something she couldn't. But that was baby brain — sleep deprivation, hormones, nursing, constantly monitoring needs, plagued with worry, fear, overwhelmed by love, hours, days, months just disappearing. It was a fog you felt your way through.

Sweating, breathless, Rain found herself on the path that led to the playground, even though the last couple of times she stopped there after her run, she promised herself that she wouldn't go back. The other moms who gathered there — they talked about strollers and pediatricians, tummy time, swaddling, milling organic baby food, and colic. Some talked about their husbands, apparently clueless buffoons who'd impregnated them and then continued with life as it was before, who *still* thought they might get laid every now and then. They talked about their single friends who had *no idea.*

Rain didn't talk much — she listened. That was her gift, to keep her mouth shut and hear what other people were saying. That was the way of the news writer — observe, ask, listen, report. But she often left the group feeling anxious, eager to get home.

Still, Rain pulled the stroller up to one of

the picnic tables as if drawn to the communal nature of the gathering in spite of herself. She gave Lily her sippy cup and retrieved her own water bottle. She put some Cheerios in the stroller tray — which she'd just cleaned, thank you very much. She'd gotten a look last time from one of the more tightly wound mommies in the playground group — what was her name? Gretchen. *Aren't you worried about germs?* she'd gasped. She'd put her pretty, conspicuously ringed, gel-manicured hand to her chest in a gesture of dismay, her face a caricature of concern. Rain had fought back the unreasonable urge to punch her.

No. Rain was *not* worried about germs. She was a career news writer and producer, among other things. She was worried about lots and lots of things — North Korea, racism, the long-term fate of the #MeToo movement, the sex slave trade, global warming, letting go accidentally of that jogging stroller and watching it career into traffic. And other things — *lots* of things imagined in vivid detail, Technicolor detail so bright that it could take her breath away. They had a state-of-the-art security system installed in their house, even though she knew — she *knew* — that the incident of stranger crime against children, home invasion and abduction was a statistical anomaly. She had very personal reasons for wanting that level of security. But, no, she was no germophobe. Was that a word?

Did you know, Rain answered Gretchen — a bit snippily, *that normal exposure to germs helps your child's immune system develop?*

Emmy, one of the other playground mommies, had chimed in with a grave nod: *Rain was a reporter. She worked for National Radio News.* Gretchen had pretended to be distracted by her phone, unimpressed. *Oh, really,* Gretchen said absently, staring off at the playground. When *was that?*

Today, some of the mommies with older children gathered around the playground. Toddlers tended to hang out in the sandbox. Lily was *just* walking, more like cruising, so Rain didn't always take her out of the stroller unless she got restless. She pushed over to the group, parked the stroller with the rest.

"How was your run?" sang Gretchen, casting her an unreadable look.

Funny how such an innocent question could have so many layers. Gretchen looked at her with a smile. Tight-bodied, tiny, with bright green eyes, a blond pixie cut, Gretchen had something icy beneath the surface, something sharp. Somehow Rain felt acutely

43

aware of the size of her own thighs, the sweat on her shirt, her forehead. Gretchen looked positively dewy, her white shirt crisp, her skinny, skinny jeans faded perfectly. And that ring. Holy Christ. How many carats was that?

"You *jogged* here? Good for you," said Emmy.

Emmy, mom to a six-month-old girl named Sage, used to work in book publishing, an editor who'd had a couple of best-selling authors to her credit. She still worked freelance from home.

Emmy's thick auburn hair was pulled up into a high ponytail, eyes shining with intelligence. "I haven't worked out in months. My boobs are huge."

"Stop it. You're gorgeous and you know it," said Rain. She *was* — even in sweats, unshowered, a little spit-up on her hoodie. Her skin was peaches-and-cream perfect, hair shiny with health. When her little one started to cry, Emmy lifted the baby from her pram, then proceeded to whip her breast out right there in front of everyone.

Gretchen turned away, clearly embarrassed.

"Oh, what, you've never seen a boob before?" said Emmy. Her face lit up with mischievous glee.

44

"The *kids*," said Gretchen.

"Oh, *they've* never seen one before?"

Emmy's laugh was mellifluous, contagious, and Rain laughed, too.

"I'm done with that little shawl thing," said Emmy. "I'm just whipping it out wherever now. You don't like it? Look the other way."

"I couldn't nurse," said Gretchen stiffly. "I have inverted nipples."

"Inverted nipples? Ouch," said Beck, joining the group.

Beck was the youngest mommy. Married to her high school sweetheart, with two toddlers (Tyler, two; Jessa, three and a half) at twenty-six, she had another one on the way. Rain thought of her as a career mom. The rest of them did something else first, or wanted to be something else, too. If Beck wanted anything else, she hadn't mentioned it.

"Did you hear about that guy? The one who killed his wife last year?" asked Emmy. "Markham?"

Gretchen shook her head in distaste. "We don't watch the news at home. Too *stressful.*"

"Someone killed him," said Beck, voice low. Then, "About time."

Lily started to fuss. Gretchen moved over

quickly as if the baby was hers, lifting her from the stroller with a quick glance to Rain for permission. Rain nodded easily. It was funny, how natural certain things were with other moms — maybe it's what kept her coming back to the group. There was something communal about the gathering, comforting. Someone always had wipes, or Cheerios, or was willing to bandage a knee, had a soothing word. Fraught in some ways, with a weird undercurrent of competitiveness, but definitely communal.

Lily sat contentedly chewing on her tiny hand, happy on Gretchen's hip. Gretchen cooed and swayed, smelled Lily's baby hair. Lily was hungry. Rain's breasts were engorged. She wasn't about to whip it out like Emmy. She was not there.

"It was probably the father," said Emmy. "Remember him at the trial? I've never seen anyone so heartbroken."

Rain had *been* there. She hadn't *watched* the trial on television like the rest of the country. She'd been in the courtroom. Gillian reporting, Rain writing and producing. The sound, no, the *pitch,* of his voice stayed with her — the rage, the pain. It was primal. A father who lost his daughter, powerless to bring justice. His hoarse screaming connected with every nerve ending in her body.

Rain had just learned she was pregnant a few weeks earlier; she was only beginning to glimpse what it was to be a parent. She just had the slightest flicker of what it might mean to have to protect another person. And fail.

"I would have killed him on the spot," said Emmy. "With my bare hands."

Rain stayed silent, though that ache was almost unbearable. She needed to get home, put Lily down for her nap and get in front of her computer. She still knew people. She could make some calls. It was her story.

"Or the brother," said Beck. "He said it on the courtroom steps, right? When you least expect it, we're coming for you."

It was organized, Rain almost chimed in. It wasn't a rage killing.

But she didn't say anything. Because.

Because, she reminded herself, she wasn't in news anymore. She was in — diapers and wipes, Cheerios and sippy cups. What she did now was Lily. What she used to do was ancient history; it was pathetic to cling to what you used to be, wasn't it?

She lifted Lily from Gretchen's arms and sat beside Emmy. She took the little shawl from her pocket, put it on and started to nurse. She felt Lily latch on. There was a blessed release, a flood of milk and oxytocin. No one ever told you that your body would ache when your baby was hungry, that your breasts might leak when she cried, about that intense physical bond.

"Good for you, girl," said Emmy.

Gretchen folded her arms and turned away. Rain wanted to tell the other woman that it was no big deal that she didn't or couldn't nurse, that it was just another thing they held out there for you. A brass ring that you might or might not be able to reach. Something they wanted you to try for, and feel like shit if you couldn't grab. Honestly, if it hadn't been easy for Rain, maybe she wouldn't have done it either. So basically, she nursed because it involved the least amount of work for her. She stayed home because — well, for a hundred reasons. Only one of which was crystal clear a year later with some of that hormonal fog finally clearing — Lily Rae.

"My brother-in-law is a cop over in Jessup, where the Markhams lived," said Beck. "He said that the Feds came in this morning and took the scene from the local police."

Alarms jangled in her head. *The Feds. Why?*

"Oh?" she said with faux nonchalance, turning to Beck.

But Beck's phone rang, and she turned

away, lifting a finger and casting her an apologetic look for the interruption.

Rain lifted her milk-drunk baby and put her into the stroller.

"Gotta run," she said, strapping Lily in.

It was a Bumbleride, an insanely expensive gift with a message from her father.

Keep moving, kid, read the card. *Don't let this slow you down.*

Rain had only seen her father a couple of times since the baby was born. She needed to check in with him, let him spend some time with Lily; she just didn't have the energy after their last visit — when she'd gotten the clear message that *he* certainly believed that she had let the baby slow her down, that her career — and therefore her life — had come to a grinding halt. He didn't seem to get that there was more to life than work.

"Have a good one, honey." Gretchen gave her a weird look, something oddly victorious.

Rain was halfway home before she realized that she was still wearing her nursing bib (thank god!) and hadn't put her breast back in her shirt. Christ. *Really?* She hastily refastened herself. When she glanced in the stroller, she saw that Lily had drifted off. She hustled home, praying she could get

49

back and get an hour online and on the phone before Lily woke up.

THREE

Greeted by the hush of her tidy house, Rain parked the stroller in the foyer. Lily was sound asleep, head lolling to the side. With another cup of coffee from the carafe, Rain hustled upstairs to the home office.

The keyboard, the screen in front of her, it was her instrument — the right strokes, the right words, she could piece together a symphony of information. She searched the web, scanning the various news sites, a couple of the crime blogs she liked. The Markham story was in circulation, the same few sentences — that Markham, tried and acquitted for the murder of his wife, was found dead in his home early this morning. But there obviously weren't enough details yet to run a full feature on any of the big networks or major newspapers. She poked around on local news sites — no witnesses, no leads, no suspects at this time.

Or the Feds were withholding information

from the media.

There should have been more — a lot more. Images of news vans gathering around the Markham house, interviews with family members, neighbors.

Maybe Markham killed himself, she thought. That was less of a story. An unsatisfyingly abrupt ending to a sad, unjust tale, and the kind of conclusion for which people usually had little sympathy or interest. But it would have been reported. Suicide. End of story.

She picked up her phone, dialed a number she knew by heart and waited.

"Wright."

"Hey."

"Rain Winter," he said. He had a way of saying her name that made it sound like song. "Long time."

She and Christopher had been friends — sort of friends — since before he and Gillian were a thing. (In fact, Rain had introduced them, and was a little sorry she had. He hadn't been good to Gillian, and Rain was still pissed about it.) Rain had been a young crime beat reporter at the city paper; she'd been working her first big story about a serial rapist. Chris was the lead detective, one of the few guys — inside the newsroom or out — who didn't treat her like a pet, didn't call her "kid," didn't wear that snide smirk that some older men wore when young women tried to do what was once upon a time a job held only by men. He never once told her that she was "too pretty to be writing about crime."

"I thought I'd see you last week at Gillian's birthday party," she said, trying to keep it light.

He issued a grunt. "Gillian doesn't want to see me," he said. "Even if she thinks she does."

Gillian's gathering had been a rare — only — solo night out for Rain, baby and hubby back at home. It wasn't exactly how she imagined it. She'd been nervous, checked the monitor and home security cameras about a hundred times to see Greg crashed on the couch, Lily sleeping peacefully in her crib. She'd spent most of the evening comforting her friend.

"Just like a man," Rain said. "To think he knows what a woman wants."

Silence. She was used to waiting for him to talk. He was king of the awkward pause. "Did you call to talk about Gillian?"

"Markham."

"Thought so."

"Well."

"I'm not your guy anymore," he said.

Street noise carried over the line, horns and voices, a distant siren. "Feds came in today. The scene is closed. Strict information control. The press conference has been moved to tomorrow, if they give one at all."

"Why?"

One of the burning questions, the one that always interested her the most. Who? What? When? Where? All important. But "Why?" In *news* it didn't matter so much.

But in *story* — *Story* with a capital *S* — it was heart and soul.

"What do you care?" he asked.

Lily stirred downstairs, the sound carrying up to Rain. Ticktock.

"I thought you were out," he said. "Home with the kid full-time."

She heard it, the weight of judgment. A little flame of anger lit inside her. Some people judged you for staying home. Others judged you for wanting to work even though you had taken on the all-sacred role of mother. Rain had never been overly concerned with what people thought. But even she felt the trap of it, how nothing was ever quite good enough. Was there always someone waiting to put you down?

"I'm producing a podcast," she said. Why did she say that? That was the furthest thing from her mind. Impulsive, reactionary.

That's what her dad always said about her. But he meant it as a compliment. "A crime podcast. You know — long-form journalism."

"Seriously?"

"Why not?"

"Exactly," he said. "That's what everyone says these days, *why not?* Anyone can do it."

"I've made my bones," she said easily. Ten years investigating, writing and producing news, she *had.* "Besides — these days — podcasts? That's the only *real* journalism left. Everything else is bought and paid for, beholden to advertisers and their agendas. It's called democracy, remember that old idea? Freedom of speech. Not speech controlled by whoever happens to be paying the bills."

She didn't realize she'd felt so passionately about this. She *didn't.* She just didn't like being marginalized.

"Most of it's crap."

"Most of everything is crap."

He issued a little chuckle, reminding her that he had a grim, serious face. A heavy, deeply lined brow and a searing, pin-you-to-the-wall kryptonite-green gaze. He had a cop voice, granite-cold and just as hard. But when he smiled or laughed, his whole face lit up like a kid on Christmas morning. She wished she was sitting across from him somewhere. It was so much easier to get what you wanted in person.

"You got me there," he said.

Rain walked to the top of the stairs. She could see Lily's chubby little legs, perfect pink toes kicking. Ticktock. Ticktock. Rain had left Lily's squishy book in reach, hoping it would buy a little time when Lily woke up. She heard it crinkle as the baby picked it up and made a happy coo. Score. She'd just earned herself about four minutes.

"Come on," she said. "You must have something."

He sighed into the phone. He just liked to argue for the sake of arguing. She could relate; a good verbal sparring session was one of the most satisfying encounters you could have with a man — especially when you won. And cops, even though they pretended otherwise, loved to talk — it was downright painful when they couldn't tell you what they knew.

"All I can say is that it wasn't a rage killing like you'd expect. It was organized, clean. Someone planned it."

She already knew that. "That's what you told Gillian."

"Yeah," he said. "And the Feds moved in

this morning, took over the investigation."

Both pieces of information she already had. He was holding back.

"What else?" she pushed.

She heard a car door slam on his end, footfalls. There were voices, another phone ringing. Lily was making noises downstairs, fishing for Rain.

"Okay, look," he said finally. "All I know is that they think it connects to another case they're working. An older one."

"What case?"

Another long pause. This time she thought he'd hung up, which he also did quite a bit. Then, "Google the Boston Boogeyman. That's it. That's all I can say."

A jolt through her system. She knew the name. Knew it well.

She realized that she was gripping the phone so hard it actually was making her hand ache. Release. Breathe. Rule number one of news investigation: just keep asking questions.

"How was Markham killed?" she asked.

"Nope."

"Come on."

"It'll be out there soon enough," he said. "You'll have to hear it in the news along with all the other civilians."

Ouch. That hurt.

"Shot?"

"Hey," he said, his voice going softer. "What I hear — it's yours, okay? I promise. I'll call you."

He always promised that, and he'd never once made good on it. It was just a way to get off the phone.

"So, you just don't know?" He knew. Of course he did. Why wouldn't he tell her?

"Goodbye, Winter."

"Why don't you give her a call?" Just a hook to keep him on the line. Gillian and Christopher weren't good for each other and they all knew it.

"Gilly?" he said. No one else on earth called her that. "I'm not sure I'm the man she deserves."

He sounded a little sadder than she would have expected.

"Maybe you should let her decide."

"Good luck with your *podcast*," he said.

Rain ended the call just seconds before Lily started crying. She sat on the top step for a moment, buzzing with frustration.

Then she got up and went to Lily, unstrapping her and carrying her back up to the nursery.

It was another world. Stars on the ceiling, a white-and-blue ocean mural on the wall. The nightlight projected buttery-yellow sea turtles that languidly circled the room. The gauzy shades were always drawn, casting the room perpetually in a peaceful milky light. Lily was warm and soft in Rain's arms, smelled like the lavender shampoo Rain used on her every night. The baby's eyes glittered, smile big and gurgling.

"Hello, sunshine," Rain said, peering into her daughter's perfect flushed face.

She sat in the glider, rocking and nursing again. It was hypnotic, the quiet of the room, the warmth of her child, that flood of oxytocin, the low sound of waves from the noise machine. Her frustration eased; the belly of fire cooled.

It was enough, wasn't it?

Maybe. If this room, pretty and safe, was the whole world.

But it wasn't.

Laney Markham would have had this. But her husband, a sociopath, brutally ended her life, and the life of their child. Then, he escaped justice, walked free while Laney's brokenhearted father raged. And Laney's mother sat stoic, pale and rigid, as though the blood had stopped moving through her veins. Grief had turned her to stone; it was more devastating to see than the father's fury.

That was it. It was the case that did her

in. The ugliness of it; she was sick with it, like a flu she couldn't shake. Gillian's words knocked around her head for weeks and months.

Bad people win. They win all the time.

When just a few weeks after the crushing acquittal, Greg asked if she would consider staying home with the baby for a while, she agreed, surprising him — and herself. Money would be a bit tight, but whatever. She worked in news; layoffs were always looming. Money was always tight.

She gave it up — the work that had defined her.

Now, Markham was dead. She felt a tickle of relief. A sort of justice had been delivered, something in line with her good-always-triumphs-over-evil belief system. Murder? Suicide? Home invasion robbery gone wrong? Accident?

A federal investigation underway. A connection to the Boston Boogeyman.

Let it go. It's not your story anymore.

Lily gazed up at Rain and started kicking her legs happily.

Or is it?

FOUR

The rain knocks on the tin roof and the sound of it always makes me think of you. Not because of the name you gave yourself. I never called you Rain.

The sound reminds me of your childhood home. I used to love that old house, how it was deep back in the woods. Rooms dim, with wind chimes on the porch. Your father still lives there, doesn't he?

Your mother seemed always to be cooking, some black-and-white movie playing on that tiny portable television perched on the kitchen counter. Your father's study smelled of leather and cigarette smoke.

I'd marvel at his shelves and shelves of dusty books, the typewriter on the rickety wood table by the window. He had a computer, of course. But he'd write on that old thing and give your mother the pages to enter into "the box," as he liked to call it. His keyboard clatter echoed down the hardwood floor of the hallway. I loved his tall thinness, the way his suit jackets hung off his broad shoulders. He was a writer, a real writer. You were often mad at him because he cared more about the page than he did about you, or so it seemed. I think you were wrong about that. You didn't see the way he looked at you. As if you were a princess and a unicorn and a rainbow all rolled into one perfect girl.

My house was different, sprawling and frigid, filled with light, professionally decorated, museum white and gray, expensive pieces of modern art chosen by my mother not for love, or because she had any idea what was truly beautiful, but because it "went with the room." My father only cared about numbers. My mother, I'm not sure what she cared about then, before. Afterward, she had a kind of awakening, became someone else. But then, they worked all week, lay by the pool all weekend. They watched television in bed at night with the lights out. Sometimes I'd wake up and it would still be on, its blue glow flickering through the crack of the door left ajar. There were no books in my house, except in my room. My parents didn't read. They didn't have time, they said.

Your parents used to play cards with us.

Your mother had an art studio in the garage. We'd all make a big mess out there — drip paint on the floor, get it all over our clothes, the walls, each other. She'd only laugh and tell us that whatever creation wound up on the canvas, that it was beautiful. Your dad gave us a summer reading list. We saw him on the news sometimes, came across articles about him in magazines. You didn't seem impressed; you were used to his brand of fame. But I was awed by him. Hey — remember that horrible review, written by some former friend of his? He sulked about it for days, muttering, shutting doors too hard. Your mother told us to play outside, not to hang around the house that week. But then the keyboard started clattering again. Because that's what you do when you're a writer, I guess. You just keep writing, no matter what they say about you.

I'm rambling.

Does that happen to you? Do you get lost in the memories of who we were before?

Today, the black fingers of despair tug at me. They always do in the days that follow one of my — excursions; there's a heavy grayness that settles. A sense of loss.

In the planning, there's so much energy and tension, the intensity raw and alive. And then when it's done, some engine inside me sputters and dies, gears grinding to a halt. In that silence, I return to that moment right after I called to Mrs. Newman and just before I heard the sound that stopped me in my tracks on that dirt path to the woods. And I wish and wish anything had turned me back toward home.

But, as you have told me more than once, we can't go back. Everybody knows that.

The rain is heavy, which is odd for this time of year. Maybe if it were cooler, it would be snow. The water sluices down the window as I build a fire in the great room. It's too hot for a fire. But I haven't built it for warmth.

Article by article, I burn the clothes I wore last night, the gloves, the balaclava. And soon, everything I brought into Markham's house with me is gone. The car is hidden. There's no trace of me.

Who am I? I often wonder the day after. Sometimes there's even regret. What have I done? What does this make me? In the planning, in the hunt, in the execution, there's nothing like that. But after, there's a heaviness I carry. You told me once that the thoughts I harbored, the things I couldn't let go, that it was *wrong,* that nothing good had ever come from wanting revenge. But what do you know about right and wrong?

When the clothes are burned, I brew some coffee. I boil water and pour it over the grounds, the liquid trickling into the carafe through the brown filter. The Chemex, it's elegant, simple. It's the way your father brewed coffee. I used to admire him. I guess I still do, even after everything.

When your heroes reveal themselves as human, it exposes your own flaws, too. Naivete, mainly, a willingness to believe in someone, something. Do you remember that book signing he did in that tiny store off of Main Street? We were kids then, but we tagged along with your mother. His big bestselling days were behind him. But his fans turned up in droves, repeating back lines to him that he'd long forgotten writing. In print, they referred to him as the father of dystopian fiction. Remember how people stood around the small store, how hot it was, how the line snaked outside and down the street? His flop of white hair, those round specs. I thought he was the coolest man alive.

I drink my coffee and watch as the fire dies to embers, everything reduced to ash. I look at the row of his books on my shelves. All of them signed, first editions. They're worth quite a bit, I think. Not that I'd ever part with them. Not that I'd ever part with any piece of you, or anything that connects back to the time when we were young together. The last safe place.

Upstairs in my study, I get online, start scrolling through the news headlines. I miss seeing your name in print every day, Rain Winter. All your stories, even when later you started producing and editing instead, had a certain energy to them. A quiet authority. You let the facts tell the tale, never hyping, never proselytizing even in that subtle way that some journalists do. I loved the longer pieces, when you dug in deep to your subject, the characters at its heart. It was personal; I could tell.

You're still trying to understand, aren't you, in your way? I am, too.

I scroll through your social media feeds. A picture of your baby. Really? You and Greg, a selfie in the park. Come on. Your professional sites are wastelands of retweets and shares. On Insta there's an artful shot of one of those smoking martinis, some party, moms' night out. Christ. How long can you go on like this? I might have predicted it, though. Your retreat into the cocoon of domesticity.

That look on your face when Markham got off. It wasn't despair, exactly. It was more like a bitter resignation, the look of a child who discovers there's no Santa. A part of you knew it all along. You shook your head slightly; your mouth dropped open just a little. You folded into yourself. You gave up on justice.

You were back there in the woods with me. Remembering.

Anyway, if I know you, you're on fire today. That's not why I did it. But I'd be lying if I said it wasn't part of the reason. There was no rush; I could have done it anytime over the next few months. But your social media posts are downright depressing.

Come back to life, Lara.

My phone buzzes and the sound moves through me like electricity. The front gate.

I touch the app to activate the camera and see a black sedan with a young woman sitting in the driver's seat. There's someone beside her, but I can't see a face, just the thick thighs of a large man, a hand with a wedding ring. Interesting. I don't get many visitors out here.

"Can I help you?" I ask.

She says my name. Her voice is husky, eyes hidden behind mirrored sunglasses. She holds her identification up to the camera.

"We have a few questions about a case

we're working on," she says. "I'm wonder-ing if you can help us."

I could ask for her to identify her partner. But even through the rain and the grainy camera image, I can see her credentials are legit. There have been other visits from people like her over the years.

I buzz her in and listen to the gate slide open with a squeal.

FIVE

Turkey tenderloin rubbed with herbs and sweet potatoes in the roasting pan, cooling on the stove, a kale salad tossed, wrapped and sitting in a bright red bowl in the fridge. Table set for three. Lily happy nearby with her blocks on the living room carpet — gotta love the open-plan room.

At the kitchen table, laptop open, Rain scrolled through her contacts and paused when she came to the name that had been kicking around in the back of her head.

She took a deep breath and dialed.

"Well, well," he answered. "I'm surprised, and I'm not surprised."

"Hey, Henry," she said, already regretting her choice.

"How's the weather, Rain Winter?"

"No complaints." Rain watched Lily contented at play in their pretty living room; she *didn't* have any but the most banal complaints. She was happy, mostly. Happier than most, maybe. Just a little restless. Still with that belly of fire.

"I saw that *a*-dorable picture you posted on Facebook last night of your little princess covered in sweet potatoes. How cute."

A little jangle of unease. "Are we friends on Facebook, Henry?"

"Uh, no," he said. "We're not."

He laughed a little into the silence that followed. "Oh, *wait*! Did you think it was *private*? Your little personal page under your married name? Come on, Rain. You know better than that, don't you?"

She didn't even want to ask. "How do you have access?"

He made a little tsking sound with his mouth.

"I can't tell you that, Rain. Sorry. Or should I say Laraine? Laraine Mitchell, your suburban mom avatar."

She smiled despite his obnoxiousness. She knew, of course, that her Facebook account, or really anything she did online, wasn't secure. There was Firesheep, spyware, cloning software. A keylogger could capture each keystroke you made on your computer, revealing every password and login. Henry, dark web mole, probably had a hundred back alleys around the social media sites. She logged on quickly and scrolled through her friends. There he was, his wide face and glasses, Cheshire cat grin filling the thumbprint photo. She didn't remember adding him. But maybe she had. He was likely just messing with her.

Most people couldn't stand Henry. But she kind of liked him. He was out there. He was smart. He said what he meant, right or wrong. He had skills — information, access, contacts.

"Meanwhile," he went on. "The Twitter feed of Rain Winter, former writer, editor and producer of National News Radio, former crime journalist extraordinaire, daughter of once-lauded-Pulitzer-Prize-winning-now-disgraced-writer Bruce Winter, lies fallow except for the occasional lackluster retweet. Weekly. Friday afternoons usually. Very little on Insta, but you were never great with that. Too cute for you, right? Following your digital footprints, or lack thereof, I'd say you had dropped out completely."

"Maybe I have," she said.

"So, this is a social call?" he said. "You want to grab a pumpkin spice latte and trade parenting tips?"

She was pretty damn sure Henry Watt wasn't married with children. She clicked on his page and it was totally blank except

71

for the ID photo. "This account is private," read the gray type.

"Wait, let me guess," he said. "Markham."

"Know anything?"

She pulled up Henry's website, started scrolling through. He was a professional news troll, a tipster with varying degrees of accuracy, and the owner, writer and editor of a blog that focused on crime and conspiracy theories, a newsletter that reached hundreds of thousands, and more than one person she knew went to him when all their other leads ran cold. Rain thought of him as a kind of mole, round-bodied and beady-eyed, connected through a network of murky tunnels to other creatures of the dark web. His tips had led her into mazes that came out nowhere, but sometimes he was dead-on.

"Who's asking?"

"I am."

"I mean — why? For what organization?"

Guys like Henry were the very reason real journalists didn't consider indie blogging or podcasting. Because news, real news, was about facts and nothing else. It wasn't about theories, and maybes, and best guesses. It wasn't about running a story because you wanted to be the first to tell it and checking your facts later. It wasn't about having an idea and finding people who agreed with you. You didn't write and print your ideas. In fact, as a news journalist, you didn't have ideas at all. You reported the facts, and let the facts tell the story. That simple. Something that had been lost in the fake news, social media information age. Still, sometimes you needed a renegade, especially when legitimate sources had closed to you. Or when you were on the outside looking in, like she was now. "I want to know," she said. "Just me."

"It's personal?"

"Yes."

"I'm not sure I believe you," he said. "I didn't think the whole stay-at-home-mom thing was going to work for you. You have too much baggage."

A little jolt of annoyance caused her to act on impulse.

"You know what, Henry? Just forget it."

She ended the call, heart thumping with frustration. He called her right back. She let it ring and go to voice mail. But when he called again a minute later, she answered.

"Don't lose your temper," he said. His voice had lost some of its smugness.

"What do you know, Henry?"

"I might have someone on the inside."

Henry's network was invisible, an army

comprised of the people who didn't get noticed. He wouldn't know the coroner, for example, but he might know the coroner's assistant, or even the janitor. He might not know the detective working a case, but he'd know the IT guy working at the precinct.

"Who?"

"Let's just say he's in cleanup."

"Okay."

"Except there wasn't much to clean up."

"Meaning?"

"Whoever did the job on Markham laid down tarps, almost as if he was trying not to make a mess, was meticulous about the scene. There was little physical evidence, some blood splatter from the victim. Obviously, they're still waiting for the trace evidence analysis. But they aren't hopeful that anything significant will come back."

She realized suddenly that she was holding her breath. She released it, loosened the grip she had on the phone.

"How did he die?"

She asked but she had a feeling she already knew.

"He died the way Laney Markham died," he said, his voice low and solemn. "Bound, gagged and stabbed more than twenty times with a serrated hunting knife."

She stared out the window to the street

outside; a blue minivan cruised by, turned into her neighbor's drive. The branches of the oak swayed, raindrops tapping at her window, and Lily stacked blocks with intent focus.

A toxic brew of disgust, anger, relief bubbled. And, yes, that dark excitement — a feeling that shamed her somewhat. And was there also a not-so-small part of her that was glad Markham got what he deserved?

"Like the Boston Boogeyman," she said. "Killed the way he killed."

A pause, the tap, tap, tap of fingers on a keyboard.

"You've done your homework," he said.

"Don't I always?"

"You do. You always do," he said. "And just like someone else we know."

Rain didn't say anything, braced herself for the sound of his name.

"Eugene Kreskey," Henry said when she didn't.

The sound of it sliced her, every time.

There weren't many people who remembered Rain's ugly history. It was big news once, but it had faded in the bubbling morass of horrific crimes since then. Greg and, of course, her father knew. Gillian. And somehow, years ago, Henry had unearthed the horrible thing that happened to her when she was a kid. Not that it happened to *her,* exactly. It should have but it didn't.

"Is there a connection?" she asked, trying to keep her voice level.

"Feds think so," he said. "That's what my guy said."

"Between all three?"

"There might be others, too," he said. "Two others, to be precise, that fit the parameters — someone got away with something vile. Then didn't."

"A vigilante."

"Yeah," said Henry, voice gone soft with admiration. "Exactly."

"Do you have files?" she asked.

Another pause, that tap, tap, tap again.

"What are you working on, Rain Winter?"

It didn't do any good to bullshit guys like Henry. They knew the truth when they heard it.

Lies had a vibration, they tingled in the air, electric. A certain kind of person — Rain thought she was one of them — could feel it. That's why she liked Henry. He might be a little crazy, sometimes wrong, but he was no liar. And he knew how to follow the questionable channels you sometimes had to take to the truth.

"I don't know yet," she admitted.

A pause, more tapping. "I'll send you what I have."

Lily's tower of blocks fell, and the baby issued a little cry of frustration, her face crumbling into a comical frown.

"That's not a monitor, is it?" said Henry. "Tell me you're not using one of those things. You know anyone can hack into those, right? The audio *and* the video feed? And those home security cameras. Oh, my god. I'll send you my blog."

"Thanks, Henry," she said. "I'll look forward to those files."

"They're watching," he said ominously. "Never forget that."

She sat a moment after ending the call, Henry's words bouncing around her head. A text from Greg startled her back to the present.

Sorry, babe. I'm running late. Don't hold dinner.

The words pulsed on the screen in front of her. She wasn't surprised, of course. But there was a flutter of disappointment; the house felt eerily quiet.

Rain and Lily ate together, Lily's version of the meal cut into small bites and spread over her tray. The baby had a little plastic fork and spoon, neither of which she could be bothered to use unless to toss one onto the table, or the floor, or, fascinatingly, as a brush for her hair.

"Maybe we'll go for a ride in the car tomorrow," she told Lily, wiping the baby's mouth.

Lily banged her spoon, sending some food flying. "Car! Car!"

Rain was going to take that as a yes.

After dinner, still no sign of Greg. So, she gave Lily a bath, the things Henry said swirling, the story already taking shape the way stories did, arranging themselves into a digestible narrative. Where did she need to go first? Who did she need to see?

As she changed Lily's diaper, dressed her for bed, she felt the eye of the baby monitor on her and glanced back to look at its glowing red light. She reached over and turned it away.

Once Lily was down, Rain texted Gillian. She hesitated, fingers hovering over the little keyboard. Then, Feel like taking a little road trip?

If she knew Gillian, her friend was on the treadmill in front of the television.

Hmm. What did you have in mind?

What did she have in mind? This story would have to begin at the end. Steve Markham's end.

She typed: Let's pay our final respects.

Rain didn't have to wait long.

Ha. I knew it. She's baa-aack!

Six

The flames in the fireplace licked and danced, crackling. Rain had made it not for warmth but just to look at it, stare into the flames and sip on the glass of white she'd poured herself while she waited for Greg.

Rectangles of light slid across the wall. Someone in the driveway. She stood and went to the window, watched her husband emerge from the SUV.

The slouch to his shoulders, the slow way he moved, standing a second to rub at his temples before retrieving his bags from the back seat — he seemed so tired, run-down by work, by new parenthood. From a distance, for a moment, the shadow of his form was unfamiliar, as if she were seeing him for the first time. She wanted to run to him. Instead, she opened the door and went to stand on the porch.

He paused at the bottom step, looked up at her. The cool of the day had turned downright chilly, a light wind tossing his hair.

"Sorry," he said. "I tried to get home earlier."

It was his default greeting lately. Rain felt a wash of compassion. He *was* working all day, and she was here in their safe, happy home with the baby. Yeah, it was hectic, all-consuming, a bit thankless. But it could also be peaceful, joyful, quiet — just the two of them. He might have a freedom that she no longer had — the freedom to come and go as he chose. But he faced different challenges — deadlines, the endless pressure to be right, to be first, an asshole boss, slackers on his team.

All the things she thought she wanted to leave behind.

She walked down the steps, wrapped her arms around his neck and kissed him long on the mouth. He dropped his bag, and wrapped her up, lifting her a little off the ground.

"How was your day?" Rain asked, pulling back a little.

He kissed her again, soft, sweet, that familiar heat rising between them.

"Better now."

The day, the things she'd learned and done, buzzed around her head. She led him inside. It was late, after nine, his dinner warming in the oven. She'd taken a shower, dressed, done her makeup. Usually, by the time he came home she was in lounge-wear, hair up, contacts out and glasses on.

"Did I miss date night?" he asked in the kitchen, grabbing her from behind as she took the food from the oven. "You're beautiful."

"I just thought you deserved to remember what I look like in something other than my pajamas," she said, plating his food.

"You're beautiful in pajamas, too."

He took a seat at the kitchen bar and she poured him a glass of wine.

"How was your day?" he asked. "How's our girl?"

She ran down the day — the jog in the park, the mundane tasks, activities, how much Lily was talking. He ran through his — a clash with the on-air talent, technical issues, still no word on the promotion he was sure to get.

It was their agreement, that someone be home. Home and kids had to be someone's primary job; it *was* a job. They'd chosen this and neither of them was supposed to complain. (Of course, they both did, all the time.) But they'd agreed to an audit at the end of the first year. How was everybody

82

doing? How was the money situation? Was everybody happy? That conversation was overdue. She put his plate in front of him.

"Hear anything today about Markham?" she asked, trying to segue toward that topic. She felt a flutter of nerves. She wasn't sure why.

"I heard the Feds took over — which I thought was a little odd," he said, watching her. "We sent a crew over this afternoon, but no one's talking. We were only able to run a small segment. You?"

"I made a few calls, did a little research."

"What did you find out?"

She told him what Christopher had told her, about her chat with Henry, about the press conference tomorrow. He nodded, rubbed at the stubble on his chin. Of course, he knew it all. He was downplaying. He'd lived the Markham case with her. He knew it had its hooks in her for all kinds of reasons.

"What?" he said when she was done. He tapped his head. "What's going on in there?"

"I was just thinking."

He offered a curious frown. "I know that tone."

"I want to follow this new angle of the story."

"Follow it?" he said. He took a bite of turkey. "Hmm. This is good."

"Doing some follow-up work."

"Freelance?" he said, mouth full.

"Something like that," she said. "Something long-form. Like maybe a podcast."

The word felt awkward, even silly now that she'd put it out there. And the look on Greg's face — something between confusion and disbelief — didn't help.

These kinds of things — podcasts, blogs, the self-published book — had a bad name in the industry. The internet had essentially killed traditional news, lowered all the standards for reporting, writing, editing. It undermined the educated, veteran journalists who cared about things like ethics and *The Chicago Manual of Style.* People were getting their "news" for free on social media, not necessarily interested in accuracy or correct grammar. It was a problem to be sure. But there was a renegade part of her that thought: Didn't the establishment need to be toppled every now and then? If the voice of the people wasn't necessarily polished or vetted, didn't it still deserve to be heard?

"There are people doing it well, legitimate long-form journalism," she said. "I have the experience, the contacts. I'd seek advertisers, maybe hire someone to help me produce and edit."

He looked down at his plate, pushed some food around.

"Have you seen our bank account?"

Outside a car drove too fast past the house, revving its engine needlessly. The teenager up the block; Rain kept meaning to talk to his parents about his driving.

"Or I could take it to NNR," she said. "Not full-time again. But just this. Just this story as a feature. Andrew said I should pitch him whenever I had an idea."

She breathed to release the tension in her shoulders. Greg stayed quiet a moment. He shifted off his jacket. When did he go so gray around the temples?

"What is it about this story?" He said it like he already knew the answer, and maybe he did. "Can't let it go?"

No. She couldn't let it go. It had been eighteen months since Markham was acquitted, just over a year since she came home to be with Lily full-time. It was the story that broke her, that made her lose faith.

She'd been thinking about this all day, since early this morning. She didn't just choose to be a stay-at-home mom. She chose to walk away from work that stopped making sense. And she was okay with that. Until today. Until someone killed Steve Markham.

"There's no story here," he said. "You get that, right? It was the brother or the father. Hell, maybe it was even her mother. Still waters run deep and all that. They'll figure it out pretty quickly. Anyway, Markham's *dead.* Just like if someone killed him in prison. A few segments, maybe a larger feature about the whole case somewhere. Maybe even a true crime book. But, really, death is the abrupt end of the story. There's no *mystery.*"

He took a few bites in silence.

"Do you remember the Boston Boogeyman?" she said finally.

"Of course," he said. He wrinkled his nose in disgust. "The guy who abducted and murdered three boys over a five-year period in Massachusetts."

"And walked free."

Greg's fork hovered between plate and mouth. A muscle twitched in his jaw as he watched her, remembering. "And then was found murdered in his home about a year later. Just like Markham. Just like —"

He let the sentence trail. Neither one of them liked to say his name, as if it was a spell, a conjuring. Greg frowned instead, and she watched his gears spin, making all the connections, seeing the possibilities, the size and scope of the story. A newsman through and through. His shoulders straightened a bit.

He took a bite of kale. "You think there's a connection?"

"I think the Feds think there's a connection."

He had big brown eyes, with girlishly long lashes. His gaze could be sweet, loving. It could also pin you to the wall with its intensity.

"So, Markham's not the story."

"He's a piece of a much bigger one. Like you said. That story's over."

"So, what are you telling me?" he said, chewing slowly. "That you want to go back to work?"

She peered down into her wineglass. Did she? Was that what she wanted?

She was about to answer and ask for his help. But then Lily issued a wail through the monitor that startled them both. She moved toward the stairs, grateful to break away from the conversation, started to climb.

"Hey, Rain," he said, coming to stand at the bottom of the stairs. "Just one question. Is this about the story? Or is this about —

what happened?"

The question sent a jolt through her body, caused heat to come to her cheeks. She froze on the stairs.

"You don't have to answer," he said, bowing his head and resting a hand on the banister. His tone was gentle. "Just think about it."

She kept moving up to the nursery.

SEVEN

In the dim of the nursery, Rain rocked Lily, who was sound asleep again in her arms. She could have exited a while ago, but she hadn't. She needed that warm body next to her heart. She wanted to stay in the pretty quiet of the baby's room, just for a while.

She rubbed at the deep scar on her right calf, which had been aching since her run. But maybe it wasn't the exercise that caused it to throb.

What happened.

It was buried so deep that she never even thought about it anymore. Almost. Sometimes it surfaced in dreams when she was especially stressed or overtired. Sometimes it came back to her at odd moments — maybe it was a song from that time, or the smell of wet leaves, that certain pitch of a child shrieking in that way that could be delight or terror. Then it came back. Just this clutch in her throat, a hollow that opened in her middle. It was a hundred years ago, a million. But it wasn't. It was yesterday.

Back then they played. Out on the streets riding bikes with her friends, they had the run of the neighborhood. She walked through the acres of woods between developments, thick green above, ground sun-dappled and littered with leaves, and waded in the cool water of clean creeks. With her best friends, Tess and Hank, she rode to the corner store in the summer heat for ice cream, cicadas singing, heat rising off the blacktop in waves. Quiet afternoons leaked into evenings, the light turning that certain kind of golden orange reserved for summer. She'd arrive home dirty and hungry, with bruises and scrapes, tired just because they'd been in motion all day, running and falling, wrestling, riding, climbing. Her body used to ache, tingle with fatigue when she crashed into bed. And wasn't there a kind of bliss in physical fatigue?

She'd eat at the table with her mother, sometimes her father on the rare night when he stopped work at a decent time. Summer-night dinners were burgers, or steak, or chicken on the grill, and fresh corn on the cob, fluffy green salads, buttery baked potatoes. Tess and Hank were at her place a lot for supper. Both of Hank's parents worked big jobs in the city; they were never around. Tess's father had left when Tess was small, and her mother was an ER nurse at the big hospital in town. She was often around during the day, leaving Tess alone in the evenings or for the late shift. Sometimes Tess stayed with Rain's family. Only Rain's mother stayed home, cooking, cleaning, driving them around.

After dinner, maybe they went out again, played with the other neighborhood kids. Flashlight tag. Fireflies in jars. Shrieks rang through the night, squeals of laughter. Eventually, always, someone started to cry. Then moms were on the porches, hands on hips. Time to go inside. Do it again tomorrow.

That's how Rain grew up, anyway. Most people seemed to think that kids had lost something, that freedom to roam, to play unfettered. But Rain knew better. Kids lost their freedom for a reason. Because it wasn't safe to roam.

But they didn't know that then. They didn't know anything.

"My mom doesn't want me to cut through the woods anymore," said Rain that day, twelve. "She wants us to take the long way around if we're going to meet Hank."

She stood on the edge of the road. Here it turned off onto a dirt path that ran between two neighborhoods. The dirt path would carry them over a stone bridge, through a stand of trees, until it let them out by a field. From there it was another five minutes to Hank's house.

"The street is more dangerous, don't you think?" said Tess with a shrug. "More cars lately."

That was true. There was a hairpin turn with one of those mirrors mounted up in the tree so you could see who was coming from the other direction. But there were lots of teenagers driving. They drove too fast, were looking at the radio or at each other, anything but the road ahead. A kid had been struck on his bicycle last summer. He was okay, walked around with a cast for a few weeks. They all signed it.

It wasn't a hard-and-fast rule, as Rain saw it. More like a mention over breakfast.

Stay out of the woods, okay?

Why?

Mom paused like she did when she didn't want to answer, looked over to Rain's father, who was hidden behind the newspaper.

Just listen to your mother, darling. Her father rarely had rules, or chimed in on her mother's. In fact, if her father ever told her

92

to do anything, it was to question the rules, ask anything, push the boundaries. *Believe half of what you see,* he was famous for saying. *And nothing of what you hear.*

"Besides," said Tess. "It will take forever."

She was right. It *was* a long way around, two big hills, an extra fifteen minutes, maybe more. And it was hot. Just before ten in the morning and it was already blazing. They didn't have their bikes. Tess had a flat and her mom said she'd fix it over the weekend. So they were on foot. The sun was bright, and the creek was babbling. She saw the red flash of a northern cardinal, heard its cry of alarm. It was a fairy-tale forest, a place they knew as well as they knew their own backyards.

"Fine," said Rain, following her friend onto the path.

No cell phones. Rain thought about that a lot now. If they'd had phones, how would that day have been different? Would she have called her mom? Would their mothers have been tracking them the way people did now? Maybe her phone would have rung just then: *I told you to stay away from the woods! Come home this instant!*

But there were no phones to ring. Just two girls, twelve going on thirteen. Neither one of them especially cool. Smart, A-students, but naive, sheltered. Tess had braces and enormous glasses, wore her mousy blond hair in braids; Rain, in braces, too, her black hair was wild, untamable. She couldn't shimmy the rope in gym class to save her own life. Rain already knew she was a writer, like her father. Tess, an accomplished horseback rider, as at ease in a saddle as she was on a bicycle, was certain she was going to become a veterinarian. And Hank, who they were on their way to meet at his house because he had a pool, well, he was just a comic-book, video-game nerd. All he wanted to be when he grew up was a super-hero. They were merely waiting for him to get bitten by a spider, or fall into a vat of toxic sludge, and emerge with his powers.

"What's wrong with the woods, anyway?" asked Tess. She was rail-thin, coltish, prone to tripping. "Since when can't we walk through?"

Rain looked at her jagged cuticles. She wasn't clear on her mother's reasoning. "My mom just said."

They almost didn't see him; the big man sat as still as a boulder by the side of the creek. They might have walked right over the bridge and passed him without noticing — if not for the dog.

■ ■ ■ ■

"Rain?"

She practically jumped out of her skin, adrenaline rocketing through her. Lily whimpered, shifted crankily in her sleep at the sudden movement. Greg stood over her, a hand on her shoulder.

"Did you fall asleep?" he whispered. He lifted Lily from her arms, kissed the baby's head softly and placed her in the crib. He stood watching their little girl.

Rain came to stand beside him, and he turned to her.

"I'm sorry," he said. "I shouldn't have said that. It was a low blow."

He put his arms around her again and they stood swaying, turtles from the night-light dancing on the walls.

You were right, she wanted to say but didn't. *It* is *about what happened.* Everything Rain had done since that day was about *what happened.* How could it not be?

She let the comfort of the room, her husband's arms, the present moment wash over her. She pushed that day, and everything that happened after, back down into the box where she kept it, and locked it up tight. She envisioned herself throwing the key down a deep well.

Don't let this slow you down, kid. Her father had issued this directive right after, and at critical moments since. *If you let it get its claws into your haunches, it's over. Remember that.*

She'd been running. Fast as she could. Why did she always find herself back there?

"Whatever you want to do," Greg whispered. "Whatever you need, I support it."

"Thank you," she said, holding on to him tight.

But wasn't there a part of her that wished he'd stop her? That he'd tell her no, that Lily came first, and they'd agreed someone should be home full-time. Wasn't there a part of her that wished he'd keep her from following that trail into the woods? Again.

They stood there awhile, holding each other, watching Lily, the big, sweet-faced moon hanging from the ceiling watching them. Her eyes drifted outside to the street, where she saw the headlights of a sedan switch on across the street. The car sat idle for a moment, then pulled away slowly. Her heart thumped.

It's nothing. It's no one, she told herself. Even though a part of her knew it was a lie.

EIGHT

Do you see me? Do you know it's me?

He loves you. That's obvious as I watch you hold on to him, sway in the dim light of the nursery. I shift in my seat, stare at the monitor in my hand, its glow shining blue on the dash, on the door. I'm happy for you, believe it or not. I didn't think you two would actually get married, let alone stay married. Of course, it's early days. Still, you seem to get each other. It's not perfect — I've heard the two of you fight, and fuck, make up, argue again. But it's healthy. It's real. When he kisses you, I turn the monitor off.

I start the engine and drive away.

You know what I remember about that day, Lara? Everything. Every detail.

I woke shivering because my parents kept that house as cold as a fucking icebox, didn't even bother turning it up when they left for work. They were both gone, as usual, when I got up.

Remember that feeling? That summer feeling. You open your eyes and there's absolutely nothing to do. The day stretches ahead, leisurely and beautiful. No school, no responsibilities, no chores in my case — hey, there was a cleaning service for all that — just the blissful freedom of the unsupervised adolescent.

I knew you guys were coming, that we'd swim. There'd be pizza and video games, and some stupid movie. I figured we'd ride our bikes back to your place. Your mom always made dinner; my parents might not come home until eight, carrying fast-food burgers or fried chicken in greasy white sacks — they loved their junk food, didn't they? Remember how we'd eat that later, too? Eat at your place, eat again at mine. Your dad would come for you, so you wouldn't ride home alone in the night. Sometimes you'd just leave your bike and get it the next day.

I had a stack of new comics that my dad brought the night before from his favorite shop in the city. I read one — Batman — as I ate a huge bowl of Cocoa Puffs, then drank the chocolate milk that was left behind. The way we ate. Remember how we'd ride to the general store and buy bags of junk — gum and candy bars, those peanut butter cookies, and cheesy puffs, potato chips in cans. We'd just sit on the sidewalk and eat it all. I look at those old pictures and we were all so skinny. I guess that's the magic of being a kid, right. Eat whatever you want. No consequences. Until much later.

I remember the sunlight glittering on the pool. The birds singing in the backyard. The hum of a lawn mower from across the street. There was a note from my mom: *Get out and do something today. Don't just lie around in front of the television. Love you!*

Later, she blamed herself. She should have been home. If she had been — The way I see it, there's plenty of blame to go around.

The last time I wrote, you told me that you didn't remember much of anything. You told me that you didn't *want* to remember. That's when you asked me to stay away, to stay out of your life. If you could go back and relive that day, change things, you would. But you can't, you said, so you had no choice but to move on. You politely suggested that I do the same. Move on.

It's so easy for you.

Not so easy for me, of course.

What if I hadn't gone out looking for you and Tess? What if I had, instead, called your mom, asked for you? She'd have known that you weren't where you were supposed to be. She'd have come looking. It's like you said, you can drive yourself crazy running through all the scenarios, all the ways things could have been different.

You can really drive yourself crazy.

The air smelled of cut grass, and the gravel driveway crunched beneath my sneakers as I left the house. My dirt bike lay where I'd dumped it the night before on the grass. *Someone's going to steal that thing,* my dad complained the night before. *And I'm not going to replace it.* But like all spoiled kids, I knew if it did get stolen — which it wouldn't — that he'd bitch a blue streak then get me another one eventually. Anyway, nothing ever got stolen, not in that neighborhood. Everyone had everything they wanted and then some. No need to steal. We didn't always even lock our doors, would forget to close the garage sometimes. We felt safe. Remember that? Remember what it was like to feel so safe that you didn't even know what it meant not to feel that way?

I pulled the bike up from the damp ground, didn't even bother wiping it off. Just hopped on it and headed toward the dirt road. Your mom told you not to cut across anymore. But I figured you guys, especially Tess, were too lazy to go the long way. The air on my face, hot and humid. The sudden coolness when I was on the dirt road, under the tree cover. A squirrel skittered in front of my bike. I swerved to avoid it. Mrs. Newman waved from the window over her kitchen sink. *Hey, Mrs. Newman!* I called back to her.

I heard something then, something high-pitched and out of place, came to a skidding stop on my bike and listened. Birdsong, and wind in the leaves.

Right there.

I go back to that place. Because even though I convinced myself that it was nothing and I kept going, I remember the way the hair came up on my arms, that sudden stillness inside, the urge to freeze and listen. That's instinct. That's the brain picking up on something, a note out of the symphony of normal life. The way ahead was dark. I think I even looked back at the way behind me, the sun-dappled road home.

If I had spun my bike around, then what? Then what?

From the way you talked about it, I could tell that you've had a lot of therapy. I have, too, believe me. Years of it, shrink after shrink, well into adulthood. After something rips your psyche apart, they try to stitch you back together. The physical wounds, they've healed. Even the scars have faded.

But whatever got broken inside, it's still not right. Do you feel the same way? I suspect you do. I see it in you, too, Lara. That look, the one I see in the mirror. A kind of emptiness behind the eyes, a strange flatness. You've seen the things that make all the other things people do seem meaningless.

Do you feel as if there are two of you? The one who's living out her life — working, having relationships, going to the grocery store, cooking, reading. The person you would have been if it had never happened. And then there's another you. The one who survived but is still somehow trapped in the nightmare.

I don't know. Maybe it's just me.

I was a child, you wrote. *And I acted out of terror and extreme trauma. Even though I wish things had been different, I don't blame myself. I have moved on to try and live a whole and happy life. She would have wanted that for us. Don't you think?*

I get that. I hear that. They give you the language of survival. The phrases you are meant say to yourself, words like a bridge over the bottomless gully of despair. I have those words, too. I dole them out to others now in my work with trauma victims, mainly children and adolescents. That's the work that the whole and healthy part of me does; I help children who have suffered find their way back to normal, or forward to a new normal. It's good work. Gratifying and healing.

So I get what you're trying to say. And part of me even agrees, that one way to honor Tess is to live out the lives we've been given.

But no, I don't think she would have *wanted that for us.* I mean, think about it. I'm fairly certain that if the choice had been put to her, she would have *wanted* one of us to take her place. I think she would have vastly preferred, as anyone would, to be the one picking up the pieces of that summer morning, trying to live a *whole and happy life* in the wake of a terrible event that she *survived.*

I think she would have wanted *one of us* to die instead at the hands of a monster. Personally — and I know you'll find this hurtful — I think it should have been you.

He came for you, Lara. Not her. And if it hadn't been for me, he would have gotten *you.*

Don't bother to thank me. It's far too late for that.

I key in the code to my gate and pull up the long drive. My own house is empty. There's no one waiting for me at home, no one to hold me when the ghosts come to call. I sit in the car for a while. I can still hear the sound of you humming to your daughter — did you even know you were humming? I let the sound of your voice fill my mind.

NINE

Rain saw the dog first, a German shepherd that sat still and stiff as a sentry beside the big man. Large, mostly black but with tawny fur on the legs, belly and around the eyes. She'd seen the man before. Somewhere. Where? She felt a flutter of unease in her belly.

"Good morning," he said.

He seemed nice enough, a slight smile playing at the corners of his mouth. He pushed his thick black glasses up his nose, stayed where he was beside the creek. Just sitting. He wore a black jacket, too hot for a summer day. His hair was long, pulled into a loose ponytail, his beard thick and long. He was heavy, very overweight.

"Good morning," said Tess sweetly.

Rain didn't say anything, just moved quickly toward Tess and grabbed her hand, started pulling her away.

"We're late," she said.

"Didn't your mom teach you to be nice?" asked the man.

She bristled, annoyed. In fact, her mother had not taught her to be nice, and neither had her father.

"My *mom*," she snapped, "told me not to talk to strange men in the woods."

She got in trouble sometimes at school, for speaking out, for talking back. *That's your father in you,* said her mother, not angrily. She didn't get in trouble at home for that sort of thing. She could say what she wanted to her parents, speak her mind, give her opinion. She was allowed to get angry, to yell even. She was allowed to be sad, frustrated, to cry. Her mom was a big believer in letting it out and talking it through. Rain's mother taught her that even though the world always wants girls to be nice and sweet, quiet, hold it all in, you don't always have to be that. *Own your feelings. Speak your mind. Know your boundaries. Protect them.*

The big man stared, displeased she could tell, though she couldn't say how since his face didn't change. Then he released a low whistle and that big dog trotted over to block their path to Hank's. Rain tugged Tess closer.

The beast stood panting in front of them,

106

legs wide, head low. He wasn't big. He was *huge.* His eyes were black, his tawny chest wide and muscular.

"Don't worry," said the man, not moving. "He's friendly."

The dog bared his teeth and started to growl.

It was a bright golden morning, sun washing in through the gauzy drapes, painting the room. Lily cooed happily on the monitor. The tendrils of the nightmare clung, pulling Rain back into the gloom.

She took a few breaths to calm herself. That place. That dog. Why was she back there? Never mind, scratch that. She knew why.

The bed beside her was cold and empty. Greg had left a note: "Thought it was better for you two to sleep. Rough night."

It was nearly 9 a.m., an epic sleep-in by current standards. It *had* been a rough night, Lily waking twice, emitting suddenly and inexplicably that high-pitched wail perfected by babies everywhere to fry each nerve ending in their exhausted mothers' bodies. Rain had nursed Lily back to sleep once, then paced the hallway for what seemed like hours after the baby woke a second time. Teething? Who knew? There'd been some late-night (or was it early morning) lovemaking — or was it just a dream? Did women dream about making love to their husbands? Maybe not. Her head throbbed.

"Maamaa," Lily sang over the monitor. "Ahhh. Ohhh."

It took an hour to get herself together, about fifty-six minutes longer than it used to take. She showered with Lily in the bouncy seat, found a pair of jeans she could squeeze into, a button-down shirt that didn't gape over her boobs, dressed, dug out the messenger bag she used to carry with her everywhere, packed the camera and the portable digital recorder, a fresh Moleskine and package of Pilot V5 pens. Ready. Then Lily — fed, changed, diaper bag stocked, snacks, toys, strapped into her car seat. Okay.

Sitting in the driver's seat and looking at Lily, red hair glinting gold in the morning light, Rain briefly wondered about the wisdom of bringing a baby to a crime scene. A crime scene that, with the help of Henry, and her willingness to break rules and sometimes laws, she and Gillian planned to enter.

But what else was she going to do? She hadn't left Lily with a sitter yet, though

Mitzi kept offering. She wasn't about to start on a whim. This was a whim, wasn't it? The beginning of a story no one had asked her to cover? She'd just have to make it all work, right? *When the road isn't laid clear before you,* her mother always said, *forge your own path.*

Admittedly, this probably wasn't what she had in mind.

The drive went quickly, traffic light, the day clear. She knew the way. She'd been where she was going before, too many times.

She and Gillian had stood among the throng of reporters always gathered outside the Markham house during Laney's disappearance, then when she was found. Sweltering afternoons, and long nights, emotions high. She remembered so clearly the feel of it — the dread, the fatigue, the intensity of every new piece of information, the tragic unfolding of the story. They'd lived it — barely going home, eating and sometimes sleeping in the news van. Her life, Greg especially, sorely neglected.

No crowds today as she approached; the Markham house had an air of desertion and the street was quiet, the overgrown and neglected yard edged with black-and-yellow crime scene tape. An empty squad car sat in the driveway, and a dark sedan blocked the property from street access. The message was clear: stay away.

Halloween decorations abounded on neighboring houses — striking a different tenor than those on her own street. Here, lawns had been turned into graveyards, skeletons hung from trees. As she pulled up the block, a grim reaper stood sentry by a tilting mailbox, a giant inflatable spider dominated another small yard.

Rain parked past the house, something tingling. A strange déjà vu, as if she'd played this scene out already, an odd sense of unease. She went around to the back to unpack Lily and put her in the sling.

Diaper bag over one shoulder, work satchel over the other, she approached the familiar white van. Gillian and their long-time driver, Josh, were in the cab, bent over something Rain couldn't see, Gillian talking, Josh nodding. They looked up as she approached, and both started waving.

Gillian emerged, svelte in a white pencil skirt, and blue silk blouse, heels. She tossed her honey hair, gazed at herself in the side mirror, leaning in close to examine her skin. Gillian out in front, Rain behind the scenes. That's how it had always been, and how they both liked it.

"Oh, wow," Gillian said, eyes falling on

Lily. "You brought Lily."

Rain shrugged, looking at Lily, who gazed up at the falling leaves, pointing. "I don't have a sitter."

"Of course," said Gillian, giving her a serious, thoughtful frown. "Right."

How *was* this going to work? She hadn't exactly thought it through.

But Gillian was already cooing, lifting the baby from the sling, Lily kicking her legs with happiness. And Rain was greeting Josh, a big man with a full, prematurely white beard and glittery blue eyes. Jeans, flannel shirt, faded denims — he was rough and ready just like always.

"I had a feeling you'd be back sooner rather than later."

Why did everyone keep saying that? He pulled her into a bear hug, which she gratefully returned. This was one of the things she missed most about work — her friends.

"I'm *not* back," she said. "I'm just along for the ride."

"Oh, sure."

"So how are we going to do this?" asked Gillian, balancing Lily on her slender hip. She and Rain locked eyes, mind-melded, then looked at Josh.

He raised his eyebrows. Late forties, father of three, the man you called in any crisis, always awake, always at the wheel and ready to go before anyone else.

"Toys, books, snacks?" he asked, regarding the baby. Rain handed over the diaper bag, which he easily slung over his shoulder.

"All right, Miss Lily," he said. "Let's do this."

And of course, Lily, the effortlessly friendly little spirit that she was, happily went to her new friend, grabbing ahold of his beard. Hard.

"They always do that," said Josh, wincing and carrying her to the cab.

Gil ducked under the tape and Rain followed, moving quickly, with purpose, as if they belonged there. That was key, always look like you knew where you were going — even when you were essentially breaking and entering. Good girls don't get answers.

Gillian knocked on the door, just to be sure the house was empty. And it was, just as Henry had promised.

"Crime scene techs are done," he'd told her. "According to my source, FBI left this morning. They'll have a patrol car there tonight, just to keep away any lookie-loos. My guy can leave the side door open for you."

"Thanks, Henry."

"Don't get caught," he warned. "And if you do, don't mention me."

"Come on."

"What are you looking for? Do you even know?"

"I'll know it when I see it."

Gillian and Rain walked over to the side of the house, Rain faster in her jeans and sneakers than Gillian was in her heels. She always dressed as if she was about to go on camera. Rain, on the other hand, would be in her pajamas everywhere she went if it were socially acceptable.

"This is where the second part of our story begins," Rain said, standing at a paint-splattered door with a rickety knob and a small glass-paned window covered with grime. She had the portable digital recorder in her hand.

"In the early hours of October 2, an unknown assailant broke into the house at 238 Pine Drive and killed Steve Markham."

Rain felt her heart race, wondering if this was how the killer got in. They pushed inside to a musty garage, moved past a parked silver Mercedes-Benz, some stacks of boxes, a humming furnace.

"When he was acquitted of the murder of his wife, we thought that was the conclusion of the story," said Gillian. This is how they did it: investigated together, took pictures, wrote notes, made snippet recordings. Later, Rain would weave together the full piece, write it, Gillian doing the reporting.

"I guess someone wanted to revise the ending," said Rain.

They found the interior door unlocked, pushed it open and stepped into a small laundry room. There was a strong odor in the house — mold, garbage, something else — a chemical edge, something that tickled the inside of Rain's nose.

She already had her camera out, stuck the recorder in her pocket, started snapping pictures.

A small house, tastefully decorated with budget items from Target — that kind of pretty, faux-distressed, almost modern look that was so in style. Laney Markham was a nice girl, and her house reflected that — a worn teddy bear on the couch, photographs of her family, a pretty collection of shells and candles on the dining room table, pretty dishes all in a row. They were always careful to keep her top of mind in their reporting, never wanting her life to be overshadowed by how she died, or by the man who killed her.

Gillian took the camera from her. Rain

scribbled notes. Their work together was silent and quick. They wouldn't need pictures for the broadcast — if there was one — but it would help Rain when she was writing.

"In here." Rain walked into the living room. "Henry said he was killed in here."

There should be some electricity on the air, shouldn't there? Some energy that set their skin to tingling. But it was just a quiet living room, some furniture clearly removed. The only evidence that someone had died was a thin spray of blood on the carpet that had been taped off in black, a chunky geometric outline around an organic splatter, like a macabre modern art installation.

"What are we doing here?" asked Gillian. She looked pale suddenly. It wasn't like her to get squeamish. They'd seen so much. The horrors people do. They knew it too well.

"We're documenting," said Rain. "Like we always do."

"For what?"

"For the rest of the story."

"Are you back?" asked Gillian, letting the camera dangle from the strap around her neck. "You know Andrew wants you to come back."

Andrew Thompson, executive producer of National News Radio Morning Edition, a bespectacled salt-and-pepper hottie who was equal parts ambition and brilliance. Rain had loved working with him, even though he was a major pain in the ass — an exacting editor, a ruthless fact-checker, a steely perfectionist.

He'd tried to talk her out of quitting, dropped the occasional email asking how was the life of the stay-at-home mom. Her job was waiting for her; she knew that.

"*I* want you to come back," Gillian said.

Before Rain could answer, Gillian's phone pinged. She glanced at it, then back to Rain, frowning.

"Someone's coming. We have to go."

Rain glanced out the window; a black sedan was pulling up behind the news van. Gillian headed for the door, but Rain grabbed the camera and took one more look around — a quick loop through the bedrooms, the kitchen. She snapped more photos.

What was she looking for?

They'd start the feature here, in the house, the day after. They'd work their way back. She could already feel it — the pace, the tendrils that reached into the past, the big questions at its center. She took a photo of the blood splatter.

She was about to follow Gillian when she

saw it, a red glitter out of the corner of her eye by the window, under the curtain.

"Let's go," said Gillian from the laundry room. "We're going to get arrested — again."

They couldn't get arrested, not with Lily here. Greg would kill her.

She pulled back the curtain. There in the mesh of the carpet was a bright red crystal heart about the size of a quarter. The blood started rushing in her ears, the room tilting a little. No. It wasn't possible.

"Rain!"

She grabbed it and shoved it in her pocket, chasing after Gillian.

"What were you looking at?" asked Gillian as they exited into the yard. "You're *white*. What's wrong?"

"Nothing. I just thought — Nothing."

"Hey." Gillian stopped her, her bright blue eyes turning on Rain like interrogation lamps. "What's going on?"

"I'm — not sure."

The fine lines around Gillian's eyes deepened, her brow furrowing with worry.

"Rain, what aren't you telling me?"

But then another ping on her phone had Gillian pulling her toward the street. The sedan, which had been moving slowly up the street, sped up and disappeared from view.

"Sorry," said Josh as they approached. "False alarm, I guess."

"That's okay," said Gillian. "Not much to see after all."

There were things that no one knew about her. Not Gillian, not Greg. Not even her father. In fact, there was only one person who knew her completely. That secret self, that stranger inside, hid the crystal heart in her palm, clenched her fist around it so tightly it started to hurt.

TEN

"Didn't your mom teach you to be nice?"

"My *mom* told me not to talk to strange men in the woods," she said.

She wasn't scared yet. But Tess was; she took hold of Rain's arm. But really, she was still Lara then, Laraine Winter. Laraine was a name her father made up, part Lawrence, part Lorraine, his parents. He'd insist always to people, continuously annoyed by their failure to do so, that it be pronounced LAH-raine. Not LOR-raine, which is how people always said it. He was annoyed when she started calling herself Lara.

It's common, he'd sniff.

That's the point, she said. *I just want to be like everyone else.*

The name wasn't exotic or cool the way he imagined it. It was just — awkward. She hated it. But her father didn't like to be edited.

Her mother spoke up. *Let her call herself*

119

what she wants to, she said. *Not everything is about you.*

"Lara," whispered Tess, pulling her close.

The dog blocked their path from the bridge. And as he stood there, panting, with a thin line of drool trailing from the curl of his lips, she felt the first lick of fear, a desire deep and primal to run for home.

"Call your dog off," she said.

Tess was making a small sound. The three of them joked that Tess was Piglet, and Lara was Tigger. And Hank, of course, was Eeyore, sometimes Pooh. At another moment, she would have laughed about that sound Tess was making. Except it wasn't funny.

"He won't hurt you," said the man.

He was disgusting. Big and slovenly, dressed all in black, with a bushy, unkempt beard and thick black-rimmed glasses. With effort, he'd pulled himself from his crouch. He was enormous, too, well over six feet tall.

"Call him back," she said, this time making her voice deeper and louder, the way her mother had told her. *Say no like you mean it,* Mom had taught her. *A certain kind of man doesn't hear any other tone. "No" shouldn't ask for permission to exist. There's no question mark after it.*

But the man just laughed. It was almost a

giggle, childish. She and Tess had their arms looped together, and in unison they started stepping backward, eyes trained on that dog. As they put distance between them, it bared its teeth, growl growing deeper. Tess started to cry.

"Tess, don't run," she whispered. "Whatever you do. Don't run."

"Oh," said Tess, a single note of pure fear. "Oh."

"You better stop moving," said the man. He lumbered his way up the bank. He would never be able to catch either one of them; she could see that. That's why he had the dog. Tess had practically fused her body to Rain's, and Rain gripped her tight. Her heart was a bird in the cage of her chest, throat sandpaper. Acutely she felt her own smallness, their isolation. She looked around for help. They were alone.

The black dog moved closer. Rain felt Tess pull away, start to unlace her arm. She tried to hold on to her, but her friend had gone blank with terror. Flight. That's what Rain saw in her friend's face, the blank terror of someone about to flee.

"Go, Wolf." His voice was a stern command.

When the dog started moving, Tess broke and ran. Rain tried to grab for her friend, but she couldn't hold her. The dog moved past Rain in a black blur. The man just stood on the edge of the bridge, his face blank, unreadable. His breath came ragged, a horrible wheeze.

What happened next was just a series of ugly sounds and images in Rain's memory. Tess yelling as the dog grabbed hold of her calf, taking her down. Rain running toward them. Fur and flesh under her fingers as she tried to pull the dog off Tess, beating at the soft fur, feeling the muscles under her fists. A yelp, a sound that was nearly a roar, then teeth on her arm, then on her leg, a terrible tearing of her skin.

Tess scrambling away, blood trailing. Her own screaming. Then a vise grip on her shoulder, fingertips hard as stone. She was knocked to the ground, looking up into that face, moon-white above the beard, eyes glittering with glee. It almost looked like he was going to scratch his shoulder, the way he moved his arm in that direction. But the backhand that connected with her jaw, shattering it, knocked her out cold.

Rain took a deep breath, coming back to the present — her bedroom, Greg's deep-sleep breathing. She moved in close to her husband and he wrapped her up in his arms without waking up. She held on tight, centered herself, matched her breathing to his.

I am not that girl. I am not in that place. It is behind me, part of my past. I survived.

Three a.m.: the hour of alchemy. Not the dead of night where sleep might fall back over her like a cloak, the light and energy of morning still distant, too far to draw her into the next day. Here, at 3 a.m., all her best ideas and her worst fears, worries, doubts mingled, an acidic potion of sandman dust, and whispers, and bad imaginings. Henry's words — *like someone else we know* — an earworm that moved through her brain.

Eugene Kreskey was never far, no matter that he was dead, or that she'd buried him deep. He was always there.

She reached for the monitor, switched on the screen and looked at Lily, so peaceful, so safe and loved beyond measure. Her heart rate started to slow. So much therapy; so much talking. It was her father who suggested that she put that day in a box and lock it up tight, and never, ever open that lid.

"My father — who you never knew — he drank," he told her. This was months after. Her grades were down; she was waking

123

nightly in terror. She was having daily meltdowns over nothing. It wasn't just the day in the woods, the horror of it. It wasn't just her injuries — a jaw that clicked even after it healed, the scars from the dog on her leg; it was the loss of everything — Tess, Hank, the girl she was. She couldn't figure out how to fit back into the world.

"When he did, he was a different man," her father said. "He hurt me — badly."

He did a thing he'd always done, circled one forearm with the long fingers of his other hand and rubbed. That night she noticed a scar, a deep gouge in the skin of his wrist.

The idea that someone could hurt her father had baffled Rain. How did you hurt the moon? That he had been a boy once, vulnerable, seemed like a lie, like the stories he made up for her about boys and girls who built jetpacks that took them to Saturn, who hunted dragons in the woods, who rode dolphins to a secret world under the sea.

"I could think about those times, about who he was and what he did, and let them define me," he said. "But I don't. I lock those memories away deep inside where they can't hurt me."

"How?"

"When they come," he said, "you imagine

124

them written on paper. Then you fold that paper and shut it inside the box. Lock it and throw the key down a well."

She tried to imagine doing that. Did she feel better? Maybe a little.

She'd never met her father's parents; they'd both died before she was born. There were some grainy black-and-white photos, a wedding portrait. They looked thin-lipped and severe.

"Do you hate him?"

Rain had so much hate in her heart after that day in the woods. It was a monster just barely caged in her brain, raging, knocking things around. She didn't know how she could live with that much rage in her; it was a black fog over her life. Everything that once seemed beautiful or fun or funny was just ash. Who would she be now if her parents hadn't gotten her the help she needed? She didn't know, didn't want to know.

Her father took off his glasses, those eternal round specs. "I did hate him — then. But now I understand what it's like to have demons. To let them control you. I forgive him."

He looked at her uncertainly, like maybe he was worried he'd said too much. It was late; he'd woken up with her after her nightmare, made her some warm milk. Now they sat on the porch together, looking up at the starry sky.

"I can't forgive him," she said. "I won't."

"No," he said gravely. "That's different. I won't forgive Eugene Kreskey either. How can we?"

He reached for her hand. His hand was big and strong, enveloping her own.

"Look," he said. "Let's keep it practical. When the memories come, say this to yourself — *I am not that girl. I am not in that place. It is behind me, part of my past. I survived because I am strong.*"

But it wasn't true. She'd survived because she was weak. She'd tried to explain this to her therapist, to her parents. No one seemed to understand that. *You were a child, Lara. What else could you have done?* She could imagine at least a million scenarios where things could have gone differently. Still, that mantra, it worked. It never failed to give her a little jolt, a boost out of the mire of her memories. Rain guessed the old man wasn't a total failure as a father. Maybe she was too hard on him.

Finally, she just gave up on sleep. Who needs it when there's coffee?

She extracted herself from the warmth of

her husband's arms and left the bedroom. She checked on Lily, then went to the room she and Greg used as an office, sat at her desk and checked her email. Nothing from Henry. She sent him a message, knowing him to be a chronic insomniac, and definitely not one to complain about 3 a.m. missives. Just a subject line: Did you forget about me?

She hesitated before going down the rabbit hole of social media. Did she really want to open that browser and get sucked into the vortex of Everyone Else — all the pretty lies, half-truths, curated moments, bravado, faux-humble braggadocio. Had she ever emerged from a social media romp with her self-esteem intact? No.

But she went anyway, wading through the lives of old school friends on whom, but for social media, she'd never have laid eyes again, colleagues who were doing (way, *way*) better than she was — or so it seemed, former editors she'd never really liked, distant cousins she hadn't seen in a decade. The cavalcade of filtered images — trips to Venice, recipes for a Tuesday night, pots prettily bubbling on stoves, perfectly decorated rooms, pictures of children in all manner of comic mischief.

Rain's own picture of Lily covered in

sweet potatoes had earned her 250 thumbs up, hearts and laughing emojis. She was pathetically pleased, started scrolling through the comments. A note from her old friend, journalist Sarah Wright: What a cutie! Motherhood is the most important job in the world! The heart-eyed emoji! Rain clicked on Sarah's page.

Honored and stunned that my feature on the opioid epidemic has been nominated for a Pulitzer Prize in Journalism. Am I dreaming?

Rain already knew about the nomination, of course. It was everywhere. And Sarah deserved it. She'd been working her ass off for decades. So, how was it possible to be happy for someone — because Sarah was a great person and a stellar journalist, and her series was, simply put, brilliant — and yet still feel a dump of despair so total that you almost needed to lie down. Sarah's kids had been more or less raised by nannies and by Sarah's mother — a fact over which Sarah herself had voiced poignant regret and had even written about. According to Gillian — who knew everything about everyone — Sarah's daughter had just dropped out of Princeton and was living in

Sarah's basement. Sarah's son, according to Gillian, didn't even speak to her.

Women make choices, said Gillian, single and childless, *by choice. We must. Do you want a Pulitzer Prize? Or do you want a happy kid? Men don't have to make those decisions. There aren't as many judging eyes on them.*

Rain was ashamed to admit that she wanted both. Why couldn't she have both? Wasn't it just giving in to think you couldn't do or have it all?

Anyway, Rain wasn't online to bring forth her daily — or nightly — existential crisis.

She clicked on Gillian's Twitter feed.

Why isn't there more information on Steve Markham's murder? read Gillian's tweet. *The Feds aren't talking. What gives?*

Her post had earned nearly a thousand likes and even more retweets.

Indeed, thought Rain. *What gives?*

She searched, scrolled through old articles about Markham that she'd read a thousand times. Old news from the investigation, the trial, his acquittal, his book deal, media appearances. Chatter online — women in love with him, feminists decrying the injustice of his acquittal, profiles on the crime blogs, and those sites dedicated to murder and murderers. Then the cursory stories about the recent discovery of his body. Nothing

129

new, no threads to pull. Like Greg said, the sad end to an unjust story. Unless.

Her fingers hovered over the keyboard, then she entered a name into the search bar. She clicked on the first link:

The Boston Boogeyman Wayne Garret Smith, youth counselor, beloved in his community as an advocate for underprivileged boys. He ran an after-school sports program at the local recreation center for nearly twenty years. Smith received awards, grants, was featured in area papers for his tireless work on behalf of young men just like he had been. Orphaned at ten, he was raised as a ward of the state, never adopted, emancipated from the system at eighteen. He joined the army, went to college, married, had two young girls. He was an American success story, someone from the twisted beginnings of abuse who came through to thrive and help other young men, too.

Rain scrolled through newspaper articles, images from the trial, pictures of the three boys who went missing over a five-year period in the Boston area. (It was suspected that there were many more, but their bodies were never found. He had access to boys —

his center a place where runaways could seek shelter for the night, get a hot meal, come for clothes or a shower.)

When the police brought Smith in, they had a rock-solid case: damning physical evidence in the form of trophies — a Spider-Man watch, a tattered old bear — not to mention the graphic photos Smith had taken himself. But Smith claimed his civil rights had been violated — that any admissions he'd made had been coerced, that he'd been brutalized by police, that the arresting officer had failed to Mirandize him, evidence had been planted.

After a lengthy trial, Smith's high-profile attorney managed to establish enough reasonable doubt that he was acquitted. It was a travesty of epic proportions, the kind of case that haunted cops, crime beat reporters and prosecutors alike.

A year later, after an anonymous tip, Smith's body was found in an abandoned barn deep in the woods on the outskirts of Boston. He died the way his young victims did — bound, in mortal terror, tortured, violated and humiliated. No physical evidence, no witnesses, suspects or leads. The killer was never found.

A little red 1 appeared over her mail icon. She clicked on it and there was a message from Henry. Subject line: For Your Eyes Only.

A burst of adrenaline. She clicked on the email and saw a slew of attachments: police reports from the Smith and Markham murders, crime scene photos, civilian security camera images.

There's not a whole heck of a lot to go on, he wrote. But this is everything I have on the Boogeyman, and the Markham murder, gleaned from inside contacts, and other moles like me — those of us watching from the shadows, the invisible.

As a writer herself, Rain appreciated his flair for drama.

He went on: Some of the civilian cams are interesting. You know how everyone has those doorbells now, the in-home cameras, doggy watchers?

Yes, she knew them well.

An image was captured, he wrote. Useless for identification but compelling nonetheless.

Finally: Nothing on Kreskey, of course. Those files are too old to be digital. You'll have to go back to Detective Harper for those details.

Detective Harper. Another name that moved through her like a shiver.

What did you find today?

Nothing much, she lied.

She'd put the red crystal heart in the back of her underwear drawer, wrapped in a piece of silk. She'd been puzzling over it. The police would have found it when they searched the place. No way they could have missed it. Which meant that someone put it there *after* the technicians had left. She briefly toyed with the idea that Henry might be fucking with her. But then she dismissed it. It was one of those things that no one knew about her — almost no one. She could barely bring herself to think about it, what it might mean, the only person who could have put it there. How could he have known that she'd be there to find it? She locked it all up tight, in the box where she locked all the other memories on which she didn't want to dwell.

Can we make a deal? wrote Henry. I give you what I find, and you keep me in the loop, too? I get an exclusive interview with Rain Winter before your big reentry into the world of investigative journalism?

Deal, she wrote back. Even though it was a promise she might or might not keep.

I almost believe you.

Rain clicked on one of the links and saw a grainy image of a hunched figure wearing a backpack, hooded. He must have turned toward a security light; the shot revealed a mask — feathers, a beak. A hawk.

She stared at it a long time, another dark memory jangling around in her brain, a kind of tension in her shoulders. She clicked through some of the other images, but they were shadows, the figures just amorphous blobs.

She opened a bunch of other images. She'd seen the crime scene photos from the discovery of Laney Markham's body, among others. She'd been to morgues, watched bodies carried away in bags. Bodies reduced to trash, lives brutally ended. She didn't get squeamish or overwhelmed the way some people did. Not anymore. She had learned to put a distance between herself and the horrible things she'd seen in her life. She'd had no choice.

Now, she opened file after file, reading, looking, remembering. It was a rabbit hole. She disappeared.

"What are you doing?"

She didn't see Greg come in, and his low, sleepy voice sent a jolt through her. He slumped in the chair opposite the desk, rubbed at his rumpled hair, a shadow in the dim room. He was holding Lily, who had her head against his chest.

"Research," she said. The screen was a collage of horrible images — the blank, remorseless face of Wayne Garret Smith, the innocent smiles of young boys, the crime scene photos of Markham and Smith. Looking at it, her baby on the other side of the screen, she was suddenly ashamed.

"Was she crying?"

"You didn't hear her?"

She'd left the monitor in the bedroom, hadn't carried it to the office with her. Still, the baby's room wasn't that far away. She would have heard. *Should* have. She had a laser beam focus; when she was involved in something, the world disappeared. Her mother used to rage at her father for just this trait. *The house could burn to the ground. And if you're writing, we'll all die before you notice and maybe not even then.*

This disappearing act had been the source of many an argument in her own marriage, and even before. Rain would miss dates with Greg, forget to call, just leave him hanging at restaurants and parties. *Why does he put up with it?* she'd wondered, sure he would break up with her at some point. But he didn't break up with her; he stayed with her, understood her and finally proposed. *Maybe this big diamond on your finger will remind you to call when you're going to be late.*

"I think she's hungry," said Greg now, rocking the baby.

She closed her laptop, got up and took Lily from Greg, returned to the nursery.

"I'd feed her, but it doesn't look like you pumped any milk?" he said from the hallway.

She sat in the glider. "It's okay," she said. "Try to get a little more sleep."

Greg hovered a moment, dropped a hand on her shoulder, then left the room.

"Are you hungry, little bunny?" she asked.

Lily gurgled happily, looking up into Rain's eyes. The baby's gaze was deep and alert, smiley. Rain felt as if she could see all the layers of the girl, the woman her daughter would become. Smart, sweet, brave, full of mischief and questions.

The sun was lighting the sky from beneath the horizon. How long had Rain been in her office looking at images of murder and death, misery and loss? Must have been nearly three hours. Lily cooed, then latched on. Rain rocked them back and forth, back and forth, thinking of the man in the hawk mask.

ELEVEN

They're gone. I've answered their questions the best that I can; they've scribbled their notes and nodded at my insights, hungry for anything I might be able to give them in the absence of any evidence at all.

I'll admit to feeling a little badly as I brew some tea. (It was peppermint you ordered the last time we met, peppermint tea with honey. It was too hot, and you sipped it gingerly, getting up the courage to tell me that you didn't want me in your life anymore. At all. Not as a lover. Not as a friend. But you didn't unfriend me on Facebook. Does that mean there's still hope, Rain Winter? Just kidding.)

The strawberry blonde FBI agent was so earnest and fresh-faced, still with hope, that straight-bodied righteousness that only young law enforcement people seem to carry. They are fighting for right with gun and shield, intelligence and perseverance.

The older ones start to sag a bit, though, don't they? They get those exhausted shiners under their eyes that no amount of sleep will ever fix, the gray pall of late nights, cramped spaces, bad food, injustice cramming its big fist down their throats at every turn.

Her partner had a bit of that. Large guy, silent, graying at the temples. He had a paunch. I didn't love the way he looked around my living room, staring at my books, looking into the fireplace. It was clear that it had been recently used, full of ash and spent logs. Did he wonder why I had the fireplace burning? In fact, I didn't love the way he looked at *me.* A cynical frown, a watchful quiet.

But I liked her pluck. That's sexist, probably that's what you'd say. What's pluck, after all? When a woman is assertive where she should be shy, questioning when she might be acquiescent, hard when she should be soft? Yes, *plucky* is a bit — what would you say — condescending. But then, I'm a man, and we're all misogynists in our deepest secret hearts. We fear you for how much control you have over us, even when you don't know it. Your words, not mine. I have nothing but respect for women, truly. I vastly prefer their company over the companionship of men.

Still, I haven't always been the man you deserved. I regret our last night together, Lara. I play it over and over in my mind, thinking of everything I could have done differently.

But there's no point in going back, is there? Isn't that what you said? We can't change the choices we made or the consequences of our actions. So why do the memories never fade?

I still so vividly remember that eternal suburban smell of cut grass and wet leaves. It was hot already but there was a coolness in the shade in the trees. The cicadas were humming already; they'd get louder as it got hotter.

I heard your voices as I drew deeper into the woods. My heart lifted, like it always did when I heard your voice.

I was right, I thought. I knew the way you two would take. We knew each other so well then, didn't we? We all accepted each other completely the way only our childhood friends do. Later, friendships change. Girls and boys, there's another layer suddenly. Adults, their focus shifts to work and family. Friendships become a lower priority. But as kids, those relationships define us. We love each other so fiercely. Of course, my love for you was deeper still.

At first, I thought it was the two of you laughing. But then I heard that off chord; it was almost as if even before I intellectually knew that you were screaming, the sound touched something primal in me.

What did I do? When confronted with a threat — we fight, we flee or more commonly we freeze. We don't have a lot of control over which; this is a limbic response of the brain. It is beyond personality or choice. It's hardwiring.

I froze, listened.

Then I pedaled as hard and as fast as I could in the direction of the sound. That's *my* hardwiring, to jump into the fray, I guess. Even though I was the skinniest kid in our class, regularly bullied and picked on through grade school and middle school, taunted as gay, and for only hanging out with girls — namely you and Tess.

As I approached the bridge, my brain had a hard time processing what I was seeing. A huge man, all in black, accompanied by the biggest dog I'd ever seen. It was the stuff of nightmares and for a couple of seconds I thought: *Wake up, wake up. This is not happening.* There was blood. Tess was screaming. You were still and silent on the ground, curled up on your side. And then he hit

Tess, threw her over his shoulder like she weighed nothing, which she didn't. She didn't weigh a thing — a dragonfly, a flower petal of a girl. He grabbed you by the wrist and started dragging your unconscious body over the ground. You were slack, a rag doll, blood trailing from your mouth in a line.

Looking back, what I should have done was run. I should have gone for help. The nearest house was minutes away on my bike. Good old Mrs. Newman. She would have heard me screaming as I rode, she'd have the phone in her hand by the time I got to her porch. We *all* might have survived if I'd done that. Kreskey's car was parked a good mile away, we'd later learn. The police would have been on him before he made it there with you. You'd have woken up and maybe fought again.

But I didn't do that. I climbed off the bike and grabbed the pump that was mounted on the bar. PS — this is *not* an effective weapon. I would learn that too late.

"Hey," I yelled. My voice was high-pitched and weak. "Hey, let them go!"

And I ran, yelling like a warrior, toward the man who was trying to hurt my friends.

Later, one of my many, many shrinks postulated that it was my obsession with superheroes, my video-game addiction, and my penchant for the heroes of spy movies and novels — *Mission Impossible,* Bourne, Bond — that contributed to the idea that I could take on and best a man like Eugene Kreskey. He weighed in at two hundred seventy-five pounds; I was barely over a hundred. He stood over six feet tall and was by all accounts preternaturally strong. My arms looked like Wikki Stix; you and Tess were both taller.

Kreskey was a violent sociopath, newly released from a psychiatric facility and living alone in a house he'd inherited from his deceased parents. And of course, there was the dog, a vicious, abused German shepherd he'd trained to hunt. Wolf — who I'd get to know well.

I agree with that shrink. What did I know then about real violence, about true evil? My mind was filled with fantasies — about myself, about the world. I was fully indoctrinated into the lie of good-always-triumphs-over-evil, even when good is an ant and evil is a mountain. There was *no way* the hero ever lost. And in that scenario, in my adolescent mind, I was the hero. I was going to save you.

Of course, I never had a chance; I know that now. It only took a single blow to the jaw, Kreskey's favorite backhand strike. All the power of that giant shoulder radiating into the knuckles. My jaw shattered; I was instantly stunned into submission.

Wow. The pain. How it blasts down your neck and up to the crown of your head. It steals your breath, your voice. I know you understand. That first time that anyone ever hits you?

I had a slight advantage in that I'd been in a fight or two on the playground, so I knew the shock of it, the flood of adrenaline, the rage, the *fear*. But those playground wimp-fests didn't prepare me for real violence, the intentional action of an evil man wanting to do irreparable harm. Your whole body goes into a chemical revolt. I bled and bled, lay there weeping in pain, helpless. He dropped you to deal with me; he couldn't take us all. Then I was the one being dragged, Tess still over his shoulder. I thought she might be dead. Her head was tilted. I'd never seen skin so white. Her hands just flopped around. She wasn't wearing her glasses.

He grunted, angry, his moon-face red.

"Find *it*," he yelled at the dog. "Bring it to me."

It. He meant you.

Because when I looked around, you were

143

gone, Lara. Laraine. LAH-raine, as your father was quick to remind anyone who dared to mispronounce it — because it was about him, wasn't it, *your* name? The dog ran back behind us, and Kreskey kept walking, lumbering really. He muttered. *Stupidlittlebitchstupidlittlebitch.* He was slow, plodding, crazy as a shithouse rat. His breathing was a painful wheeze. He thought you got away, that you were running for help.

His grip on my wrist was steel, a vise. My efforts to pull away were pointless. I know you know what it's like to be utterly powerless, to be sick with terror. I couldn't move my mouth, the sounds coming from me were animal, strangled. I choked on the taste of my own blood, retching.

The dog came back without you; Kreskey picked up his pace best he could, that fat fuck. I was glad, I was, and yet I hated you. *Lara,* I wanted to scream. *Lara, help us.*

Because I *saw* you as he dragged me away, a shivering black shadow in the hollow of a tree down by the riverbank. Your white, white face, it was blank, your eyes were unseeing, your body was quaking. I know now — years later, a doctor who has extensively studied trauma and its effect on the brain, the psyche — that it was shock, that you retreated to another place in your mind.

You would sit there like that for the next twelve hours until they found you, while Kreskey got farther and farther.

You ran, Lara.

You ran and hid.

And Eugene Kreskey took us away.

TWELVE

Why was she doing this? She hadn't seen her father in months.

The rural road twisted and wound in front of her, the canopy of trees so thick above that her headlights automatically turned on. Lily napped in the back seat. Rain glanced at her in the rearview mirror that was trained on the baby instead of the road behind her, something Greg would notice the next time he took the car in for service. *It's not a baby-view mirror,* he'd admonished her last time. *You're supposed to be watching the road, not the kid.*

The closer she got to the place where she grew up, the more tension she felt settle into her body, the shallower her breathing became. But that's where she was headed with her story, wasn't it? The road home was a journey into the past. Maybe that was why she was going to see her father. Or maybe it was just that there was something that drew her back home, to her father, when she had questions she couldn't answer. Wasn't there a part of you that always wanted to go back to the time when you thought your parents knew everything?

The crystal heart was in the pocket of her jeans.

She turned onto the long drive to the house where she grew up, taking the rocky, potholed path slowly, hoping not to wake Lily. The house, when it crept into view, was ramshackle and gray, yard a crazy tangle, dominated by a large twisting metal sculpture. Her father had the piece commissioned for some ridiculous sum and it had sat, rusting in the elements, for twenty-odd years.

The statue was an eyesore to begin with, sharp-edged and menacing. Now it just looked like a piece of neglected junk, akin to a rusting old jalopy, or a dilapidated lawn mower.

It was exactly the kind of purchase that drove Rain's mother crazy and was a part of the eventual undoing of her parents' marriage. Wasteful, pointless expenditures that frittered away their earnings. The money from his novels came in chunks. There would be months of excess, extravagant trips, lavish gifts, then long dry spells. Her mother worked as a teacher, trying to create stability — financial and otherwise — for Rain. She worked, and managed the house, and Rain's life — while her father stayed in his attic office, or went on book tours, or spent months at writers' retreats.

The sight of that sculpture put an uncomfortable squeeze on Rain's heart, thinking about how her mother worked until the year she died. She got almost nothing in the nasty divorce from Rain's father, but still managed to save money for Rain's education with enough left over so that Rain had started her life with a "fuck you" fund — the most important thing a woman could have: the ability to walk away from a shitty man, an exploitative job or any other situation in which she felt helpless and trapped.

Rain stepped out of the car and listened. A chickadee issued a sweet, low whistle and the chimes sang on the porch, wind rustling the leaves. She heard the tap-tap-tap of the woodpecker. Though she'd left this place at sixteen when her mother and father finally divorced, she never stopped thinking of it as home.

Her father, tall and thin, a hurricane of silver-white hair, black shirt and pants, emerged from the house, stepping onto the porch. He lifted a hand, unsurprised, though she'd given him no warning, and it had been nearly half a year since last she'd visited. It was another place she kept promising not to visit again — too many sad memories, her dad too difficult — yet here she was. She walked toward him, leaving Lily in the car with the windows open. He walked the path, grass as tall as his thighs.

"I thought you'd come," he said when he reached her. He took her face in his palms, kissed her gently on the head. Then he walked past her to peer into the car at Lily, who was sound asleep, head tilted to the side, snoring a little.

"She's just like you," he said after a moment.

"Is she?"

Lily always just seemed like herself, this magical gift from the universe, not like Rain really, not like Greg. There were flashes of her husband — in her smile and in her frown, in the color of her eyes. But Rain didn't see herself in Lily's face.

"You don't see it?"

"Maybe around the mouth?" It didn't pay to argue with her father. He was never wrong.

He squinted at her from behind his glasses. "It's in the *spirit*."

Something about this made her smile.

"We can sit on the porch," he said. "Until she wakes up."

She sat on the old rocker and watched the car, while her dad went in to get them something to drink. The ghost of her mother was everywhere here, kneeling in the overgrown garden, staring up in disbelief at the monstrosity in their yard, standing on the porch looking for Rain to come up the drive on her bike. Rain tried not to think about her mother's final days in hospice, the dim room, the sound of her breathing, how quiet and slow the world became. Everything that was important — school, grades, internships, her trauma, her father's disgrace — slipped away behind a curtain of grief. He was there for them then, even if he hadn't been any other time. He was there, a hand on her shoulder, by her mother's bedside, whispering to her. He was the husband and father in Mom's dying days that he had never been when she was well.

"I regret so much," he'd said to Rain after the funeral.

Don't be angry with him, her mother said once. *He is only the man he knows how to be.*

"It doesn't matter, Dad," she'd said. There was an ache in her chest for him, for both of them. "She knew you did your best."

"I did," he said. He bowed his head and took off his glasses. "A poor showing, but, yes, unfortunately, my best."

Now he handed her a cold glass of lemonade, which she couldn't even believe he had. It was good, tasted fresh and sweet, tingling. There was a woman who came in twice a week, did the housework, the grocery shopping for him. He'd mentioned it the last time they spoke.

"How's motherhood?" he asked.

"All-consuming," she said. "Wonderful, exhausting, frustrating as hell and totally blissful."

Her father demanded total honesty. He could hear the ring of lies and half-truths, dug in until he got the whole story in all its terrible, shimmery, dull and beautiful layers. She wouldn't dream of bothering with the pat answer.

"Was it a dig?" she asked. "That damn jogging stroller."

"Not a dig," he said with a slow shake of his head. "An encouragement. A reminder."

"Hmm."

He gave a chuckle, looked at his glass. The wind chimes sang.

"You know, your mother was a better writer than I ever was — really in every way.

Whatever small amount of ability I had was dwarfed by her talent."

Lilian Rae Winter wrote about love, motherhood, failure, regret. Her characters were layered — wise, flawed, human. They hurt each other, did wrong, were redeemed. She'd had a few books published, as well, small literary novels that were well reviewed and sold a smattering of copies. Rain had them on a shelf in her office, opened the pages when she wanted to feel close to her mother's love, her wisdom.

"Compared to you, we were both hacks," he went on.

"Stop."

He lifted a palm. "Talent doesn't know itself."

Rain sat up from the slouch she was in. She didn't like to think that Lilian had given things up because of motherhood, because of her selfish husband, that her life hadn't been all she'd hoped.

"She didn't want your life," said Rain. "Gone all the time, dogged by fans, lauded then slammed by reviewers, living and dying by the numbers you couldn't control."

She listened to the wind, for the sounds of Lily waking.

"But she missed *the writing*," her father said. "Which she didn't have to give up, but did anyway. There's always time to write, if you want it. Story creates a space in which to be told."

Just like a man to think the world was simple, that story made a place *for itself.* That you didn't have to juggle and bargain for every moment of free mental space, for energy.

"Maybe if you'd been around more," she said, unable to resist a dig herself.

He drew in and released a long breath.

"Maybe," he said with a nod.

"So — it *was* a dig."

"Like I say." He turned to face her. The lines around his mouth and eyes had grown deeper, his skin crepey and soft. But he was still handsome, still a smile turned up the corners of his mouth — in, as always, on the cosmic joke of it. "It was just a reminder. You have a gift. A calling."

She laughed a little. He'd always said this to her — her gift, her talent, her calling. It seemed like this idea, like so many of the ideas he had about his only daughter, was more about "The Bruce Winter" than it was about her. What would it be like for the great writer to have a child who was just normal, who had no special place in the world? As much as she wanted to believe that there was more to her than had so far

153

been revealed, she was fairly sure there wasn't.

"You saw the news?" she said, changing the subject.

"I did," he said, watching her. "What are you thinking?"

She ran down what she knew so far, her conversations with Chris and Henry, the files Henry had sent her, her visit to the Markham house. She didn't tell him about the crystal heart; that was hers alone. He listened carefully, rubbing at his chin.

"Have you talked to Greg?"

"He knows I want to follow the story."

"Does he know you took Lily to the Markham house?"

She shook her head. Sins of omission. She'd been guilty of it before; it had almost unstitched them — more than once. And here she was, doing it again.

"Why this?" he asked. "Why now?"

Something about the way the leaves rustled brought her back there again.

The truth was, she didn't remember much. After that first blow, there was just a series of images, sounds, vivid but disjointed. Where the dog had bitten her, she saw the bright red of her own torn flesh, even the incomprehensible white of bone, the pain had yet to register. She heard Hank

154

issuing a warrior's scream that was abruptly, brutally silenced. She wasn't even sure then where he had come from. Tess over the shoulder of a giant, hanging, a rag doll. Hank, limp and pale being dragged by the wrist. The labored sound of the big man's breathing. The smell of rot. Her clothes growing damp. The sun sinking. The sound of birdsong. Darkness encroaching. Then the sound of her name, and Hank's, and Tess's. Knowing that she was the only one who could answer, but she didn't have a voice.

The world was far and fading fast. She'd lost a lot of blood from those dog bites; the one on her leg would take more than fifty stitches. A plastic surgeon would be called but the scar of that bite would mar her leg forever. Her jaw was broken, both eyes swollen and black; she had two broken ribs. And she was the lucky one. By far.

Years of therapy, a career that let her dig deep into crime, trying to understand why people did what they did to each other, and yet, and yet, psychologically, in many ways, she was still where she was when they found in her the woods, twelve hours after Kreskey took her friends.

"I'm thinking there's a connection," she said in answer to his question. "Between

155

Markham and the Boston Boogeyman."

"And Kreskey."

She nodded, felt her chest tighten. "Yes. Maybe."

"Three men guilty of horrible crimes, all of whom escaped justice."

"Until they didn't."

"It's a good story," he said. "Who will you cover it for?"

"I don't know," she said.

She remembered this feeling, the feeling of bringing something to her father and waiting for his reaction. Her mother loved everything Rain said and did; even her mediocre outings were met with enthusiasm from her mom. And so Rain learned to never be afraid, that it was okay to try and fail and try again. A beautiful lesson that had served her well. But her father recognized good work when he saw it. There was a special look on his face, a certain tone. Even now, an accomplished person and a mother herself, she craved it.

"I wonder," he said quietly.

She waited. He paused, took a sip of that lemonade. She did the same — it was cool and tart, reminded her of days long gone — sitting with her mother playing cards at night. They never had a television. She watched nonstop at Tess's and Hank's, but at home it was books and art, cards and board games. They'd sit on the porch and listen to the owls, watch the stars, talk about this and that, or nothing. Sometimes they just sat. Did people still do that?

"I wonder if this is really the story you want to tell."

She felt that flutter of annoyance, of disappointment that was so familiar in her father's presence. She wanted him to say what her mother would have said: *Write your way in. If the story is there, you'll know it.*

"What does that mean?"

He looked at her, waited. She stared at him until he dropped his gaze, took off his glasses and rubbed at his nose. He still wore his wedding band. Her mother never took hers off either.

"You told me to lock it up tight," she said. The words tasted like gravel in her mouth, gritty, dirty. "I did that."

"I did tell you that," he said. "I've since revised my thinking on that matter. These days I have a lot of time to reflect."

There was a stack of books on the table by the rocker. *The Snow Leopard, The Prophet,* a volume on northern birds, *The Wisdom of the Sufi Sages, Zen and the Brain.*

"A lot of the mistakes I made in my life were due to the things I didn't want to examine about my past. There's power in telling the story. You know that, don't you?"

"The story's been told."

"Not by you."

"I'm not the one to tell it."

"There's no one who can tell it better," he said. "This story, the one you've brought to me. It's *that* story. Surely you see. Because if these crimes are connected, that's the beginning."

Lily started to cry, her voice carrying over the distance between them, as thin and distant as birdsong. But Rain felt it in her body. She got up quickly, eager to get away from the conversation. But her father put a hand on her arm.

"I'll get her," he said, hopping up. He seemed so happy, she didn't have the heart to stop him. She figured she'd hear Lily start to wail as some weird man she barely knew lifted her from her car seat. But when he came back, the baby was happily smiling in his arms. She'd go to *anyone,* obviously. Weren't babies only supposed to want their mommies? He had the diaper bag over his other shoulder, looked like a natural with it.

"She knows her grandpa, doesn't she?" he said.

"Ba! Ba!" Lily enthused.

"Baba! Yes! That's a perfect name for me,"

her father said, clearly pleased.

Rain's heart was still knocking with annoyance, with an odd kind of fear. She followed her father inside, his words bouncing around the inside of her skull. She was forced to ask herself the worst question she could imagine asking: Was her father right?

To tell the story she was thinking about telling, did she have to dive into her own shadowy past, as well? Was the reason she couldn't fully move on from that day in the woods that she'd never really told it? She hadn't narrated her experience; she'd buried it. Now it was digging its way up and through her psyche. It was a child's memory. Maybe she needed to face it as an adult.

"Where did that come from?"

Her father had placed Lily in a high chair she'd never seen before. It looked ancient but sturdy.

He looked at her with a smile. "It's yours. It was in the basement."

She put her hand on it. It was solid wood with bunnies carved into the seat, a tray that fit in neatly like Jenga blocks. No strap. She had no memory of it.

"See, it pays to be a hoarder," said her father. He went into the diaper bag and retrieved the little plastic container of Cheerios, her sippy cup. "All this minimalist garbage about getting rid of all your things, clutter clearing. Clutter is life!"

"Why did you take it out?"

Lily bounced happily, shoved a few Cheerios in her mouth. She was fixated by her "Baba" — maybe it was the glasses. The kid couldn't take her eyes off him.

"Last time you came, I wasn't prepared," he said. "I think it was uncomfortable for you. Maybe that's why you didn't come back until now."

It *had* been uncomfortable. But it wasn't because there hadn't been a high chair. Her father and Greg had started talking about politics, disappearing into their man world of conversation that seemed to take precedence over everything in their immediate environment. Lily had been fussy. And Rain's father seemed annoyed that Lily was making noise, interrupting his thoughts. He'd looked embarrassed when she nursed. The place was an obstacle course of junk. The baby couldn't walk yet, but what about when she could? The house was dirty — like really dirty, floor gritty, dishes in the sink, coffee table covered with magazines, newspapers. She suggested he get someone in to clean; he'd been offended.

Rain felt like her father barely even looked at her, was disapproving of her choice to

160

stay home with Lily. Then the stroller came in the mail. *Don't let this slow you down.* What a clueless, male thing to say, right?

"I did get someone in to clean, too," he said. "Did you notice?"

He'd mentioned it before, the last time they talked. He was repeating himself. But he'd always done that.

It *was* clean, cleaner than maybe it had ever been. She opened the fridge; it was stocked and organized. There were no dishes in the sink, flowers sat in a vase on the windowsill. There was a dish towel folded on the counter. Other things started to come into focus. His sudden consideration for her; his enthusiasm for Lily. His questioning of past choices. There was a lightness to him, something new.

"Dad?" she said. "Are you seeing someone?"

"No, no," he said, waving at her. "Nothing like that."

She waited.

"She's just a friend," he said. "The woman who came to clean. We became friends."

She was equal parts amused and annoyed. A girlfriend? He was seventy-five.

"You know, I think I like the idea of this long-form journalism they're doing — podcasts and such. There's a freedom to that — you're not beholden to advertisers, editors who fear for their jobs, you can create your own brand. You've made your bones — you have a name, credibility. Have you thought about that? Why not strike out on your own with this? Then maybe — best case — it gets picked up by a bigger outlet."

She was embarrassingly pleased to have her father's seal of approval.

He hadn't written anything in years, but he was still up on the publishing industry, was current, informed. Well, maybe he was writing; he just hadn't published in more than ten years. Not since he'd been accused of plagiarism, right before Rain's mother died. The accusation, made by a student who'd claimed her father had stolen his idea and work he had submitted, was dismissed in court. But the scandal, the humiliation, the court appearances, on top of losing Mom, had been too much for him. He swore off the industry, swore off teaching, and more or less became a hermit. He did the occasional interview. Last year the *Times* took pictures of his writing studio in the attic, the place where he'd written every novel. That last book, which critics said was his best ever, was a huge bestseller. He didn't have to work again after that.

She watched him dangle a set of keys

before Lily, who laughed happily. The kitchen was warm and sunny; this visit couldn't have been any more different from the last one. "What are you working on, Dad? Anything?"

"I'm working on being a better man, Laraine." LAH-raine. "How am I doing?"

She couldn't help but smile. She leaned in and gave him a kiss on the cheek. Lily laughed.

"Great, Dad. You're doing great."

She walked over to the window and stared at the metal sculpture. She really hated it.

"Speaking of clutter," he said. He disappeared, and she heard him move lithely up the steps to his office. It was quiet a moment and then he returned, in his arms a stack of papers and files.

"What's this?"

"It's everything," he said, putting the stack down on the kitchen table. "It's every newspaper clipping, every courtroom transcript, every letter we received from supporters, all my notes, even my diary from that time."

"You were going to write about it?" she asked. Now that she thought about it, she was surprised that he never had.

"I thought about it once," he said. "I hoped it would be a catharsis, a way to exorcise all the demons and the pain of it.

But I could never access it. And now I know why."

"Why?"

"Because it's your story," he said, resting a hand on the stack. "And only you can tell it."

She felt the weight of it, the air in the room suddenly over-warm.

"So, what's the story, Laraine? What are you going to tell them?"

"I'm going to tell them the truth," she said, surprising herself.

Most of it.

THIRTEEN

When I woke up it was pitch-black at first. And so quiet; the only sound was my own wheezing breath. It was cold, too; wet concrete beneath me. I knew that stink right away, the mold of a northern basement. A persistent damp that sinks into everything.

My body didn't feel like my body. It shook uncontrollably. Oh, and the pain. It was like the worst earache, the worst toothache, times a million. What did we know about pain then, beloved children of the suburbs, private schools and parents who for all their minor flaws and mundane failures loved us to distraction? We'd barely been yelled at. Even our teachers weren't allowed to be mean anymore.

If not for the steady diet of comic books and horror movies, the ideas that got me into the whole mess in the first place, I might not have survived what came next.

Or that cop — remember him? — the one

who came into the school and told us what to do if we were taken. *First, don't let them take you.* That was lesson number one. (I know you remember that one, Lara.) *But if he gets you,* he told us, *break all the rules. Anything anyone ever told you about being good, and not making a scene, and obeying the grown-ups in your life — toss that right out the window. Be bad. Yell and scream. Fight. Make a mess. Tear things up, flood toilets and bathtubs, smash drywall. Anything that calls attention.*

Remember how he taught us to punch out taillights — if we were in the trunk of some psycho's car. It was a surreal presentation, but no one laughed. We didn't even joke about it afterward. Because it was scary as fuck. People were out there. People who wanted to take you and do unspeakable things to your body.

Something weird happened to me in Kreskey's basement. In extreme trauma, especially in the very young, the psyche can split. People generally think of this as a bad thing. It can present as psychosis, or dissociative states, even catatonia. But most trauma experts agree that this split can sometimes be a gift, as a stronger self emerges to protect the weaker aspects.

In the fearsome dank black of that basement, a darker, stronger, bolder version of me was born. I might never have met him otherwise. I can't say I like him, or that I'm glad we have had occasion to know each other. I also can't say I'm not grateful to him.

The Hank I was when Kreskey took us — he, alone, wouldn't have survived what came next. I wish I could have left the Hank who emerged in that basement behind when I didn't need him anymore. But that's not the way these things work usually.

It's about fifteen minutes before my last session of the day. And from my office window, I see her car, a black sedan, pull into the lot and just sit, waiting.

Patrick, my four o'clock patient, notices my attention waver and I think the last bit of the session suffers some. Children of trauma are finely tuned to shifts of expression; they see everything. It's a survival mechanism. When raised by an unpredictably violent parent, the abused child learns to watch every movement, every microexpression, to listen for every shift in tone or even breath. They become watchful adults, unusually intuitive to the point of being empaths.

Patrick is a gifted artist, obsessed with the

human form, the face especially, the eyes. I feel the heat of his gaze our whole hour together; most of my other patients stare at their hands, the floor, the art and objects hanging on my walls. Not Patrick. Patrick's father abused him physically and psychologically, brutally, relentlessly. He bears the scars — a broken nose that didn't heal quite right, an arm that wasn't set properly gives him pain, a burn on the side of his neck, still red and angry. Patrick's father killed his mother brutally as the boy, beaten nearly senseless, watched, helpless.

His aunt and uncle took him in, and they are getting him the help he needs. I don't know what lies ahead for him. He's quiet, folded into himself most of the time.

"How are you sleeping?" I ask.

It's just over a year since his mother was killed.

He shrugs. "The night is a good time to work."

"Sleep is a healing force in our lives," I tell him. "Our brains rest, skills set, our cells heal and regenerate."

"It's a dark doorway," he says.

He has deep brown pools for eyes, a thin line of a mouth. Lately, under my suggestion and with the encouragement of his uncle, he's discovered exercise. He was emaciated when we first started speaking. His body has grown toned; he's gained weight. His aunt thinks there might be a girl he likes; he's asked her to his senior prom. All promising things.

"Nightmares still?"

He nods, looks out the window. I follow his gaze and my eyes fall on the car.

What does she want now?

When I look back, Patrick's watching me with a frown.

"What?" he asks.

"Nothing," I say. "Sorry."

He reaches for his portfolio and hands it to me. I open it.

The images are, as always, disturbing. A woman's face without eyes, an open screaming mouth. A boy cowers at the end of a long, shrinking hallway, just visible as a drooling monster sets upon him. A severed head. A pile of gore. Thick charcoal lines of black and shades of bloodred. He and I have talked about them in depth. Who is this woman? Why does she not have eyes?

"These are just the images from my dreams," he has explained. "I don't know what they mean."

No wonder the kid doesn't want to sleep. He's admitted to feeling angry at his mother. Even after his father beat them, she

169

always forgave him. She turned away from things that were happening to Patrick, made excuses to doctors, to teachers. *It's like she couldn't see what he was. Like she was blind or wanted to be.*

I explained to him that people who accept abuse in adulthood often come from abuse in childhood. That if it forms them, they might forever equate violence with love.

He asked me early in our work together: *Am I him? Will I hurt the people I love?*

It's a good question. What makes us who we are? Is it nature or nurture, or more likely some impossibly complicated helix of both of those things? I've been working with some of the most traumatized, the most broken among us, for a while now. I don't have the answers. No one does. Some of them are in prison. Some of them overcome and go on to lead healthy lives. Others languish in a misery maze — unable to love or be loved — that seems to have no exit.

I think we make choices, or can. I think the fact that you're even asking the question means that you can be a better man than your father was.

Which is just a shrink way of saying, *I have no idea, kid.*

"Walk through that doorway, frightening as it is," I tell him. But I'm distracted. Why has the young FBI agent returned? "There's no other way out. Face down those dream demons. And we want to avoid sleep deprivation."

After Kreskey, the nightmares were the worst thing. Yes, a dark doorway. I scribble the phrase on my notebook; it's a good one, accurate to a fault.

"Never get too hungry, too angry, too lonely, too tired," says Patrick. He has a slow way of talking, draws out his words. He's repeating something I've said to him many times.

"That's right." It's an AA thing but I think it's a good rule of thumb for pretty much everyone.

"If you have nightmares and wake up, continue to journal or draw," I remind him. "Bring your work to me and we'll discuss it next week."

At the bottom of the stack of drawings, there's the portrait of a girl. She has lavish copper curls and sea-glass-blue eyes, a smattering of freckles. Color, light coming in from a window. She lays a hand on a tabletop.

"Who's this?"

"Amanda," he says.

"Your prom date?"

He blushes and smiles, a rare thing. It's

the first drawing I've seen from him that isn't unsettling. I'll take this as another promising sign.

"This Saturday, right?" I say. "Bring pictures next week. Have fun and be safe."

Then he's gone. I watch from the window as he leaves the building, climbs into his aunt's waiting car.

Brenda, my receptionist, would have left after she greeted Patrick. She leaves at three to pick up her daughter at school, except on Wednesdays when we see the late patients. I watch as the red-headed FBI agent and her partner leave the car and enter the building. A few minutes later, there's a knock on my outer office door.

"Sorry to bother you again," she says. She wears a cool smile. This is our second time talking about her case. "Agent Brower. My partner, Agent Shultz." Maybe she thinks I have a poor memory. I don't.

"Anytime," I say, stepping back to let them both come in.

I lead them past the foyer into the room where I see my patients. Agent Brower sits but Agent Shultz stands as he did in my home last time. Again, he goes right to the bookshelf.

"I don't mind admitting that we're floundering a bit," she says, leaning forward on

172

her knees. "In the absence of physical evidence, we're trying to create a profile."

"You still think the two crimes are connected?"

Last time she was here, she wanted my consult on whether I thought the vigilante murders of Steve Markham and Wayne Garret Smith were connected.

"In reviewing other cases, we think there may be more."

"Oh?"

"Two years ago, a man charged with the beating death of his wife and stepson was acquitted on a technicality. Six months later, someone beat him to death. And then there's a case you'll be familiar with, doctor."

"Let me guess," I say. "Kreskey."

"That's right," she answers. "I don't mean to bring back bad memories."

Her eyes are almond shaped, trained on me. She laces her fingers, long and thin. Her nails are cut short, and filed square, unpolished. She is slim, but her legs and hips are muscular. A runner.

I almost smile. Instead I bow my head. "Trauma like that," I say. "It doesn't leave us. We adapt, learn to live with it."

"Is that why you do the work you do?"

She doesn't know what she's asking.

"It helps me to help others, yes," I say. But there are other reasons.

She nods solemnly, unlaces her fingers and leans forward.

"I think we might have a revenge killer," she says. "Someone murdering people who are guilty of crimes for which they've not been punished."

I sink into the chair behind my desk.

"There's no real precedent for that, is there?" I say. I said as much during our last visit.

"That's what I wanted to discuss further," she says.

She's young, I realize in that moment, really young. It's a thing you don't really encounter until you reach a certain age. Where people in authority positions are younger than you are. And though she carries herself with confidence, I see clearly in that moment that she's struggling. Self-doubt, a bit of angst.

"I see."

I am a bit of a celebrity, if I do say so myself. The surviving victim of a child killer, I then went on to earn multiple degrees in psychiatric medicine and abnormal psychology, specializing in victims of trauma. I am a bestselling author, an expert witness, a media consultant and an occasional source for law enforcement agencies — though not usually the FBI, who are quite proud of their elite behavioral sciences unit. (They even have their own podcast now.)

I put on my glasses, and rock back in my chair a bit. Agent Shultz has taken a book off my shelf. I can't see which one it is.

"Most serial offenders, as we discussed last time, are motivated by deep-seated needs and compulsions. It seems unlikely to me that someone might be motivated again and again to kill for revenge. It takes an intense amount of planning, a dehumanization of the victim, a tremendous and burning desire to kill. And serial offenders are exceedingly rare, by the way. Usually when a crime of revenge is committed, it's passionate, full of rage and hatred. You'll be looking to the families of the victims for these crimes."

"No," she says with a neat shake of her head. "These were not crimes of passion. They were meticulously planned, seamlessly executed, with not a shred of physical evidence left behind."

"Hmm."

"If not for the proliferation of home security cameras, we'd have nothing to go on at all."

She slips a file from her leather case and

rises to slide it across the desk. There's a photo inside, grainy and green, indistinct — except for a hooded form wearing a bird mask — feathers, a curved yellow beak.

"That image was captured the night of the Markham murder."

She hands me another file. "This is from the Boston Boogeyman murder."

Another grainy image, another hooded form in a bird mask.

I put them side by side, make a show of looking closely at each.

"I see," I say, pressing my glasses up a bit.

"I just wondered if you'd take some time with these. Give the connection some thought."

"Of course," I say. "Anything else connecting the cases? Any other details, no matter how small, could help me."

"I'll get you copies of the files if you think you have time to look them over."

"Like I said, anything I can do."

When they are gone, I allow myself a moment to stare at the images. How fucking stupid can you be? Those cameras are everywhere; I should know that better than anyone.

I am aware of Tess before I look up and see her sitting where Patrick was a few minutes earlier. The girl I see today is not as you remember her, Lara. She's not a girl with braces, with a funny, awkward kind of beauty. She is tall, willowy, so much like her mother, Sandy, with straw-blond hair. She often wears black — a dress with high boots, sometimes jeans and a charcoal top. Tess.

"Do you think they know something?" she asks.

She looks worried. Remember how she always worried about everything. She hated roller coasters, and never wanted to watch all the scary old movies we were dying to watch when my parents weren't home — *The Exorcist, Jaws, The Texas Chain Saw Massacre.* I was Eeyore (sometimes Pooh) and you were Tigger. But she was Piglet — fretful, nervous, but so sweet. She still worries.

"I don't know," I say.

When they came the other day, I assumed it was just to ask for my opinions, my insights into their case. Something was a bit off this second time.

The sun has gone down and the room has grown dusky. When I look over to Tess again, she's gone.

177

FOURTEEN

Lily fussed all the way home, overstimulated and out of routine. By the time they were pulling into their driveway, Rain was exhausted. It was dark, but she was still surprised to see Greg's car in the garage, the door standing open. It was more than an hour before he usually came home.

She saw him silhouetted in the doorway a moment, and then he stepped out and came to help her with Lily and her plethora of baby gear. How could one little person need so much stuff?

"You're home early," she said, handing him the diaper bag.

"Where were you?"

She didn't love his tone. Taut, a little cool. He worried, she knew that about her husband. He had his reasons — legitimate ones. She'd made mistakes, big ones. She hadn't always been honest with him. Even now, there were things she hadn't told him that she should have. Those sins of omission.

Still, she bristled a little when she felt like she had to account for her whereabouts; she had an independent streak, like her father, didn't like answering to anyone.

But that wasn't fair, was it? Now that she was the mother of Greg's child, his wife. That was part of the territory.

"I just went to see my father," she said, trying to keep her voice light. What started as a whimper when Rain took Lily from the car seat was blossoming into a full-blown cry.

"Everything all right?" he asked over the din.

He slung the diaper bag over his shoulder while Rain shifted Lily, patted her back. There was that frazzled feeling so familiar now — too much on her mind, the baby crying, her breasts engorged.

"Yeah," she said, her frustration rising. "Is it okay with you if I visit my dad? Should I have asked for your permission?"

Lily's cry escalated, now an angry wail that was growing in pitch.

Greg rolled his eyes, an action he knew she *hated.*

"It would have just been *nice* to know you wouldn't be home," he said. "I left early tonight so that we could eat together, give you some time to go to the gym — or whatever."

Now guilt, which made her angrier. "There's this brilliant device? It's called *a phone.*"

"I've been calling for an hour."

Lily took it up another notch. Rain bounced the baby on her hip, which honestly only seemed to annoy Lily more. Rain started swaying side to side.

"But we don't talk and drive, right?" she said. Her tone was sharper than she intended. She wasn't angry with him. "Especially not with the baby in the car. I have that Do Not Disturb while driving thing on."

She'd disabled the Find My Friends app, too. So, if he'd tried to find her that way, he would have received a "location unavailable" message. It wasn't personal. She wasn't trying to hide her whereabouts from her husband. Today.

She simply didn't like the idea that her phone knew her location every second. When had they all given up their freedom of movement? Henry had a whole rant about the location services on your phone, too.

They're always watching. Never forget that.

Rain moved into the house, with Greg

right behind her, and saw the takeout on the counter. Chinese from her favorite spot, way out of his way home. Another even sharper note of guilt joined the cacophony in her head.

She moved through the kitchen to the stairs, dropping her purse as she went. Lily was in full-scale meltdown, and Rain's head was going to explode.

"Let's get you fed, in the bath and straight to bed," she said, keeping her voice soothing and light. "Okay, baby? You're so tired."

Thankfully, Greg didn't follow her upstairs, just stood at the bottom and watched her climb. She turned back to him at the landing, and there was something unreadable on his face.

She nursed the baby, then bathed her. In the tub, Lily was sated and quiet, happily splashing in the warm water, the dim light.

Her visit with her father, the things he said, the images still dancing in her head from Henry's email. It all receded as Lily settled, happy again, splashing and cooing. Lily used chubby fists to rub at her eyes as Rain lifted her perfect baby body from the tub, dried her with her duck towel, kissing her toes and belly button.

While she was nursing, Greg came in and kissed the baby on the head.

"We should talk," he said quietly.

He lingered a moment, watching them. She waited for a comment about her nursing, but instead he offered her a sad smile, and left the room.

Downstairs, he'd set the table and was waiting for her with a glass of wine.

"I should have called earlier," he said when she sat. "To let you know I was coming home."

"And I should have called to let you know what we were doing today," she conceded. "It was a spur-of-the-moment thing. I'm sorry."

She took a big sip of wine, felt the warmth of it move through her, ease some of her tension.

"I'm worried, Rain." He closed his eyes and rubbed at the bridge of his nose.

Something about his tone was off, and then her eyes fell on the stack of letters next to his plate.

"When were you going to tell me about these?"

He laid his palm on the pile and regarded her, brow furrowed.

"Where did you find those?" she asked, a tightness in her throat.

He sighed. "In the drawer of your desk."

She could get angry about that, she guessed. Violating personal boundaries and all of that. Snooping was low, wasn't it? But it wasn't like that with Greg. Plenty of couples she knew led these weirdly separate lives — different bank accounts, phones that were off-limits to partners, locked offices, password-protected computers. But she and Greg were entwined — she'd have no qualms about sitting at his desk; his email browser was always open. He might answer her phone.

That he was in the drawer of her desk wasn't a big deal; that's where the checkbooks were. There were no off-limits spaces. In fact, she kind of had a thing about that. She remembered the room that belonged to her father, the one they were never supposed to enter. It came up again and again in her parents' arguments. *You'd rather be in that room than anywhere else in the world. What goes on up there, Bruce?* Rain didn't want secret spaces and locked doors in her marriage to Greg. They were best friends first, then husband and wife.

That she'd not told him about the letters, *that* was a big deal. She'd meant to. She wasn't really even hiding them. Why hadn't she told him? Why had she kept them? Worse — why did she read them, sometimes more than once? Shame was hot on her cheeks. Another drink of wine. No good words to say.

"I don't know what to think about this," he said when she stayed silent. "I'm — concerned."

"I don't answer but he keeps sending them," she said, finally.

He pointed at the address. "He knows where we live."

"Yes."

"How?"

"I don't know," she admitted.

She had been unsettled when the first letter arrived — after they'd had Lily, after they'd moved. But she hadn't been surprised. And wasn't she even a little relieved?

"But," she said quickly, "it's not like that. He's not going to *hurt* us."

Why did it sound like she was defending him? She put her hand in her pocket and touched that crystal heart. Greg cocked his head and squinted at her, the look of the skeptical newsman. It would annoy the crap out of her if she wasn't so far in the wrong.

"We're — you know," she said, looking at Greg, trying to grab his eyes. He distanced himself when he was angry, went behind what she thought of as his journalist face — which was stern, seeing, skeptical. She wanted him to understand but she wasn't sure she even understood herself. "Bound — by what happened."

"No," said Greg, leaning forward. He wasn't one to yell or bang his fist on the table. But he might as well have. The sudden intensity in his gaze pushed her back. "You're *not*. You're bound to *me,* to *our daughter. Not* to him."

No, no. That wasn't true.

She was bound to the present, to the future, with her family.

With Hank — the boy who was taken when it should have been Rain or Lara or LAH-raine or whoever she was — with Hank she was lashed to the past.

She sat there for nearly twelve hours, she'd later learn, huddled in the wet hollow of the tree. It didn't seem like twelve hours or twelve minutes. It was a space that existed without time, a dream, a twilight between life and death. She was bleeding profusely — another couple of hours and she would not have survived. But it might have been a year, or five minutes. She'd separated out from time, stayed suspended by pain, terror and shock so far out of the realm of her nearly twelve years of life experience.

The giant in the woods, the evil dog; she'd

been bitten, struck — her jaw shattered — watched her friends be beaten, dragged away. Dusk fell; she drifted in and out of consciousness. Then her name on the wind. Even then, she didn't dare call out. She dug herself deeper inside the tree, the black, wet womb of its hollow.

"Hey, Lara Winter, is that you? Everything's okay now, kid," said the police officer when he came to kneel in front of her. Detective Harper. She'd come to know him well over the years. "You're okay."

But it wasn't true, and she knew it even then. There was who she was before and who she was after. She would never be that other girl again. And nothing could be okay now.

He reached a hand to her, but she huddled away from him even though his eyes were kind and he seemed strong and good.

He stood and started yelling. "Here! I need the paramedics. I've got the Winter girl!"

She heard a woman scream and she knew it was her mother. And still no words could come. The Winter Girl, someone with arms like dead branches, covered in ice, hair and lashes icicles, frozen and half-dead. That was the image those words put in her mind. She wondered before she blacked out again if maybe she was dead.

Then there was a crowd, her parents hovering, holding each other. Tess's mother stood frozen, arms wrapped around herself, her face blank and pale. Rain was in and out, lifted, carried. Pain a distant siren. She heard her own screaming.

Her mother weeping in the ambulance.

Detective Harper was there, too: *Lara, honey, I know you're hurt. But you have to talk to us. Where are your friends? What happened?*

The words came then in a tangled rush, everything, everything she could remember — shouldn't have been in the woods, he sat by the creek, the dog, big, enormous, a disgusting beard and thick ugly glasses, a monster, he walked north. She knew the direction because of where the sun was in the sky; her father taught her to always know where she was.

The man in the woods. Did she know him? Had she seen him before?

Yes.

Where?

She couldn't remember.

Think. Think. Try, baby, try, urged her mother.

No one said that Tess's and Hank's lives depended on it. But she knew that.

"I know how hard this is," said Detective Harper. They were at the hospital; he ran beside the stretcher down a hall where people shouted. "Where did you go the last few days? Who did you see? Try to remember, Lara. Help us find your friends."

Tess and Hank. They needed her to remember. Through the pain and terror, she pressed. Summer days. Hot ones. Nothing to do. Her father wanting her to come while he ran errands, she didn't want to go but did anyway. Because she loved any attention he had for her.

And then she remembered.

At the garage where her father got their car serviced. She went with her dad, under protest, and waited and waited and waited in a room that smelled like gasoline, filled with ancient magazines for old people, wood paneling and a sweating, struggling air conditioner. Even the vending machine looked spent, its wilted offerings unappetizing and off-brand. Her father talked forever with the mechanic who was apparently a fan of her father's work. They talked and talked in the other room, endlessly, like grown-ups do, about nothing.

"Dad, can Mom pick me up?"

"Just a minute, LAH-raine, darling."

She felt his eyes on her before she saw

him. He lingered in the shadows, watching through the window that separated the waiting room from the garage. He lifted a hand, looked at her with a strange blankness. She ran to be with her father, hung on him until he couldn't ignore her anymore. But it was just a moment. She forgot him as soon as she was back in front of the television at Tess's.

"Where was this?" Harper asked her father.

He looked stunned, confused, uttered the name of the garage.

"Good work, girl," said Detective Harper. "You did it."

The detective ran from the room. Her mother held her. Her father dipped his head into his hand. She remembered the flickering fluorescent lights, the scratch of the gurney sheets, the pain.

"Will they find them?" she asked. "Is that enough to find them?"

Her mother tried for a smile, but it burst into a thousand little pieces and she started to cry again.

"Let's hope so, darling," her father said, coming up behind her mother.

She heard accusation in his voice, she thought, a vague disappointment. He later said that no of course not, that he was stunned by the events, absent, mind reeling. She believed him. But then, that's how it felt. They wheeled her away, voices soothing. A mask came down over her face, and she was gone.

Hank came home. Not Tess.

Eugene Kreskey was arrested.

The things he did. Even now, even when it had all been laid bare in articles and books, documentaries, crime blogs. She didn't allow herself to think of it. She couldn't. When she remembered her friend Tess, it was just as she always was — laughing, always ahead of Rain, pigtails swinging.

Rain wasn't well enough to go to the funeral.

Tess was dead. Her body buried. She'd found the news impossible to process. How could she grasp that a girl who'd been her best friend all her life was simply — gone? Not on the phone. Not sending goofy pictures of herself via email. She wouldn't sleep in the creaky trundle bed or sit in front of her in math class. Her funny pigtails. Her big glasses. She was a ghost.

And Rain was shattered — physically weak, psychologically battered, her jaw reconstructed and wired shut. A plastic surgeon had stitched her leg and there was more surgery ahead, but that scar would be there forever. A twisting, textured relief map of her horror. Years later, her hand would find it under desks and tables, in bed. Sometimes when she was bare-legged, she'd catch someone's eyes fall on it. And she would remember.

Days passed, one gray day after another. Her parents took her home. Everything seemed different, the house, her room, all her dolls and toys. She felt like it belonged to someone else. There were visits from the police, a seemingly endless string of questions.

It's my fault, she thought. *He was there for me. He followed me. I ran away. He took them instead.*

She wanted to see Hank. She begged, day after day until finally she and her mother climbed in the car. No one came to the door when they rang at his house. She stood there, kept ringing. The red door. The slow, deep chimes of the bell. The rustle of leaves and the whistle of the chickadee. She left the card she brought. Inside it simply read: "I'm sorry."

When they were back in the car, she saw him. He stood in his window, a slim and nebulous form behind the gauze of the curtain.

She waved to him and he didn't wave

191

back, just moved back from view, let the curtains close.

"Is he alone in there?" worried his mother. "Did they leave him alone? Surely not."

He knows it's my fault, she thought. *He hates me.*

Because they were minors and had been so traumatized by events, their testimonies were taken in chambers with the judge and the lawyers, shown on video to the jury. They weren't asked to testify sitting feet away from Kreskey. Hank's family moved away before school started the next fall. She didn't see him again, not for a long, long time.

"It's the stuff of nightmares," said the doctor who helped her survive the trauma of her experience, Dr. Maggie Cooper. "You were trapped in a nightmare."

"If I'd run, I could have saved them."

"If you'd been able to run, the dog might have caught you. Maybe you'd all be dead."

"I hid."

"Of course you did," she said. "Your brain, your psyche wanted you to survive. You couldn't outrun his dog — you couldn't have overpowered him physically. You only had one option. Hide from the monster. You're a survivor. If not for what you told the police, they might not have found your friends. Hank is alive because of you."

"But not Tess."

Dr. Cooper's office was always warm and cozy, a comfortable place to bare all. The doctor didn't cry like her mother, or rage like her father. She listened.

"There's only one person to blame for that, Lara. And it's not you."

"They're both gone," she said. Misery was a fog that wrapped around her. "Hank. He wouldn't see me, and now he's gone. He hates me."

"He's filled with rage, suffering trauma just like you. He hates, certainly he does. It may even be directed toward you because you're safe. But none of this, not for a single second, is your fault."

"He saw *me* in that garage," she said. "He came for *me*. But I ran."

The doctor waited a beat and then repeated what she'd have to say a hundred times.

"There is only one person to blame for what happened to the three of you. It's not your fault, Lara."

Slowly, slowly, she came to see that it was true. She healed. Her body. Her spirit. She was the lucky one.

"Call me Rain," she said to the doctor. "That's what I want to be called now."

"Rain," said Greg. He looked down at the pile of letters and back at her. "Make me understand this."

Greg was a good man, and she could share herself with him. But she often didn't, especially when it came to Kreskey and Hank. It was a wound, raw and deep. Exposing it to anyone, even someone gentle who loved her, was painful. What her father had taught her about locking it away had served her, allowed her to live a life. Why was it all banging on the lid now?

Because it's time, her father said. *It's time to tell the story, to own it. Otherwise, and I have come to understand this too late, it winds up owning you.*

"I can't," she said to her husband. Fear was the lock on the box, and for Rain, it was still fastened tight. "How can I make you understand when I don't understand myself? I'm sorry."

She looked at the letters and wanted to snatch them back. Would he throw them in the trash, try to burn them? How could she try to stop him?

"There shouldn't be secrets between us," he said, rising. The letters in his hand.

194

He handed them back to her, locked her with that intense gaze. When she didn't say anything — what *could* she say? — he left the room.

FIFTEEN

Life goes on.

It's such a pat phrase, such a well-worn truth that you almost don't even hear the words. It's only when your own life has come to a grinding halt that you understand the cruelty of it. In the aftermath of trauma or grief or loss, life goes on for everyone else. But not for you.

Later, one might come to understand it differently. Life is a river, it washes over you, washes the past away if you let it. If you forgive, let go, move on simply, day by day, one foot in front of the other, even the worst things can be left behind you. They fade away. This is what I tell my patients. And I believe it. At least part of me believes it. Half of me.

The next time I saw you, I was twenty-two, already working on the first of my graduate degrees at Columbia. You, in your senior year at NYU, were working on your journalism degree. It was your father's book signing at the big Barnes & Noble on Union Square. Remember? I know you do. The old man could still pack a house. (You know the rumor was that after the accusations, he paid that kid off, and helped him get a book published. That's why his student dropped the charges against your father. I'm not sure I believe that. Meanwhile, that kid's book, it sucked. So derivative of Bruce Winter it was embarrassing. I can't imagine your father plagiarizing such a hack writer.)

The event was standing room only. You were up in front, the good daughter — attentive, smiling.

He was with you, leaning in and whispering to you occasionally, his hand on your leg. Greg. I could see it in him — a little controlling, isn't he? Possessive as hell. He knew what he had and he wasn't about to let you get away. Your body language wasn't aligned, though. Greg leaned into you, but you — ever so slightly — leaned away. He took your hand, and you let him. But then you unclasped your fingers a few minutes later. Maybe I was reading too much into it. Seeing what I wanted to see. But I suspect you've never loved him the way he loves you.

I'd already been watching you. I stalked you on social media. I knew where you lived. Your schedule at NYU, what time you crossed Washington Square, how you stayed in the library late to study on Wednesdays. How you were with him almost all weekend, most weekends. He was so — I don't know — clean-cut, a journalism major like you. A runner. Your choice surprised me. I always figured you'd go for someone edgier, cooler. Someone more like your dad. But maybe it was stability you craved — after the trauma and violence of your near-abduction, the divorce, your mother's early death. Your father, his issues with money, his mental and emotional absence — maybe you wanted the opposite. Greg — does he have a creative bone in his body?

That night I noticed you wore a skirt, your legs bare. A couple of times you reached down and rubbed at that scar, the place where Wolf bit your calf to the bone. You do this when you are anxious, nervous, thoughtful.

I didn't expect you to recognize me. By the time I was twenty-two, I'd shot up to nearly six feet, weighed over 200 pounds, all muscle. When I wasn't watching you, all I did at that point in my life was study and work out. I started practicing the martial arts during my freshman year in high school and by the time we met again, I was a skilled practitioner of kung fu and bukido. I was two years into my parkour training then. Unfortunately, I was always a little too big to ever achieve the agility one needs to leap around an urban landscape without breaking my neck. I gave this up, though those skills sometimes come in handy.

I wore my hair long, sported a full beard. I suppose I was hiding. From the world, from myself. In my center, there was a burning core of anger that no amount of therapy could extinguish. You would later claim that this was not so for you, but I could see it in you. In those blue pools you have for eyes, sunny on the surface, shadow beneath. It's a theory I have: only those who embrace anger, who accept its raw power into their lives, survive extreme circumstances.

"Leave her alone," urged Tess. She was always with me then. "Let her live her life."

I never answered her in public. I'm not completely crazy, Lara. I get that other people can't see her.

I stood near the back of the room and listened without really hearing. I just watched the back of your head, that silky raven hair, the way he dropped an arm around your shoulders — loving, protective. Yes, I realized, that's what you wanted. Someone who protects you, someone who's there. I was surprised because when we were little — before — you were always the fierce one. *You* were the defender, the protector. You stared down the bullies, comforted Tess when she'd been mean-girled. You stood up to Kreskey and Wolf that day at first. I guess that's one of the things he took from you that day, that faith that you could stand up for yourself. You couldn't, not that day. None of us could.

I stood near the back as the crowd filed out. You lingered near your father as he was mobbed by fans, signed piles of books. I watched as you kissed Greg goodbye. He would be off to the library to study, because that's what he did on Thursday nights. A straight arrow.

I was surprised when I felt your eyes on me. Even more surprised when you started moving toward me. I'd have moved away, quickly blending into the crowd and disappearing as fast as possible. I had come only to see you, not to be seen by you. But I'd waited too long, lost in watching you. It was just me standing there alone against the wall.

"Hank?" you said.

I almost said no, no, you're mistaken, sorry. But we had locked eyes and I'll admit I just froze.

"It's you, isn't it?" Your face. So wide open, that smile turning up the corners of your mouth. You were happy to see me. Another surprise.

"Hi, Lara," I said. My voice sounded deep, awkward. I wasn't used to being seen, not the way you were seeing me.

"I call myself Rain now," you said.

"Rain," I said stupidly. Of course, I knew that. But you'll always be Lara to me.

Did you know that I've loved you since kindergarten? Did you know that I've never loved anyone else?

You did something I never would have expected. You threw yourself into my arms, wrapped me up tight. I must have felt so stiff, so awkward. The shock waves of your gentleness moved through me, so unaccustomed was I to anything but a fighting touch at that time.

Then I felt something release and soften inside me, and I embraced you. The delicate form of your body against mine, the warmth of you. The clean, light scent of your hair. I held you tight. God help me, I almost wept. You brought me right back to the me I used to be. Someone I'd almost forgotten.

"I'm so sorry," you said, breathless. "I'm so sorry."

■ ■ ■ ■ ■

"Dr. Reams?"

My receptionist, Brenda, cuts a slim figure in the doorway. I've told her a thousand times to call me Hank, but she won't. She's one of those old-school people who stand on ceremony. I appreciate her for her astounding efficiency, foresight and competence. She manages my schedule with dictatorial zeal, but also with a deep compassion for my patients, for the sensitivity of the work.

"You have the afternoon blocked off for research. But Patrick's aunt called. They need a session."

"What's going on?"

"Apparently the dance did not go well," says Brenda, pushing up her red-framed glasses with a manicured nail. "He's in a bad place."

I feel a wave of disappointment for him, run through by a wide skein of worry. "Have him come in."

"Do you need me to stay?" For some of my more unstable patients — who I mainly don't see here in my office — Brenda likes to stay until we close up. Patrick did have an outburst here once, early in our work together.

Is it that late? I've zoned out, something I'm prone to do more and more lately. A glance at the clock reveals that it's almost three, her usual departure time.

"No," I say. "Go get your girl. And have a good night."

"My mother can get her if you need me." Brenda has her russet hair back in a tight ponytail, wears a simple black sheath and polka-dot scarf. Her brow knits with concern, but I wave her off.

"I'm fine," I tell her. "Go home to your family, tell Ryan I said hello."

They are the rare intact healthy family, balancing careers, a child, their marriage. I'm not going to be the one who messes with their well-oiled machine.

"If you're sure," she says. "I'll leave the outer door open on my way out."

My internet browser is open to the file I was reading. I ate lunch at my desk. Half the sandwich still sits in the wrapper by my keyboard. The article I was reading, about the effects of early childhood trauma on physical health later in life — I've only read a few paragraphs.

How long have I just been sitting here?

That's when I notice there are other browser windows open. I'm surprised by what I see there. Shocked, actually. I click the windows closed one by one, my hand shaking. The crime scene photos provided by Agent Brower — gruesome, bloody — disappear one by one. Kreskey. Smith. Markham. How long has he been looking at them, that other side of me?

It reminds me.

Sometimes I forget. I'm not entirely well.

SIXTEEN

Little had changed about the one-story ranch house where Tess had lived, not the buttery-yellow color, not the simple landscaping of squat shrubs, lined with the same type of perennials planted and removed each season, replaced and removed again. Even the red aluminum mailbox seemed to tilt on the same angle. Maybe it was a little worse for wear.

Rain pulled into the gravel drive and sat, taking it in. The trees were taller. Some of the other houses on the block had been renovated. But if she blurred her eyes, she could see it all just as it had been, Tess waving manically from her bedroom window, or sitting on the brick stoop, waiting for her. She'd come running when the car pulled into the driveway, already talking about one thing before Rain even stepped on her walk.

As Rain sat now, the door swung open and Tess's mother, Sandy, stood there, smiling.

For a moment it was Tess, the way she might have looked now — with long blond hair, willowy and tall. Sandy came out with arms wide.

"Oh," the older woman gushed when Rain climbed out to greet her. "Look at you!"

They embraced, and Rain had to bite back a rush of emotion. The scent of her shampoo brought back a vivid sense memory — lying in bed with Tess, her mother kissing them both good-night.

"And look at *that baby*!"

She took Lily as soon as Rain got her out of the car seat. Lily, of course, was all smiles.

Sandy had been the youngest of their mothers — and definitely the coolest. Funny and pretty, she'd turn up the radio in the car and sing along (not like Rain's parents, always listening to some talk radio show on the public station), watch soaps and music videos on summer afternoons with them (not make them go outside like Hank's dad). She didn't have that many rules, let them eat whatever they wanted. At Tess's place, they could stay in their pajamas all day, have the leftover pizza for breakfast. There was always something just light and easy about her; she seemed less grown-up than Hank's or Rain's parents.

She still had that lightness, that youthful

bounce to her step as she bustled about, offering Rain coffee, getting Lily settled.

With Lily on a blanket on the floor, a pile of blocks in front of her (Tess's old toys), Rain and Sandy sat on her couch, chatting about Sandy's work at the hospital, how Rain was doing at home full-time.

"It's been a little over a year," said Rain. "It's been good — for all of us."

"I didn't think you were the stay-at-home-mom type," said Sandy, giving her a long look.

"What type is that, exactly?" asked Rain, really wanting to know.

It was a thing she heard over and over and wasn't sure she understood. Was there a *type* that could stay home, a *type* that couldn't?

Sandy shrugged, pulled at the length of her still-blond hair. Again, for a second Sandy was Tess. It would have been like this, wouldn't it? Maybe Tess would have had children of her own. Maybe they'd be at the park together with their kids, out to lunch. She pressed down a wave of helpless sadness. All the things that could not be changed.

All around them there were pictures — Tess on horseback, Tess and Rain on the swings, Tess as a baby. Printed photos, fading with age. She remembered how they used to take photos, bring the roll to the photo shop, go back a week later to see what they'd captured. Everything was instant now, digital, forever floating in the cloud. Weren't all those images less real somehow?

"Some women take joy in it, some don't," Sandy answered her question. "That's all. No judgments. I am a fan of being true to who we are. Not everyone can do it, the full-time mom thing. It's more demanding than most other things, the stakes very high."

"I do take joy in it," said Rain quickly, almost defensive. She did. Why did she always have to prove it? Nothing in life was perfect, no choice ever exactly the right one. Wasn't that true of everything? Even if she'd chosen to stay at work, wouldn't that be fraught, too?

"But is it enough for you?"

Now it was Rain's turn to shrug; she glanced over at Lily, who was happily banging and cooing. It was a question you didn't dare ask, wasn't it? "It's not really about me. It's about Lily."

Lily agreed with a bang of a big red block, and a happy laugh.

Sandy got down on the floor and helped her stack.

"Fair enough," she said. "Me? I never wanted anything else. I went back to work because I had to support us. I would have been happy with a bunch of kids, making cupcakes and shuttling them all over. Even as a little girl that's all I wanted."

Rain believed it. Her own mother had said the same thing. Sandy handed Lily a green block.

"You said you wanted to talk," Sandy said, leaning back and letting Lily stack. "About this?"

She shook her head. The coffee was strong and rich. Rain was grateful, as always, for the rush of caffeine.

"I wanted to talk about Kreskey," she said, his name sticking in her mouth. She hated the way it sounded on the air. "About what happened to us, to him. Do you mind if I record?"

"Back to work after all?" said Sandy, nodding her assent.

"Maybe."

Sandy wasn't one to shy away from this topic; she'd talked to Rain even when her own parents were still too raw to process, too sick with fear and anger and grief and all the things that might have happened to Rain but happened to Tess instead.

But Sandy always took it head-on, never turned away from the brutality of it. She found some reserve within herself to comfort Rain even though she'd suffered the most unimaginable possible loss.

"Eugene Kreskey was a very sick man," Sandy said, bowing her head. "Deeply, terribly disturbed."

A psychiatric nurse, Sandy had that way about her — the one Rain saw in law enforcement, health professionals, soldiers. These were the people who stood on the front lines of humanity. They knew something about life, about the human condition that other people couldn't grasp. It either made them hard, or it filled them with compassion. Sandy was the latter. "He was the victim of terrible abuse and psychic trauma as a child. I forgave him long ago."

Sandy had mentioned this before, that she'd forgiven Kreskey. It was a thing that Rain didn't understand. How do you forgive someone who did what he did? It was part of that whole Zen thing that eluded her. Forgiveness. It might be overrated.

"And you three were in the wrong place at the wrong time. I look back and think you all had too much freedom. We thought the world was a better place than it was. We thought you were safe — no, we *knew* you were safe. And we let you go too far, too young. That was our failing."

It was a similar thing she heard from her

own parents, how they'd failed. But it was Rain who hadn't followed the rules, Kreskey who'd lain in wait for them. Rain who'd hidden while he took them away. How could she forgive him? How could she forgive herself?

"Do you remember when he was released?" asked Rain, pressing the conversation forward.

Sandy nodded, leaned back against the edge of the couch. The sun from the window danced on her hair. "You and Hank were in your twenties by then."

"Kreskey came back here," said Rain. "To a halfway facility not far from his childhood home."

She nodded again more stiffly this time, her face gone grim and still. "That's right." Then, "Why this? Why now?"

She told Sandy about the story she wanted to investigate and write, one that reached into a past she'd sought to bury. When she was done, Sandy sat a minute, staring at a picture Rain had seen so many times that she'd stopped seeing it. Tess, Hank and Rain, lying on the ground, heads together, Hank smiling broadly, Tess squinting, Rain laughing with mouth wide. Sandy had stood over them and taken the shot from above — green all around them. She remembered the bright blue day, their laughter. They'd been bored and told Sandy. She suggested they go outside and join the Cloud Appreciation Society.

What's that?

It's when you lie on your back and notice how beautiful is the world.

The air was warm that day, the breeze light. Those high cumulus summer clouds towered, growing gunmetal gray inside as they watched. Later it would storm. All those days were so vivid still.

"I always found it interesting," she said. "The work you and Hank chose for yourselves. You an investigative journalist, Hank a psychiatrist. Like all these years, you're still just trying to understand what happened that day. What do you think will happen if you can put together all the pieces?"

Rain didn't have an answer for that.

"You were working that day," she pressed instead. "We were supposed to go to the mall. But you got called in to the hospital. What do you remember?"

Sandy pulled her legs in, wrapped her arms around them so she sat in a ball.

"I remember kissing my daughter goodbye in the morning, sitting on the edge of her bed, touching her hair. Remember how silky it was? I told her what I told her every day

212

— be good to yourself. Be good to others. Be careful and kind."

She stared down at the floor a moment, then went on.

"Then I went to work, resentful as hell that I couldn't spend the day with you two," she said. "It was days like that when I hated her father the most."

Sandy was still in college when she'd had Tess and married Tess's father — a drummer in a local band. The marriage imploded while Tess was still a baby. Tess's dad was mostly absent, showing up now and then for the grand gesture — an American Girl doll (which Tess hated), once a trip to Disney. When Tess and Rain were older, he took them to a Red Hot Chili Peppers concert once.

Tess hated her dad a little, but was giddy with excitement when he'd called, or sent her something in the mail. She deflated when afterward he disappeared again. Now, a parent herself, Rain could see how totally messed up it was. But then — it just *was.* That was Tess's life. And Rain often found herself wishing that *her* dad would buy extravagant gifts and take them to concerts and amusement parks — museums and summers overseas didn't quite cut it. The fact that at least her father was there mostly

— when he wasn't traveling for work, or locked in the attic working, or drifting about, "thinking" — didn't seem like much at the time.

"I remember thinking on the way to the hospital that the real stuff of parenting is in the details, the day-to-day," said Sandy. "I felt like a failure for having to work when other women could stay home."

"You were never a failure."

But Sandy's gaze had grown distant. She was back there, and Rain felt a spasm of regret for having opened this door into the past.

"The day is a blur after that," she said softly. "Until the call came. The rest of that day and night, the week, and the year after, her missing, her found, the funeral, the trial — well, it's every parent's nightmare, isn't it? It's a tunnel I walked through, kept looking for the light of forgiveness, which I knew was the only way I'd survive it. I remember that I wanted to survive, which is odd. Because — why? Any mother would rather die than face that pain. But there was something alive inside that wanted to stay that way, even without her."

Lily started to whimper, maybe sensing the change in their mood, their tones. Sandy picked her up and nuzzled her. Predictably,

Lily cuddled right up. Sandy reached into a bin under the coffee table and pulled out a small stuffed frog, handed it to Lily, who regarded it seriously.

They sat quiet a moment. Outside somewhere a lawn mower hummed.

"And when Kreskey was released?"

Sandy stroked Lily's hair.

"Hank came to see me."

This was news to Rain. She couldn't imagine Hank coming back here, to this town, to see Sandy. The rage he carried inside, it was a force. It had frightened her when they came to know each other again. She couldn't be in the same room with it.

"He did?"

"Do you still talk to him?" Sandy asked.

"No," Rain answered, bowing her head against the complicated rise of feeling. He talked to her endlessly in his letters. But she didn't talk to him. "He's so —"

"Broken."

"Yes."

"He wanted something that we can never have," said Sandy.

"What's that?"

"Justice," she said.

"But justice was done."

"Was it?"

"Kreskey is dead," said Rain. "Someone

killed him, the way Tess died, in the same place."

"Is that justice, Lara?"

Rain didn't bother to correct her. She would always be Lara to Sandy, to Hank. She'd always be LAH-raine to her father.

Rain was the name she gave herself. It was her survivor's name.

"Isn't it?"

"Do you feel better? Does Hank? Did Tess come home? Can I turn back the clock and not go to work that day, take you girls to the mall instead?"

Rain didn't say anything, just looked around the room, which was the same as it had always been, cozy, safe, a fat Buddha on the coffee table, a Tibetan singing bowl, two papasan chairs, the same velvety couch.

"Justice is a modern concept," said Sandy. "In ancient cultures, time, life, is a continuum, no beginning, no end."

"No justice?"

Sandy smiled, patient, loving. "Justice is not for this plane. Punishment, yes. Consequence, certainly. For someone like Kreskey, damaged beyond repair by violence and trauma. How do you break something that's already broken? How do you repair something that has so many critical pieces missing?"

Lily issued a noise that Rain recognized as a shift in mood.

"How did you feel when he died?" asked Rain.

Lily started to fuss again, and Sandy handed her over. Rain fished through her bag while Sandy sat silent, retrieved her shawl and started to nurse. So much for weaning.

"Sad," Sandy said finally. "Sad for the horror of his life, that more evil was done. Sad that it didn't make a damn bit of difference to anyone or anything except to make the world seem a little harsher, uglier than it already was. Violence is never the answer. I believe that with all my heart."

Rain told her about the other men — Smith and Markham. How she thought there might be a connection, someone looking to deliver justice in a world where it was in short supply.

"Do you know the concept of karma?" asked Sandy when Rain was done. Lily had fallen asleep in Rain's arms.

"Of course," she answered, glad for the warm weight of her sleeping daughter. "If that's not karma, I don't know what is."

Sandy shook her head and pulled her legs into a half lotus.

"Karma is about balance. It's about the

natural order of the universe, the delicate dance of light and shadow. 'An eye for an eye' is not a karmic concept — that's a misconception. What happened to those men, it's just more darkness. We fight violence with more violence and only more violence follows. We dig our grave deeper and deeper — there's no end."

Rain saw Tess everywhere — lounging on the couch, digging snacks out of the cupboard, half sliding down the banister that led to the living room, homework spread out on the coffee table while she slouched on the floor.

"How often do you talk to him?"

"Hank? Not as often as I talk to you," said Sandy. "He calls on her birthday some years. Sometimes on the day she died. Sometimes he comes by, brings tulips or Oreos."

Those things were Tess's favorites. She thought tulips were the happiest flower. And that skinny kid could pack away Oreos like nobody's business.

"Part of him never moved on," said Rain. "He's still back there."

"I'd say that's true of all of us, right? Or we wouldn't be talking about this today."

She nodded toward the digital recorder.

"Did he ever talk to you about what happened to Kreskey?" she asked.

Sandy looked away, down at her finger-nails. "No."

"Sandy."

The older woman looked up at Rain, eyes shining.

"Don't go down this road, Lara." Her voice had gone low with warning. "He can't move on. But you can. Look at that baby, asleep in your arms. She's the future and that's where you need to be headed."

Shame warmed her cheeks — again. The baby — that's all that mattered. Seemed that everyone kept reminding her of that. Sandy, her husband, Gretchen on the playground. Her father had the opposite warning — *don't let this slow you down.* She was Lily's mother, an awesome responsibility, an earth-quaking love, a profound gift. But she was still Rain Winter, survivor, journalist, a woman with a lot of questions about the world, about her own life. Couldn't she be all the things she was?

"I'm Lily's mom, present and in love," she said, holding her daughter. "But I'm myself, too. I can be both."

In the comfort of Sandy's living room, she felt like she was acknowledging the feeling out loud for the first time. You were allowed to be both, weren't you? She managed to

219

put herself back together without disturbing Lily.

"I get it," said Sandy with an assenting nod. "Just take my advice and be *that* first. Because nothing else matters if you fail your child."

She flashed on Laney Markham's father wailing, her cored-out mother. She picked up the recorder from the table and switched it off, stowed it in her bag. The air in the room had grown heavy, the past a hulking form in the corner draining all the light from the room. They chatted anyway about breastfeeding, and jogging strollers, both of them grateful for the mundane.

Finally Rain stood and moved toward the door. Sandy followed, embraced her at the threshold, kissed Lily on the head.

"Did he?" Rain asked again. "Did he ever talk to you about what happened to Kreskey?"

Sandy drew and released a breath. She still looked so young, same creamy skin, same jewel-blue eyes, high cheekbones and toothy smile.

"You have nothing to feel bad about, you know that, right?" Sandy laid a hand on Rain's cheek. "You survived that day. You might not have. Why do you want to go back there? Don't. Okay? Don't go back."

■ ■ ■ ■

Rain carried Lily back to the car and strapped her in. She sat in the driver's seat a moment. It was still early. Lily stirred, kicked her legs. *If she wakes up, we'll go to the park. If not, one more stop,* she thought. Lily's head lolled to the side; she stayed asleep. Rain put the car in Reverse and headed north. It wasn't lost on her that Sandy never answered her question.

As she pulled onto the main road through town, the phone rang, Gillian's number flashing on the dashboard caller ID.

"Don't be mad," Gillian said by way of greeting.

"Okay," Rain answered, drawing out the word.

"I might have mentioned the story to Andrew."

She was instantly mad. "Gillian!"

Andrew. She could almost see the gleam in his eyes at the thought of this story.

"He wants us to do it."

She was less mad. "What does that mean?"

"He said we can do the story as a podcast — a long-form, character-driven series. He'll produce. Well, he will if the network accepts his pitch. And when has anyone turned down golden boy Andrew Thompson?"

"Wow," she said, a mingle of excitement and worry doing a dance in her chest.

"Our terms to be negotiated, of course."

Some of her guilt for following the story dissipated — at least she might be bringing some money in. This wasn't just a passion project, her own personal grudge match, dredging up a past she couldn't forget, hurting people in the process. It was a real story for a major network.

"Are you mad?" asked Gillian.

"Yes," said Rain without heat.

"I'm sorry," said Gillian. "It was too good not to pitch. This is big, Rain. It's your story, but it's bigger than that. It deserves more than some indie project that gets buried in the app store."

"I'm not even sure I'm up to doing this," she admitted.

"You are," said Gillian. "Of course you are."

There were lots of layers to the story, personal things she wasn't sure she was ready to face or share. There was a mystery, an investigation. It looped in a man with whom she shouldn't even be involved — for a million reasons. She wouldn't have pitched it to the network. If they accepted, she'd lose control of the story. It would take on a life of its own, sweep her along with it. Still, there was that dark tingle of excitement — that deep drive to get to the heart of the story, even if the truth was the most painful thing of all. It was a big story. A career-maker. Yes, she still wanted that. It felt good to admit that she did.

SEVENTEEN

Agent Brower is back — again. It's my morning without patients, the one I usually reserve for study and research. On these free mornings, I might review my patient notes, connect with colleagues to talk things through — patient issues or challenges. Maybe I'll even have a session with my own therapist. We all have them, you know. No one needs a shrink more than a shrink. Later, I'll go to the hospital to see one of my more troubled souls, then take evening sessions in my office.

I'm edgy, distracted.

I spent most of the night reviewing Agent Brower's files, going over her notes. I'm gratified to report that they have very little to go on. Those images from the home security cameras, even the short video. They're grainy and blurry, the person unrecognizable. Masked. Moving fast. He's not identifiable in any way.

Using what she has, though, I've created a loose profile for her, developed some theories. Former military or law enforcement, someone young, strong, intelligent. Someone who has been disillusioned with the system, who considers himself above the law, but working in tandem with its underlying philosophies. He's following some code. Likely, he would not be married. He might have a criminal record.

So, when I see her face on the camera, I'm ready. I buzz her in and go to the kitchen, put on a pot of coffee.

"If you don't get caught, maybe it's time to give this up." Tess.

She has been worried, all night, pacing as I put together my notes for the FBI, a disingenuous activity if ever there was one. My profile is not purposely misleading. There are some elements of truth to it.

Tess has never been a big fan of my dark activities. After all, she's Sandy's daughter, all about love and forgiveness, karma, and the balance of the universe. The things I've done — the things *he's* done — it's just more of the same as she sees it.

"At a certain point," she says. I pour the not-quite-boiling water into the filter. "You're just one of them."

But no. I'm not like them. I wasn't born,

like Kreskey. I didn't come into the world damaged, my mental illness deepening through trauma and abuse. I don't seek out innocence and destroy it. I was made, by Kreskey. Now I *unmake*. I am a doctor. I remove the cancer, even though I have to make a cut to do it. Sometimes we must harm to heal the world.

"Bullshit," says Tess easily. "You like it."

She's right. I have grown to like it. The truth is I'm not sure I want to stop. I know he doesn't.

"I wonder if you *can* stop."

That's a different matter, one upon which I don't like to dwell. Who is in control? Who is the real Hank Reams — me or him?

Tess wears a long white dress today, a sundress like the one she wore sometimes in summer. Her feet are bare, and her hair is loose, strands of sunlight gold. She would have been a beautiful woman. Not as beautiful as you, of course. Different. She stands, disapproving, by the door as I open it for Agent Brower, who is alone today.

"Thank you for seeing me again," she says. I direct her toward the couch, where she sits perched on the edge. "I feel like I've taken up a lot of your time."

What's your story, Agent Brower? I find myself wondering. *What is it about your life*

226

that has you chasing monsters? We all have our reasons. Most of us don't come to this work without them. It takes drive and ambition to become these things — doctor, law enforcement agent, investigative reporter. There are grueling trials, failures, sacrifices. I wonder what's driving this young woman.

"This is my job," I say. "I'm happy to help if I can. No partner today?"

"He's following up another lead," she says vaguely.

"I see. Coffee?"

"Please."

Is there something about her that reminds me of you? Or is it just that you are rarely far from my thoughts. No, I think it's the practiced facade — as different from you as flame is from jade, silk from metal, sunlight from moonbeams. But that still surface belies a wildness beneath, that's what you both share.

She follows me down the hallway to the kitchen.

Does Greg know about us, Lara? Your husband. Does he know about our time together? Does he know the side of you that you revealed to me? About our correspondence — albeit a one-sided endeavor? I've always wondered about that. How much of

227

yourself you share with him.

You made your choice. And to be truthful, it was the right choice.

Because Greg is the kind of man you marry, right? Handsome, stable. He's a big guy, well built. He loves you, anyone can see that. He's attentive to you, to the baby. He carries your bags. He does the grocery shopping — I'm guessing when you can't get out during the day. But he's not a big personality, not like your dad. He doesn't have some huge ego that needs to be stroked and fed. He doesn't crave the spotlight, doesn't need to be the most interesting man in the room. He's perfect for you. Really.

I still wonder. Do you love him as much as he loves you?

If I were your confidant, or your priest, or your shrink, I'd have advised you to marry Greg. Certainly no one with half a brain would recommend that you throw in with the man who shared your dark past, who was still mired in it. Who'd been changed by it. No matter how you felt about him. I'd tell you to marry the man who loved you best. Because marriage is less about that kind of knock-your-socks-off, head-over-heels thing than it is about compatibility, patience, warmth, respect. The hot stuff burns out fast, but the other qualities endure. They deepen. Or so the research suggests. I, obviously, wouldn't know.

For me, there has never been anyone but you.

That night when we found each other again — we left the bookstore and found a table at the restaurant on Seventeenth Street, some unknown spot with a fireplace — I go back there again and again. The way the candlelight lit your skin, your shining eyes, the silken ink of your long hair. The way you tugged at it. Your pink lips. I loved you when we were children, but that love stayed buried deep. It was alive that night, its heart still beating.

We talked and talked, catching up on years — a lifetime really.

Then you said, your voice hoarse with emotion: "I'm so sorry for that day. If I'd listened to my mother, Tess and I would have gone the long way. Then I sat there, in shock, for so long. If I'd been stronger, I could have fought with you. I could have run for help. But it was hours. I don't remember anything after he hit me. I've carried it with me."

The man who sat across from you, the student of human psychology, he understood. We always imagine ourselves as heroes. But the truth is that shock and terror are a brain event. The limbic responses of the brain, it's hardwired, biological, the personality doesn't control them.

"You were a child," I said. "There was nothing you could have done. You were bleeding. Your jaw was shattered. Lara, please, it's not your fault."

You put your head in your hands and wept then, shoulders shaking. I saw your pain. Even the monster in me was soothed. Any anger he harbored faded to dust, for a while, anyway. And then we were standing, you in my arms. And then my mouth was on yours, the salt of your tears on my tongue. We took a cab back to my place, holding each other. We barely made it up the stairs.

I pushed us inside, fumbling with the key. My place was a Lower East Side dump, high ceilings, little furniture, piles of clothes, and books stacked, my laptop open on the kitchen table. As we made love over and over on the futon, we listened to sirens outside, and the shouts of drug dealers. From my window, I could see a fire burning in a barrel in the abandoned lot across the street. Our bodies melted into each other. I felt whole again that night. I felt like the boy I was before Kreskey broke my psyche in two.

Do you remember? Do you think of it,

that night?

You were on top of me, your body pale as the moon, your hair a river almost to your flat belly, your head tilted back in pleasure as you moved, languid, rocking.

It's pathetic to say that there has never been anyone but you.

There have been other women, one-night stands, half-bearable dates that led to soulless sexual encounters. There was a girl in school who I think tried to love me. Recently a woman who, in another lifetime, might have been the one.

But no, Rain. No, Lara. It's only ever been you.

There was such hunger between us, such a desperate, aching wanting. Did you ever have that with Greg? Have you ever cried while making love to him? I honestly doubt it. We are connected by the evil that leaked into our lives that day; it's twisted around us like a vine of thorns. I know you feel it, too. It hurts but there's a pleasure there, too, a deep intimacy. You don't have that with him.

Why am I thinking about you when Agent Brower sits at my kitchen table, staring at me with wide, earnest eyes?

"Do you think it could be the same person?" she asks, snapping me back to the present.

Yesterday, I wondered if she suspected me. Now, I think not. She looks tired. Her nails, which were perfectly manicured, are a bit frayed at the cuticles, as if she's been biting at them. I'm glad she came alone today. I'm tired of the silent, hulking presence of her partner. There's something I don't like about him.

"I'd say it's doubtful," I answer. "As I mentioned, there's little precedent for a serial offender of this type."

"But the images," she says. "The masked person at both scenes."

"True," I concede, trying to look thoughtful. "It's just that in my experience, serial offenders have a driver, some deep need they are trying to fulfil. These crimes, they're all very different. Various regions. Different types of crimes. Different execution."

That's not the word I intended to use but she seizes on it.

"But that's just it," she says. "They're all *executions*. Guilty men, or men widely perceived to be guilty, who escaped justice. They're calling him that now. The Executioner."

"So, the bureau thinks it's a serial. The same person."

"They do."

"According to the file there's no physical evidence, nothing linking the crimes."

"Just the images. The meticulous nature of the scenes. The victim profile."

I nod, pretending to consider. "So, let's say it's the same person. What's the driver, the thing he needs?"

She puts a thumbnail to her mouth, then pulls it away, sits on her hand. Her eyes are a kind of stormy gray blue; she has her hair pulled back tight from her face. She's so young, practically looks like a teenager.

"Justice? Revenge?"

I nod, encouraging. "But usually those things are very personal."

"So, something has been done to him. He's been wronged in some way."

"Or someone he loves has been wronged."

"He's angry," she says. "Maybe angry at the system for failing to bring justice."

"So he endeavors to bring it himself. That's part of the profile I've developed — on the off chance that we are looking for one man."

"He watches the news, waiting." She's deep in thought.

I lift my eyebrows. "Maybe he's even in law enforcement. Or the military. Given the precision with which he carries out the crimes, the lack of evidence."

She raises her eyebrows, nodding. "That's come up."

We go on like that for a while. I do feel bad. Because, really, we're on the same side. Except that we're not. I am not about to let them catch him.

"It would take a tremendous amount of arrogance, don't you think? To do what he does," she says, musing.

"Arrogance."

"To imagine that you know better, that it's your right to deliver justice. To be so sure of yourself that you'd kill another person."

"It does take arrogance to kill," I admit. "A belief that your needs come before the needs of others. In fact, that your victims are less than human. That whatever needs they might have don't even rank."

"He's a psychopath," she says, meaning it clinically rather than as a judgment. I bristle a little at that, but drink from my cup of coffee so that she doesn't see it on my face.

"Yes," I say. "Most likely."

"But he knows right from wrong."

"No one disorganized or distanced from reality could kill like this."

The crime scene photos are spread out between us. They're gruesome. I admit it's shocking, the things he does.

I feel him banging around inside me sometimes, just looking for a reason to come out. He's wild now, howling. He doesn't like the things she's saying about him. That he's arrogant. A psychopath. He hates it even more because it's true.

"It's cold-blooded and calculated." Her voice has gone soft.

I look down at my own hands. His hands. I feel a wave of nausea. I only have the vaguest memories of those moments, flickering images, soundless, on an old film reel.

"What do you think the mask means?"

"A bird of prey," I say without thinking.

"I did a little research. The mask — it's a kind of hawk."

"Oh?" She's smart, this one.

She pulls out a sheet of paper from one of her files. She has a scent, something clean and floral. I know the fragrance. Wait. What is it? Lavender.

"At the bureau, like I said, they're calling him the Executioner. But I call him the Nightjar, a bird of prey that hunts only at night."

"Ah," I say. "Interesting."

"You said he needs a driver, something deep inside that compels him to kill. If that's true, then I think he was a victim of something awful. I think there's more to it than just revenge, or even justice."

I watch her. There's that flicker of wanting. Like me, like you, Rain. She's trying to understand. I wonder again what's driving her. I plan to find out.

"What do *you* think he wants, Agent?"

Something on her face changes with my tone. Maybe it came off as condescending — I've been accused of that before. I didn't mean it that way. In fact, she's a bit too close to the bone. She's quiet for a moment, then she starts gathering up her files, puts away her notebook. Her energy has shifted. It's gone still and careful.

"I think he's trying to keep them from hurting anyone else."

She pins me with her gaze for a moment. Then continues to organize her materials.

Now it's my turn to go quiet. I see her gun in its holster under her blazer. It seems too big for her, out of place on her person.

"How did you feel when Kreskey was killed, Doctor?" she asks when she's finished packing her things.

I hand her my file with my notes, theories, possible profiles. I lean back and sigh, meet her eyes.

"I was in the middle of getting my doctorate when that happened. I understood a lot about the human mind, about the brutality of Kreskey's life. I wouldn't say that I'd forgiven him, exactly. But I knew he was a victim of terrible abuse."

"How did you *feel*?" she asks again. There's an intensity to her stare.

"Relieved, I suppose," I say. "One less person in pain, one less person to create pain. Not everyone can be cured — some people suffer and make others suffer until the day they die."

"If you'd had the opportunity to kill him, would you?"

I smile at this, as if she's a child who knows very little and understands far less. What's she playing at?

"I tried," I say. No point in hiding it; the account of my ordeal is out there for anyone with a computer. "I nearly succeeded. I wasn't strong enough, though. I was just a kid."

"Someone finished the job," she says.

I don't know what she's getting at. I maintain the easy, disinterested posture I've been holding, leaned back, hands in pockets, comfortable slouch.

"So he did," I say, watching her. "But it didn't change what happened, if that's what you're wondering. It didn't undo the damage or erase the memories."

"You didn't feel better."

"No," I admit. "I didn't."

She seems disappointed, slouches a little. I want to ask her: What happened to you? Tell me. What is hurting you? What are you trying to understand? But I don't. And she tells me she'll be in touch. There's no warning, or indication that she suspects me in any way. But there's something just off in our interaction, a strange new vibration. What did I say? What did she intuit from our conversation? What will be her next line of inquiry?

When I close the door, Tess sits on the hearth.

She's a girl in pigtails again, with those ridiculous glasses and a mouth full of metal.

"You should have told her that you felt worse afterward," says Tess. "You should have told her — that's when you knew."

"Knew what?"

She looks up and she's as I last saw her. I turn away, heart thumping.

"That he was *never* going to feel better."

EIGHTEEN

The Kreskey house. It was still there. In Rain's mind, it had been torn down. Or maybe it had burned, set on fire by vandals. What other fate could a place like that meet? No one would ever live there, surely. She expected an empty lot, or a burned-out shell. But from the road, she could just catch sight of it. It sat empty and sagging, the peaks of its roof jutting above the tree line. It was still there, intact.

Rain sat in her car at the edge of the drive, wondering if she'd completely lost her mind. Coming here. Bringing the baby. She could envision the ashen look of worry and disapproval on her husband's face, pretty much the look he'd given her last night when she told him that she couldn't explain herself to him. He'd gone to bed angry, left this morning without saying goodbye. He didn't even know that she'd taken Lily to Markham's house, that she was about to enter into negotiations to go back to work. She was a bad person, a horrible wife. She might be a shitty mother, too. But she was a good journalist. That much, she knew.

Rain cast a look at her sleeping baby, then took the digital recorder from her bag, hit Record and pulled up the drive. She was fine with the ambient noise of tires on the road, her own breath. There was a certain aesthetic to it; the realism of it appealed. If she was going to do this, she was going to get in deep, warts and all.

"While I sat in the hollow of the old tree, bleeding, in shock, barely aware of myself, Eugene Kreskey brought my friends, then twelve-year-old Tess Barker and Hank Reams, back to the house he'd inherited from his parents," she said.

"It's still here, sitting on an isolated property in this rural New York town. Within its walls, I'd learn at his trial, the young Eugene Kreskey suffered. As a child in this place, he was starved, beaten, locked in the basement for weeks at a time. There are no records that he was ever sent to school."

She brought the car to a stop, regarded the abandoned, dilapidated house.

"Kreskey was twelve when a carbon monoxide leak killed his parents," Rain said.

"A hiker, on the trails behind this house, heard the sound of his screams and called the police. The year was 1990.

"Locked in the basement, he'd been spared the fate of his parents. He was in the house with his dead parents for a week, before the hiker's discovery. It was suspected but not proved that he was responsible for the accident — the furnace in the basement was cracked, might have been faulty."

She paused here, thinking, wondering what it was like to be Eugene Kreskey. A child, a victim of unspeakable abuse at the hands of his deranged parents. He was a baby once, just like Lily. She tried to imagine him, locked in a basement, starving, alone in the dark, his parents dead upstairs. She couldn't get her head around it.

"At the time of his first hospitalization, Tess, Hank and I were not quite toddlers," she went on. "We each lived within five miles of this house. Kreskey was made a ward of the state, treated, and housed for the next ten years. He was released, deemed fit to hold a simple job and live alone, a year before the three of us encountered him in the woods just a mile from my house. He was twenty-two years old."

Rain brought the car to a stop and stared,

241

took a few pictures with her phone.

"Doesn't it sometimes seem like places hold energy? This house — shingles falling, windows cracked, red siding peeled and puckered — looks as if it has never been a home. Only bad things can happen here."

She clicked off the recorder, glanced at Lily sleeping and rolled down the windows. She stepped out of the car, started recording again and walked toward the house, footfalls crunching and loud in the quiet.

"Since Kreskey's arrest, this house has sat empty. An examination of public real estate records reveal that after a decade of taxes in arrears, the county seized the property. But the house stands, and the property has not been sold. Local kids, of course, say it's haunted. That on full moon nights, you can see Tess running through the brush. Sometimes she's just a floating light, they say. Sometimes you can hear screaming."

She moved closer, came to stop at the stoop and looked up at the front door, which stood ajar. There was a sign pasted there, stating that the property was owned by the county, had been condemned. Trespassers would be prosecuted.

"Eugene Kreskey came for *me* that day," she said.

She paused a minute, surprised by a sudden rush of emotion. Then went on, "He'd seen me a week earlier at the garage where he worked when my father brought his car in for service. He'd been educated by the state, learned a trade, was good with his hands. His ability to earn a living was part of the reason for his release. He'd never shown a tendency toward violence."

The woods around hummed with the sound of insects and bird chatter. The sun was high in the sky, the temperature had risen. Sweat beaded on her brow.

"His boss was a distant cousin who wanted to give him a chance after all he'd been through — the abuse, the death of his parents, most of his life in a hospital. That's why he was working at that particular garage."

She had her reporter voice on, something low and soothing that didn't match her everyday voice. It let her keep a distance from what she was saying. She didn't feel the quaking inside that she usually felt when she told this story. Which wasn't often.

"Kreskey had use of his cousin's car. He spent the next week following me when he could. He told police that I looked like a nice girl, and he just wanted to talk to me. But it turned out, he said in the transcript of his police interview, that I was a little bitch with a smart mouth and it made him angry. That I fought. I hurt his dog. I ran. So he took the others — to punish *me.*"

She imagined music here. Something slow and morose, with a light note that might communicate hope.

"Ten years later, after Eugene Kreskey was released again from psychiatric care to a halfway facility nearby, someone killed him. Here in this house, where he assaulted Hank Reams, and killed our best friend, Tess Barker. He died the way he killed — a victim in terror and unspeakable pain."

She paused again, watching the grass blow and the trees bend in the wind, casting shadows on the house. She tamped down the rise of anger; it was an acidic pain lodged in her throat. All the ugly pieces fitting together.

"Since then, two other men, both accused killers who many believed escaped justice, have been murdered in ways that mimic their alleged crimes."

Another pause, another breath.

"Is there a connection? The FBI seems to think so. Is there a vigilante at work? I'm Rain Winter. And since in many ways this story begins with me, I intend to find out."

She clicked off the recorder. It was a decent start. She'd edit and rewrite, rerecord. But that was the lead. Her father was right; this was her story. The one maybe she'd been trying to tell with all the other stories she'd told. She felt something like relief, a thorn pulled from her paw.

A movement in the brush caught her eye, and she felt her body freeze.

She cast a quick glance back at the car, all the windows wide open, and she could just see the top of Lily's head, her little toes. Feet still. They were the first thing to start moving when she woke up. When Rain turned back, there was an old woman standing among the grass. She wore a wide-brimmed hat and carried a walking stick, a pack on her back. Around her neck was a camera with a long lens.

"Hello," Rain called with a wave.

The woman nodded, and then kept walking.

"Excuse me," Rain called.

Rain followed, but the woman was surprisingly fleet-footed for someone so small and frail-looking. She was down by the creek by the time Rain moved into the trees, across it and gone by the time Rain reached the bank. The water babbled and sparkled.

"Hello?"

The woman was nowhere in sight. Something cold and fearful moved through her.

"Hello?"

Then a sound, shrill and terrified, shot through her like a rocket.

A blood-curdling scream of pain, connecting with every single one of her nerve endings. *Lily.*

Rain turned, the old woman forgotten, and ran with every ounce of strength and breath she had back toward the car.

Every step was an eternity, every foot a mile stretching on and on. Rain crashed through the trees, a branch lashing at her face. She raced past the house, the car only seeming farther with every step. How had she come so far?

"Lily," she screamed pointlessly. *"Lily!"*

When Rain finally reached the car, the baby was bright red and wailing.

A black wasp, impossibly big and menacing, like something out of a comic book.

It was still on the baby's leg as Rain swung open the door, the site of its sting swelling, angry scarlet. Rain swatted it away with her bare hand and the thing fell dead to the ground. Lily's wail was a siren.

"You're okay, baby. Mama's here."

Rain's whole body shook as she dug out the Neosporin and a bandage from the first aid kit in her diaper bag. At her touch, the baby's wails amped to ear-shattering levels.

Lily's leg was too swollen; it wasn't right. It seemed to balloon and grow redder before her eyes.

Heart racing, breathless, the rest of it was a blur: the race to the emergency room with Lily screaming and screaming; her run inside; the baby being whisked away from her by a nurse as Rain followed, desperate, arms outstretched.

"What happened?"

"A wasp. She was stung."

"Allergic?"

"I — don't know. I'm not allergic. Her father's not."

The nurse was quick and efficient, taking Lily, removing the stinger, applying a compress, all the while soothing with gentle touches, soft words; Lily's crying quieted to whimpers, the redness and swelling going down quickly. As Lily calmed, Rain's body was so weak with relief, she almost passed out.

"There we go, little one," said the nurse. "There we go."

She swabbed Lily's leg with something, then held up the stinger for Rain to see.

"That's a nasty one," said the nurse.

Lily wailed, reaching for Rain. The nurse handed her back. Rain held her baby, rocking and rocking, as the nurse bandaged the site, handing Rain an ice pack that came from she didn't even know where.

"Oh, Lily, Mommy's so sorry that happened. I'm so, so sorry."

More whimpers, Lily's head nuzzling into Rain's neck.

"There you go, Mom," said the sweet nurse. An older lady with kind eyes, she rubbed Rain's shoulder and Rain, to her embarrassment, started to cry with relief.

"Everything's okay now, you two. Bad wasp."

Bad mom, thought Rain. The world's worst mom.

"I'll give you two a minute," she said. "Get the doctor in here to take a look."

She nodded gratefully, couldn't get any words out.

I left my baby in the car while I chased after some old woman in the woods, she wanted to say but didn't. *What was I chasing? What was so important?*

Sandy's words rang back, hard and accusing. *Because nothing else matters if you fail your child.*

"Oh, Lily," she whispered. "Mommy's so, so sorry."

"Make me understand this, Rain."

She hated that, again, her husband was

forced to utter this sentence.

Greg had built a fire, and it crackled, comforting and warm. Lily was sleeping, none the worse for wear from her ordeal. Rain was a bundle of nerves; head pounding, neck aching. Guilt sat heavy on her shoulders, her heart.

An open bottle of wine sat on the coffee table between the facing couches. She was already on her second glass, but he hadn't touched his. His face was tight with worry, some anger there, too. She didn't blame him. She'd come clean about everything — her research, where she'd been with Lily, the offer from NNR. Not the crystal heart. No, not that.

"Please," he said when she stayed silent.

She'd called him from the hospital, and he'd been there in under twenty minutes. She could have lied to him about what happened, said it happened in the park or while she was driving. But they didn't do that. She didn't lie to Greg — not since they'd been married. Sins of omission didn't count, did they? The letters. The heart. He didn't need to know about those things; that's what she told herself. He'd only worry.

Fidelity is more than what we say, it's even more than what we do, her mother had written in one of her novels, *The Widow,* about a woman who'd lost her husband only to find that she never knew him at all. *It's who we are in our relationship, it's about sharing the nether regions of our hearts.*

"I don't have any excuses," she said. "I went from Tess's place to the old Kreskey house. I was just following the story. My story."

"Your story," he repeated, a low note. "And in telling it — what?"

"In telling it . . . I release it, finally," she said. "I own it and control it."

Yes, that was it. That was the truth of it.

"You know," he said, shaking his head. He looked down into the glass as if he might see the future there. "I wish I believed that. I think in some way, you keep going back there because on some deep subconscious level you believe it should have been you that day. That Kreskey should have gotten you. That you should be dead, Tess alive, Reams unharmed."

"He came *for me.*"

Greg dipped his head in his hand for a moment, then looked up at her.

"You had a right to survive him, Rain," he said softly. "You all did. But you got lucky. I'm sorry, but that's not a reason to carry guilt for the rest of your life."

250

Wasn't it, though? She drained her glass and poured herself some more. She was tipsy. It felt good, some of the day's tension draining.

"What would you tell Lily if she were sitting where you are now?" he went on. "Would you tell her to fight a monster or run for her life? Would you want our twelve-year-old daughter to take on Kreskey?"

The thought made her sick. "Of course not."

"Then you can't hold little Lara Winter responsible for what happened to them."

I've got the Winter girl! Detective Harper's voice bouncing off the trees. She was still that girl inside, frozen, half-gone.

"I have to do this," she said. "Anyway, we could use the money."

He couldn't argue with that.

"What about Lily?" he asked.

"I'll work it out." Her voice sounded weak, uncertain.

"Like you did today."

She leaned forward to defend herself, then sank back. She could still hear Lily crying. She'd left her baby alone in the car to chase after some weird old woman in the woods, on the abandoned property of the man who killed her childhood friend, while she was "investigating" a "story" that no one had

251

officially hired her to tell. She wasn't sure she could forgive herself.

"It will never happen again," she said. "It was an unthinking moment — I got carried away." Just like her father. Just like she always did when she was following a story.

She lifted a palm when he opened his mouth to protest.

"I'll get help," she said. "Just part-time. Lily comes first. That's my promise to all of us."

He was quiet for a moment, and she stared into the fire, her mind drifting back to Kreskey's house, that old woman, the things Tess's mother had said — and hadn't said. *Don't go down this road.*

"What about *him*?" said Greg.

"Hank?" she said. "We're tied together by the past. That's all."

She moved over to her husband, slid in close beside him. He was stiff for a moment, then wrapped her up in his arms, rested his lips on the crown of her head. He was the first safe place she'd found in her life. Upright. In charge of himself, but not controlling. Frugal, but not cheap. Studious, but not lost in his head. The opposite of her father.

In his letters, Hank accused her of choosing the safe man over the man she really

252

wanted. But it wasn't true. She loved Greg because he was good and strong, because his love was all light. She chose him because he was nothing like her father, nothing like the man Hank became — nothing like Rain.

She saw the darkness in Hank almost right away. He was not the boy she knew. Still, she knew him immediately. The man in the back of the room at her father's book signing, hair long, a thick, full beard. He'd grown tall. She could see the muscles straining against his leather jacket. The pull to him was magnetic, irresistible. She pushed her way through the crowd around her father, toward the back of the room where he stood.

"Hank?"

Beneath all the layers, he was there. The boy she loved, the one who raced into the woods to save her but couldn't. She remembered his sweetness, how funny he was, what a brain, a comic-book, video-game dork. How he had this kind of delicate beauty — almost girlish — even though he was skinny with fine, high cheekbones and straight white teeth that never needed braces.

She ran to him, to that boy, but a man — someone so different — took her into his arms. That night, she still thought about it. All the time. Too often. That heat, that desire — it was white-hot. She couldn't have resisted if she tried.

She remembered the way her father looked at her when she left with him, his eyebrows raised in warning. *Don't fuck up, kid.* That was his other favorite piece of advice.

After the café where they talked and talked, about how his family moved him to Florida after Kreskey, how he tried to forget the past. They followed each other on Facebook; he never posted, and never responded to her posts. But he knew all about her. He'd been watching, he admitted, too shy to reach out. What if you wanted to forget, too?

They barely made it back to his place, groping each other in the cab, up the stairs to his apartment. Her encounters before that had all been so — polite. Gentle, respectful, halting. Hank took her, and she wanted him to. They were up most of the night.

The way he watched her; the boy was gone. There was a man, a stranger, muscular and powerful beside her. She felt his strength, his need. Half his face was cast in shadow.

"Do you have that with Greg?" Hank had

wanted to know. It was after three. How many times had they made love? She lay beside him on his futon, the street noise loud outside. Someone yelling. The blaring of a horn. "Does he make love to you like that?"

"No," she admitted. "It's different with us."

It *was* different. It was light and good, healthy. She and Greg — there was laughter, play, genuine pleasure in being together. But no, it was nothing like it was with Hank.

"Good," Hank said. His voice was gravel as he moved in closer. "That's better. Because this thing? It could be dangerous."

He kissed her deeply, and though she'd been about to leave, she let him. Then he flipped her on her belly and took her from behind — deep, desperate, leaving her weak and spent when they were done.

But almost as soon as they were together, she was pulling away from him already. There was a black place inside him, an abyss that she could feel tugging at her. He connected her to her basest self. Sometimes she saw him, the real boy, the one she'd never stopped loving. But he was lost, buried deep in the woods of their past.

And it was always going to be Greg. Because Greg was the guy you married.

■ ■ ■ ■

"What worries me," said Greg now, "is that this is not about you, not about what happened, not about telling the story, and finally healing."

His voice was a sad whisper. She didn't say anything, just held on to him — his kindness, his gentle strength, his faithful love, his adoring fatherhood. A good man anyone would be lucky to have as a husband. Maybe she didn't deserve him.

"What worries me is that this is about *Hank Reams,*" he said. "And if you chase him, you won't be able to come back."

She looked up at him, put a hand on his jaw, which was rough with stubble.

"This has nothing to do with him," she said. They probably both knew it was a lie.

He held her a moment longer, then rose, leaving her. He had circles under his eyes; she felt a sudden distance between them. She watched as he walked out of the room. She wanted to chase after him, try to make him understand. But she let him go, listening as his footfalls faded up the stairs.

NINETEEN

I have a small office here at the psychiatric hospital on the outskirts of town. I think it used to be a generously sized janitor's closet, but it works. There's a narrow window, enough room for a desk and a chair. The desk is bare; I carry my laptop and notebooks back and forth with me in a leather satchel that reminds me of the one your father used to carry. It was a gift from my parents when I got my PhD.

Today, I am here to see Ashley. She's been my patient for over a year now, and in that time, she's wasted away to almost nothing, attempted suicide twice. If you ask me, her life is like a daily suicide attempt — as she slowly starves herself. Though since she's been here, she's been better. Some color has returned to her cheeks. Last week I made her smile.

This is not what you think of when you think of a psychiatric hospital, not the kind

of place where we house people like Kreskey — there are no gray corridors lit by
fluorescent lights, no metal doors with tray
slots and glass run through with wire. Here
at Fieldcrest there are gardens, well-
appointed rooms, a chef who grows his own
produce and herbs on the property, there's
a library, art therapy room, a meditation
space. It's more like a spa, a retreat from a
world that is cruel and unfeeling. Ashley's
here for clinical depression, though like
most of my patients she has no simple, one-
word diagnosis. People always want a name,
a pill, a cure. But the human psyche doesn't
always fit in a tidy little box, as we both
know.

Her trauma was the accidental death of
her father, one she witnessed as she was a
passenger on the back of his motorcycle at
the time. After her last suicide attempt,
wrists slashed in a hot tub, I thought it
might be time to take her out of her home
environment. The cuts were shallow, but her
mother was away (though I'd suggested it
was best that Ashley not be alone). If not
for Ashley's boyfriend, we might have lost
her.

I wondered how she'd fare away from her
mother; it's part of the reason I recom-
mended a stay here. True to my suspicions,

she's gained weight, opened up more in session, has started painting. Her mother is grieving differently — which is to say drinking, staying out at night, sleeping around, sleeping all day.

Today I see Ashley in the dayroom, a sun-drenched space filled with cozy couches, fresh flowers, shelves lined with books. There's no television here, no Wi-Fi. Here we shut out all the crazy-making chatter of our day-to-day world. It's so hard for the strongest among us to stay sane, isn't it, under the conditions we have come to think of as normal?

Ashley reminds me of you in some ways. The sweetness of her smile, an innocent twinkle that belies the sharp wit, the dark thoughts. Like you, she's authentically both — light and shadow. Maybe like all of us.

"I've been thinking today that maybe I don't want to die after all," she says when I sit down. Since she's been here, she's stopped pulling her hair back into the painfully tight ponytail she usually wears. She's ceased gnawing at her fingernails.

"That's good news," I say easily. "What has led you to this change of heart?"

"In meditation class, the teacher asked us to dwell in a place of gratitude. I asked her, 'What the hell do I have to be grateful for?

I'm in a mental hospital.' "

"Good question."

"She said, 'Today, someone who was clinging to life lost the battle against a grave illness. That person would have given anything for one more day, one more hour, one more breath. You might start by being grateful that you can draw air into your lungs. It's okay to just start there.' "

"And that resonated with you?"

"I never thought about it that way."

I am not sure if she's being a smart-ass or not. She's capable of great snark. But I think I see a change in her, something softened, something more relaxed.

"My dad," she says, looking down at her hands. "He wouldn't have wanted this for me. He'd be mad that I tried to throw away my life, when he would have done anything, I think, to hold on to his."

I don't say anything right away, just nod. The less you say in session sometimes the better, otherwise it can become about you. She's quiet a moment, then wipes at a tear.

"It was, you know, like an aha moment."

I had a moment like that once.

When I woke up in Eugene Kreskey's basement, I thought I was dreaming. I was lying on concrete and there was nothing around me that I recognized. Odd shapes in

260

a shadowy space, some light leaking in from a high window. He hadn't even bothered to tie me up. The pain in my head, my jaw, my leg, my back. Sometimes those breaks still ache in the rain and Christ, it brings me right back to that basement. I can still smell it.

"Mom," I whimpered. "Mom."

We always want her, don't we? Those of us who were lucky enough to be loved by our mothers. She's the one who picks you up, dusts you off, cleans up your wounds and sends you back on your way. No one else ever loves you like that, not really. She's the one you want when things go bad.

Then I remembered — the woods, the dog, the monster of a man. Panic ramped up my breathing, brought me wobbly to my feet. It was so goddamn quiet.

Remember what he said, that cop. He said: *No matter what, don't let them take you. And if they do, fight like your life depends on it. Because it does. Break all the rules, don't listen, don't be polite, make a mess, make a scene. Anything you can do to call attention to your situation, do it.*

It was such an abstraction then, something from a movie, something so outrageous it was almost funny. Though I remember looking around that assembly and everyone so silent, staring. No one, not even the bullies and the troublemakers, made a sound.

But I was frozen, afraid to open my mouth.

"You have to get out of here." Tess stood in the corner of the basement. She was still and calm. "He's coming for you."

"Tess." I was so relieved to see her, moved toward her quickly.

But then she wasn't there at all; I was alone. To this day, I don't know if she is a product of my addled brain, or — something else. I moved over to where she was standing and there was a box of tools. A screwdriver, a saw, a rusty hammer.

I was shaking. My body quaking with fear and pain; my jaw, my head, my arm. I wept with it, unable to stop. I was so weak, I could barely lift the hammer. But I put it in the pocket of my shorts, took the screwdriver. Then she was at the top of the stairs.

"Use the screwdriver to remove this doorknob," she whispered, urgent and sure. "Then run. And, Hank? Do not look back."

By the time I got to the top of the stairs, she was gone again. My mind, shattered, just accepted her as she was, whatever she was — a friend who was trying to help me. In the black, it was impossible to see the knob. But I felt the screwdriver into the screw head, and slowly, painstakingly, I turned, and turned, and turned, until the knob fell off and the door swung open.

The house was rank, smelled of mold and garbage. It's funny how children of privilege experience the world — our homes are attractive and safe, things are clean, rooms bright. We think it's all like that — every house, the world, clean and safe. Even when they tell us that it isn't, we don't believe it.

Kreskey's house was a hovel. Stacks of newspapers lined the walls, dishes spilled out of the sink, naked bulbs hung from wires in the ceiling. It was a maze of junk, old computer monitors lined up against a wall in the kitchen, furniture stained and sagging, walls yellow. It was a horror-movie house, nothing like anyplace I'd seen.

I limped quietly, trying to stifle my breathing, ignore the pain, looking for a door, a window. The back door in the kitchen was boarded shut, the windows, too. I saw Tess standing again; she motioned, silently urgent, and I followed. There it was. The front door. I broke into an unsteady run, hope giving me strength. That's when I heard it.

The low rumble in his chest, guttural and ferocious. Wolf.

He was lying by the door, got to his feet

as I approached.

I froze. I had the hammer and wished I'd brought the saw.

I had one of those aha moments: fight or die.

Maybe this is not quite the same as Ashley's breakthrough. I've had other light bulb moments, too. But this one has served me best.

"Have you — ever had a moment like that, Dr. Reams?" asks Ashley now.

"I have," I tell her. "I think all of us on the path to wellness have those moments. They're like stepping stones, the places where we find a foothold to bring us to the next stone."

"Did you ever want to die?"

I am open with my patients. Most of them know my path, my history. I think it helps them to know that someone survived extreme trauma and came out the other side, healthy (ish) and whole (sort of). Naturally, they don't know the whole story.

"I did," I tell her. "For a long time after, I didn't understand how I could live a life."

"Did you try to kill yourself?"

"No," I say. "Because of my parents, at first — my mom especially. Later, for other reasons."

She bows her head. "What other reasons?"

I shrug. Here I must veer from the truth a little. "For all the reasons people don't want to die. Life has promise. Love. The joy of just being alive — food, music, the sky, the stars. You'll get there, too."

A thirst for revenge. An idea that I can help people with what I've learned. The desire to cut what cancer I can from this sick world.

"I miss him so much," she says. "I think a part of me died when my dad did. Maybe too much of me."

I know what she means.

"We all lose a part of ourselves when someone we love dies," I tell her. "But we can heal and go on living. We can live well, love, experience joy, and it doesn't mean that we didn't love the person we lost. It means we loved them so well, that we do what we know they'd want us to do. Live and be happy."

"I know he'd want that." Her voice is just a whisper.

"Of course he would."

"You're such a hypocrite," says Tess from over by the towering vase of fresh hydrangeas. Today she's dressed in faded jeans and a peasant blouse, her gold hair flowing. "You should start taking your own advice."

I ignore her.

■ ■ ■ ■

Later, the day has grown cold and a deep gray. I have been carrying that heavy cloak I always don *after.* I feel like I'm standing on the edge of an abyss, and that howling empty place, it calls to him, hums a deep B-flat, that hypnotic note of the universe. I could live this life of study, of helping people over the void of despair and into the light. I could maybe even love someone other than you, Lara. But increasingly, he's in charge. His desires and appetites attracting more and more of my attention.

I want to go home. But instead I'm going to run an errand. I get in my sensible, affordable car and drive. He never stops thinking about you.

"Can't you just let her live her life?" asks Tess from the back seat. "She chose Greg. Accept it."

I can accept it. Of course I can.

It's him.

He's the one who can't let go.

TWENTY

Rain's head pounded, her limbs felt filled with sand. How was it possible to be so god-damn tired all the time?

The bed beside her was empty. Greg had tossed and turned until late, finally deciding to go sleep in the guest room down the hall. She'd pretended to be asleep when she heard him leave. He was angry with her still. Worried, too. She didn't blame him.

Then she lay awake thinking, her thoughts a manic tumble — the dilapidated house with its door ajar (Could she get permission to go inside? Could she handle it?); the strange old woman (Who was she? Why had she run away from Rain?); how she'd failed her daughter (What kind of mother leaves her child alone in a car? In that place, no less?); about Eugene Kreskey (a monster, a victim, her worst nightmare); about Tess and Hank (Did you ever have friends like that again? Gillian probably came closest.

But no, there was a love there that gets lost when adulthood sets in). How many hours had she spent just turning it all over in her head?

You got lucky, said the ER nurse. She'd heard that phrase too many times. *Lily had a large local reaction to the sting. But it wasn't life-threatening.*

The older woman had dropped a hand on Rain's shoulder.

"Take it easy on yourself," she advised. Rain looked up into a set of velvety eyes, the kind gaze of a woman who'd seen it all. "You can't be watching every second."

Can't you, though? Rain wondered. *Shouldn't you be watching every single fucking second? Because that's all it takes. One second.*

She heard a rustling on the monitor, something strange that caused her to sit up, then a soft cough.

"Good morning, sunshine." Greg. "Let's see that boo-boo."

Lily's voice was soft, an inquiring coo.

"Oh, it's nothing," he said, indulgent, sweet. "You're a tough girl, just like your mommy. Let Daddy get your diaper and your breakfast. Mommy could use a little rest. And look outside — the sun's not even up. You're such an early bird, aren't you?"

He was talking to Rain, she could tell. He knew she was listening. Encouraging her to chill a minute. *Thank you,* she thought, lying back down.

Rain listened to him talking to the baby softly, sweet nonsense, the zip of the diaper tabs, the *whump* of a diaper falling into the empty bin. "Oh, how nice, the wipes warmer! Back in *the day,* our wipes were cold! Ice-cold! I remember — what a shock it was."

The baby issued a fascinated coo.

Then they were gone, walking down the steps, the floorboards creaking. Rain lay a moment, then grabbed her phone from the drawer by her bed, started scanning the news sites.

The FBI press conference was just a regurgitation of things Rain already knew; Gillian had attended. There were still no leads on the Markham murder — no physical evidence, no witnesses, investigation ongoing. No mention of a possible connection to Smith and Kreskey. The story was already going cold in the media. Markham's death was a pointless coda to a sad, tragic, unfair story. His death changed nothing, and no one wept for him.

Christopher and Gillian had both returned her calls late yesterday, neither with anything new to report — except that they were meeting for a drink last night. How did that go? she wondered. There was about an eighty percent chance that they'd slept together. She'd hear all about it tonight when Aunty Gillian came to babysit for Lily. Her heart lifted at the thought of seeing her friend. She'd lay it all out, they'd talk it all through.

After trying and failing to fall back asleep, Rain pulled on a robe over her pajamas, pulled a brush through her hair. In the mirror, she barely recognized herself. Would she ever look like a normal person again, someone not frazzled, puffy and sleep-deprived?

Downstairs, Greg and Lily were at the table. Greg with the newspaper open, Lily surrounded by cereal and cut-up bits of strawberry.

"Hello, munchkin," she said, pouring herself a cup of coffee, then leaning in to kiss Lily on the head. He handed her the arts section without a word.

"I'm sorry," she said. She wasn't even sure what thing she was apologizing for — the letters she'd kept from him, breaking the contract of the stay-at-home mom, neglecting their child. For everything.

He blew out a breath, rubbed at the bridge of his nose.

"No, I am," he said, folding up the paper. She sat beside him, looped a hand through his. "I know who you are, Rain. I know what drives you. And, you know what, it's part of the reason I fell in love with you. I've always admired the passion you bring to your work. If you need this, for whatever reason, let's make it work, okay? It's great that they are interested in the project at NNR. We *could* use the money. But when the story is done, let's move on — from it, from *him.*"

She nodded, then looked at Lily, who was delicately placing one Cheerio in her perfect pink mouth.

She didn't know if she could do both things. Or if she wanted to. Maybe it was another one of those lies they sold you, another one of those brass rings. Maybe they wanted you always overextended in the reaching, always face-planting. You can have it all! If you just try hard *enough.* But what if you couldn't?

"What about Mitzi?" asked Greg. "She's offered. We both like her, former kindergarten teacher, beloved grandmother. And right across the street. Probably not an ax-murderer, right?"

She was way ahead of him, planned on

giving her a call when Greg left for work. "I'll talk to her today."

The knock at the door startled them both. Lily's happy face fell into a frown.

"It's 6 a.m.," said Greg. "Who could that be?"

Rain's whole body went stiff; she couldn't even say why. As he got up for the door, she reached for him. *Don't answer it,* she wanted to say. Which was crazy — of course he had to answer the door. He patted her hand and she got up after him.

There was a young woman at the door, a big man behind her, both unmistakably law enforcement — conservative, hard-bodied, serious. Rain stood right behind Greg, who kept a hand on the door, an arm between Rain and the people on the porch.

"Laraine Winter?" The woman stared right at her, held out her identification. FBI.

"I'm Agent Stephanie Brower. This is my partner, Agent Brian Shultz. Can we come in?"

"What's this about?" asked Greg, moving his body now in front of Rain's.

"This is about the murder of Steve Markham," she said. "We have some questions. Ms. Winter, you covered the Laney Markham murder trial as a journalist. We're hoping you can help us."

But there was more. Rain could tell by the intent way the agent stared at her. She had watery blue-green eyes, strawberry blond hair pulled back tight from her forehead. She knew. Rain could always tell when someone knew her history. There was a certain wondering, watchfulness. She pulled her robe tighter. She wasn't going to feel bad about being in her pajamas at 6 a.m., but she wished she was dressed.

When Greg didn't move, Rain put a hand on his arm. "It's okay," she said. "Come on in."

"Sorry for the early hour," Agent Brower said, stepping inside. Her partner was like a hulking shadow, silent.

"Can we get you some coffee?" offered Greg, stiffly polite.

"No, thank you." Her partner also lifted his hand to decline. Agent Brower smiled and waved to Lily, who bounced enthusiastically in greeting. That kid. Was there anyone she didn't like?

"Let's sit in here," said Rain, motioning to the living room.

They all sat, and Agent Brower launched into her questions right away: Was there anything about the investigation that she hadn't reported? Had she received any threats, or been witness to any threats against Markham?

"It was long-form journalism," Rain said. "So we had the luxury of in-depth reporting over a long period of time. We didn't have to cut anything important, or relevant. We didn't receive any threats, but I'm sure Markham had plenty, including those issued publicly by Laney's family."

"Was there anyone suspicious in the courtroom?" the agent asked. "Someone who was there daily? Someone who caught your notice."

"There must be surveillance footage, right?" If Agent Brower noticed her deflection, she didn't show it. "The room was full of reporters, cameras, as well."

"We're sifting through all of that now," she said. "But I was wondering if you observed anyone, or anything odd."

"No," she lied. "I didn't note anyone unsettling, suspicious."

Why would she lie? When it came to Hank, it was second nature, some deep desire to protect him. He'd been in the courtroom a number of times; another thing about Hank she'd kept from Greg. It had come as a shock to see him, so many years after their last encounter — both of them adults with careers, ostensibly having moved past the horror movie of their past. He was there when the verdict was handed down. She supposed it had something to do with his work. Certainly, he wasn't suspicious; he was a psychiatrist, an expert witness who'd testified at numerous trials. They'd avoided each other, never spoke. Their last encounter had been an ugly one. She didn't want to talk to him again. Ever.

The letters had started shortly after the Markham trial ended. The first one was an apology for the way things had gone between them, for the things he said.

The agent watched her a moment, then: "You were one of Eugene Kreskey's victims."

"One of the lucky ones," Rain said. There was that word again.

"You're aware, of course, that someone killed him," said the agent. She'd leaned forward a little; Rain had shifted back in her seat, closer to Greg, who took her hand. "Like Steve Markham, he was killed the way he killed."

"I did take note of that," she said. Her voice sounded thin, too soft. She cleared her throat and deepened it. "In fact, I am considering writing a story."

"Have you started your investigation?" Agent Brower asked, her eyebrows raised.

"I've done some early research," said

Rain. "Do you think there's a connection?"

"Do you?"

"I'm not sure yet," she said. "Seems possible."

Agent Shultz still hadn't said a word. He stood and walked over to their bookshelves, lifted one from its place, then turned back to Rain.

"Are you still in touch with Dr. Hank Reams?"

He held one of Hank's books in his hand: *Surviving Trauma.* "We correspond occasionally," she said. "We're not close."

This was as near to the truth as she could get. She wondered if Greg would chime in. *He's obsessed with her. She had an affair with him, before we were married but while we were dating. I asked her to choose and she chose me. And yet. And yet. He sends her letter after letter. We suspect that sometimes he watches her, though we've never been able to prove it.*

But Greg stayed silent, his eyes on Rain.

Lily yelled, testing her voice from the high chair. In the open-plan room, they could see her from her seat, still happily playing with her breakfast. *Clunk.* Her sippy cup tossed. A happy shout, loosely translated to: *See what I did!* Greg got up to retrieve it.

"He's agreed to help us with this case,"

Agent Shultz said. His voice was deep, almost gravelly.

Rain battled that scattered feeling she had too often — trying to pay attention to what was going on, one eye on Lily, one part of her brain worried about Greg, another part wrestling with the bad memories, fears, regrets, that thoughts of Hank always stirred up.

"It's his area," Rain said carefully. "I'm sure he'll have a good deal of insight."

"He's helped us quite a bit already."

As a journalist, Rain thought she was pretty good at reading people. She listened — to what was said, and what wasn't. She watched bodies, posture, eyes. She caught the microexpressions, the ticks, the uncommon phrase. But Agent Brower was a tough customer — face still, gaze intense, seeing, but eyes revealing nothing. Her body was relaxed, but she moved quickly with deliberation.

"You didn't say if you thought the two cases were connected," pressed Rain.

"Like you say," she said. "It seems possible."

"Do you have any physical evidence linking the two crimes?"

A slight smile, the upturning of one corner

of her mouth. "Now you sound like a journalist."

Rain matched her smile. "I am that, I suppose. Among other things."

"Dr. Reams says that a serial killer — not that I'm saying that's what we have — is most often motivated by deeply personal drives. Compulsions he can't control. This type of crime would be unprecedented."

"A killer who hunts killers."

She shrugged. "That sounds like a headline."

"What are they calling him at the bureau?" When Agent Brower didn't answer, "Come on, they always have a name."

"I call him the Nightjar."

Because of the mask, Rain thought. The hawk mask. A bird that eats insects. That hunts at night. Nice.

"Did you have any suspicions when Kreskey was killed?" asked Agent Shultz. "Any thoughts on who might have done it?"

"To be honest — no," said Rain. Another lie. "I was just glad he was dead."

"A journalist without questions, without theories. I've never met one."

"Trauma." Rain pointed to the book still in Agent Shultz's hand. "It can get its hooks in. It takes time to find wholeness again. I was still running away from Kreskey, trying

278

to forget him and everything about him. When he was killed, I only felt relief that I didn't have to share the planet with him anymore. And I only recently started asking questions. About a lot of things."

There was more truth to that than she'd intended.

Agent Brower looked chastened. "I'm sorry," she said. "I didn't mean to be flip."

"If I think of anything that helps," Rain said, "or if I come across anything in my investigation, you'll be the first person I call."

Agent Brower held Rain's eyes a moment, then nodded lightly. "Thank you for your time."

Agent Shultz carefully replaced the book. Agent Brower handed her a card. And then they were gone. Rain sank into the couch as the door closed, drained, mind racing.

Greg stood holding Lily, looking out the window as the agents in their black sedan pulled away through the overcast morning.

"Are you ever going to be free of this?" he said softly, half to himself.

She looked at them, her beloveds. They were good — solid and innocent, the foundation of the life she'd built. She felt separated from them, on a raft floating out to a treacherous, stormy sea.

No, she thought. *I don't think I am.*

TWENTY-ONE

He was so thin. Wolf. All bones and teeth. Starved. Beaten. Locked up in the dark. Just like Kreskey, he'd been made vicious by neglect and abuse. When I looked into his soulless gray eyes, I swear I saw it. All the layers of his pain and fear and sadness. I know you remember him. He wanted to be good, don't you think? Deep inside, he wished he was a good dog. But he wasn't. He was a beast.

We stood a moment, the cluttered filthy hall between us, his eyes shining in the dim. I was aware of the rise and fall of my chest, air coming in through my throat constricted with fear. Then he charged, his nails scrabbling on the hard wood.

I fought him, Lara, with every ounce of strength and will I had left in my skinny, broken little body. I punched him, bit him, screamed at him. I felt chunks of his fur come off in my hands, his teeth on my legs, my arms. He yelped with pain, more than once. You know, I don't think his heart was in it; he grew weak quickly.

When I finally got my hand around the hammer I took from the basement, I raised it up high. Then I brought it down hard so that it connected with his skull. That was an ugly sound, metal on bone. I think he was glad. He shuddered with relief as life left him, and then his big body sagged on top of mine, both of us bloody and spent.

I felt the second he stopped breathing. I think I freed him from a life of suffering. Silence. I shoved his body off mine and pulled myself up — which, looking back, was a small miracle. I must have been running on adrenaline and pure mortal terror — the breakfast of champions. I reached for the front door and twisted the knob.

Can you believe it? It was open, unlocked. I swung it wide, blinded by the white of the shining sun, by the wide expanse of green that lay out before me.

This is what I think.

Within us, there are layers of self. If things go well, the whole and healthy self, the flawed but basically decent self emerges, grows, is nurtured and heads out into the world. If things go badly, other selves, the shadow selves that might have remained dormant, emerge instead. Sometimes we need them, those dark ones within. We can't survive certain circumstances without them. It's just that once they're out, you can't always get them to retreat.

I could have run in that moment. I should have. Looking back, that would have been the right thing — to go for help. I think Tess might be alive if I had. Instead. Instead — I turned around, that hammer still in my hand and I went back to try to save Tess. I wasn't going to leave her there. Not the way you left us. I see that as the last moment I might have survived undamaged. Injured, traumatized, changed even, yes. But not split.

From somewhere above I heard a rhythmic banging.

I climbed the stairs and moved toward the sound, which I soon discovered was coming from behind a closed door at the end of the hallway. I still dream about that hallway sometimes, the filthy floor, grit crunching beneath my sneakers, the dingy walls. I put my hand on the knob, my breathing ragged, my whole body shaking with fear, pain, exhaustion.

When I look back, I remember as I pulled the door open a bright light pouring out of the room. A liquid gold. There is some type of sound — a siren. But there's nothing else there. What I saw, what followed in the hours before the police finally found us. It's not accessible as a linear memory. Sometimes there are flashes — in that hypnagogic space right before I fall asleep. I see a floor covered with blood. I hear my own terrified screams. I have scars. I know you do, too. Sometimes my hand finds them — on my arms, my neck, my legs. It's a blessing, that blank place. I tell my patients who don't remember the details of their trauma that they are the lucky ones. As a doctor, I do not push into memory, or recommend hypnosis. If your mind has created a blank space for you, it's because you can't handle what's there. Be grateful. I'm sure he remembers, but I don't.

The next thing I recall is the police breaking down the door.

Kreskey's face was a bloody mask when the police took him out.

"You fought him, son," someone said — maybe it was the EMT. "Good for you."

You never go home. Not after something like that. That cop, he told us, never, ever let them take you. I understand now what he meant. If they take you, you never come back, whether you survive or not.

■ ■ ■ ■

"You're over the line," says Tess from the back seat.

"Is there a line?"

That thoughtful pause. Remember how she used to do that. Kind of cock her head to the side, push up her glasses. "Isn't there?"

I leave her there, shut the door and step out into the night.

I shoulder my pack. Pull up my hood.

She's right. This one's a little different. There has been no lengthy trial, no obvious travesty of justice. There's no mountain of irrefutable evidence. There's just one child's suffering, her not-quite-reliable claims, the lingering suspicion that there might be something not quite right happening on this isolated property.

And maybe, maybe there's something else.

Dare I admit it?

An appetite.

TWENTY-TWO

Gillian swept into the house rather than arrived, a beautiful bluster, laden with bags, gifts for Lily, for Rain, her overnighter, her laptop case.

"Ugh," she said as Rain helped her unload. "What a week!"

Something about the sight of her friend made all the tension Rain was holding in her body just melt away. Roommates, coworkers, partners in crime, they'd seen each other at their best and worst. Gillian was a hold-your-hair-while-you-puke, tear-drying, belly-laugh, potato-chip-binge bestie. She filled the room with her warmth, her good humor, her scent of lilacs.

"Where's my girl?" said Gillian, dropping to her knees in front of Lily. "There she is!"

Lily bounced up and down in her swing, vibrating with excitement.

"Oh, my goodness, you're such a grown-up girl," she said. "So *pretty.* But no!

You're brilliant, powerful, in charge. Forget about pretty. Pretty is boring."

Rain laughed, putting the gift bags on the table, Gil's luggage by the stairs.

"Mommy and Daddy are going to have a date! And we're going to have a girls' night! Yay us!"

Lily giggled, delighted, as Gillian gave her a big smooch.

Rain and Gillian lay on the floor with Lily and spent a while chatting about office politics, and how their former boss was facing harassment allegations (handsy asshole), Gillian's new subscription to Stitch Fix, and how she wanted to buy some Bitcoin. It was the usual exuberance of both of them talking nonstop, one topic bleeding into the next, tangents taking over the conversation. It had been like this since college; they couldn't stop talking when they were together.

When Lily got fussy, Rain took the baby up for her nap. She came back down to find her friend was making coffee. Gillian knew her way around their kitchen as well as Rain knew her way around Gillian's.

"Tell me," said Gillian. Rain held the monitor, watched Lily fight sleep.

"What?" Rain suddenly felt weary, sank

into a seat at the table and let Gillian take over.

"Don't even," said her friend. "You've got circles under your eyes — you're pre-occupied. I know that look. Tell me what you've got. Chris told me you two have been talking."

"Oh, did he?" she said. "Over drinks?"

"Don't even try to redirect," she said lifting a palm. "That's not going to work with me."

Gillian carried over coffee, slid her tall, lean frame into the chair across from Rain. She was sporting some pretty dark circles herself. Rain noticed the lick of one of her tattoos snaking out her sleeve. It was a snake that wove around her arm. She almost always wore long sleeves when they worked. Gillian regretted that tattoo, bitterly, a drunken night in college, hanging out with the wrong guy. But she'd stopped short of having it removed. *I have too many scars already.*

Gillian put a hand on Rain's, and it all came out in a tumble.

The papers her father had kept, how she'd been poring over them, her visit to the Kreskey house, what happened with Lily, the FBI visit that had her feeling off-kilter and nervous. Gillian listened in that way she

288

had, leaning in close, chin in hand, as if all her focus was on the sound of Rain's voice. Nodding. Making all the right affirming noises in all the right places.

When Rain finished, Gillian was quiet, traced the rim of her cup.

"This is the perfect story for us," she said finally. "You know that."

Of course she knew. This was exactly the kind of thing that they could sink their teeth into together, a long, looping story that spans decades, a mystery, so many questions.

"Andrew's pitching it next week," said Gillian. "They're going to say yes. Are you ready for this?"

"I think so," said Rain, gazing at Lily through the video monitor.

Gillian gazed out the window, took a drink from her cup. "Have you talked to him?"

When Rain didn't answer: "He's the logical next person to talk to. I'm sure you realize that."

Rain told her then about the letters. How he wrote every couple of weeks — long, eloquent missives. Gillian didn't seem surprised, just gave that thoughtful nod she was so good at.

"What do they say? What does he write?"

Rain shrugged. "Memories of that day.

Things he holds against me. Sometimes apologies for the way things ended between us. Musings. Mundane things about his day, his life. Sometimes he's angry. Sometimes he's nostalgic. Like an old-fashioned correspondence. Except that I don't answer him."

Rain retrieved the stack from the drawer in the kitchen where Greg had put them. She handed them to Gillian, who thumbed through them, reading.

"Letters," said Gillian.

"What?"

"Handwritten, on this thick stationery paper. This beautiful, long-form prose."

Rain peeled open one of the envelopes. Had she told Greg she didn't really read them? She did. She read them over and over.

His handwriting was neat and beautiful, still somehow masculine. His sentences, about his isolated house, his work, were somehow soothing as if he was writing about another place and time when things were quieter, more peaceful.

"The common mode of modern communication, especially among the dating set, is texting," said Gillian. She picked up her phone, which was on the table beside her. She'd tapped on the home button at least three times since they'd sat down; Rain had

done the same. Everyone was always checking, checking, checking. What were they all
waiting for?

"You meet someone, you get a text," said
Gillian. "Maybe you hook up. Then it's
more texts. More hookups. Or not. You get
ghosted. Or you stop answering."

Gillian took her phone, tapped it a couple
of times, then handed it to Rain.

Hey, we met last night. You said you
wanted to connect again. Drinks tonight?

Can't tonight. Tomorrow?

Sounds good. Where and when?

I'll text you tomorrow.

Great.

What time tonight?

Sorry, can't. I'll text you.

Ok. LMK if you have time later this week.

Hey, what's up? Are you out and about
tonight?

291

Hello?

Hello?

Ok. Whatever.

"Sad, right?" said Gillian. "This hollow, stripped-down way we talk to each other now."

"You blew him off?" Rain handed her back the phone.

She shrugged, looked at the phone, bit her lip. "I guess I did. I wasn't that into him."

She was still in love with Chris; Rain knew it. Gillian knew it. Everyone else fell a little short. They'd get into that whole thing in a minute. Gillian twisted a long strand of hair, looked out the window.

"But Hank's writing letters — long, detailed, personal," she said. "Expensive stationery, black ink."

"He's a psychiatrist, a writer," said Rain. "Communication is important to him. He's kind of a throwback, too. No smartphone. He had a flip phone when I knew him. He didn't text."

"Why is he still writing to you?" she asked. "What does he want?"

Rain knew the answer. He wants to be

known. It's what everybody wanted, wasn't it? People want to be seen, to be understood, accepted. Hence the cultural social media addiction — everyone vying for attention, creating a persona posted for approval.

She put a finger to the thick ecru envelope. His letters, his poetic descriptions, his long, flowing sentences, his thoughts about patients (whom he never named), the world in general, they lulled her back to the place she occupied with Hank in those few torrid weeks when she was sneaking around behind Greg's back, before she acknowledged that there was — another side to him. Gillian saw it immediately, warned her off. *You have a good man who loves you, who you love. Don't throw it away for this guy. He's not right.*

It was late when Hank's call came in and she left her dorm room to go to his Lower East Side loft. Greg was studying that night. They'd had an early dinner together and she knew Greg wouldn't call again that night; that he wouldn't drop by.

She'd almost told Greg at dinner, almost broke up with him. Whatever was happening with Hank, it was getting more intense. Even when she was with Greg, she was thinking about Hank. It wasn't right. Her feelings had swept her away, fast, downriver; she wasn't sure she could get back. Wasn't sure she wanted to. Hank connected her to a part of herself that she'd forgotten.

When she got to Hank's building, he buzzed her in and she climbed the dingy stairwell, pushed through the open door to his place. He was standing by the window, his big, muscular body in silhouette against the blue-black night, the light coming in from the streetlamp.

"Hey," she said.

He turned to face her. There was something hard about his expression. Something dead in the eyes. She felt a flutter in her chest, which was silly. Because she knew him. It was as if she'd always known him. Preschool through middle school. He picked her up after she fell off her bike and helped her home to her mom. She defended him against Max, the school bully, got a detention for swearing. She wrote his book reports; he helped with her math homework. Hank was in love with her, always had been. It was just something she'd always known, even before she knew what it meant to be in love with someone.

"What is it?" she asked, moving closer even though something inside told her to move away. The door closed behind her.

"We've never talked about it," he said. "Not really."

"About what?"

But she understood. It always lingered in the air between them. That summer afternoon when the world changed.

"About what happened to us. I never told you the details."

"No," she said. That complicated swell of feelings — a sick fear, shame, anger — it all rose up from her belly into her throat.

"What happened to Tess, to me," he said. "At Kreskey's house."

"I read the transcripts," she said, sitting at the rickety kitchen table where he studied. "Not then. But later."

They'd each given their testimony in chambers, just the attorneys, their parents, the judge. They were spared the courtroom; the media largely left them alone. Hank's family left town shortly after. Rain's family stayed. When she returned to school she felt embraced, people were kind — teachers, even the other children.

Eventually, what had happened became a kind of folklore, a ghost story — for everyone else. She became a character in a story that might have happened, or maybe not. Unbelievably, as the years passed it faded for her, as well. That day in the woods took on the gauzy quality of a nightmare. There were the scars, the dreams from which she woke screaming, the anxiety she felt around strange men, her strong attachment to her mother — she never went to another sleepover after that. But over years, with therapy, with the help of her parents, she *recovered*. She moved forward. There was guilt in that truth, too. She lived her life while Tess could not.

The years passed. By high school, kids were sneaking out to the abandoned Kreskey property, claiming it was haunted by the ghosts of the parents who'd abused and tortured him there. They'd died from carbon monoxide poisoning, an "accident" that almost killed Kreskey, too. If only.

Hank sat. "I want to *tell* you."

She shifted back from him. Everything about him was off, his expression, his body language. Wrapping her arms around her middle, she nodded. She owed him, didn't she? To hear his story, from his own mouth.

She was weeping by the time he was done. They both were.

He brought her back there with him — what he saw, what Kreskey did to Tess, Hank's battle with Wolf, the inside of the house. It wasn't a nightmare. A thing that might never have happened. She could hear

and smell and taste that day — Tess screaming, the blood in her own mouth, the sound
of the dog, the scent of rot from the tree
where she hid, the wet leaves, how the
gloaming settled, and she couldn't move.

The look on Hank's face, the anger, the
hatred, the blame — everything she imagined in her grimmest suspicions of how he
must feel about her — was there.

"I am sorry," she said, shivering. "I was a
— child. I was in shock."

"We were all children," he said.

She got up from her seat and began to
move, still facing him, back toward the door.

"He's going to be released, Lara. Did you
know that?" he said. "I got a call today from
Detective Harper."

She had known Kreskey's release was a
possibility, that it might happen that year.
But no, no one had told her that Eugene
Kreskey was about to be released. A chill
moved through her, drained her of energy.
She leaned against the wall.

"Do you ever think about it?" he asked.
"Do you ever wonder about who lives and
who dies and why?"

She didn't say anything.

"Who makes those decisions?

"He came for you," he went on into her

stunned silence. "Why did he get Tess instead?"

"I don't have the answer to that."

"Was it because you were stronger? Because you fought, and she didn't?"

"It's all so complicated," she said. The images came back. The bridge — how Tess wanted to cross through the woods, and Rain had her mother's warning in her head. How she gave in out of sheer laziness. Kreskey by the creek. Wolf. "Those moments are a blur. But we both fought, and we lost. He would have taken both of us. Except you showed up."

"And then he got me instead."

His gaze was relentless. She felt small and ashamed before him. She knew what Kreskey did to him; she'd seen the scars on his body, touched them with her hands.

"I don't remember how things unfolded." Her voice was just a whisper. How many hours had she spent in therapy, working through that day. But there it was, alive and well, a hollow within her. "How I got away."

"What were you thinking when you watched him drag us away?"

"I wasn't thinking anything," she said. It was the truth. "I was gone, out of my mind in shock. I barely remember how things happened."

"Have you forgiven yourself, Lara?"

"No," she said truthfully.

Something changed on his face. He bent forward into his palms. When he looked up again, the hard mask had dropped, and it was Hank again.

He sat up straighter, looked around the room as if confused. When his eyes fell on her, he got up from his seat and moved toward her, outstretched his hand.

"Hey," he said, clearly unsure of what was happening. "When did you get here?"

She moved back from him, closer to the door, the strangeness of the moment expanded. What was happening? What had just happened?

"What's wrong?" He reached for her. "Hey — are you crying?"

"Is this a joke?" she said.

He seemed afraid suddenly, seemed to realize he wasn't wearing a shirt. He grabbed one that was hanging over the couch, shifted it on. He went to the refrigerator and grabbed two beers, popped the tops and slid one across the counter to her. She stayed where she was, watching him.

"I — uh," he said, looking down at the floor. "I don't seem to be able to orient myself. When did you get here?"

He looked at the clock. "Is that the time?"

She wanted to leave, but she stayed. She sat at one of the counter stools, took a deep drink of the beer he'd offered.

"You called," she said, wobbly inside. "I came."

"How long have you been here?"

"Awhile."

"What did we talk about?"

"Kreskey," she said. "About what happened to us — to you."

He rubbed at the crown of his head. "Why do you look so — scared?"

She didn't know what to say. He was Hank again. The man she'd been with earlier; he was someone else — voice, body language, energy. Utterly other.

"You were someone else," she said. "Someone with so much anger toward me."

He shook his head. "No."

He paced back and forth a couple of times.

"What's the last thing you remember?" she asked.

"I got a call from Detective Harper," he said. "Do you remember him?"

She nodded, the detective who'd coaxed the memories from her, the one who saved Hank.

"He told me that Kreskey was going to be released."

"And then what?"

He sank into the couch. "It's a blank. I don't even remember how the call ended."

"Has this happened to you before?"

He just sat, didn't answer. She grabbed her coat from the chair.

"I'm sorry," she said. "I'm sorry I ran and hid. I'm sorry I wasn't more or better or stronger that day. I'm sorry for everything he did to you and to Tess. I've carried it with me. If I could go back and change a hundred things about that day, I would."

"Lara." Notes of sadness, regret.

"Instead I have no choice but to accept that I survived and that she didn't. That Kreskey, a deranged man, did horrible things to you that have damaged you. But I was a frightened kid. I was badly hurt. I wish everything about that day had been different. But the one thing I can't do is go back and change the past. I have moved on. You should, too."

He turned, his face ashen, so sad. "Don't leave," he said. "Of course I don't blame you. Please."

But the words he'd spoken, the things he said — they were a poison. Every time she looked at him, she would hear them. She'd know that in some nether region, beneath his affection, he hated her. She'd seen the hatred burning in his eyes, etched into the lines of his face. He blamed her. She couldn't look at him again.

"Goodbye, Hank."

She left, letting the door close behind her, and ran down the stairs.

"Part of him is still back there," she told Gillian now. "He's still trying to understand what happened to us."

"Part of him?"

"There are two of him," she said. "The doctor, the writer, the commentator — he's well and whole. He helps people through trauma, has used his experience to do good."

"Okay." Gillian wore a concerned frown.

"But there's a part of him that's still filled with rage — at Kreskey, at me."

"When you say a part of him, you mean —"

"There are two Hanks."

"You're scaring me," said Gillian. "Like he's dissociated? Split?"

"In a sense, maybe," she admitted. "It's *that* Hank, I think, mostly — or sometimes, I don't know really — who writes to me."

She started flipping through the letters. "Why?" Gillian asked after a bit. "Why do you keep these? Why do you read them?"

Rain picked one up, stared at the crisp,

buttery pages filled with his beautiful hand-writing.

"Because he's lonely," she said. "Because he's the only other person alive who was there that day. And because part of *me* — a big part — wishes I could go back and save him."

"But you can't," she said. "Like you told him. We don't get to go back, only forward."

"I know."

Gillian drew in and released a deep breath. There was worry on her friend's face, but also the dangerous excitement of a journalist staring down the barrel of a big story. That was the power of the work — when you investigated the truth, when you put the words down on the page, you ordered the chaos of the world. When you took control of the narrative, it stopped controlling you. She hoped.

TWENTY-THREE

The Hero's Journey. There are plenty of heroes in our human mythology and myriad journeys on which they have embarked. But it's only one story. A young man — yes, in classic mythology it's always a man — hears the call. He is made aware that an epic task is his to accomplish. He rejects the calling — he is too young, too weak, unable. But the call is relentless, and finally he must answer it. And so begin the trials — the struggle, the pain, the loss. All of this strife prepares him for the final battle, where he faces his ultimate foe either within or without. He has been made strong by all that he has endured. He is ready for the great battle.

My journey started with Eugene Kreskey.

He'd been hospitalized already once before we knew him, after the death of his parents. It was widely believed that he had attempted a murder-suicide, rigging the gas furnace so that the house filled with deadly carbon monoxide gas. But it couldn't be proven, and he wasn't charged. He was raised in the system; which I'm guessing was a far better deal than being raised by sadistic monsters who kept you in a basement for twelve years. I've read the case files. He was docile as a lamb, no sign of violent behavior. Arrested development had him operating on the emotional level of an adolescent; he had an IQ of about 70 — not disabled, but able to comprehend about as much as a twelve-year-old.

He was released at twenty-two, a caseworker assigned to visit him at home and work, and went to work in his cousin's garage. That's when he saw you, Lara.

He followed you, we know now. Maybe for weeks that summer. He knew your routines, how you spent your days. He watched your bedroom light go out at night.

What is it about you?

He told his doctors that you looked like the girl who visited him in his dreams — raven-haired, white skin, those pale blue eyes. Snow White, he called her. The fairy-tale princess who loved dwarfs. You don't have to be Freud, you know, to figure some of this shit out. She loved him, this girl in his dreams, when no one else did.

The lonely, stunted Kreskey said you smiled at him, sweet and innocent. An invitation, he thought. He wanted to bring you back to the house where his parents tortured him. He imagined that you'd cook and clean for him, tuck him into bed, read to him. You'd be the sweet, pretty girl mother he never had. But you fought him, and you hurt his dog, you had a nasty mouth, and you weren't nice at all. And he was angry. He never wanted Tess, or me.

He was declared unfit to stand trial for the murder of Tess, for our assault, my abduction, unable as he was to differentiate between his dreams and reality, the voices inside and outside his head. He was a paranoid schizophrenic, truly. But after ten years of medication, therapy and work release, the powers that be considered him ready for a halfway house. Supervised living, a room of his own, a job as an office-building janitor.

I could not accept that. *He* couldn't.

As you know, I was a student then. A year from my PhD, writing my dissertation on the gift of the split psyche, how it can allow a traumatized mind to survive horror and abuse. How, even if it never quite returns to wholeness, a traumatized psyche with adequate therapy and sometimes medication can function in society. Who would know about this better than I? Though I guess some might argue that I'm not exactly functioning.

After my school day, making sure I stayed on top of my workload, in the evenings I drove north. I started shadowing him.

He was even bigger than he had been, a great, lumbering ogre. He'd lost his hair. His skin was gray, flesh hanging, eyes dead with medication. He moved as if carrying a great weight around his shoulders, a yoke — stooped, gait slow and dragging. For weeks, he only moved between the halfway house, a grim block building outside town, and the contractors' office where he was the night janitor five miles away. A van drove him to his job and picked him up.

Then, one night, I watched as he left the office building on foot through the back door. He walked the mile and a half back to that house, the house where he brought Tess and me. He stayed there for nearly two hours. Just standing in the front yard, staring. What was he thinking? What voices was he hearing? Then he lumbered back, finished his work. The van picked him up at 5 a.m., hours before the workers returned for the day.

I knew what I had to do. I wasn't about to

let him hurt another living soul. That other part of me wouldn't be able to live with it.

There is the world you live in, Lara, and there is the world I live in. You live in the light. Your happy family. Your friends. Your career ambitions. Yes, I know you still have those ambitions. That belly of fire to know, to understand, to dig in deep, find and tell the stories of humanity. You may be on a little domestic vacation, but this whole stay-at-home-mom thing? It's not for you. Not that there's anything wrong with it. Quite the contrary. The world would be a better place, I think, if someone stayed home, if it was someone's full-time job to be there, especially in those early years when we are formed. What would the world be like if everyone had a loving parent at home, someone happy and contented, someone who loved and nurtured, cooked and cleaned? Of course, that's not the world. Among the young people I see, there is so much horrific abuse — physical, verbal, psychological. More than that, there is neglect. A turning away from our children — as we indulge ourselves, succumb to our vices and addictions, worship our material goods, stare unceasingly at our devices, climb and climb that corporate ladder. We tell ourselves that we do it all for them. But we don't. They don't need the toys, and the iPads, and the Range Rovers. What they need is our attention.

I will say that I admire you, Rain. I see the way you are with her. Attentive, loving. I don't see you staring at your phone like the other mommies on the playground. I saw one woman, glued to that thing while her baby clung to her leg and cried and cried. As if to say, what are you looking at? Why aren't you looking at me? When she finally picked the kid up, the child reached urgently for the phone. What's so special about this thing? she must have been wondering. Why does Mommy look at it more than she looks at me?

I watch you jog with your stroller, pushing her around the park. You are a beautiful girl, always have been. Not that plastic, Barbie blonde. Nothing revealing. Nothing flashy. Snow White. You beguile with your beauty, your goodness. I know why Kreskey watched you. Why he wanted to take you to his little house in the woods and keep you for himself. That, above all, is the fantasy of the neglected man. To be loved and cared for by beauty and goodness. To have that mother's love that was withheld.

My mother loved me. She stayed home awhile, went back to work when I went to school. She read to me and held me when I cried. She bandaged my knees and taught me how to stand up for myself when the bullies brought me down. My dad played catch and took me to the movies. He checked on me at night. That boy, *that* Hank. He is well; he survived and thrived. It's the other one, the one formed in trauma. He's the problem.

My patient today is Grace, a bulimic. She's also a cutter. With a razor she hides in her sleeve, she slices at the inside of her thighs.

"Why?" I asked her in one of our earlier sessions. "What are you thinking when you make the decision to hurt yourself?"

She seemed surprised, as if no one had ever asked her why she would do such a thing. It surprised her to think of it as a choice. At first, she didn't know how to answer. She stayed silent and I waited, let her process the question and its implications.

"It quiets the other pain," she said finally. "The pain inside."

"Does it work?"

Another moment or two of silence. "Maybe for a while. But there's always more pain."

"When you're in pain, hurting inside,

what other choices are there besides taking a razor to your flesh?"

It was a breakthrough for her, the idea that she had a reason for doing it, and a choice not to hurt herself.

Today she sits in my office. Fuller, pinker — healing. She always curls herself up in a ball, as if she is trying to make herself as tiny as she can be. Her mother is a cold and graceful beauty. She drips with diamonds and expensive fabrics, one of those women who exudes confidence, an easy comfort in her own petite and perfect body. Grace is a beauty, too. Her blond hair a wild mane, her limbs long and coltish. *She has been given everything.* It was the first thing her mother told me. *All of me; I stayed home with her, have always been here. There's been world travel, every material thing and opportunity money can buy. Why wasn't it enough?*

It was enough, I assured her. It's not about that. Mental illness is not about that. We are all an impossibly complicated web of biology and circumstance, nature and nurture. The event that cripples one child, gives another child wings. The trauma that breaks one person in two, imbues another with a supernatural strength of spirit. We cannot apply intellect and logic to our

311

humanity. We can only try to understand ourselves, to heal the broken, to make strong again the injured.

Grace lifts her skirt for me and shows me her thighs. She's not teasing me, though many of my young female patients have. I am not a man to Grace, just a kind teacher, a friend. Her thighs are creamy and white, her scars fading.

"See?"

"Very nice," I say. "No uncontrollable urges?"

She shrugs, tugs her long hair around the back of her neck, strokes it on one side.

"I breathe," she says. "I say my mantra. *I am enough. I am more than enough. I don't have to be anyone else but who I am.*"

We came up with that one together. There are some drugs, too. A light dose of anti-anxiety meds, which I'll wean her off slowly. Sometimes I use medication to take the edge off, but I like to teach my patients techniques for managing anxieties and chaotic thoughts. I teach them to meditate, to journal, to draw. I encourage punishing exercise for some, especially my young male patients. Physical exertion, and the brain chemicals that flow from it, the exhaustion that follows, work beautifully to quiet the mind. I am a distance runner, taking winding trails through the woods, along the twisting roads of this town, up into the foothills of the mountains that surround us. Sometimes when I'm at my most anxious I can log nearly sixty, seventy miles a week.

"Nice, Grace," I say. "Good work on yourself, kid. You seem a lot stronger. I'm super proud of you."

She smiles broadly. If only more grownups knew: it's okay to push, but a little praise goes a long way with kids.

"Thanks, Dr. Hank. Thanks for helping me."

After she leaves I do the invoicing, filing. I type up my notes. I am organized and efficient. I always have been — a good student, a good doctor. I was a good friend, too, wasn't I? A good lover. I might have been a good boyfriend, husband, father. Don't you think so, Lara? Might have been.

I keep the Toyota in a parking garage about an hour away. I drive my red Volvo there and park it. I am mindful, watchful, have been since the FBI knocked on my door. I don't think they're watching me. As the days have passed, I've come to think that Agent Brower really was just looking for help, looking for someone who might know what seems unknowable. Why people do the things they do? Isn't that what we're really all trying to figure out — detectives, doctors, writers? Aren't we all just trying to unravel the mysteries of ourselves?

She hasn't visited again, or called. Still. I have been keeping to my routine. The hospital. My office. Home. I am not seeing anyone. You are my only friend. (And you're not much of one, are you?) Sometimes I take my secretary to dinner, or on our late night we'll grab a drink before she heads home to her family. I monitor the outdoor security cameras at my home, keep my eyes on the rearview mirror. If there's a tail on me, it's a very good one. And I don't think anyone's that good at anything these days.

Still. You can't be too careful. I leave the parking lot and jog the mile to my gym. Through the park, the town center. It's a quiet little town, not many people around this time of night. The gym is in an old warehouse. It's not your usual chain with brightly clad hard-bodies and blaring music, television screens on every machine and in every corner. There's a big boxing ring in the center, an area for free weights, a couple of rows of treadmills and bikes for cardio. This is a serious bodybuilding gym — lots of cops and firefighters, EMT guys, martial artists.

"Doc," says the young woman at the desk. She's as big as any man I know, muscles ripped, neck thick, mousy hair shorn almost to the scalp. I'd say sexual abuse in childhood, if I had to hazard a guess.

"Marin," I say. "How goes it?"

"No complaints." But her eyes are sad. It's always in the eyes if you know how to look. Not just the eyes, but the muscles of the face that jump and dance ever so slightly.

"What's it today?" she asks.

"Shoulders and back."

"Let me know if you need me to spot."

"Will do."

I have a brutal and punishing workout regimen, in addition to my running. It's the only way I can keep him in place, exhaustion. I'll be an hour and a half tonight, working lats and traps and deltoids. Rows, pull-ups, deadlifts. I'll go as heavy as I can, work to shaking failure. Then I'll do forty minutes light on the bike, run back to the car. I have a trainer here, too. I see him twice a week — he keeps me limber, working out on all the planes, twisting and balancing so I don't get tight and stiff like some of the guys here. A couple of guys will get into the ring with me. A couple of them beg off; fighting, the adrenaline, it brings out another side of me and some people can sense it, though I've never lost control here.

When I'm done, I realize I'm the last one and it's ten minutes past closing.

Marin sits patiently at the desk, her bag and coat by the door. She pushes back on the office chair, which looks like it's about to snap under her weight, reading, I see as I get closer, a copy of one of my books: *Surviving Trauma.*

"Sorry about that," I say. "Lost track."

"Happens to me all the time," she says. She holds up the book. "This is helping me. Thank you."

I nod. "I'm glad."

I reach in the pocket of my coat and hand her a card. "I have a practice," I say. "If you need to talk."

She smiles, takes it. "I can't afford that, Doc."

"We can work something out," I say. Her eyes slide away from mine, and I realize how it sounded. "I mean — pay what you can afford kind of a thing."

She presses her lips together. "Thanks."

She won't take me up on it. I can tell; some folks don't want to talk. Can't trust. Don't have the words. Don't want to hear those words on the air. And that's okay, don't you think? Don't you wish you never had to tell a soul what happened to you? Don't you wish you could just forget?

"Can I walk you to your car?"

She gives me a look, a kind of smiling up and down. She's got a couple of inches and maybe even a couple of pounds on me. "No offense, Doc. But can I walk *you* to *your* car?"

I have to laugh. "Fair enough."

I tip an imaginary hat to her and step out into the cool night.

By the time I get back to the garage, I'm sure they're not following me. I leave the Volvo in the lot and get into the Toyota.

Tess is there as I pull onto the street, sitting beside me. She's a child tonight, thin and shivering. I am grateful to her, you know. That she's here with me this way.

In a disaster-stricken Japanese town called Otsuchi, there was an earthquake followed by a tsunami, which precipitated a nuclear plant meltdown, and over ten percent of the population was lost. A young man installed a disconnected rotary telephone booth in his backyard, a way to call his lost beloved cousin and deal with his grief. He called it a wind telephone. After a while, others from the town started to come, everyone trying to find some way to reach out to the many

317

people lost. I heard about it on NPR. It struck me, how we hold on to each other, how we are so desperate to find those who have been taken from us.

I know you still think about her, too, Rain. Because that time together, those friendships, they were special. Grown-ups dismiss the love that children share. But there is nothing purer, no love more accepting, no affection more complete than the love among young people. You don't know yet how much pain there is on the other side of it. You haven't learned to hold back the biggest part of yourself so that you can survive the end of things.

Maybe that's why I can't let her go. Why I can't let you go. I've never cared about anyone as much since. You told me that you found it sad. Maybe, you said, if I'd built a life, I wouldn't be clinging to the past. But I wonder.

"Let me go," Tess says. "Let this go."

"I can't."

"You can't?" she asks. "Or *he* can't."

"There's less distance between us lately."

"Maybe you should see a shrink about that."

We drive a long time; it's late. "What would you tell a patient who was behaving like this?" she asks.

318

"I couldn't condone it," I admit. "This is criminal behavior. I'd have to advise my patient to stop immediately. I'd have to turn him in to prevent him from harming others."

She nods solemnly. "Physician heal thyself."

"I saw Lara today," I tell her.

"She doesn't love you," she answers.

She was always so honest like that, remember? Never cruel but just an innocent stating the facts. "She never did. Not even when we were little, and you stared and stared at her, tried to hold her hand at the Valentine's Day roller-skating party that time.

"Or that crystal heart you gave her for her birthday," she says. "Remember how proud you were of that, how you shopped and shopped for the perfect thing. What did she do with it?"

"She left it," I admit. "She forgot about it."

Tess nods meaningfully. It still hurts. How sad is that? We were ten.

"And she just liked that goth kid who wrote that horrible poetry and didn't even know she existed."

I remember. That guy. He was such an asshole. What did you ever see in him?

"She might have loved me, later when we

met again."

Those weeks with you, they're like a film reel I play in my mind. Your scent, your skin, your body in my bed, the sound of your laughter, the silk of your hair. It was a glimpse at the world that was still there waiting for me — love, a family, children. Helping people in order to ease my own pain. Not the other things — the obsessions, the secret plans.

"But not him," she says. "You let him scare her away."

"No," I say. "He is not lovable. He's a dog on a chain."

"I was the one who loved you," she says softly. "I love him, too. He tried so hard to save us."

She reaches out to touch my face. Her fingers are ice on my skin and I shiver. She looks wounded, then disappears, stardust. I watch the empty seat beside me. I'm not a hundred percent sure what she is. A haunting. A hallucination. A manifestation of my deep and total aloneness. I don't dwell on it for long. She is what she is, I guess.

Physician heal thyself?

Easier said.

The house is isolated — as it would have to be. So I park the car just inside the hidden drive, pulling it close to the trees so that it can't be seen from the road. Then I walk through the woods.

The temperature is dropping. Winter comes later in our age of global weirding. But the cold arrives like an ambush, bringing all-new superstorms, like the "bomb cyclone" that's expected to hit later this week. Or maybe there are just new names for these things, some marketing department somewhere cooking up phrases to incite maximum dread. Keep people afraid and you keep them consuming, stockpiling supplies and buying generators.

I know my way around this property now. I know all the exits and entrances to the big house. I understand that there's another structure here, as well. But I've yet to find it. That's why I'm here. A patient of mine was a foster child here; she's made claims that no one believes — shocking stories of starvation, children locked in rooms for days, physical and psychological torture. There have been investigations that turned up no evidence. The girl, a damaged young thing, has a reputation as a pathological liar. She has a rap sheet of petty crimes — shoplifting, possession of marijuana, attempted prostitution. But I know the look of trauma. She's broken. The question is —

who broke her? And can he (or she — yeah, sometimes) be stopped from breaking others?

As I make my way through the woods, I hear her shuffling footsteps behind me.

"It's just an excuse," Tess says. "He's aching to do it again. And I don't think you can contain him."

Maybe she's right.

TWENTY-FOUR

Gillian waved from the doorway, a slim figure in a rectangle of light. Lily was already asleep, Rain having nursed her and put her to bed. She was a sound sleeper. If Auntie Gillian didn't go in there too often, checking and poking around as she was prone to do, Lily would sleep through the night.

They hadn't even pulled off their street before Rain was checking the app. Lily lay on her back, arms ups, head to the side, mouth agape. The sleep of the innocent, deep and peaceful.

"You're not checking the app already," said Greg, looking over. At the stop sign, he took the phone and stared at the baby a moment, then at her.

"Sorry," she said.

Date-night rules: don't just talk about the baby. Don't compulsively check the monitor. Don't succumb to the constant fatigue and go home early. Devices on Do Not Disturb except for Gillian's number. No social media posting.

"What did our parents do?" asked Greg. "They didn't have any tech, not like there is today."

"I guess they just did what they did," she said. "Figured if there was an emergency someone would call."

What if her parents *had* had that tech? Maybe she, Tess and Hank would all be raising their children together in the same town, like so many of the people she knew. She saw their posts on Facebook, kids going to the same schools as their parents, same community fairs and soccer games. Mini versions of the people she knew, playing in the same parks, visiting the cider mill in fall, the sheep-shearing festival in spring. Maybe Tess would have married Hank, on whom she'd had a lifelong crush. Maybe Hank would have stopped staring at Rain and noticed Tess one day.

"What are you thinking about?" asked Greg, resting a hand on her leg.

"Nothing," she said, looking at him, trying for a smile. "Just zoning out."

"So, how's the story coming?" he asked. "Did you hear from Andrew?"

The space between them was still tingling,

charged with the energy of his worry, his anger about the letters, her guarding of this thing she wanted to do, maybe for the wrong reasons, her guilt about Lily, the visit from the FBI, her sins of omission. He hadn't brought up the letters again, though they were fluttering in the air. What was there to talk about, really? She'd lied or omitted something important. She hadn't made excuses or even really apologized. He was angry, confused — of course he was. She didn't know how to make things right. She'd been able to explain it to Gillian, but she wasn't sure Greg would understand.

She had a feeling it wasn't going to be the best date night they'd ever had.

In fact, sometimes date night just turned into fight night, the only place they had that wasn't sucked up by work or parenting. So everything they held inside came out in a rush; they'd wind up parked somewhere screaming at each other.

Sometimes they wound up parked some-where — at the overlook, once in the park-ing lot of the closed library — and fucked in the back seat — raw, desperate, tawdry. Then, laughing at themselves, they'd grab fast food, or go to a bar and have a couple of drinks. Once they took an Uber home. Thank god Gillian had been there to wake up with the baby.

"He's pitching it next week," she said. "I'm taking it slow until then."

It was a half-truth. She wasn't taking it slow. She'd connected with Henry, reached out to an old colleague who'd started a very successful podcast. She'd purchased a few URLs — rainwinter.com, winterstories-.com, murrayandwinter.com and a few others. She'd created a timeline, compiled a list of people she wanted to interview. All of this in down moments while Lily slept, or was occupied with her toys, eating in her high chair. She was doing this, with or without NNR. It was a runaway train inside her.

She fought the urge to check the app yet again, even though it hadn't even been a few minutes. She looked at her husband instead, that wild mop of hair, that presidential jaw, the impressive span of his shoulders. She gripped his hand, wound her fingers through his. *Remember to touch each other,* one article on "Keeping your marriage alive after the baby!" advised.

Often, still, they couldn't keep their hands off each other. Even after so many years, just the sight of him could make her jittery with desire. "When you're both focused on the baby, it's easy to forget about each other," the article warned. Why did she even read that stuff?

But just that simple action caused him to smile, caused some of the tension in her own shoulders to relax. His tone was softer.

He made the turn, drove through town.

She turned up the heat; she felt chilled to the bone. The temperature had taken a steep drop. Halloween decorations glittered — witches on broomsticks, bats, and cats with arched backs hanging from the street-lamps. The little square had been turned into a pumpkin patch. On weekends, there was a farmers' market — cider and maple syrup candy, bags of candy corn on offer. She and Gillian were taking Lily tomorrow; it was Greg's morning to sleep in.

"So, I did a little research today," he said. "About Kreskey."

She was surprised, and not. She knew the way his brain worked, a lot like hers. Probably he went into the office after the FBI visit and, stewing, he started researching the thing that was irking him, trying to figure out the puzzle of the past that was always pushing its way into their present.

"There's a lot of information about him," said Greg. He kept his eyes on the road, but she saw a muscle working in his jaw.

"Yes," she said, feeling that familiar tingle

of unease she had whenever she had to talk about him.

Kreskey, for whatever reason, was one of those killers with a following. Though he wasn't technically a serial killer, there was something about him that kept people returning to his story. There was a documentary that had aired on one of the big cable networks, a slew of features, and he had his own page on a particularly sick website called thekillernextdoor.net, devoted to high-profile murderers, their histories, current status. On this site, the perpetrators had followers, fan clubs. Those living might submit a blog from prison. Rain had spent far too much time on that site, often came away feeling vaguely sick and slimed.

"Detective Harper," said Greg. "The officer who saved Hank and brought Kreskey in, then investigated Kreskey's murder ten years later. He's still alive and living near your father."

"How old is he now?" she asked, though she already knew the answer.

Rain remembered him as an old man when she was a young girl, but maybe in that way that all adults seem ridiculously old, almost living on another plane of existence in the mystical world of the "grown-up." Only once she was a grown-up (allegedly) did she realize how close they all were to childhood, how plenty of people were still living there, clinging, in fact, to that place. Herself included.

"He's in his seventies," said Greg. "Long retired from the department, but still working as a PI. I thought he might be a good connect for you."

Detective Harper was the first person on the list she'd compiled. They'd talked a number of times over the years, were connected by the events that had transpired — his finding her, the years that followed. They shared something that few people did. But she didn't want to make it seem like she didn't want or need Greg's help.

"Thank you. That's a good idea." Then, "I'm sorry. I know this is hard for you."

Greg had taken them to the overlook and put the car into Park. They sat, looking at their glittering town in the distance. Looking at all of the points of light, she wondered which house was theirs.

"I'm sorry, too," he said. He squeezed her hand. "I get that it's *way* harder for you."

He bowed his head a moment, and she waited. Then, "I get mad, so frustrated — because I can't protect you. I was on there, that website, reading about him, about the abuse he suffered as a child, how it turned him into a monster —"

The sentence came up short; he shook his head tightly in frustration. "I want to *go back* — you know? Stop it before it all began. Save you. Save your friend Tess. Even Hank. If I could just lift that one moment out of all of your lives. It's stupid. I couldn't protect you then — in a lot of ways I can't protect you now. How, then, do I protect Lily?"

He pressed his mouth into a tight, angry line, looked away.

"That's who you are," she said, rubbing his shoulder. "You're a fixer. A protector. But we can't always protect each other. All we can do is love each other."

"It's not enough."

"It has to be."

"And Kreskey," he said after a moment.

"What about him?"

He traced a finger along the line of her jaw, pushed the hair back from her face.

"The abuse," said Greg. "The police found him in the basement. They kept him in there, for days and weeks, no food, no sunshine. He was *twelve*. He'd never been to school. His mother had taught him how to read and write, claimed she was home-schooling him for religious reasons. He'd only seen other children at the grocery

330

store. He had broken bones that had healed wrong, scars from cigarettes that had been put out on his flesh. His right eardrum had been pierced by something. What if you could go back even further, and save *him*?"

His words bounced around the car.

What if?

If only.

That black spiral into nothing.

"The investigation into Kreskey's murder," said Greg after they were quiet for a while. "It was — cursory."

"How do you mean?" She felt her body stiffen a little, forced herself to relax.

"There wasn't a lot of energy put behind it," said Greg. "There were a few lackluster interviews, other ex-cons at the halfway house, doctors who treated him, a woman whose land edged the Kreskey property."

The wizened old woman with her hat and stick, the camera around her neck. How swift she'd been on the path through the trees, how quickly she'd disappeared. Was it her?

"What's her name?" asked Rain. "The neighbor."

"Greta Miller."

"Is she still alive?"

"She's still alive," he said. "She still lives in the house next to the Kreskey property."

"Did she see anything that night?"

"That was the strange thing," he said. "There was no recording or transcript from her interview. I mean, things get lost in small departments. No one is as organized or meticulous as you'd hope, especially when you go back that far. But everything else was intact."

Greta Miller. What did she see?

"But no one was ever brought in, no one charged. No leads. No real suspects."

He went on, "In a way, it reminds me of the Markham murder. The story is already out of the news, the investigation 'ongoing.' You know? No one cares. It's like — good riddance."

Yeah, good riddance.

In recovery, she'd struggled with the idea that Kreskey still thought about her. He could still dream about her. She existed in his fantasies, as if a version of herself was trapped within him. She used to wonder: What does he do to me in his dreams? She could still hear his voice, feel his hands, the hard shock of his fist. When Kreskey died, the part of her he kept in his fantasies died, too. She was free.

"But it's just this cycle of abuse, violence, murder," said Greg. "If we never understand it, we can never lift that next Kreskey out of

332

his circumstance, or save the next Hank, Tess and Lara."

"Maybe that's why I do what I do," said Rain. "That's what my father thinks, what Tess's mom thinks."

"You're trying to understand."

"Yes," she said. "Because monsters live and thrive in the dark. Hank, too, I think. I think we're both trying to understand, to fix, to prevent."

He stared ahead, nodded lightly.

"So," Greg said, reaching to the seat behind and retrieving a thick file folder. "Here's all my research so far. I'm in — I'll do what I can. I'm behind you. I support you — we'll make this work. We'll make sure Lily gets everything she needs. And that you do, too."

She took the file, held it in her lap, opened it and flipped through the pages, then closed it again and looked into the face of her husband. She knew it represented a lot of hours he didn't have, phone calls, requests for information. She leaned in and kissed him, long and deep.

"About the letters," she said when she pulled away. She'd put them back in the drawer where she kept them. She didn't want them. She couldn't let go of them. "I shouldn't have kept them from you."

"Why did you?"

"How can I make you understand something I barely understand myself?"

"I get that you're connected to him," he said. "And not in a way you chose, exactly. I get that part of you feels you owe him something. But you don't owe him, Rain. We need you, Lily and me. We need you here with us. I already told you, long ago, I won't share you with him."

Greg knew almost everything about her time with Hank. She'd told him, wanted him to know her, all her flaws, mistakes she made, the demons she wrestled. He was angry, hurt, and for a time she thought she'd lost him. But he forgave her. *We are all flawed, aren't we? We all make mistakes.* He told her some things, too. A girl he'd kissed at a bar one night. A lie he told her. Small things, compared to what she'd done. She forgave him, as well. They walked into their married life together clean, mostly. Some feelings, some details she kept to herself.

"I'm here," she said. "With you. With her. I promise. I love you."

He reached in and kissed her hard, then that killer smile. "Prove it."

She did.

Later that night, Gillian asleep in the guest room, Lily in her crib and Greg snoring, Rain took the file into her office, started sifting through the documents there — police reports, news articles, pictures and articles as far back as the week it all started. There was even a picture of herself she'd never seen, looking small and scared, tucked into the arm of her father as they climbed the courthouse steps so that she could deliver her in-chamber testimony. She barely remembered that time, lost in a fog of trauma and sadness. The girl in the photo looked like a stranger.

Rain entered Greta Miller's name into the search engine. A website was the first item.

She was a wildlife photographer, specializing in birds. The image of a crow on a fence post, a snowy field behind, the yellow of his eye a striking brightness in the grayscale, dominated the home page. That eye, sharp and seeing, seemed to stare off the screen right at Rain.

Something outside caught her attention — what was it? A light, a sound? Some kind of sixth sense? She moved from the desk and over to the window, staying off to the side.

Pushing back the drapes, she saw it. There, parked across the street, down a bit, a beige Toyota Corolla. She could just make out the thick form of a man in the driver's seat.

Her heart jumped and started to race.

She slipped over the hall runner and crept down the stairs. By the time she got to the door, disabled the alarm and opened it into the night, the car was pulling away, slow and easy. She watched as it disappeared into the night, breath shallow.

Wake up Greg and cause him a fit of worry? Call the FBI agent and say what, that she thought Hank was stalking her in his spare time? And if she was wrong, cause him even more heartache than she already had. Call the police and tell them she'd spotted a suspicious vehicle? Actually, in this neighborhood — safe and wealthy and quiet — the cops would come, take her seriously, make a report, even be kind and concerned. But then what?

She stood in the cold, watching the night, hugging herself tight, aware of a gnawing sense of dread.

TWENTY-FIVE

Detective Harper was an old man now, with a full head of snow-white hair. He greeted them at the door to his modest house, embraced Rain as if they were old friends. He seemed smaller than Rain remembered him. In her memories, he loomed large — a towering figure with a booming voice. But he still moved lightly and easily, was healthy and fit. He still had that bright, intelligent gaze, the ready smile.

"It's good to see you," he said. "We haven't talked since —"

"Since Eugene Kreskey was murdered."

He looked down at the bricks of his stoop, then back at her, his gaze intent.

"Long time now," he said.

She introduced Gillian, who stood beside her. He took her hand, gave her that goofy look that men get when they like what they see.

"I listen to your morning broadcast," said

the detective. "The station has a liberal bent that I don't love. But I love the sound of your voice."

Was the old guy flirting?

"Thank you so much," said Gillian, amping up her high-wattage smile. She knew how to work a source.

"Are you sure this is a good time?" Rain asked.

"If you want to go back there, Miss Winter," he said, "I'll go with you."

She didn't *want* to go back there. She had to.

Rain and Gillian had taken Lily to the pumpkin patch, then left her with Greg. It was Gillian who pushed for the interview with Harper today, after reviewing Greg's findings that morning over coffee. Rain felt a deep reluctance to see him again. Though he'd been the one to save her, his face was etched into the memories of the worst days of her life. And for a number of reasons, she'd have preferred to talk to him alone.

But Gillian had a way of making things happen. She'd hassled Rain until she made the call; Harper surprised her by agreeing to see them that afternoon. She was caught in the current of the story. That's what happened. Hadn't she known that?

He led them down a dim hallway, into his

living room.

They sat on a sectional with built-in recliners and cup holders, across from a huge television, a flat screen that took up most of the wall over an ancient credenza. The walls and the surfaces around were populated by pictures — grandkids, she guessed, Harper with the town mayor, a wedding portrait where he looked impossibly young and virile, his bride an angel in white. Harper with his platoon. Vietnam, was it? She seemed to remember that. Sports memorabilia, pennants on the wall, medals of commendation, his detective's shield in a shadow box, all the detritus of a life someone enjoyed living. The window looked out onto a big backyard shaded by old-growth trees, a swing set and sandbox sat waiting for play.

"Mind if I record?" asked Rain, placing the device on the coffee table.

There was a definite beat as he held her with that gaze again. The wary cop. "Where is this going to air?"

"We're not sure yet," said Gillian. "This will be part of a larger feature, a history of the Tess Barker murder, and an exploration of how it might tie in with the vigilante killings of Eugene Kreskey, Wayne Garret Smith and Steve Markham."

"Vigilante?" he said, leaning back. "Have there been developments on those cases?"

"No," she said. "No yet. As I say, we're just exploring connections, possibilities."

"In my experience, when the media starts looking for connections, people get hurt," he said. "And when it comes to cold cases, it's usually a postmortem of the investigation where the local cops wind up looking like idiots."

"It's not that kind of story," she said. Gillian leaned in, smiled this particular brand of smile she had — polite, so sweet. Those big eyes, the intimate way she touched his arm. Rain watched the old guy melt.

"And you'll get a chance to hear the final product before it goes live. If it ever does."

Which is not to say that you'll be able to change a word of it, of course. But she wasn't obligated to say that. You talk, we report. Those were the rules, and everyone knows it, even if they don't like it in the end.

Text from Greg, the third one in an hour: Where's Moon Bear?

Look under her crib?

Got it!

Detective Harper gave Rain a nod, and

she pressed Record.

"Let's begin at the beginning. Tell me about the first time you saw me."

He closed his eyes a moment, as if accessing the memories. Rain remembered, too, seeing his face, clean-shaven, kind eyes.

Hey, Lara Winter, is that you? Everything's okay now, kid. You're okay.

"We got the call around noon," he said. "Your mother, she'd called over to your friend Hank Reams's house. When there was no answer, she went looking. When you weren't there, she started driving around the neighborhood. It was Hank's bike. She saw it fallen by the path to the bridge. She went to the nearest house and called the police."

Rain nodded. It jibed with everything she knew, had heard or read a hundred times.

"We mobilized very quickly," he said. "Missing kids, a small town. We had most of our people, some guys from other area departments, about a hundred volunteers, as well as some of the fire department out in those woods within an hour or so."

He shook his head. "The clock starts ticking right away, as I'm sure you know. You have five hours to bring them home alive, they say. We created a circle, started talking to everyone we could find."

Outside, the sun moved behind a cloud and the room dimmed.

"But it was nearly dark by the time we found you. You were right there. How did we miss you?"

He stared into the middle distance.

"I still think about that, you know, those hours, that ticking clock. How could we have been faster? What difference would have been made in two hours, one?"

Rain felt the familiar rise of emotion; she bit it back.

Indeed, what difference would there have been if Rain had managed to run, to even answer the voices she heard calling for her? An hour earlier, according to Hank, and Tess would have survived. He would have escaped the worst of his ordeal.

But she was frozen, deep in shock, her voice encased in ice inside her chest. The Winter Girl.

"It was just luck that I found you, you were buried so deep in that tree. I saw this flash of something, the last light of the day came out from behind the clouds and there you were. Huddled. I won't forget the way you looked."

"The way I looked?"

"Your eyes," he said. "I've seen that look on men after combat — men much bigger and stronger than you were. They've seen and experienced horrors that changed them. They check out, go blank. It's almost like a brain reboot, you know? When they come back online, they're someone else. I wanted to cry — I remember that. You were so young. That look didn't have any place on you."

"PTSD."

He gave an assenting nod. "Yeah, that's what they call it now. After Vietnam, they gave it a name, a list of symptoms, ways to treat. And that's all good, a way for people to get help. But some of those guys, it was too much. Meds, therapy. But some things you can't unsee. Some things just stay with you. You either live with it. Or it haunts you. Or you let it kill you."

He leaned back, the chair creaking under his weight.

"It's like you didn't die there on the battlefield, but you *did*. You just didn't know it."

He went quiet; Rain and Gillian waited. Outside there was shouting. Kids she'd seen playing in the street. Laughter. Then, distantly, a siren. Her mind drifted briefly to Greg and Lily. What if there was an accident? A fire? *Stop it,* she told herself. *Focus.*

"It took us a couple more hours to coax you back, to find out what you'd seen, what you knew. Honestly? I wasn't sure you'd *come* back. You were hurt — badly, drifting in and out of consciousness. You shook, like you were the worst kind of cold. I thought, she'll never get over this."

He looked at her, his gaze level, seeing.

"But look at you," he said with a fatherly smile. "You're all grown up. Family, good job. That's the one good thing from all that. That he didn't get all of you."

"Because of you," said Gillian. "You saved her, and Hank."

"Like I say, it was luck," he said. "The luck of the way light moved in just that moment. Mind if I ask, why now? Why do you want to go back?"

She opted for a bit of honesty. You couldn't get people to open up to you if you weren't open yourself. She'd give him as much as she could.

"The murders of Steve Markham, and also the Boston Boogeyman. They have me thinking about Kreskey. It's brought me back to that time and place — a time and place I've buried deep. It has me asking questions about justice, and what makes men like Kreskey, and what unmakes them. And . . ."

344

She let the sentence trail off.

"No matter how many times we go back, we can't change what happened," he said. "Sucks, right?"

"I still have a lot of guilt about that day," she said, though she hadn't intended to. She felt Gillian's eyes settle on her.

Harper regarded her, his eyes full of facets and layers. He knew things about her that no one else did, not even Gillian.

"There's no shame in survival, Miss Winter. It's what we're all doing, every day. The brain — they didn't get this for a long time — it does what it needs to do to keep the rest of you living. It's not about will or bravery or any of that. You were a tiny slip of a kid. You hadn't run, you'd be dead, too. Where's the justice in that?"

The grandfather clock in his foyer chimed the hour.

"So, at a certain point," she said, moving on, "I remembered where I'd seen Eugene Kreskey before, who he was. And then —"

He sat up from his reclined position. "As soon as you mentioned the garage, along with your description of him, we knew. Kreskey had been on our radar since his release. We all remembered him. Then it was five of us like bats out of hell, racing for that house. I remember feeling like it was a

345

hundred miles away, that the car couldn't go fast enough even pedal to the metal. The road just seemed to get longer, and longer.

"Then we got there. We knocked, identified ourselves, but then we just blazed in through that front door, breaking about a million rules. We didn't care — we were just thinking about those two little kids."

Rain sat breathless, listening.

"What a place, I swear you can still feel the energy there — all that pain and death. It's like it radiates out of the ground."

She was a pragmatist — didn't believe in ghosts or hauntings. When people talked about *energies,* she kind of glazed over a little. But she knew what he meant; she'd felt it, too. The malevolence of that place; it was still on her skin.

When she looked back at Detective Harper, his eyes had filled.

"What he did to that girl. What he did to her. She wasn't even a person to him. She was a doll. And Hank Reams. Man, just an hour sooner."

Rain felt her eyes fill, too, with the rush of just *wishing* that one thing had been different that day.

That Tess's mom hadn't had to work.

That they'd listened to Rain's mom about not crossing through the woods. That one

346

of them had a phone. That Hank had run instead of trying to save them. She bowed her head into her hand, felt Gillian's arm on her shoulders. Maybe this was a mistake. How could she tell this story well when it still hurt so much? When the memories still burned.

Gillian took over, asking questions about the arrest, the trial.

"So," she asked finally. "What was Kreskey like?"

"He was a child, you know that," Harper said. "Kreskey. I mean, he was a monster — huge." He lifted his arms wide to signal Kreskey's girth.

"He had the glazed stare of a sadist, a sickness deep, deep inside. But he could barely read or write, he had zero education before the age of twelve, not even a television in that house. He didn't know who the president was. When he was left in the interrogation room, he asked for crayons and paper. Soft-spoken, shy, very polite — 'please' and 'thank you.' "

"Did you give it to him?" asked Gillian. "The paper and crayons."

"We did," said the detective. "We wondered, what would someone who just murdered a child and tortured two others, what in the goddamn world would someone like that draw with crayons?"

"What did he draw?" asked Rain, even though she already knew the answer.

He looked at Rain, lowered his eyes. "He drew pictures of Lara Winter. Over and over and over. Sweet pictures — playing with him, making cookies with him, walking through the woods."

Rain had seen them, most of them. She'd asked Henry to show her after he told her about them; reluctantly he sent her instructions on how to access the dark web, find the images. Harper was right; they were the drawings of a toddler, two-dimensional, facile. He was a child, a deranged murderous child.

"It was — sad, I guess. Unsettling. Kreskey was a sick fuck — pardon my language. There was no helping that guy, his hardware was damaged — irreparably."

"So, when he was murdered ten years later," said Rain. "How did you feel?"

Harper shrugged, his features hardened a little. He cast Rain a look and she averted her eyes.

"I guess I'd be lying if I said that there wasn't some sense of relief," he said after a moment in thought. "I fought against his release from the psychiatric prison, even into that controlled work release facility.

348

That was a minimum-security situation. I think they figured that he was so docile, so heavily medicated, that he wasn't much of a threat."

"But you didn't feel that way."

"I thought it was only a matter of time before he hurt someone else. We were aware of him, let's put it that way."

"You had someone watching him."

Harper looked uncomfortable. "Well, there wasn't manpower for that. And even if there was, we wouldn't have had the over-time hours in our budget. But some of us watched him in our spare time. We organized a group — it wasn't enough. But it was something."

She could feel Gillian seize on this.

"Wow," said her friend. She was queen of the controlled gush — not over the top, sounding totally sincere. "That's really amazing. That you all took time from your life to watch him, to protect your town."

Predictably, he swelled a little. "The job doesn't end when you go home. You never stop being a cop, even when you retire."

"Was anyone watching him the night he was murdered?" she asked.

Rain caught just the flicker of a smile on Harper's face.

"No, not that night. Unfortunately, there

was a gap in our surveillance. My grandson was graduating from high school, one of the other guys had date night with his wife. Kreskey had, in fact, been kind of straight-arrow since his release. To be honest we were less worried than when he'd just been released. I mean, the guy *was* so pumped full of meds, he was like the walking dead."

"You investigated the murder," said Rain.

He sat forward in his chair. "Yeah, if you can call it an investigation."

"Meaning."

"I mean there was no evidence, no witnesses. Whoever did it planned it, executed with precision and left no trace of himself behind. We did everything by the book — interviewed neighbors, a couple of the more dangerous guys at the facility where he resided. We watched the house for a while. We never had a single lead or suspect. The case is cold."

He nodded toward the kitchen. "I've got my old files back there. I still go through them sometimes. Your case, Tess, Hank, Kreskey. It's still with me, as I can see it's still with you. Some of them, you can just never let go."

"Can you tell us how he was killed?" asked Gillian.

He gave Rain a look, like — *You really*

want to know? Rain already knew the answer. She just wanted him to say it for the story.

"It didn't look like he put up much of a fight, which I didn't get. Kreskey was a big guy." He lifted his hand, fist clenched as if he were holding a weapon. "A knife through the heart."

Rain was surprised at a sudden rush of nausea, a sheen of sweat popping up on her brow.

"I'm sorry," he said, maybe catching her expression. "When you know what people can do, it changes you, doesn't it?"

It does, thought Rain. *Of course it does.*

"Did you have any theories about who might have killed him?" asked Gillian.

Something came down over Harper's face, a kind of veil, a shield.

"No," he said flatly. "I don't have the first idea. Like I said, we did everything by the book. Sometimes you just don't get the answers you want."

"We were able to get some of the transcripts of the people you interviewed. There was one missing. Greta Miller, the Kreskeys' neighbor."

Detective Harper chuckled. "Greta," he said. "I don't know what happened to the transcript, but that was a short interview, as

351

I remember it. I can look in my file, but I didn't have many notes from that talk. She didn't want to see us in the first place, finally answered the door, then claimed to have seen nothing, basically threw us out. Said no one ever came when she called about kids partying and making a mess at the Kreskey house, and why should she help us?"

"So, she could hear people out at Kreskey's from her house?" asked Gillian.

"Doubtful," he said. "Sound carries sometimes, foggy nights. But she was always out on those trails, taking pictures of birds. She's a bit of nut, if you ask me."

He circled a finger around his temple.

"Won some awards, though, kind of a big deal in her field, I think."

Rain's phone pinged again. She took it from her pocket.

"Sorry," she said.

She won't take the breast milk you pumped, and she's really fussy. When will you be back??

Rain felt a flash of annoyance. They hadn't even been gone two hours. Could he not manage a couple of hours?

The retired detective took advantage of

her distraction and got up to leave the room. "Can I get you girls some coffee?" he tossed behind him.

Gillian raised her eyebrows at Rain. "Everything okay?"

She showed the phone to Gillian, who rolled her eyes. There was that brutal tug-of-war between the two parts of herself, again.

"Let me help," Gillian called after the detective, following him into the kitchen. She could record on her smartphone — which was no doubt on Do Not Disturb.

I need another hour, she typed back to Greg. We're in the middle of an interview.

She watched the dots pulse. Oh. Okay.

There was attitude in that text. Just two simple words and, somehow, he'd managed to communicate that he was overwhelmed, wanted her to come back. What happened to *I'll do anything I can to help*? Man up, honey.

She turned down the notification volume at least and followed Gillian and Harper into the kitchen. Pushing through the doors, she felt like she'd passed through a time machine into the seventies — old linoleum floors and ancient avocado appliances in need of replacing. On the counter, a battalion of pill bottles.

"I've talked to a lot of cops," Gillian was saying. She sat on a green swivel chair, leaning on a Knoll-style glass-top tulip table. "And I've never met one who didn't have a theory on the cases still keeping them up nights."

"Not this one," he said. "And don't misunderstand. It's the kids, what happened to you all, that still bothers me. Not Kreskey."

He turned to face them both, Gillian and Rain now seated at the kitchen table. "I know it's not very PC or whatever. These days the liberals run the show, it's all about prisoners' rights and what makes us tick. Rehabilitation. Education. Job training. But there's something that cops, soldiers, some doctors know that other people don't seem to get — or don't want to get."

"And what's that?" asked Rain, inching Gillian's recording phone closer.

There was a coldness to Detective Harper that she'd seen in him before.

"That some people are better off dead."

TWENTY-SIX

"It's there," she says. "I swear it is."

"I believe you."

I do. I do believe her. Or, anyway, I believe that she believes it. But my search of the property revealed nothing. Just the house, where I've never seen anyone come or go. There was no other structure. I was out there late looking, and I'm exhausted having barely clocked three hours of sleep. She doesn't know any of that, of course.

This girl, she's so thin and so tense, I just want to cover her with a blanket. Her foster mother, Jen, younger than most, loving and concerned, sits out in the waiting area. This is an emergency session because Angel has been having nightmares — night terrors really, where she wakes screaming and inconsolable.

Angel claims that her former foster family abused her, and that other children in their care were also abused. Her new foster mother reported Angel's claims to the police a while back, and no one's done a thing. There was a cursory scan of the property, an investigation into the family that housed her before the couple she's with now. But no evidence has been unearthed to corroborate her story.

"There was still someone else there when I ran away. A boy."

"What was his name?"

She shakes her head. "I don't know. He was younger than me, I think. He didn't talk much. He had a birthmark on his shoulder that looked just like a heart. So, I called him Val, short for Valentine."

She's very creative. That's what makes her a good liar.

"He's in my dreams — alone and scared, Dr. Reams," she says. "Someone has to save him."

She leans forward, her eyes wide and desperate. There's an off note; I just can't place it. It might be that she's used to being disbelieved, discounted. It might be that she's lying, making up stories for attention. I have an open mind.

"I'll make some calls," I say. "I'll push for a closer look."

"What if it's too late?"

We both know how it feels when help

356

shows up too late, don't we, Lara?

"All we can do is try."

She leans back, pulls her legs up onto the couch and hugs herself into a ball. She stares out the window and I'm aware that the fall color show has faded, leaves brown and falling. Soon the trees will be bare. Winter. The Winter girl, isn't that what they kept calling you in the media?

"We're not just throwaways, you know," says Angel, suddenly angry. "Because our parents didn't want us, or they were too fucked up to raise us. We're *people.*"

"Yes," I say gently. "Of course."

"But, like, *you see that,* right? How people just don't care. If no one finds him, and a year from now someone stumbles on his bones — there'll be tears and flowers and all of that. But no one cares enough *right now* to look for him."

"People do care — I do. Your foster mother, Jen, she said they've started the proceedings for your permanent adoption. She cares about you. I think you know that. It's the institutional processes that can make the system seem inhumane. But, trust me, plenty of people care."

She shakes her head, eyes going hard. I didn't love the blank look of anger on her face. She's too young to be so jaded, so worn down.

"Do you think she's telling the truth?" her foster mother, Jen, asks me, after Angel is hypnotized by her new iPad in the waiting room. If I could tell parents one thing it would be to get rid of those devices, or at least strictly limit them. They're turning our kids into a generation of addicts.

I'm careful about how I answer, because I do believe something happened to Angel at that foster home. I'm just not sure what. "I know that she believes it," I say. "I could be wrong, but I don't think she's lying."

"She's so *fragile,*" Jen says, a tear escaping and trailing down her face before she can wipe it away. "I just want to help her get whole and look to the future — with us."

I hand her the tissue box; I go through a case a month.

"We'll get there," I promise. "She's strong."

Jen and her husband, William, are dream fosters, affluent people who couldn't have children of their own and looked to the system of abandoned older children rather than to private or overseas adoption for a baby. It's a hard road they've chosen, one that may lead to heartbreak.

"I was in the system," Jen tells me. "Did I ever mention that?"

"You didn't," I say. "But I guess it explains your desire to bring Angel into your home, into your life. Most people wouldn't have the strength or the patience to manage a troubled girl."

She nods, dabs at her eyes.

"I bounced from foster to foster," she says, clutching her leather bag to her middle. You wouldn't know it to look at her. She looks like a woman who came from privilege, who doesn't know anything else — fine features, expensively coiffed and dressed. "Finally, I aged out, worked my way through college, where I met William. We built a life, a family, just the two of us. His family have more or less adopted me — I have sisters and cousins, parents. I want to give that to someone else. I *was* Angel. Inside maybe I still am."

"She can learn a lot from your strength and resilience," I say. "Talk to her. Tell her about your experiences, even the painful ones. Sometimes it helps more than anything else to see someone thriving and well on the other side."

She smiles gratefully.

"You're a nice man, Dr. Reams," she says. "Are you married?"

I am taken aback by the question. It's not about me. It never is. That's one of the

359

things I like so much about my profession, I can disappear in the helping of others. I am trained to observe my feelings, distance myself from them, to focus on the people in my care. And people in pain, especially children and adolescents, are not prone to worrying about others. I am a sounding board, a strong and comforting voice, a well of advice and instruction. I am not a person with needs and feelings.

"I'm not," I say, feeling myself flush. There's some shame to this fact. I have closed myself to that kind of life — the life of husband and father, of lover, even friend. I have given myself over to other things — my work mainly, my darker activities. Plus, there's my old friend, the one who even now I can feel tugging on my consciousness. He is not comfortable with intimacy; strong emotion makes him harder to ignore and control.

Hank, my mother laments. *You're such a handsome man, financially comfortable, kind. Why can't you meet someone?*

She wants that, for me to love and be loved. I have stopped wanting that for myself.

"I hope this is not inappropriate," Jen says. "We're having a party for Angel, kind of a welcome thing where she can meet friends and family. We'd like you to come."

She slips a card across the small end table between the couch where she sits and the chair that I'm in.

"I'll try to make it," I say. "Thank you."

I look at the invitation, pink and printed. "Join us to welcome Angel into our home and our life."

"This is a nice thing," I say. "Important for her."

"She seems tense about it. She's worried people won't like her. I told her that they will, of course. But it's not really about them and what they think — it's about her getting to know the people who are going to be a part of her new life."

I understand Angel's fear. Those marked by trauma always feel apart.

"Someone who hasn't had a lot of love or attention might feel uncomfortable with it at first," I offer. "I think she'll grow into it."

I know how Angel feels. Intimacy can be painful, the closeness, the comfort of it. If you're always waiting for it to go away, you almost can't stand to have it in the first place. That's how I felt with you, Lara. Our pleasure, those deep moments we shared, the union of our bodies, it was as much agony as it was ecstasy. I think I always knew he'd hurt you, that I couldn't stop

361

him. Now I just try to keep him from hurting anyone else who doesn't deserve it.

"I'm not pushing her? Trying too hard? William thinks I'm hovering too much."

"Pushing is okay, as long as you comfort her if she falters, and help her keep trying after that."

"It might help if you were there?" she says. Shyly, a question.

"I'll be there," I say.

I look at my planner, an old-school leather-and-paper behemoth that sits on the desk. The weekdays are packed, every single section filled with scrawl. The weekends, on the other hand, are totally blank into infinity, page after page of nothing. *Live your life, Hank. Love, laugh, find someone, start a family. Jesus, get a dog. That's how you honor Tess. Not like this.* That was your sage advice the last time we communicated. A long time ago now.

I pencil the party in, the time, the address. It's not really a personal invitation, I tell myself. It's more about helping Angel through a transition that might be uncomfortable.

"Are you going to keep looking into it? Angel's story."

"I have one more person I can call."

She'd stopped hugging her bag, put it on

362

the ground and leaned forward.

"I was wondering if we should just let it go?" Worry etched into her brow.

"Why?"

"Because I want her to move on. If something did happen there, and she was a witness, doesn't that just hook her into the past, keep her reliving trauma and abuse?"

I get it. She wants to speed Angel on the road to wellness, to a kind of normal. But here's the thing — you can't just take the intact pieces forward and try to glue them into a person. You have to bring all the broken, shattered bits, as well. If something happened to Angel there and no one ever deals with it, and worse, no one believes her, that's a wound that might not heal. I tell her as much.

She listens, nods slowly. I can tell by the way her eyes dart to the left, she's accessing memories. By the drain of blood from her face, I can tell they're not good ones. Then, "But we don't always get justice, do we? Wrongs aren't always made right. And bad people get away with the worst things — all the time. Do we cling to that, use it as a reason to not move forward into whatever life we may have ahead? Do we stay broken because the people who broke us didn't get what they deserved?"

The heat comes up to my cheeks and I find I can't meet her gaze, drop my eyes to a faceted paperweight on my desk. When the light strikes it just right, it casts rainbow shards on the wall behind me.

Yes, I thought, not without a twist of shame. *Yes, in fact, some of us do just that.*

TWENTY-SEVEN

Really?

Her husband's hair was a crazed tousle, shirt dotted with mashed avocado, and the kitchen — the aftermath of a kid hurricane, a colorful muddle of Lily's plastic dishes, sippy cups, utensils, Greg's coffee cup and lunch plate. The floor, an obstacle course of toys.

"Wow," said Rain, putting down her bag. "Four hours?"

"I think I'll head upstairs and pack," said Gillian diplomatically.

Greg handed Lily over and collapsed on the couch with a great sigh.

It would have been funny if it wasn't also kind of annoying. Was the hardwiring just different? The whole caregiving thing just not in the male DNA?

Rain wiped the baby's face, then set about cleaning up the kitchen with Lily balanced on her hip. It took about a minute to clean up, wipe up, even with Lily grabbing for everything.

"It's not like it's *hard,*" he was saying, arm over his eyes. "Not in a bad way, it's just that it's so *totally consuming.*" He was incredulous.

"I didn't even take a shower," he went on, as Rain picked up the scattered toys, tossed them in the wicker bin. "I mean — I couldn't."

Four hours. Rain smiled, balancing Lily, closing the dishwasher, starting it.

"Dada!" said Lily, giggling, pointing at her father.

"I get it," she said, trying to keep the sarcasm out of her voice. "It's a pretty massive tour of duty. I'm sure you'll get better at it, the more you do it."

He peered at her from under his arm.

She stopped short of thanking him. He wasn't the babysitter; he was Lily's father. Time with your child wasn't a favor, or an added item on your task list. It was the life of a parent.

When she looked back over at Greg, he'd fallen asleep. How did he do that? Fall asleep the minute he sat down, in the middle of a conversation? Just — out. The hardwiring — definitely different. Anyone who thought otherwise did not have a husband or a child.

She left him snoring, carried Lily upstairs and gave her a bath. But her thoughts were still on Detective Harper, the look on his face, the things he'd said.

Some people are better off dead.

Cold words, hard and full of judgment.

But was he right?

Was the world a better place because people like Markham, Kreskey and Smith were no longer in it? She shampooed Lily's hair while the baby happily splashed her duck.

Images swirled, crime scene reports and photos, the man in the hawk mask, the memory of Detective Harper's face as he peered into the tree hollow. Agent Brower and her searing stare, her questions. Those piles of documents — newspaper clippings, transcripts, notes — from Greg and her father.

What was the heart of this story? Revenge? Justice? Was someone trying to get even? Or trying to save the world from evil men? Was there a connection? Who? What? When? Where? *Why?*

She lifted Lily, who wailed in protest at being removed from the warm water, and then dried her perfect chubby little body — that creamy skin, her perfect feet and starfish hands. The round of her cheek, the scent of her silky hair. Rain tenderly moisturized her skin, the baby giggling now, staring up at her with glittering eyes. Into the diaper, the onesie, legs kicking. *Mamama-mama.*

Could a child this loved, this cared for, turn out to be a monster?

Greg had mused last night, *What if you could go back even further, and save* him? Sometimes it seemed that life was just questions without answers.

Later, with logs crackling in the fireplace, and big glasses of wine between them, she and Gillian pored over their notes all over the coffee table, analyzing Detective Harper's interview, listening to parts of it, playing it for Greg.

"He's hiding something," said Greg.

"We thought so, too," said Gillian.

"But maybe it's just that he did a shit job, you know?" Rain offered. "Someone, as he saw it, did the world a favor. He didn't look very hard at who that might have been."

Greg shrugged. "Maybe he's right."

"That's messed up," said Gillian, ever the idealist, the humanist. "He was a person, killed in cold blood. No one has that right. I'm sorry, Rain. There's no excuse for what he did to you and Hank, and Tess. But who has the right to kill him? If we all go around killing the people who do wrong, then who are the good guys?"

"What's right, then?" said Greg. "That the taxpayer foots the bill for the rest of his life, a child killer?"

Rain stayed silent. They didn't get it, not really. It was all abstract to them. They'd never felt his hands on their flesh, or the hands of anyone who wished to do them harm. They'd never looked into Kreskey's eyes and saw what she'd seen — pain, rage, a kind of vicious fear, sadness. It was primal, filling her with terror. But it was human, recognizable. That's what people never wanted to imagine, how close we all are even to the most murderous and deranged. Did she think Eugene Kreskey deserved to die for what he did? Maybe. Maybe not.

Gillian took a long sip from her wineglass, stared into the fire. She had her bags packed, waiting by the door. Rain knew she'd call an Uber in a bit and head home; she'd seen her texting more than a couple of times while they were cooking, under the table. They'd been so wrapped up in the story that they hadn't talked about Chris Wright at all.

Glancing out the window, she saw a van

move slowly up the street. She thought about the car she'd seen last night. She had enough distance from all of it that it seemed like she'd overreacted. A common car, probably nothing.

Or maybe it *was* him. Watching, always watching.

It didn't unsettle her the way it should. The way it surely would Greg. If he knew, he'd call the police. *It's stalking,* he'd say, *which is just the beginning of something worse.*

His watching. The letters. It was his way of staying with her even though they couldn't be together, not in this life. Not in the life that Kreskey had created for them. It would be impossible to make anyone understand that.

She walked to the window while Gillian and Greg chatted.

The street was quiet, no strange cars parked. No stranger lurking in the shadows.

There were two Hanks. The one who had moved on, and the one who hadn't. Where was he tonight?

She rejoined her husband and friend, popped open her laptop and scrolled through the Instagram feed she'd found. Greta Miller had a lovely, peaceful feed of northern birds — the chickadee, the red-tailed hawk, the robin, the swallow, the American crow. The images were crisp and detailed — the shining texture of blue-black feathers, the glint of a beady eye, shiny as glass, the delicate grasp of a clawed foot on a birch branch, an owl, fluffy and ferruginous, peering out from the hollow of a tree.

Rain had called Greta Miller. The phone number she'd managed to unearth from the online directory just rang and rang and didn't allow her to leave a message. There was an auto-responder to the email account listed on Greta's website that stated quite clearly that Greta didn't answer mail, that images were for sale at a local gallery and that assignment queries should be directed to her agent at Lang and Lang, in New York City. She was semiretired.

Rain felt the agitation of the modern world. Didn't everyone want to be instantly available all the time? Couldn't the internet connect you to anyone in a millisecond? She left a message on Instagram; Greta Miller apparently couldn't be bothered with Facebook or Twitter.

An introvert. And thank goodness for them. Every journalist knew that they are the only ones paying attention. The only people who aren't hypnotized by their devices, not chattering away on the phone, not staring at some pointless app, or playing some time-sucking game. They're watching.

Rain googled, scrolling through images of Greta Miller herself. The only pictures of her were from the early 2000s. She was slender and petite as a young woman, fine-featured with doe eyes, russet hair, starkly arched eyebrows — it could have been the same woman she saw in the woods. But she couldn't be sure. She'd have to do it the old-fashioned way, show up for a visit.

"So," she said, looking for a distraction. She snapped the laptop closed. "What happened with Chris?"

Gillian peered at Rain over her phone with a cryptic smile. "Wouldn't you like to know?"

"I thought you two were done," said Greg, draining his second glass of red.

"We are," Gillian answered, sounding final. She twirled a honey strand of hair. Then, "Or we were. The truth is, I don't know what we're doing."

"Is that who keeps texting you?" Rain pressed.

Greg cleared his throat. "This sounds like girl talk. I'll go check on Lily. Then I'm going to veg out in front of the game."

He leaned in to kiss Rain on the head, then tossed a wave to Gillian.

"You're lucky," she said when he was upstairs. There was that phrase again. *Lucky Rain Winter.* "He's a good one."

"He could have been yours," Rain reminded her. Gil dated him first, then moved on to someone else — the tattoo guy, actually.

She waved Rain off with a laugh, and a sip of wine. "Oh, no, why would I choose the smart, kind, upstanding man when I could have the bad boy who talks me into a tattoo I'll regret for the rest of my life?"

"Chris is a good guy," Rain offered.

Gillian wrinkled her eyes at Rain. "Is he, though? Sometimes he seems like a good guy. Sometimes he seems like an asshole. Distant. Uncomfortable with real intimacy. Controlling, a little. Then absent."

Maybe we all have multiple selves. The trick was finding someone you could live with — all of them.

"You slept with him?" nudged Rain.

"He's hot," Gillian said with a roll of her eyes. She leaned back, stretched lean arms over her head. "So, *so* hot. That's the problem. When he puts those hands on me, I melt."

"I think maybe you love each other." She meant it. Which didn't necessarily mean that it would work. "I hope he steps up and

373

acts like the man you deserve."

Gillian raised her glass to Rain, and they clinked over the coffee table. "Here's to the men we deserve."

"Cheers," said Rain.

"Okay, so what's next?"

"I'll see Greta Miller."

"And I'll proofread the proposal and outline you put together and get it to Andrew for his meeting."

Teamwork.

"Thank you," Rain said.

"For what?"

"For being you," Rain said. "For being a great friend, a partner in crime. All of it."

Gillian hung her head a moment, was a little teary when she looked up again. "No, my friend. Thank *you.* I have to be honest — this last year without you. It has *sucked.* Big-time. I'm glad to have you back."

Rain helped her get her stuff together, and they waited on the porch for the Uber.

"Just be careful, okay?" said Gillian.

Rain looked out into the night. No mysterious car drifting up the street. No monster lurking in the shadows.

"Careful?"

"He's quicksand," she said. "You know that. You have a life, a good one. Don't let him pull you under."

Rain didn't need to ask her friend what or who she was talking about. *Of course I'm going to be careful,* she could say. Of course she wasn't going to let Hank or this story ruin her wonderful life. But she didn't bother pretending she didn't know what a dangerous path she was on.

"He won't. I promise." It felt like a vow she had no way of keeping.

"I promise," she said again.

TWENTY-EIGHT

Must be something in the air; my patients are all struggling. My otherwise quiet Saturday is filling up with emergency sessions.

Peter, despondent after his disastrous homecoming date, has locked up like a vault. We spent a silent hour in my office while he sketched the events of the evening. The sketches — charcoal on thick white stock — practically radiate his despair, his feelings of helplessness. In the final sketch, he sits alone, head sunk into his hands. I get it. He has no idea how to be in the world, how to navigate the treacherous terrain of relationships.

"I'm sorry your night wasn't what you expected," I tell him, again. "Try not to take it personally. In the history of school dances, I promise that you're one of a legion whose night has gone horribly wrong. It's nothing you did."

Nothing. Not even an eye roll. I'm not crazy about his flat affect. I've asked his distraught aunt to call me tonight if he doesn't snap out of it. It's been a week. Wallowing like this, sinking further into despair, instead of moving away from it, not a good sign.

Grace has started cutting again. Her mother found the telltale cotton balls dotted with blood in her wastepaper basket.

"It's my fault," her mother confesses over the phone. "I let her back on Instagram for an hour. She begged, and I relented. She said that she felt like a freak, isolated from everyone she knew because she wasn't online. That she was better, stronger. So I gave in."

"It's not your fault," I tell her. "You do your best, we all do. The choice is hers. We can only try to help her make better choices. Give her the tools to deal with her anxiety."

"We're the first generation of parents to deal with this," she says. "I wish I could take all her devices and set them on fire."

"Kids have always struggled to find their place in the world," I tell her. "But, yes, social media, the internet in general, is making it harder because their friends can present these fake perfect feeds of their lives, because there is so much information, not all of it true. And it's so hard for kids to understand that what they're seeing is not the real thing."

"It's hard for all of us," she says, sounding wistful and lost.

You remember what it was like, don't you, Lara? To be so unsure of who you were, and where you fit into the bizarre social structure that is teen culture. I think it's worse now. I wouldn't want to be a teenager in the age of social media. Try being a real person when everyone around you is an avatar — a multidimensional girl in a world of air-brushed paper dolls.

"Bring her in," I tell her. "I can meet you at the office at two if that works."

"Thank you, Doctor."

I'll be late to Angel's party, but that will have to be okay.

When I hang up with Grace's mom, I dial another number. I am still saying *dial,* are you? I don't know if they say that anymore. It must mean I'm getting old.

"Andrea Barnes."

"Hi, it's Hank Reams."

"Oh, Hank," she says. It doesn't sound like she's a hundred percent happy to hear from me. I don't blame her. "How are you?"

"I'm okay. No complaints," I say. Which is a lie. I have plenty of complaints, as you well know. "How about you?"

"Good," she says, falsely bright. "Great. What can I do for you?"

Andrea and I dated briefly. It ended badly, like all my relationships seem to. I wouldn't have called her, except that she's my last resort for finding out about Angel's former foster parents. I tell Andrea about Angel's claims, give her the relevant names and details. She's quiet when I'm done, and I hear her tapping on the keyboard.

"It looks like these allegations were investigated," she says after a pause. "No wrongdoing on the part of the foster parents was discovered."

"Yes," I say. "I know."

"But?"

"I can't shake it," I say. "She's a deeply traumatized kid. Has a history of lying. There's just something about her story I can't let go. She says there was a boy there, someone they had locked in a cellar."

"According to what I see here — and the system is slow to update — there hasn't been anyone placed with them since Angel. They've had fifteen children cycle through their home over the last three years, no allegation of abuse. Looks like they have refused placements since Angel."

Andrea is a child advocacy lawyer. It's

gritty work with few untethered successes and some bone-crushing, nightmare-inducing loses. She's a passionate, determined, dogged champion of kids who have fallen through the cracks of a system that doesn't always work to protect them. She's the person you call when everyone else has given up.

"I'll look into it a little more closely," she says. "Is that what you're asking?"

"Yes," I say. "Not a favor. I'll pay your rate, of course."

"That's not necessary," she says. "But you're aware that the incidence of false abuse allegations in the foster care system is high. There's a one-in-four chance that foster parents will face one type of accusation or another."

"I'm aware," I say. "I just want to do my due diligence for this kid. And for any other kid who might wind up there."

She's gone quiet again; I hear her tapping on the keyboard. "Okay," she says. "Give me a couple of days. I'll call you."

She hangs up, and I'm left holding the phone. I'll cop to a familiar sense of mystification I have when it comes to relationships. Doctor-patient, fine. I get it; there are clear rules and standards of behavior. But friendships, romantic relationships, even family —

I'm a bull in a china shop.

I don't know exactly why Andrea distanced herself from me. It was never a clear break. To be honest, it wasn't a clear beginning. We just had a little too much to drink one night after an especially brutal court loss — a kid going back to an abusive father — and she wound up back at my place. There were a couple of dinners, a few more pleasant — I thought — sexual encounters. Then she basically ghosted me — isn't that what "they" call it now? Stopped answering calls and texts. I didn't pursue because — why? Maybe it's respect for boundaries, but maybe a big part of me didn't want to know why someone so smart, sensitive, attractive felt like she wanted to put space between us.

It's not just what happened with Kreskey.

I was awkward before — only you and Tess ever made sense. I was okay with my mom; still am. She's in Florida now, a yoga instructor with a new boyfriend who is good to her. She and my father divorced after Kreskey and our move away. She asks about you sometimes, Lara.

I don't talk to my dad as much. I always had the vague sense that my jock, engineer father was a little embarrassed by his skinny, uncoordinated, brainiac kid. *Straight As, test scores off the charts, and you can't hit a ball with a bat?* As if one thing had anything to do with the other. Even now, my degrees, books, television appearances seem to unsettle him a bit, like I am an equation that he just can't solve. In our awkward monthly phone calls, he'll bring up some team or another that's going to some playoff or another. I'll remind him gently that I don't follow sports. And it's as if that's a fresh disappointment to him every time. Chemistry. Sometimes it's just not there, even between parent and child.

If I could go back and heal my inner child, which frankly is the least of my problems, I'd tell him what I tell my troubled patients: just be yourself. It's perfectly okay to be the flawed, quirky, awkward, unique individual you are. No matter what you think, or how things appear on the surface, everyone around is grappling with similar issues. Maybe that football star secretly worries that he's stupid; maybe that superhot girl thinks that's all there is to her; maybe that kid who is even smarter than you are wishes he was superhot and athletic. Whatever you are, it's enough.

But I can't heal that lost boy. And I clearly can't heal myself, as Tess urged. I don't know why Andrea ghosted me. I'm sure it was my fault. Lara, I know you'll agree. I'm damaged goods and she's a smart woman. She probably just figured it out like you did.

After my session with Grace I force myself to go to Angel's party. The push from my car, up the walkway, to knock on the door, is gargantuan. I almost turn back twice. But I want to support Angel, Jen and William. So few of my stories have a happy ending. I want this to be one of them.

"Dr. Reams!" says Jen at the door, pretty in a pink dress, smiling. "I didn't think you would come! You're shy, aren't you?"

I smile. "Sometimes," I admit.

She ushers me inside, where a group of smiling, happy people mingle in a stylish living room. Angel is sitting with an older woman, who looks to be showing her photos in an album. There are balloons and flowers, a cake with roses, some gifts. Angel, usually wrapped up tight, knees hugged to her chest on my couch, seems relaxed, sitting close to the lady on the couch, engaged. She smiles and waves to me.

"That's William's mom," says Jen. "She's so good with Angel."

I spend the next hour being shepherded around by Jen, who introduces me as "the man who saved Angel." Which is hyperbole, of course, but nice of her to say. I chat and eat, just like a normal person. These are nice people, kind and wide open, not a whiff of dysfunction. Sure, nothing's perfect and all families have their issues. But these people are healthy — warm and giving.

"Dr. Reams," says Jen, coming up on my conversation with William. He's talking about golf and I'm nodding politely. "I wanted you to meet someone."

Oh, now I get it. The young woman Jen presents — she's lovely. Dare I say, she looks a bit like you. That raven-haired, blue-eyed combo never fails to make me weak in the knees. "This is my friend Beth."

Beth smiles, and offers her hand. She looks as uncomfortable as I am at a party, but her handshake is warm and firm. She wears a silver infinity symbol on a chain around her neck. "I've heard a lot about you."

"Beth is a clinical psychiatrist specializing in criminal behavior."

Jen may be more intuitive than she realizes.

"That's gritty work," I say.

Beth gives an assenting nod. "It can be."

Almost immediately we're looped into each other, the conversation flowing, the rest of the room disappearing. Her work,

384

how she studies yoga and practices meditation to counteract the stress, how I run and work out to manage mine. We talk about my books — she's a fan, which is always nice. The male ego thing and all of that. But it also means she knows my history. It's awkward, isn't it? When they know, and you know they know but it hasn't been acknowledged.

For a little while, with her, I forget about everything going on in my life.

But then it starts to creep up.

As the sun dips and the afternoon turns to dusk, he starts to get restless. I can feel him pacing in his cage; I try to measure my breath, distance myself from him. Still he grows agitated. We have work to do tonight.

She's talking and I'm watching her. I'm almost tempted to skip it. I could make the choice to wait on Andrea's call and go from there. Follow the right channels, the legal ones. Tess's admonitions, my own admissions about my behavior, have been ringing in my ears.

And then there's Agent Brower, her knowing gaze.

I almost ask Beth if she wants to get a drink somewhere, keep talking. It was a clear setup by Jen and it worked. But I can feel him, his tension growing, and I start to distance myself from the conversation. Like most people in our line of work, Beth is an empath, senses my shift and mimics it.

She hands me her card. "I'd love to keep talking sometime."

"Me, too," I say, handing her mine. Will I call her? I doubt it, not that I don't want to. "It's been so great to meet you."

She smiles and blushes, turns to someone else who touches her arm.

I thank Angel's mom. "Don't be mad," she whispers. "I just thought you two would be perfect together."

Mind your own business, I can almost hear him bark.

"She's really special," I say. "Thank you."

And then I'm gone, out the door.

Later, when I'm aware of myself again, it's after midnight and I'm parked in front of your house. I'm startled to see you in the window, then a few minutes later at the front door. I pull away slowly, heart thudding — at the sight of you, at the wondering of how I got here, and at what else he might have done tonight. Of what he might do in the future if I can't get him under control.

TWENTY-NINE

Guilt. Was it meant to be the primary feeling of motherhood, the underpinning of the entire experience? She was pretty sure it wasn't, that it was just some unique failing on her part. Mitzi was an angel, every mother's dream babysitter, stout and smiling, obviously gaga over Lily. Lily practically leaped from Rain into her arms. And still Rain was having an out-of-body experience as she went over the schedule she'd meticulously crafted while Mitzi looked on, nodding, with a plump, heavily ringed hand on Rain's shoulder.

"She'll probably eat the avocado and the sweet potato. If not, the pumped breast milk" (yes, she did it again, hooked up to that damn machine and milked herself like a cow) "is right here. Just run under warm water to take the chill off. You don't need to heat it."

"Yes," said Mitzi without a trace of impatience. "Absolutely."

Up in the nursery, she reminded the older woman, who had three children of her own, six grandchildren (two of whom she'd helped raise while her lawyer daughter ran her small downtown firm), and was a retired preschool teacher, that Lily shouldn't have anything in her crib except the sleep sack and her crinkly book (which Rain had allowed after Lily turned one). Even though the threat of SIDS had long since passed — especially now that Lily could roll, sit up and even pull herself to standing — Rain still strictly adhered to the "back to sleep" rules.

"I think that's everything," said Rain with a sigh.

Lily reached for Rain, and she took the baby from Mitzi, balancing her on her hip. "Ma MA." She nuzzled Lily and considered canceling her afternoon appointments.

"I know," said Mitzi, one hand on Lily, one hand on Rain. "It's hard. But remember — while it's critical to be here as much as you can, it's also important for our girls to watch us pursue our dreams, to have work that matters to us."

Another one of those brass rings. Be here all the time. But pursue your career goals, too. Be the best mom but follow your dreams. And also — be hot and sexy, always be *totally* into getting it on with your husband. Don't forget to work out, be thin, keep a perfectly organized home and clear that clutter!

"Anyway, dear, didn't you say you'd only be gone for three hours?"

"Something like that."

Mitzi looked lovingly at Lily. "I think we'll manage."

Sure, separation anxiety didn't begin in earnest for another few months, but it would have been nice if Lily had at least *noticed* as Rain walked out the door. Instead, Mitzi had her so entranced with her Duplo blocks on the floor, that after Rain gave her a kiss goodbye, the baby didn't even look up when Rain slipped out.

In the car, she checked the camera. She half wanted to find Mitzi already lying on the couch, having lit a cigarette and cracked open a beer. Then she could go racing back to save her child, and forget all about her appointment with Greta Miller, bird photographer.

But no, they were still happily playing.

"Mama?" she heard Lily say, her heart lurching.

"Mama will be back soon," said Mitzi, striking that perfect pitch of sweet and easy.

Then, a masterful deflection, "Oh! Look at this red one!"

"Oh!" said Lily, as if it were the most wonderful thing in the world. And, hey, maybe it was. Red Lego Duplo blocks were pretty damn spectacular. It should be her on the floor with Lily. What was she doing? She wasn't even getting paid yet, no guarantees that the project would even fly with NNR. She was paying someone to watch her baby so that she could do work on spec. Mom of the year.

"Okay," she said aloud to herself. She shut off the camera app. "Pull it together!"

She forced herself to pull out of the driveway and drive up the street. At the stop sign, her phone rang. Greg.

"How many times have you checked the cam?" he said by way of greeting.

"Just once," she said.

"Yeah," he said, "but you haven't even left the street yet."

"Are you tracking me?"

"Of course."

"So, I'm watching Lily, and you're watching me. Who's watching you?"

"No one," he said. "No one cares about the dad. He's just the caveman with the club. All he has to do is drag home the carcass."

"Oh, please," she said.

"Go get 'em, tiger," he said, and ended the call.

Greta Miller's place had a mile-long drive. The twisting dirt road wound through a thick stand of woods, past a wide-open pasture lined with a wooden rail fence where two horses grazed, then back into the woods.

Giant oaks shaded the road, and a deer bolted in front of her car, stopped to look at her, then ran on. She'd been going slowly; she slowed down further. That would be all she needed, to hit a deer. To damage the car on this probably pointless errand. Body work. Insurance rates jacked up.

The phone rang again, causing Rain's heart to jump. Mitzi? An emergency already? No. Gillian's number on the dashboard caller ID.

Could you not drive a mile without someone calling you?

"It's a go," Gillian said, voice vibrating with excitement. "Andrew wants you to come in so that he can make you an offer and discuss terms. I think he's sending you an email."

A flood of excitement washed away her feelings of worry and guilt. Then worry and guilt swept back, a tidal surge. Now it was real.

"Rain?"

"That's — *amazing*." She was going for thrilled. Excited. It came out sounding wobbly. But she was excited. And terrified. What was wrong with her? Motherhood had obviously turned her into a soft, angsty stress case.

"You sound — I don't know. Off."

"No," she said. "All good."

"Where are you?"

"Lily's with Mitzi and I'm approaching Greta Miller's house."

"Whoa, is this your first time leaving her with a sitter?" Then, "Are you okay?"

"Yeah." She tried for easy, nonchalant. "I'm fine."

She wasn't fine. She wanted to race home and take care of her baby, leave the other parts of herself — Lara Winter, the journalist, the dog with a bone — by the side of the road.

"Yeah, right. Okay, fill me in later," said Gillian. "Let's talk tonight after Lily goes to sleep and come up with a plan."

As the news sank in, she felt lighter, almost giddy, as she brought the car to a stop in front of a beautiful old house, with gray siding and red shutters. It was restored to perfection, with tidy landscaping and a wraparound porch, red Adirondack chairs lined up, awaiting quiet conversation and glasses of lemonade. She checked the app to see Mitzi feeding a happy Lily sweet potatoes.

She could do this. She could really do this.

Greta Miller was a dried branch of a woman, brittle and gray, and not at all what Rain expected of someone who took such beautiful photographs. In spite of the agent's warning that Greta Miller "was not exactly warm and fuzzy," Rain had still imagined someone expansive, lighthearted. Someone joyful. The images the photographer captured were moments of breathless natural beauty — one could almost hear the birdsong.

But Greta greeted Rain with a scowl at her front door, reluctantly swinging it open so that she could step into the rustic, high-ceilinged foyer. The scent of sandalwood mingled with the aroma coming from a vase of stargazer lilies on a center table.

"Thank you for seeing me," Rain said, as she followed the old woman into a grand living room — beamed ceiling, enormous fireplace flanked by an overstuffed chintz sofa, a collection of Staffordshire dogs on the mantel. All around the room, in tiny glass vessels, were birds — a fat robin, a glossy cardinal, a perky bluebird, a blue-sheened crow. Taxidermy birds, perched on branches — singing silently, or just about to never take flight, wings hopelessly spread.

"You were persistent."

Rain *had* been persistent — a slew of email, several calls, finally a call, then another email to her agent. "And my agent thought it might be worth my while to talk to you. Apparently, she's a fan of your work."

She issued the last line with a wrinkle of her nose.

"And you're not, I gather," said Rain easily.

If you were going to work in news it was necessary to have a thick skin — every story she'd ever done was met with an equal amount of praise and anger. Gillian's email overflowed daily with love letters and hate mail, threats and compliments. *It's not about you,* her father counseled when this truth was first revealed to Rain. *It's never about you.*

"I'm not a fan of the media in general," said Greta, taking a seat. She tucked herself into the corner, folding her arms around her middle. "Nothing personal."

On the mantel there was an owl, staring with stern yellow eyes. Greta had a similar gaze and held it on Rain.

"Okay if I record?" she asked.

Greta gave an uncertain nod and Rain didn't ask twice. Chances are she'd forget as soon as the conversation got rolling — which she hoped it would. Sometimes you worked for every sentence you squeaked out of someone; sometimes you couldn't get people to shut up.

"Well, I *love* your work," said Rain, glad that she could be genuine. "You really capture something special. Each of your birds seems to have its own — energy, a personality that shines through. The light, the detail. Amazing."

The woman seemed to relax a bit; a sincere compliment could work wonders.

"They do," Greta said. "They're all special, those that let me capture them." She gazed at the blackbird that sat on the coffee table between them. He had his head cocked to one side, a berry held in his beak. He almost looked like he might hop off his perch and fly away. "I rescue these, in case you were wondering."

Greta pointed at the stuffed bird in his glass cage. "I find them at flea markets and antiques shops, sometimes garage sales. I give them a home here."

"It doesn't bother you, to have them like this?" Rain asked. Frankly, she found it unsettling. She never got the whole taxidermy thing. "Your photos have so much life."

Greta smiled. "That's the comment of a young person. Everything dies."

The sun moved behind the clouds and the room grew dim, suddenly cold.

"The bird's life is a hard one," said Greta. "You've heard the phrase 'free as a bird.' But their life is a constant foraging for food, grueling migrations, evasion of predators, protecting their young. They're so delicate, so fragile — victims of human carelessness, cruelty, destruction of the environment. Flight is their gift, as is their purity, their innocence — like all animals. But it comes with a price. Here, they're free from struggle."

Greta leaned forward, tapped on the crow's glass. "They're safe."

Rain really wished Gillian was here; they'd be hooting later about the creepy bird lady. But alone, in the old woman's thrall, Rain felt chilled.

"Your home is beautiful," she said, eager to change the subject. "How long have you been here?"

"I grew up here. It was my parents' house. I've renovated, added on over the years. I have a darkroom a ways back on the property — I still develop much of my own film the old-fashioned way even though the world has gone digital. But I've lived here all my life."

"So you knew the Kreskey family."

Greta shifted and looked out the window in the direction of the adjacent property. "As much as you can know people like that," she said. "We kept our distance."

"People like that?"

"My grandfather sold off some of this land when times were hard. And the Kreskey family — this would be Eugene's grandparents — bought it for a song. This was before my time. My mother was an empath — do you believe in that type of thing? She felt energies, even as a young girl. She just knew things. She'd always sensed a malevolent energy, and we were always warned to stay away."

Rain waited. Silence always encouraged more talk.

Greta went on. "Violence is a genetic condition. If someone doesn't break the chain, it gets worse with every generation. The grandfather was an abuser — his son grew into an abuser. Eugene turned into a ghoul."

"Did you listen to your mother? Did you stay away?"

"I did," she said, nodding. "Even now, I stay away."

"I saw you," said Rain. It *had* been Greta, the woman she'd seen in the woods. She knew it right away.

"Our property connects to trails that lead behind the Kreskey house," she said with a shrug. "Let's just say I stay to my part and I don't linger."

That might explain why she was moving so fast, why she didn't stop when Rain had called to her.

"I called to you that day."

The older woman tapped her ear. "I'm a little deaf, I'm afraid. Which is convenient as I'm not one for chitchat."

Somewhere in the house a clock ticked, then prettily struck the ten o'clock hour. Rain's mind drifted to Lily . . . time for snack, and maybe a jog to the park.

"So, when Kreskey attacked us, and brought my friends Tess Barker and Hank Reams here that day, where were you?"

"I was overseas, working on my MFA at Oxford," she said. "I didn't hear about it until much later. My mother kept it from me."

"And when he was killed?"

"I was living here," she said, bowing her head a moment. "The police questioned me. But our properties are separated by acres. It's a good twenty-minute walk on trails from that place to here."

Greta's body had taken on a kind of careful tension. She'd averted her direct gaze to something off in the distance. Her shoulders had hiked. Rain felt her pulse quicken; the old woman had something to say.

"It's okay," Rain said easily. "Everyone's gone."

"Not everyone."

"What do you mean?"

"The people who killed Kreskey were never caught."

"People?"

"My mother thinks I should tell you."

"Oh," said Rain, looking around. "Is she here?"

That would make a great layer to the story, the older woman telling her perspective of the day, just a few miles from where it was all happening. But Greta shook her head.

"She died about ten years ago now," she said. "But I still hear her."

Rain nodded, pretended to adjust the recorder. "I see. You said she was an empath."

Oh, perfect. A crazy bird lady who spoke to the dead.

"She loved birds, took so much pleasure in my work. When I was a girl we used to hike through the woods. She knew every bird, every call. She knew where the owls nested, where the hawks perched. Love of nature was her gift to me. We used to go out at night quite often."

Rain took and released a breath, waited. Then, "Were you out the night that Kreskey was killed?"

"I was," she said. "I was looking for the nightjar. A rare sighting. But some birder friends claimed to have seen one."

The name sent a jolt through Rain. Was it a coincidence, or had Agent Brower already been here? She made a note to ask, not wanting to interrupt.

"What did you see, Greta?"

"I'd already seen Eugene," she said. "A few nights earlier, I saw him on the property. Just standing there, staring at the house. Naturally, I didn't confront him. I just got away as fast as I could."

"And on that night?"

"There were two people there. The moonlight was diffused by thick cloud cover, and they both wore masks. They entered the house. A while later, he showed up, went inside."

Rain felt a dump of excitement mingled with dread.

"What kind of masks?" The words came out wobbly.

"Bird masks of some kind — with beaks and feathers. I think that's why I stayed to watch at first. I just couldn't figure out what was happening."

"Greta," said Rain carefully. "Did you take pictures?"

She nodded. "They didn't turn out. I was set for a full moon. But, like I said, it was obscured."

"Can I see?"

Greta considered a moment, then got up and left the room. Rain looked around at the birds in their glass cages. All their dead eyes were on her. She fought the urge to gather her things and leave.

When Greta returned with the pictures, they were grainy and indistinct. A large figure, a smaller one, both in black, wearing masks and hoods, one carrying a pack. They walked toward the house.

"Since the first murder, that house has been overrun with vandals, kids looking to party, homeless, drunks and people on drugs. So after I snapped those pictures, I waited in the brush awhile, to see who else would show up. I thought I'd get some more pictures and call the police. Not sure why I bothered, they never did a thing about the way that property had gone to seed. But when I saw Eugene, I left as fast as possible."

"Did the police come when you called that night?"

Mentally, she thought back to the reports she'd read, those that Henry had sent, the documents in Greg's research. She didn't remember a logged 911 call.

"I don't know," she said. "I called, said there were trespassers on the adjacent property at the abandoned structure."

"You didn't say it was Kreskey?"

"No."

"Why not?"

She shook her head and gazed at her fingernails. "You know, I always felt sorry for him. I used to see him sometimes when he was a boy. I'd see him in the woods. He seemed like a gentle spirit, a lost soul. Once, he brought a cardinal with an injured wing to my mother. He stammered, could barely get his words out. Then he ran off, as if he was afraid of us. I know he was a monster

— he did horrible things. But once upon a time, he was an innocent. An innocent who someone damaged and twisted until he grew sharp and dangerous."

She didn't share Greta's sentiment. How could she? To Rain, he'd always be her worst nightmare come true. Rain thought of Gillian: *He was a person, killed in cold blood. No one has that right.*

"He killed a child," said Rain. "My friend."

"And quite likely his parents," Greta agreed. "He was a bad man, who was aptly punished. But I still remember that skinny boy in the woods, too. Somehow they seem like two different people to me."

Rain saw the softness in her then, the thing that allowed Greta to capture images of such breathless beauty, light and love. Compassion.

"You told all of this to the police?"

"To Detective Harper, yes, back then," she said. "I gave him the photos I took."

Detective Harper. He'd blown Greta off as a nut. Said he hadn't learned anything from her. That she was crazy. He hadn't mentioned the photographs; true they were essentially useless except to document that someone — two people — had been there the night that Kreskey died. Like the other

403

images captured on other nights, they were indistinct. Notes from his interview were missing. The 911 call wasn't logged.

"Do you have any idea who those people are?" asked Rain.

Greta turned that gaze back on Rain. "No," she said. "I have no idea."

Rain watched Greta a moment; the older woman was tiny but looked as strong as a coil of wire.

"I put in a bid at a county auction last month for the Kreskey property," said Greta. "I won. There were some crazies there, looking to have that house for god knows what. That property belongs to my family again — even though my brother and I are all that's left."

"What are you going to do with it?"

"Raze the house for one thing," she said. "I have a shaman friend — I'll ask him to bless and cleanse the site. Then I'll plant some trees, let nature do its thing."

Rain felt a sudden lightness. Yes, that was right. That house shouldn't still be there.

"So, if you need anything from that place, you have about a month. Then it's coming down. Sometimes you have to kill the past, let the earth take the ashes away. People create damage. But nature is perfect in its design — life, death, decay, rebirth. It heals."

"Did you ever find it? The nightjar?"

She shook her head. "No, I never did. Not that night."

"Do you have any theories on who killed Kreskey?"

"I tend not to trouble myself with the actions of humans," she said grimly. "Look at the world we live in. Look what we've done to the planet, to each other. I stay here on this property mostly and try to take care of it. I'll try to give that ugly piece of it, that bit that the Kreskey family defiled, back to the planet. Trees will grow, animals will burrow and birds will nest. When I die, all this land will be donated to the Audubon Society, and hopefully there will be peace here. Finally."

Digging into this story suddenly felt salacious and wrong. But separating yourself out from the world — that was easy. Trying to understand it, to survive it, to make it better through that understanding — that was the hard thing. *Writers explore the world on the page,* her father always said. *And readers come not to escape but to understand. We don't turn away from ugly things, we dig in. Evil thrives in the dark. If you shine the light, sometimes it just shrivels and dies.*

Greta let Rain snap photos of those pictures with her phone, and they finished talking about Greta's work, her plans for the property. The conversation grew softer, easier, and Greta seemed lighter, less stern and grim.

"I'm sorry for what happened to you and your friends," Greta said. "My mother suffered terribly, so angry at her father for selling that land, at the Kreskeys for what they were. She was such a peaceful person, so loving. She couldn't stand the thought of anyone or anything being hurt."

"It was a long time ago," said Rain. "But for me it's yesterday. I guess that's why I'm doing this story. I'm still trying to make sense of it all, the cycle of violence — Kreskey's parents, what they did, how it formed him, what he did. Then someone killed him."

Greta nodded, stared over at the northern cardinal on her mantel. So red and still.

"My mother is gone, Eugene Kreskey and his parents are gone, your friend, too. One day, I'll be gone, as will you. But this land, it will still be here. Spring to summer to fall to winter — growing, changing, thriving if it's left alone. I take comfort in that, somehow."

Rain thought of the tree in which she had hidden, that smell of bark, of vegetation, of decay, of life, how it sheltered her, hid her.

Instead of feeling shame, for the first time she felt gratitude that whatever came, she was still here now.

"If you let it, the earth will cover everything that happened there," said Greta. "Nature is full of murder, you know. The soil accepts everything, recycles it. Death brings life."

"Greta," said Rain. "Do you know what happened there the night that Kreskey was killed?"

She turned owl eyes on Rain.

"I know as much as you do, Miss Winter."

THIRTY

There's a trail behind my house and it connects to a state trail adjacent to my property.
I spend hours back there, forest bathing, as
the Japanese call it — shinrin-yoku, welcom-
ing the peace of solitude, the long quiet of
early mornings, or late afternoons.

It's odd that I would find comfort in the
woods, don't you think? It wouldn't be
surprising if the imperviousness of trees,
the sound of wind, the sight of dappled
sunlight on the ground triggered the memory of trauma. But I am at peace as I walk.

These are not my trails. I trudge through
the night, using the scant moonlight to see.
I'll try not to use the flashlight unless I have
to.

I lost myself after Kreskey. The boy who
returned in the back of Detective Harper's
car was not the same boy who got on his
bike that day — that very same day.

The way people looked at me — did they

look at you the same way? Revulsion wrapped inside pity. As if it might have been something I was, or something I did that marked me as a victim. As if I had something that they or someone they loved might catch. The words were always kind, but the eyes don't lie.

My dad. He couldn't even look at me anymore. My mother wouldn't let me out of her sight. Within months, they'd sold our house and moved us to Florida near my grandparents, to a condo on the beach. Another museum-like space with white walls and high ceilings, the jewel-green Gulf of Mexico dominating our views. Florida — land of palm trees and blazing sun, strip malls, and sugar sand, stunningly beautiful and somehow ugly, dilapidated and strange. A place that never seems to quite get it right, even though it makes no end of promises.

The ocean is going to heal us, Hank, my mother would say as we floated in the salt water. *We're going to swim every day and wash away the past.*

Always a seeker, she dove deep into her "spiritual practice," reading to me from the books of Deepak Chopra and Eckhart Tolle, Wayne Dyer. She'd quit her job in marketing, decided she was going to devote herself full-time to motherhood. My father's company had an office in Tampa. We started over in Florida's stultifying heat (my god we would just drip sweat, wilt under that brutal sun). We started over. Except that I was a ghost.

Sometimes I wondered as I floated with my beautiful mother — whose skin turned a deep golden, whose hair faded blonder, who grew thinner and toned from daily yoga — if I had died up there at Kreskey's place.

If all of this was just a dream.

I wouldn't have had the language for it then, but I think of those years in Florida as a kind of bardo — a time between two existences. The boy I was, happy and free, a hopeless geek who loved his friends and comic books, who was in love with a girl who didn't love him. (That hasn't changed, Lara, as you know.) And the man I would become, the fractured, solitary misfit who nonetheless helps (or tries to help) other injured children through their vilest days.

It was probably my grandfather who saved me, who managed to patch back together the pieces of me that survived.

We weren't close before; he'd always seemed odd, distant when he came to visit. We rarely went to Florida to see them. The old man knew about trauma; he was a veteran of the Vietnam War. He and my grandmother had a big old house — boxy rooms that smelled of mold, wood paneling, giant televisions in wood cabinets, my grandmother's watercolors of sunsets and sailboats, palm trees swaying in the moonlight — tucked into a strip of land between the Gulf and the Intracoastal Waterway. The house nearly disappeared into the shadows of the giant McMansions that flanked it on either side. Though the house was barely standing, the land was worth millions. They'd never even thought of selling like so many old-timers did during the boom.

Behind their house was a rickety old dock that wound through the mangroves and let out at the Intracoastal, offering views of Caladesi State Park and a smattering of islands. We'd lower the Boston Whaler from its creaking davits, and head out just as the sun was peeking over the horizon. We'd fish, pulling snook, sheepshead, hogfish, the occasional baby shark or grouper. The rays flopped around, jumping out of the water — dolphins would sometimes crowd around the boat. Egrets stood in the shoals, fishing just like us. In the summer, piles of cumulus clouds towered above us like distant mountains. I'd heard that bald eagles nested on Caladesi. There was a big nest, but I never saw the birds.

"It's this, too, you know."

"What?"

The old man didn't talk much, that's why I liked him, could not wait for our weekend mornings on the boat. Didn't it seem like, after Kreskey, no one could shut the fuck up? My mother, the legion of therapists, teachers, counselors — all well-meaning and kind — but their words meant very little to me then. (Words, the language of healing and understanding, would mean everything later. But not to that broken kid who had no idea how to piece himself back together, how to understand the world again.)

"There's chaos and pain, son. War. There's evil in this world. We've both seen it, what people can do to each other. What happens to the body, or can," he said that morning. "But there's this, too. Always."

I looked around at the peaceful water, the electric-blue sky, and knew he was right. It was everything, all of it, good and bad. It made a kind of sense; I figured I could live with it.

Now, hiking on this strange property, I am breathless. And this search has yielded nothing; I am back at the house where Angel was fostered, having failed to find the other structure she claimed was there. I am beginning to wonder if she might be wrong, or lying, or exaggerating. All this time, I've seen no one in the house. But tonight, there's a light on inside. I find a perch inside the tree line and watch. I think about those days when we were together again.

You agreed to meet me at Café Orlin in the East Village. You wouldn't come to my place, and who could blame you? You'd seen something in me that I had been able to hide from most others. And it scared you, as it should.

Always, even as kids, I felt like you were behind glass. A butterfly pinned to velvet, beautiful and untouchable. For the briefest moment, I had been able to touch you — heart to heart, skin to skin. (In fact, I can still feel you. Can you still feel me?) But when you showed up at the café that night, you were out of reach again.

Even at the small table, you kept your distance. Your movements were small and protective, your face still and unsmiling. It had been a few weeks; I thought you might have forgiven me. I'd hoped that the distance had softened our encounter in your mind, that your affection for me had washed over it, as sometimes happens. I'm sorry to admit that, even now, I don't remember that night in my apartment, exactly. Blurry flashes, moments, words. I know I made you cry.

You ordered a double espresso — with steamed almond milk on the side. Your go-to order. When the waitress left us, you said quietly, "I don't want to see you again after this, Hank."

You and Tess had that in common, you were always direct and to the point.

I could feel him raging inside, clanging around.

I was surprised when I noticed that your hands were shaking. That's when I saw Greg lingering outside. You have good taste; he was a handsome guy. He leaned against a lamppost reading the *Post* (a lowbrow choice for him, no?) like a character in a noir film. I realized with shock and shame that you were physically afraid of me. That he was there to step in if things got out of hand.

"The messages you left, the things you've said. They've hurt me deeply. And you're wrong. I'm not to blame for what happened to us, to Tess."

The quaver in your voice cut me. I could see how much he'd hurt and frightened you. How much *I* had. Because I can't divorce myself from him. I want to, but I can't. I

414

understand too much about the mind to give the healthy self a free pass. He and I, we're not integrated. But we're not totally apart either. Still I had to wonder: What messages? What did I say to you? Honestly, I was too ashamed to ask.

But you must have read it in my face. You were always good at that, tuning in, reading expressions. You always seemed to know what I was thinking.

"You don't remember, do you? You don't even know what I'm talking about."

Again, I just opted for silence.

You leaned in close. When you spoke, your voice was just a whisper.

"What's wrong with you, Hank?"

And I told you. I'd never told anyone, not even my parents. Only my psychiatrist at the time was beginning to suspect. I was taking medication back then, Ativan for anxiety, Zoloft for depression. I had determined that it was high emotion, anger, stress that caused me to switch over. Like that night; it was the call from Detective Harper that had unstitched me.

"You need help, Hank," you said. "Serious help."

This annoyed me; I thought you'd have more sympathy.

"Is that your boyfriend out there?" I nod-

415

ded to the window.

You nodded. "Yes."

"Does he know about us?"

You took a sip of your coffee. "He does, yes. I told him — everything. I don't know if he'll forgive me."

"He's here, isn't he?" I didn't like the sharp edge to my tone. You backed away from me, actually shifted your chair. It's healthy, you know. The healthy person protects herself from dangerous men.

"We're friends before anything else. He cares about me."

"We're friends, too. Aren't we?"

"We were, Hank," you said sadly. I saw you almost reach for my hand, then hold back. How I ached to touch you. "We were best friends. But a horrible thing happened to us, and I'm afraid that's one of the many things Kreskey has taken from us."

He was practically roaring inside. I focused on my breathing, took a sip of my chamomile tea. I try to avoid caffeine or any kind of stimulant. It's all downers for me.

I took the crystal heart from my pocket and put it on the table between us. It glittered and shone in the light, just like it had in the store when I first bought it. I remembered thinking, this is it. I'll give this to her.

416

And she'll know how much I love her.

"Do you remember this?"

"Hank."

"I gave it to you for your tenth birthday."

You picked it up and looked at it, held it up to the light so that it cast flecks of blood-red on the white tablecloth. Then you put it back on the surface.

"That was a long time ago."

"Not for me."

You wiped at your eyes, your lashes glistening with tears.

"Have you thought about just trying to move forward? I know. I know, Hank. I didn't experience the horror that you did. But when you try to stop looking back, to build a solid bridge of love, accomplishments, form new, happier memories, I believe it's possible to live a life, a good one. Even after extreme trauma."

Unless it damages your brain. Which I honestly believe is what happened to me. Not just trauma but head injury, as well. (Did you know, Lara, that there's a strong link between traumatic brain injury and psychosis? You can read my article about it in the *New England Journal of Medicine*.) Of course, they won't know that for sure until after I'm dead. Then they can dissect my brain and see what's really wrong with it.

"He's out," I said.

You looked at me and shook your head, stayed silent. But I saw it on your face, the fear, the anger. You had told me all about the letters Kreskey sent you, the ones your family received from Kreskey's fan club. You had confided in our close moments how you felt like Kreskey still had a part of you — in his dreams, in his mind. Later, I'd discover the pictures he drew of you on that website that sold the effects of murders on the dark web. I knew how much pain you were still in. How you hated him.

"I can't live with that," I said. "That he's out. Walking around free. Can you?"

I thought you'd get up and leave. Instead you took a sip of your coffee, seemed to settle. Your eyes stayed on that crystal heart.

"What are you going to do, Hank?" you asked.

I told you that, too. You didn't leave, did you? You stayed and listened.

You always want to paint yourself as the healthy one, the innocent who has managed to move on in spite of the awful things that have happened. I am the broken one. The one who cracked under the weight of it and couldn't put myself back together.

But there's another side of you, too, Lara. And I'm the only one who knows it.

THIRTY-ONE

Hands shaking, breath shallow — she was practically vibrating. Sitting in Greta's drive, she dialed Mitzi, who answered on the first ring.

"Hi, there," she said, voice low. "Lily's napping, and we've had a lovely time."

Rain drew a breath, released it. The sound of Mitzi's voice somehow managed to both energize and calm; a mother's voice. Someone who knew the world, understood its steep hills and treacherous valleys, who knew the way. She'd missed that most of all, just the sound of her mother on the phone.

"That's — wonderful." She meant it. It was wonderful to be able to count on someone. "Thank you."

She almost mentioned that she'd watched them on the camera, then realized she'd never *actually told* Mitzi about it. Was that a violation of her rights, of the unspoken trust between them? Wasn't there something just south of creepy about it? They'd have to discuss it when she got home.

"I'll just be another hour or so," said Rain. "Is that all right?"

"That's totally fine." Not a note of impatience or judgment. "You take your time."

Ending the call, she clicked back to the camera. Mitzi sat at the kitchen table with an open book and her own thermos of tea. Lily, on the monitor app, napped peacefully.

She clicked off and picked up the photos Greta had let her keep. Two people there that night, masked, a man and a woman. The back of her throat was so dry it ached. She saw Greta standing in the window, watching. Rain lifted her hand in a wave and drove away.

Yes, just like Greta said, the earth would cover it all. It would take back the land and integrate every dark thing that ever happened there.

Why couldn't she let that just happen?

"You owe me this much, Lara," Hank said.

The café was dim and mostly empty on that Wednesday afternoon. Outside it was winter gray, the air heavy with cold, threatening snow. Greg lingered on the street: she watched him pretend to read the paper,

420

glancing up at the café window every few minutes, then down at his watch.

He had been angry with her — that look on his face, so hurt and disappointed. She'd lied to him, cheated on him. But he wasn't about to let her confront Hank alone.

I'll just be outside, in case you need me. That was the moment when she realized what kind of man he was. How deep, how faithful and good. And she was grateful for his friendship even if she'd fried everything else they might have been.

"I don't owe you *anything,*" she told Hank. She took cash from her wallet, put it on the table, was about to rise. The heart rested between them, glinting like an accusation. All the ways she'd failed him, let him down, didn't love him the way he loved her.

"He's going to kill someone else," he said, voice almost a snarl. "You know that."

She almost said, *There's nothing I can do about that.* But that wasn't quite true, was it? She sank back down.

"Another Lara, another Hank," he said. "Another Tess."

She felt the drop of dread in her belly. "He's being supervised," she said. She'd had a call from Detective Harper, also from her father. They'd promised her that she was safe.

421

We're on him, Harper had promised. *We won't let him out of our sight.*

"Not well enough," said Hank grimly.

"How would you know that?"

He looked down at his hands. She knew them to be calloused and rough, but tender on her body. There was something deeply wrong with the man in front of her; why was she so drawn to him?

"I've been watching him," he said. "At night. After classes I head back out there."

"Who does?" she asked. "You or the — other side of you."

"He does," he said, shaking his head. "I do. I don't know how to explain it."

You're batshit crazy, she thought. *That's how you explain it.*

"What do you want from me?" she asked. It was more of a rhetorical question. But he had an answer.

"I want you to lure him into the house," he said. "That's it."

It took her a beat to realize that he meant it, that he actually wanted her to be bait for Kreskey.

"That's it?" she said, leaning close to him. She accidentally knocked his empty cup and it clanged against the saucer. He righted it calmly. "Are you out of your fucking mind?"

The girl sitting in the corner on her laptop

422

with her earbuds in glanced over at them.

Hank leaned back, locked her in the intensity of his stare. Something about his gaze, about the way he looked at her. He knew her. He knew her in a way that no one else had and no one ever would. He saw right inside to her shadow self. She couldn't keep his gaze. Thought about getting up and running out but she didn't. She stayed.

"You said yourself that you feel like part of you is trapped inside him — in his dreams, in his mind. That it haunts you."

The words stung because, outside a shrink's office, she had only ever admitted this to him, the sick fear that settled in her middle when she imagined Kreskey thinking about her. She regretted opening herself up to this version of Hank Reams who she'd mistakenly believed was still the boy she used to know. The words jammed up in her throat. She didn't trust herself to speak without yelling, so she sat there quaking.

"Have you seen these?"

He turned around the tablet he had with him. Drawings — rudimentary, thick lines. Horrible images of a girl being strangled, or in a garden, or screaming in terror, or caring for a little boy. It was unmistakably Rain — she recognized the line of her own mouth, the arch of her brows, her wide blue eyes.

"These were confiscated from his belongings," he said. "Harper sent them to me."

Her stomach twisted, the espresso turning acidic.

"We won't be free until he's dead."

"You're wrong," she said, pushing the tablet back at him. She didn't have to look at that. What good was it? You couldn't control what other people thought, or dreamed, or fantasized about. "We're free right now. We're as free as we allow ourselves to be."

"Are we?" he asked, grabbing her hand. She didn't yank it away. "Are we really?"

Now she came to a stop in front of the Kreskey place. She'd brought her real camera this time, a Canon Rebel EOS, and quickly set up the tripod. The ground smelled wet, the air cold. The sun was white and dipping lower, the light punching the brown leaves silver. It was beautiful here, peaceful, if not for the house that radiated a kind of menace. Once it was gone, trees would grow, animals would come to burrow, and birds to nest. The crow. The finch. The owl. The nightjar. And everything that happened here would fade away.

The thought of Lily sleeping in her crib lowered Rain's heart rate. Since Lily had been born, her only clear moments of focus had been when the child was tucked safely asleep in her crib. Down the hall was best. But, as she finished setting the camera, she figured she could work with this situation some of the time — as long as someone like Mitzi was on the case. Experienced, qualified, in control — all qualities Rain herself felt she lacked as a new mother. Was anyone "qualified" to be a parent? Were they all just muddling through?

The ground was soft, and it took Rain a moment to steady the tripod. The low, sad whistle of the chickadee carried on the breeze; a squirrel rustled through the ground cover, then scampered up a tree. In the distance, the intermittent whisper of a passing car.

She snapped a few pictures of the ramshackle structure, then set the timer and stepped in front of the lens herself. She snapped off a few more shots. Then she took the camera and hung it around her neck, headed toward the house.

She stepped up onto the rickety porch, and barely avoided a ragged gaping hole in the wood, where it looked as if someone had stepped through. *Click, click, click —*

the tilting railing, the abandoned rockers, the cracked pot that hadn't held a plant in decades.

Stepping carefully, she pushed the front door and it swung open with a nearly comical haunted house squeal.

The smell hit her first — mold and rot, garbage, something else so foul that Rain covered her mouth and nose. She thought of the things that Hank had told her about the hallway, about Wolf, about how he'd headed out the door, free, but then turned around for Tess. She could almost hear him, see him in the dim.

A scant light came from the windows caked with grime. She felt her way with her free hand and found herself at the bottom of the staircase. Her heart was thudding in that unpleasant way — fear, anxiety, the knowledge that she was acting like an idiot. She reached for the recorder, hit the record button. At least when they found her body they'd know that she'd come here, to the place where her friend was murdered, of her own accord — for "work."

She steeled herself against the smell and started to talk.

"I'm in the Kreskey house. It has been abandoned for many years and looks it. It's a shack — overrun with garbage, graffiti, the detritus of years. Hank Reams could have saved himself that day. He was hurt, yes. Had suffered. But the worst of what would happen to him lay ahead. He stood at the doorway, having killed the dog, Kreskey nowhere in sight. Instead of running, he went back inside to find our friend Tess."

She took a step, testing the stair with part of her weight. It groaned but held.

"He climbed these stairs. How brave he must have been to do that. He was a small boy — thin, so young."

She, too, started to climb, distantly aware of how stupid this was, how she shouldn't be here alone — again.

"Meanwhile, I had been rescued and was in the hospital, trying to stitch together the broken pieces of my memory. What had happened? Who had been in the woods that day? Where had he gone? From the timeline we established later, I must have remembered about the same time as Hank was standing in the doorway, making the decision to go back inside."

Another step up, the wood groaning.

"I have so much shame still for not being stronger that day. My rational mind understands the concept of shock, that I was a child, that I was badly injured and of no good to anyone. But the part of me that always wanted to be a hero, that wishes desperately that things were different — that doesn't go away."

She reached the top landing, flipped on her iPhone light.

Rain didn't believe in ghosts. She wasn't afraid of hauntings and ghouls. She was a reporter in search of the layers of a story.

Her phone pinged:

Holy shit. Are you at the Kreskey house???

Greg tracking her on Find My Friends. She'd turned it back on after their last argument, at his request. She'd meant to disable it again. Shit.

Just getting a few pictures. Heading home soon.

Rain, WTF?? Get out of there right now.

Yes. Leaving now.

She switched off Find My Friends, and flipped on the Do Not Disturb. (Only Mitzi's number allowed.)

A low groaning — beneath her, in front of her. She couldn't be sure.

Then a rustling movement.

Her throat closed up, heart lurching.

She should leave. Right now. That was obvious.

It was the last room at the end of the hall, that's what Hank had told her. The door had been ajar, like it was right now. No light at all. Her smartphone light fell on scattered cans and bottles, a broken crate. Some magazines soaked through and covered with mold. She could hear her own breath, ragged, afraid.

Why didn't she leave? Why didn't she turn around? She couldn't; she just kept moving toward the door as if it was her that day, coming back to save her friend. Wasn't that part of it, too? She wished she'd been here that day, to help them, to save them. It was an irrational idea, a childish one. But it lived in her. She put her hand on the knob and pushed inside.

THIRTY-TWO

"I did some digging."

It's Andrea Barnes, the child advocate I called about Angel's claims. I remember what her voice sounded like when we first met. It was light and flirty, always just about to dissolve into laughter. In contrast, it is now clipped and professional.

"There have been two other allegations of abuse against Tom and Wendy Walters, the couple who fostered Angel for six months late last year. A girl claimed that Tom Walters sexually assaulted her back in 2012. Then in 2014, a boy said that Wendy Walters slapped him hard enough to leave a bruise."

"And —"

"Both claims were investigated and dismissed," she says. "As you know, there is a high incidence of false reporting against foster parents."

"Which doesn't mean there isn't plenty of abuse." Three allegations against the Walters in this case, including Angel's. Where there's smoke, there's fire, I have found.

"That's true," Andrea concedes. "It can be hard to prove. Meanwhile, during Angel's stay with this family, there was no one else placed there. Angel claimed that there was a boy who was kept in a cellar, or some kind of bunker on the property?"

"That's right."

"According to state records there was no boy placed with them at that time, or since. In fact, Angel was their last foster."

"Okay," I say.

"However," she says, "I ran a search against the national database of missing children. Angel claims that the boy there had a birthmark on his shoulder in the shape of heart, is that right?"

"Yes."

"Well, searching with that distinguishing feature, I found a listing for a boy gone missing about that time, just a few towns over. He was a runaway, drug problems, fourteen years old. He has not been found."

"What's his name?"

"Billy Martin," she says. "He's been missing eighteen months."

I hear an odd humming in my head that I know is not healthy. There are little signs these days, tells — that humming, sometimes there's a kind of flash in my vision as if the lights are flickering. He's making himself known more often, trying to push me out of the way when my anxiety or anger levels are even slightly elevated.

"I reported my findings," she says. "Gave a call to the detective who investigated Billy's disappearance. It's still active — he hasn't let it go cold. I wouldn't be surprised if he reaches out to Angel."

I feel an unreasonable flash of annoyance. But, of course, she did the right thing, what she was obligated to do. That's what we're all trying to do, isn't it? The right thing. I remind myself that if there's a missing child, it's not about Angel's trauma, or even about Tom and Wendy Walters. It's not about his wicked appetites. It's about finding Billy Martin.

"Thank you, Andrea," I say.

Tess sits in the corner of the room. Today she's wearing gym shorts and a T-shirt with a rainbow on it, those silly white socks with the stripes at the top and the sneakers she used to wear. Braces, glasses, braids. She looks out the window, kicks her leg back and forth. She's whistling something. What is it?

"Thank *you,*" Andrea says. "For keeping on this when others might have given up or discounted a troubled girl's allegations. There might be something here. Though I have to admit, I really hope not."

"Me, too."

There's an awkward silence. I could ask her how she is. Or suggest maybe we have dinner. But I just don't. You know I think I would have been socially awkward anyway. I can't blame everything on Kreskey.

"Keep me in the loop?" she says.

"Of course." I struggle with what to say next. Why is it all so hard?

Then, "Take care of yourself, Hank."

She ends the call. I stare at the phone — feeling like an idiot.

"So, what are you going to do?" asks Tess. Somehow, she's found herself an ice-cream cone. Remember that farm, the dairy, how we'd ride our bikes down that dangerous twisting road, heat rising off the asphalt and the smell of cow manure heavy in the air? We'd turn off onto the farm drive and the cows would low at us, munching on grass. The ice cream there, made fresh every day from the milk of those cows. Have you ever had better ice cream? I haven't.

"I'm going back tonight," I tell her.

She rolls her eyes. "For the third time?"

"For as many times as it takes."

"What if you can't find anything?" she

asks. "What if there's nothing there?"

I look around my empty kitchen, my single dish in the sink, the container of *massaman* curry from the Thai place empty beside it. The single glass of red wine imbibed for its health benefits.

"Why don't you call Beth back?" Tess suggests.

The woman I met at the party. I've been thinking about her. This could be another one of those moments. Like that moment when I was still on my bike with the choice to turn around and ride for help. Or that moment when I stood at the doorway of Kreskey's house and could have run out across that field screaming.

Maybe in this moment, I could pick up the phone and call Beth. Maybe we'd meet for a drink or catch a late movie. Maybe she'd come back here, and who knows what might happen after that. I can almost see my way along the well-lighted, normal path. I've gone above and beyond within the letter of the law, done what needed to be done for Angel. Andrea has called her findings in to the police; if anyone is still looking for Billy Martin, they'll get out there fast.

But what if there isn't time? What if another night, another day — another hour — means it's too late for a boy in trouble?

To save his life, to save his mind.

After all, that's all it took for me, just an hour. Right, Lara?

THIRTY-THREE

She stood to leave, Hank sat staring at his cup in Café Orlin.

"Did you forget something?" He picked up the heart and held it out to her in his palm.

"Keep it, Hank," she said. "I never wanted it in the first place."

She intended it to be mean; it was not even true. But she hated him in that moment. Wanted to hurt him. She could tell by the look on his face that she had. He closed it in his palm.

"He's unstable," she told Greg in the taxi. "He needs help."

"What did he say?" he asked.

But she didn't tell Greg that Hank was planning to kill Eugene Kreskey, that he'd asked her to lure Tess's killer back to that house. That Hank had a plan, a plan for revenge — it was well thought out. He'd been to the house a number of times. He'd purchased the items he needed to carry out his task.

No, Rain didn't tell Greg.

She didn't tell anyone.

In fact, later that night when she woke sweating and weeping from a nightmare where Kreskey sliced her open and pulled out her heart, the only person she thought to call was Hank. He answered on the first ring.

"Are you okay?" he asked, voice heavy, knowing.

"No," she said, breathless. He was right there. Kreskey. Lurking in every murky corner, of the room, of her mind. She wasn't free. "Of course I'm not."

"I'm sorry," he said. "For everything. I had no right —"

"I'm in," she whispered. "I'll do it."

Rage.

Of all the emotions she'd acknowledged and examined, of all the feelings she'd laid bare for shrinks. That beast crouched inside her, unwelcome, unexpressed, but there all the same. Because deep down, beneath the cover of shame and self-blame, survivor's guilt, she knew who was responsible for what happened to her and to her friends. And she'd never stopped hating him for it, never stopped wishing something horrible would happen to him.

"And then," she went on, gripping the phone. "You and I are done."

Hank breathed on the line. Then, "Yeah," he said. "Okay."

It should have been her that day; that was the other thing she knew. Cosmically, maybe, it had been her day to die. And because of Hank, she'd lived. Now, she'd finally go to the Kreskey house to save Hank.

And this time, they'd win.

THIRTY-FOUR

The shuffling came from behind the door, a series of scratches. Then quiet again. Why didn't she turn and leave? Why couldn't she keep herself from moving forward? There was another high-pitched noise, too. She couldn't identify it, but it made her skin tingle. Something hurt or trapped? Since she'd had Lily, the thought of anything helpless in pain or in distress sliced her. She couldn't stand the thought of hungry children, abused pets, runaways, women hiding from abusive husbands. She had the iPhone camera running, held out in front of her.

The door swung open. In the corner, mingling with the shadows, she saw a form, something small and rustling. A pair of yellow eyes stared at her, startled by the light from her phone. A low yowl. A cat, black with a white chest and yellow eyes. Around her a litter of kittens.

"Oh!" she said, moving forward, crouching down. The kittens mewled and wriggled, hairless, eyes closed, and mama didn't look happy.

"That's all right, kitties," she said. "I won't hurt you."

Rain rose, backed away and didn't see him until it was too late.

Kreskey, towering and filthy, arm raised. He slipped out of the shadow behind the door and she didn't even have a chance to scream.

The blow caught her on the side of the head and she went sailing, like she weighed nothing, head cracking against the floor. The world spinning. The cat hissing, wild, right by her head. When he came at her again, the cat lunged — going straight for his face. And he issued a yell, ripping the cat away and tossing it brutally against the wall.

Then he was coming toward Rain again, howling, bleeding from the scratches on his face. She just cowered, not believing her eyes.

She was back there, back in the woods, a child, helpless.

"Get out of here," a voice roared.

Then a loud crack and Kreskey fell to his knees, clutching his head. And there was Greta behind him, her walking stick raised like a baseball bat, ready to strike again. The homeless man wearing an army green jacket skittered toward the door.

Not Kreskey. Not even close. Half the size, wailing now with pain.

"Get out!" Greta roared again. "This is private property."

Rain lay on the floor as the man rumbled out the door and crashed down the stairs, still yelling. "Bitch! Bitch!"

Not Kreskey. Just a homeless man she'd frightened.

Greta kneeled down to the cat, who was lying still, the kittens mewing in distress.

Rain leaned over and was sick.

She had a cut on her head that was bleeding, but she helped Greta with the injured cat and her kittens. They used a box that Rain had been planning to take to the recycling and made a bed with some of the nursing cloths in Rain's diaper bag. Greta rode in Rain's back seat, cradling the mother cat in her arms.

"Don't you have the sense to know how dangerous it is to venture into a condemned building alone?" Greta asked irritably as Rain helped her establish the cat and kittens in Greta's freestanding garage. "Mother knew you would go there."

Rain didn't say anything. Her head was pounding, and she wondered if she was going to be sick again. She had to go, get back to Lily. Call Greg before he had a nervous breakdown. How was she going to explain her head? Should she even be driving? The world seemed impossibly bright; the pain in her head growing more intense.

"Thank you," said Rain. "For helping me."

She wanted to get out of there, far away from the Kreskey house, from the crazy bird lady, from all the memories that were as powerful and frightening as they had ever been. She'd unlocked the box, and everything was flying out now, screaming furies surrounding her.

Still, she helped Greta get the kittens settled. The mother cat was alert but favoring her injured leg.

"I'll take her to the vet," said Greta.

"I have to go," Rain said, moving toward the door.

"It's a bad idea, you know," said Greta with a deep scowl. "This story. What you're doing. You're going to regret it."

It was another voice in the cacophony that played in her head all the way home.

"What happened?" Mitzi rushed to the door to greet her. "Oh, dear. Let me look at that."

Lily reached for Rain, arms urgent, and Rain took the baby gratefully into her arms. Oh, her warmth, her wonderful softness, the scent of her hair. The contrast of her present life and her past was dizzying. How could she walk away from this to go *there*?

The baby bounced, giving Rain a wide two-toothed smile.

"This one," said Mitzi, still frowning, worried, "is an angel. A real joy baby."

"She is," said Rain, her voice a hoarse whisper.

"Where's your first aid kit?"

"I'll get it," said Rain.

"Boo-boo?" asked Lily. Rain fought back tears, but then they came anyway — welling, falling, a delayed reaction. She pulled Lily close so that she didn't see her mommy cry. Had Lily seen her cry before? Did babies even notice that kind of thing?

"Let me," said Mitzi. A warm hand on Rain's shoulder.

"Upstairs, cabinet under the master bathroom sink. The far one."

Rain put Lily on the ground and got down with her. Lily reached for and handed Rain an *Elephant and Piggie* book by Mo Willems, rock god of children's literature. Gerald, an elephant, is afraid that he's allergic to his

best friend, Piggie. He sneezes magnifi-
cently.

Lily squealed with delight as Rain read:
"AAAAAH-CHOO!"

She let the house, the sound of her daughter's voice, the familiar smells of the fireplace, the organic cleaner she used to clean
the wood table, the light from the window
wash over her.

*I'm home. Not in Kreskey's house. Not on
the path in the woods. Not at Hank's loft.
Home — the place I make with Greg and Lily,
my little family.*

When Mitzi returned, she got down on
the floor with the two of them, nimble and
fast for an older woman. She wiped at the
blood on Rain's head. The cut wasn't very
big; she'd inspected it in the car, wiped at it
ineffectually with spit on a tissue, pushed
her hair in front of it so that it wouldn't be
obvious.

"What happened?" Mitzi asked, when she
seemed satisfied that the cut was clean.

"I — uh," said Rain. "I walked into a door.
Stupid."

Mitzi nodded, smiled kindly. She got up,
discarded the cotton ball, put the kit on the
counter. She washed her hands. "Well, be
careful, young lady. You have a little one to
watch over. You have to take care of yourself

— for her."

Most people think that a mother's greatest fear is that something will happen to her child, and that's true. But of equal horror to most mothers was that something would happen to *her*, and that she wouldn't be there to care for her baby. That thought, what she did this afternoon, it gutted her. What would have happened if Greta hadn't shown up with her stick and her inherent toughness?

"Things are harder on you girls," said Mitzi. "I mean, it was hard on us, too. Just the beginning, you know, of women being very career-minded. Me? I never wanted to be anything but a mother and wife. Which I kind of felt guilty about back then. Like you were supposed to want more, you know. And I just wanted kids.

"That's what my Bruce wanted, too," Mitzi went on. "He earned a good living and we did well enough. Trips to Disney, the Grand Canyon — Janey got a scholarship, and we had enough for Jack's education."

She came to sit next to Rain, ran a hand through her gray hair. "Janey's a lawyer, two little ones — not so little anymore. High school. But it was hard. She wanted both things."

"And?"

"She wishes she spent more time with the kids now that they're out, here and there, living busy lives with not much time for their parents."

"And you?"

"Now I guess I wonder what else I might have done," she said. "Especially since Bruce passed away, five years ago now."

She looked sad for a moment, and Rain reached out for her. The other woman squeezed her hand. She laughed a little. "I think, there are always regrets — or maybe wondering. But I guess I'd rather wonder what else I might have done, than wonder if I'd done right by my children."

Rain nodded, looked at Lily, who was on her back, holding her toes, very interested in her feet. Her legs were so chubby, her feet and hands such perfect specimens of cuteness.

"Do you think it's possible?" asked Rain. "To do both things well?"

"I do," she said, with a firm nod. "You just have to give up sleeping."

They both laughed then. They were still laughing when Greg came through the door, looking just south of frantic.

His messages. The Do Not Disturb setting. Shit.

"Look at that," Mitzi said. "Daddy's home, too!"

"Hi, Mitzi," said Greg, voice low. "Thanks for coming today."

"Well, I best get on," said Mitzi, maybe sensing the encroaching storm. "Did we say Wednesday same time?"

"We did."

"I can't wait, Miss Lily," she said, waving to the baby. "More fun on Wednesday."

Then she was off; Rain watched her slip out of the door, wishing she had a reason to call the older woman back. When was the last time anyone had cleaned and bandaged a cut on Rain's body? She flashed on the man — the imagined Kreskey — lunging for her. Greta. The injured cat. The blank-eyed birds under glass. She didn't have the energy for a fight.

He walked past them, not stopping to kiss Lily.

"What happened to your head?" he asked from the kitchen. He was still wearing his coat, took a bottle of bourbon from the liquor cabinet and poured himself a generous portion.

"AAAH-CHOO!" yelled Lily from the floor. Rain smiled at her, which encouraged her to do it again.

"I knocked it on a door," she said. She

447

really wanted to be honest with her husband, but how could she when she was acting like such an idiot?

"In the Kreskey house?" he said. "A condemned building if I'm not mistaken."

"I needed footage, pictures," she said. "It's being torn down."

"Well, thank god for small favors."

He shifted off his suit jacket, rubbed at his temples. "You blocked my calls."

"I know." She tried for sheepish. "I'm sorry."

She got up and walked over to him, wrapped him up. He was stiff at first, then folded her in his arms, buried his face in her hair. But then he pulled away, walking over to the window and looking out with his back to her.

Lily pulled herself to standing on the coffee table.

"Careful, bunny," said Rain, heading back to her. Lily fell on her bottom, rolled back and started to laugh. Rain righted her again.

"How am I supposed to trust you, Rain?" Greg said, his voice thick.

"What does that mean?" She pressed at her injury, felt the sting of it. She knew exactly what he meant and he was right.

"Trust you to take care of yourself — for us." When he turned back, his face had darkened with worry. "This story. I can't lose you to this again. *We* can't."

She walked to him. "You won't. I promise."

But the words sounded hollow, and his frown only deepened. How far could she push him? She'd asked so much of him over the years. Would he at one point just get fed up, give up on her?

"I have news," said Rain, trying for a change of subject. "Good news."

"I have news, too," he answered with a resigned sigh. "You go first."

"NNR accepted Andrew's pitch. It's a go," she said. "We're going to do the story for the network."

He looked at her, something strange on his face. "That's — fantastic."

"Is it?"

"Isn't it?"

She looked at Lily, who was cruising — coffee table to couch to end table to the other couch.

"I have to meet with Gillian and Andrew tonight, in the city. I'll go late, after I put Lily down."

He went to sit cross-legged on the floor with Lily. She joined them.

When had he started looking so tired? The circles under his eyes were purple; he was pale. She reached a hand for his face, touching the hard edge of his jaw. You forgot about your husband sometimes. Between being a new mom, all the angst and existential bullshit, you could neglect the man who was your partner, once upon a time your boyfriend, the guy who made you hot, who rubbed your back and got your coffee.

"I'm sorry," she said again, for what felt like the hundredth time. For what? For all her failings, for being a shitty wife, for not knowing what she wanted, for being stuck in the past, uncertain about the future. For the fact that his talent and hard work was less appreciated than it should have been.

He took her hand and kissed her palm, then touched gingerly the bandaged cut on her head. He always forgave her. Maybe that was the heart of true love, forgiveness for all our many flaws and failings.

"For everything."

He kissed her, soft and sweet. "I knew who you were when we got married — everything about you. But it's different now. There's Lily. You can be yourself — but *take care* of yourself."

"I will," she said.

His frown showed his skepticism. Lily crawled into her lap, and Rain held her tight.

"What's your news?" she asked.

"So, the executive producer job?" he said.

She'd totally forgotten. The job above him was open; he was a natural for the promotion, experienced, hardworking, beloved by everyone at the station.

"They gave it to someone else."

"What?" Her voice came up too high. "Why?"

Lily was watching Rain, her face gone still, almost worried.

"Al said they wanted someone more 'current,' not from hard news. Someone with a finger on the pulse of what viewers like these days. Fluffy features and wellness tips, I guess. And someone who they could pay way less than they'd have to pay me. He didn't say that, of course. But that's the size of it, isn't it?"

"So, who'd they get?"

"A twentysomething morning show producer from California," he said with a wave. "He starts next week. My new boss — some kid from Los Angeles."

She hugged him tight, still holding Lily. Sometimes things really sucked.

"Whatever," he said. "You know, I guess what's strange is that I don't even really care. I'm happy. I like what I do. I love you and Lily so much. The job's already a pressure cooker — deadlines and ratings. Maybe

451

it's okay, especially now with your thing. Sometimes, you know, things just happen the way they're meant to happen."

She could see it in his eyes, though — the frustration, the disappointment. There was worry, too. When someone new came in, who knew what else might change. She took Greg's hand, and Lily crawled from her lap to his. Some of the worry dropped away, and he smiled at their girl.

"Dada!"

They made dinner together, with Lily in her high chair tossing Cheerios as if she was playing a game, to which only she knew the rules, and was joyfully winning. A chicken stir-fry, a bottle of wine, some David Bowie playing.

Rain searched out Greg's new boss on the internet and they agreed that he looked like an ass — tight-lipped with blond curls, thick glasses — oh, come on, he doesn't really need those. In one picture, he wore a bow tie. He ran a small local morning show outside Los Angeles — the kind with local chefs in to cook healthy meals, and visiting authors on the road, best gifts for your valentine.

"He won't make it a week under the pressure of covering the sheep-shearing, and the local toolshed break-ins," said Rain.

"Yeah," Greg agreed. "Hard news is going to crush him."

By the time Lily was down, Greg was planted in front of the television — zoning out to some college game. She tried to make herself look put together, professional.

"Are you taking the car?" he said when she came downstairs. She had her tote, her laptop. She looked the part — lipstick, hair blown out. She felt the part, the way she'd always felt at work — smart, powerful, in control. She didn't always feel that way at home. Often, she felt incompetent, lost, floundering. Why was work easier than life?

"Yes," she said, dangling the keys from her finger.

"Drive carefully," he said, getting up, kissing her. He bowed his head, then looked up at her, an eye lock, hands to her cheeks. "And knock 'em dead. I'm proud of you, you know. You're brave to do this. You're smart. And you're a great mom. You got this. All of it."

There it was — one of those moments again. She almost put her stuff down, went upstairs and changed into her pajamas. She didn't have to go, did she? Not really. She could just curl up on the couch beside her husband, and that would be that. They'd head upstairs after a while, probably make love, fall asleep together.

"What?"

"Nothing." She smiled. "I love you."

Then she was outside, down the steps, climbing into the SUV. She checked her phone, made sure that Find My Friends was disabled and pulled out of the driveway.

She didn't have a meeting in the city tonight, no appointment with Gillian and Andrew. The words were barely out of her mouth, and she was breaking all her promises to her husband. But there was something she needed to do, and it was past time.

THIRTY-FIVE

Don't they haunt you? Those pictures he drew. Believe it or not, I still dream about them. Crayon Rain — your stick hair and bright pink mouth, that blue he used for your eyes, the red he used for your insides. The gore. The childish horror show of it. When I saw them the first time on the dark web, the rage — it woke him right up.

Is it a violation to hold someone in your mind? What right did he have to imprison your image that way in his fantasies? I just couldn't let that stand. It was one thing when his body was locked up. But to have him free in the world and imagining you that way? No. No.

Honestly, I was sure you would call Harper. What would you say? *I talked to Hank,* you'd confess. *I think he might do something.*

What would Harper say? He'd say something like: *Don't worry, we're on Kreskey every minute. We'll handle whatever comes up. Live your life, Miss Winter.* (He'd call you "miss," of course.)

Harper. He's one of those men. A man who knows what's right. A man who understands people. A veteran like my grandfather who knows how dark is the world, how base the human heart. He knows what men will do. And what must be done to stop them. Or to right the miserably unbalanced scales of justice. Sometimes. Just sometimes.

"What are you doing here, son?"

He surprised me that first night. I thought I was sly, that I was hidden. But he was slyer. And he had been hiding first.

"Detective Harper?"

In the woods behind the place where Kreskey was working his janitorial night shift, I'd been waiting, watching him arrive. I'd follow his progress through the low concrete buildings as the lights came on and went off. I watched as he shuffled out with the trash, tossed it into the Dumpster. He was slow, a lumbering giant. I noticed that he walked with a limp, that he dragged his right leg a little. Great hanging jowls, tent-sized clothing. His black hair hung in greasy slicks, thick glasses obscuring his eyes.

I could see that Kreskey was a medicated zombie. If I was totally honest, in the nights I sat watching, some of my rage drained. I wasn't quite there; *he* — the other one inside — wasn't quite ready either. I was bound in a tangle of thoughts and nightmares, the blank spaces where I knew *he* resided. I knew what I wanted to do, what he wanted to do. But I wasn't sure how you crossed the distance from intention to action. He came out when I was angry, or afraid. Looking at the husk Kreskey had become, knowing my own strength and physical power, I was neither.

"I don't suppose you'd believe I just happened to be in the neighborhood," I answered Harper.

"Camping?"

"That's right."

"Nice night for it."

"Full moon."

"You know they say these woods are haunted."

"I believe it."

"What's in the pack?"

A gun. A big hunting knife. A length of rope. Duct tape. A big plastic tarp. If you download Tor, the engine that gets you to the dark web, you can learn almost anything about anything. How to build a bomb. How to mark someone for assassination. How to commit a murder without leaving a trace of physical evidence. Interestingly, this is also

457

where you can find the sites that sell murderabilia, like the drawings Kreskey made of you. One sold for nearly $5000 the last time I checked. Or so they say. You can't trust anyone on the dark web. Or anyone, anywhere, for that matter.

"Camping gear."

"You won't mind if I take a look."

A moment passed between us, where I didn't hand over the bag and he locked me in a knowing gaze that made me slouch my shoulders and want to slink away like a dominated dog.

"You're out of your league, son," he said, gaze sliding away and up to the stars.

I didn't answer. As we stood there, the van pulled up and Kreskey lumbered out. A guard opened the door for him, then got back in his truck and drove away.

"What are *you* doing here, Detective Harper?"

"A few of us — retired guys, some still on the job," he said. "We're taking turns keeping an eye on our local monster. Can't have anything like what happened to you kids happen again up here."

He wasn't a big man, especially. As Kreskey had, he'd seemed bigger when I was a kid. But I was taller than he was now, much bigger, obviously in better shape, a trained fighter. But he had an aura that all other men recognized. He wouldn't hesitate to kill you; and so, he'd always win any fight.

"Problem is that there aren't enough of us to be on him all the time. There are gaps. Wednesday nights, no one's watching. Sunday nights, too."

We stood awhile, watching the lights go on and off, watching Kreskey's bulky shadow. The air was warm, smelled of green and rot. Stars blinked, milky and faded in the full moon.

"Are you sure you know what you're doing?"

I didn't answer him.

"I'll just let you know right now. It's not what you think. Not during. Not after."

I noticed for the first time that he had something over his shoulder, a camping chair, that he unfolded. It was an impossible tiny triangle of cloth hanging between three poles. No way it could hold him, but it did.

"Too old for standing around all night," he said, sinking down. "I've got this tonight. Why don't you go back to school? Live the life you have. Study hard. Drink too much. Get a job. Love someone."

I left that night. But I went back, as you know.

■ ■ ■ ■

Today, Angel's mother, Jennifer, asked if I would be present for the interview with the police detective investigating the disappearance of Billy Martin. I agreed, of course.

I've also done some of my own research. I asked Detective Harper to run background checks on Tom and Wendy Walters. They wouldn't have police records most likely, otherwise they wouldn't be candidates for foster parents. But he dug around some. Tom had a sealed (to everyone except Detective Harper) juvenile record — arson, petty theft, found with a gun in his locker and kicked out of school. Joined the military, dishonorably discharged, worked at a factory in town that manufactured ice trays, of all things.

Wendy was a high school dropout, worked at a grocery store, no record of any kind. They'd been married ten years. They didn't exactly fit the foster parent profile of older, childless couples, usually of some means, looking to help kids since they couldn't have their own. Of course, some folks were just looking for the money that came with caring for the kids. I've found this to be a rarity, though. Most people are well-meaning.

Life often gets the better of them. The stress and struggle of it all, the voices in their heads — some of them crack under the burden. Life breaks them, and they do wrong.

"How long were you with the Walters, Angel?"

They sit at the table, Angel and the young detective — earnest, bald by choice, head shaved.

Angel looks at Jen, who smiles and nods.

"A little under a year, I guess," she says. "We had Christmas there, but no presents."

I keep my place by the window so that Angel can look at me. "We?"

"Me and Valentine. I called him Val."

The detective slides a picture over to Angel. "Is this Val?"

She smiles. "Yes," she says. "I think so. He was much thinner, different around the eyes somehow. But, yeah, it looks like him."

"Was he there when you came?"

"No. He came after."

"Did someone bring him?"

"No, he was just there one night. He came in with Tom. He had a bag, a beat-up old black rucksack."

"How long was he there?"

"A week, maybe more," she says. "He was in the bedroom down the hall. He didn't

461

talk much. Didn't go to school."

"Did he say where he came from?"

"He said he ran away," she says. "That his dad hit him. That his mom never did anything about it."

"So how long was he there?" the detective asks again, maybe trying to get a more exact timeline, or trying to see if she stays consistent in the details.

She lifts her bony shoulders. "I don't know," she says. "A couple of weeks?"

"Who left first?"

"I heard him yelling one night," she says, not really answering the question. "I stayed in my room, but I watched as Tom dragged him outside. I followed."

I have heard some of this already — along with her reports of neglect, how long days in the house, neither Tom or Wendy came home. Angel got herself off to school, cleaned her clothes in a machine even though there was no detergent. She ate the school breakfast and lunch provided, knowing there might not be dinner. But she hasn't told me the details about the night that Val (Billy?) got dragged from the house.

"They walked and walked. Finally, they came to this door in the ground, like one of those cellars in *The Wizard of Oz*. Tom dragged him in there. They didn't come out.

462

I went back to the house."

Oh, I think. I'd been looking for a house, some kind of structure. I could have sworn that's what she said before. Another hole in her story.

"When did you see him again?"

"I didn't," she says. "I didn't see him again."

She's gone flat; which is something most people don't understand and why I think Angel might present as a liar. Trauma victims learn to separate from their emotions, to distance themselves from painful memories, from fear.

"I heard screaming, though."

"Screaming."

"In the night," she says. "At first, I thought it was a bird, or some kind of animal. But then I realized — someone was screaming."

I don't like how blank she seems. She's slowly folded into herself, her thin arms twisting around legs she's pulled up to her chest. Jen is frowning with worry, hovering nearby — leaning in, then pulling away as though she's not sure what to do. She's a worrier — doesn't want to overattend, doesn't want to seem unavailable. All parents should worry so much between the balance of those things.

"Angel," I say, and her eyes dart toward

me. "It's okay. You're here now, with us. The detective is trying to help."

She audibly exhales, looks at the picture in front of her.

"It's too late," she says. Her eyes go big, tears fall. Jen swoops in, gathers the girl up in her arms. "It must be too late."

"If I'm facing the house," asks the detective, "which way was the cellar?"

"You walk behind the house. There's a path you follow through the woods, there's a fork in the path. You stay to the right. It's a long way on foot — maybe fifteen minutes."

He slides another picture over toward Angel. Jen and I both lean in to look.

"Do you know who this is?"

She leans in. "That's Valentine."

The detective frowns. It's the image of a different boy — older, bigger, eyes set farther apart. Similar coloring, but with a smattering of freckles.

"Are you sure?"

She nods. Jen and I exchange a look over Angel's head.

Another picture.

"And this?"

She nods. "Yes, that's him."

It isn't the same boy in the first photo. Again, similar coloring, but this boy with a scar on his cheek, a haunted look in his eyes, one I've seen too many times — in my patients, in the mirror.

"Thank you, Angel," he says. He's good at masking his disappointment, seems to sense that Angel is fragile. "You've been really helpful."

"Are you going there?" she asks. "Are you going to find him?"

"Yes," he says. "I'm going to keep looking until I find him."

She nods, uncertain. Her eyes dart between me and the detective, watching our faces, our expressions. I keep mine encouraging, soft, head nodding. Jen offers a hand to Angel, who allows herself to be hoisted from the couch. The older woman wraps an arm around Angel, walks her upstairs, motioning that she'll be right back.

"Who are these boys?"

"Billy Martin," he says. "And two other open missing cases on my desk. Three boys missing over the last two years. All runaways, troubled. All passed through the same bus station."

I sit across from him, surprised to notice that he is very young. With the height and the glasses, the dark of his skin, he presents as older somehow. It's in the eyes, the softness of his face, the complete absence of any lines or wear and tear. There is too much weariness in his shoulders.

"It doesn't mean she didn't see him," I say. "They all have a similar look."

"They fit a profile, certainly," he says. "And that bus stop? It's right across the street from where Tom Walters works."

"Maybe she saw more than she's telling us," I suggest.

"I've been out there twice," he says. "They cooperated, let me look around. They're — weird. I don't know. Creepy people. But that's not a crime and I didn't see any evidence of wrongdoing."

He goes on. "I went to the city and checked the property survey. There's no record of that cellar she mentioned."

He shakes his head, and I can feel his disappointment, the frustration of not quite being able to do his job. "I can't go out there again without a warrant."

But I can.

I wait until late. I hacked into your home cameras, by the way. And the baby monitor. I can watch from any of my devices. How, you might wonder? Ah, the labyrinth of the dark web, with all its dim passages into the lives of the unsuspecting. Devices that capture IP addresses, spyware that turns

466

your phone into a camera, an eye always watching you, devices that easily decode logins and passwords.

If normal people only knew what was out there — what kind of people, what kind of instruction for those looking to indulge their derelictions, abnormalities, fetishes, fantasies. All the cracks and crevices that allow the wraiths to slither into your life. All you need is the box with the serial number, which you so diligently recycled in your bin down at the curb.

Greg is asleep on the couch in front of the television. He looks wrecked. Hard day? Lily is in her crib. But where are you, Rain Winter?

"Stalker," says Tess. It's not a new accusation. "You're a stalker."

I'd try to deny it, but, how can I?

"I'm protecting her." Lame.

Tess guffaws at that one. Remember "the snorter," that laugh of hers. Normally all you could get out of her was a polite smile, sometimes a giggle. But every once in a while, she really let it rip, snorting like a wild boar in the brush. You and I, we'd die, that sound so much funnier than whatever had amused us in the first place. She'd get mad at first, then she'd just laugh harder. I haven't laughed like that since then. The relief of it, how the waves wash through your body. Laughter is the same release as crying, that rush of emotion roiling through, leaving you clean in its wake.

Tonight, she's stunning. Long hair like her mother's, a flowy peasant blouse, clinging soft jeans. She lounges on the couch in my home office, on her belly, up on her elbows, legs kicking.

"She's called twice, hasn't she?"

"Beth?"

She called once. I called her back. She hasn't returned that call yet. I have found myself thinking about her — her smoky voice, the way the silk of her blouse just carelessly revealed the lacy edge of her bra, the cream of her skin. Her sapphire-blue, almond-shaped eyes, the thoughtful way she listened. She wasn't just waiting for her turn to talk, to give her opinion or share a story. There was a pleasant fleshiness to her body. She wasn't one of those women — starving themselves, hours at the gym, their bodies taking on that pulled-taut strain, that tension of trying too hard, fighting time and age, gravity and flab. Every morsel measured, agonized over. She had a plate of food, ate with gusto, drank two glasses of wine.

"I think this is another one of those

places," Tess says. "Another fork in the road."

"Oh?"

Greg groans in his sleep, turns over, putting his back to the camera. Where are you, Rain?

"As I see it, you could move on from here. Move forward in a new direction."

"As opposed to?"

"As opposed to staying on the path that keeps looping you back into misery."

I see that doorway, the bright yellow sunlight, the electric green of the grass, all of it so bright against the darkness it hurts my eyes. I could have walked through that door, and I don't know where I'd be, but not here, I think. But then — would I have become a doctor? Would I have helped all the young people I think I have helped? Among other things?

Trauma victims spend a lot of time looking back, trying to unstitch the fabric of the past. All the ways the thing might not have happened, everything they could have done differently.

"And suppose I take this other fork," I ask Tess. "Toward what? Normal life, I guess. I call up Beth, we go to dinner, maybe we fall in love, get married. Have children."

"Is that so far from the realm of possibility?" she asks. "You're not getting any younger. Could happen pretty quickly if it's right. People get married fast at your age. Why wait?"

"And so, I'm at the movies," I say. "Or on a tropical getaway with my new girlfriend. And what if there's a boy trapped in a cellar on the isolated property of Tom and Wendy Walters? What if there is more than one?"

"What if there isn't anyone?" she says. "And what if you don't have to, can't, save everyone. And what if you could have the life that you deserve?"

She speaks with uncommon passion.

"What if *this* is the life I deserve?"

When I glance over at her, she's not there.

The victims of trauma — they want it back. The time. The person they would have been if the worst thing hadn't happened. But they don't get it. The world is fractured; the mirror casts back a different reflection. And we just have to accept it. We are who we are now because of what happened then.

After a while longer, I leave my house, get in the car and drive to the parking garage. There I switch vehicles.

I am about halfway to the Walters property, armed with the new information given by Angel today, when I realize that someone's following me.

THIRTY-SIX

"Where are you?" Gillian asked, her voice echoing from the speaker. "It sounds like you're driving."

Rain didn't answer. Instead, she told Gillian about her visit to Greta. Told her about the stuffed birds, how they stared, lifeless, frozen. It didn't sound funny, as she hoped it would.

"That's creepy," said Gillian absently, probably on Tinder or whatever the dating app of the moment was. Swipe left, swipe right. That was the low to which the modern world had reduced love, the magic of human connection.

Then Rain went on to what happened in the house with the homeless man, the cat, the kittens.

"Oh, my god. Honey." Gillian snapped back to attention. "Are you okay?"

"I'm okay," said Rain. She probably should have gone to the emergency room, gotten herself checked out.

"Why would you go there alone?" she asked. "Rain, you're smarter than that."

"I just wanted the pictures," she said. Gillian made a sound like she understood.

"Two people there that night," Gillian said after a moment. "That's new."

No, it wasn't new, not to Rain. She hadn't forgotten as much as she'd pushed it deep, locked in that box her father had taught her about. She'd put that part of herself away.

That box. What her father hadn't told her, and to be fair maybe he didn't even realize it himself, is that if you lock something in a box and bury it deep inside you, it stays, rattling around in there, forever.

"Rain?"

"Yeah?"

"Are you sure you want to do this?" It was her friend talking, not her partner. "I mean. Maybe it's all too hard. Maybe it's taking you places you don't need to go."

"Maybe it's taking me places I *do* need to go."

She was opening the lid now, setting it all free, so that she could watch it fly away, a winged figure across the moon.

That night, she and Hank took the ride mostly in silence. She tried to shift as far away from him as the passenger seat would allow. Greg wasn't speaking to her, so she hadn't had to worry about an excuse for where she'd be all night. But she had one at the ready; she was going to visit her father, spend the night in her old room and do some laundry. It was something she did fairly frequently, and it would track.

But Greg hadn't called or returned her calls. And she was pretty sure that she'd lost him. It was stone in her heart; that she'd pushed away someone so good. What a cliché to say she didn't even realize how much she loved him until she'd screwed it all up. Her past had bubbled up like a noxious gas and poisoned her present.

The Henry Hudson was thick with traffic, the city disappearing in the rearview mirror. Hank was a hulking presence. When he'd tossed his pack in the truck, it had clanked heavily, and she could only imagine what was inside. Was he really going to do this? Were they really going to do this?

And yet, wasn't there also a giddy anticipation? The terrible thrill of imagined revenge tingled through her nerve endings. The idea of facing someone who terrorized you as a child and making him pay, there was a kind of comic-book justice to that. It was a Technicolor idea, bright with reds, oranges, yellows and blues, one that recast everything that came before it. It turned her from a black-and-white figure, cowering in fear, into someone powerful, ready to make things right.

She hadn't talked about her rage much. Maybe with Dr. Cooper, early on. The size and scope of her anger; it was nothing she'd ever experienced, and it didn't even feel like it fit in her body. But when she thought about Tess, about Kreskey, about how they shouldn't have even been where they were, about how a million little things went wrong — Tess's mom called into work, the tire flat on Tess's bike. The injustice of it swelled, filled her — there was a scream of rage bigger than the world lodged in her center. If she let it loose, it might shatter everything with its terrible pitch and volume.

She'd swallowed it, held it inside. Like the box.

They drove and drove. When they entered The Hollows city limits, she sensed a change in him — even though they hadn't exchanged a word in miles. He sat up straighter, the rhythm of his breath shifted.

"Hank."

He turned to look at her, then back at the road. She'd done a little research on this, what might be wrong with Hank, talked to

474

a psych student she knew.

"I mean, split personality disorder — like a *Sybil* kind of a thing where there are different personalities, characters so to speak — it's rare. Like so rare that many doctors don't think it exists," he told her over a falafel in the park. She'd dated Steve briefly in her freshman year, but the chemistry was more friendship than anything, and the few kisses they'd shared were forgettable.

"On the other hand, childhood trauma is very tricky. In extreme cases, the psyche will split. It's a survival mechanism, really. But it's more like two sides of the same coin — a stronger self emerges to protect the child self. There might be some dissociation, fugue states where one part of the self is more in control. This might lead to blackouts, foggy memories, blank spots in recall."

The park had bustled around them, but Rain was back in the tree hollow. Steve had watched her carefully, put a hand on her shoulder as if intuiting her bad memories. He was wiry, with a few days of dark stubble, big soulful eyes.

"Jung called them splinter-psyches," he said. "One part of the ego regresses. Another part basically grows up too fast in response to trauma. A kind of false self emerges. May reemerge in times of great stress later."

475

"Does one self remember the actions of the other self?" Rain asked.

Steve shrugged. "Possibly yes. Maybe not. It might be like the memories we have of our dreams — disjointed, nonsensical. Our dream self is effectively another self. It's probably best likened to that."

She remembered Hank's face, how confused he'd seemed. It *was* as if he'd awoken from a dream.

"Hank?" she said again.

He didn't even answer her.

"Rain?" Gillian still on the phone. "Are you there? Girlfriend. What's eating you?"

She parked outside the gate to Hank's property.

What in the hell did she think she was going to do? Ring his buzzer. Yeah. Yes. She was going to ring his buzzer and tell him what she was thinking, what she was remembering, what she suspected him of doing. But then what? She'd be destroying him. Ruining his life. Again.

"I'm fine," she said.

"Rain."

"Gil," she said. "I have to go. Hey, don't call the house, okay? Greg thinks I'm with you."

She ended the call before Gillian could

say anything else.

She nearly jumped out of her skin as the gate swung open and Hank pulled out; she saw his bulky shadow in the driver's seat.

Sometimes when we think we don't deserve what we have, we subconsciously set fire to our lives. I think that's what I did with your mother. Her father's true confessions yesterday — was it just yesterday? *I was so broken inside from abuse, I don't think I knew how to handle your mother's brand of love — giving, unconditional, nourishing. I'm sure I didn't deserve her.*

Maybe he'd hoped she would argue the point. But, meanly, she didn't. Lilian, her mother, was good, through and through — a loving spirit, a sensitive soul, a beautiful writer — and he was not good enough. He *didn't* deserve her. The way she didn't deserve Greg.

Beware of self-destructive impulses, Laraine. They are shadows in the psyche. We often aren't even aware of them until they've burned our lives to the ground.

In her history with Hank — both sides of him — he'd done all the chasing, all the watching. He'd come after her in the woods that day, risked his life and sacrificed his sanity to save her. He'd stayed close to her, even when she'd made it clear she didn't want him. But tonight, it was her turn to chase. She wasn't even sure why.

She gave Hank a bit of a head start, then she followed.

THIRTY-SEVEN

But no. I'm paranoid. Or at least when I come to an abrupt stop and pull over, the car behind me keeps going fast. The night is velvety, and I'm a bit off my game. I have to admit that my conversation with Tess (or myself, depending on what I think she is) has me a bit rattled. So, I don't get the plate, or the make and model of the vehicle. But it's not Agent Brower's black sedan. So that's good, at least. Our conversations have been increasingly tense.

She came by the office when I was out with Angel. "I just have a few more questions," she scribbled on a note that she left with my assistant. Her handwriting is tight and precise.

A message on my voice mail: *I just have a few more questions, Dr. Reams.* Something in her voice has shifted a little, less deferential, more hard edges.

I asked my assistant to make an appointment with her for tomorrow.

She asked about dates, Brenda told me after they'd talked.

What dates? As if I have to ask.

September 7. She asked if you'd been in Boston or the surrounding area on June 5 of last year? I told her I'd have to check your calendar.

I'll take care of it.

Dr. Reams, is everything all right?

Of course. Not to worry, Brenda. I'll turn over my calendar to her tomorrow when I see her. Tell her that.

Just one more night, just one more wrong to right, if I can. And then, and maybe, maybe I will call Beth. Maybe I will try to take back the time I've lost.

It's not too late to have a life. Is it?

And what about me?

He rattles around in his cage, pacing, wanting things that — to be honest — I don't want to give as much anymore.

What *about* you? You integrate.

Good luck with that.

This is what it's come to, Rain. My only friends are a ghost and the other side of my own fucked-up psyche. Sad, right? More than sad. Unsettling. Kreskey did kill me that afternoon, all the best of me.

I pull the car deeper off the road tonight.

There's a path by the shoulder right on the edge of the Walters property. I check my pack, shoulder it and head into the night, air sparkling with cold.

I think they've abandoned this property. The house is dark again, the yard and shrubbery overgrown. There's never a car in the drive.

I've been inside; it's nicer than I expected, with tattered antiques, an orderly kitchen. The rooms upstairs are simple and clean, with quilted bedspreads, old pictures along the hallway wall.

I've seen the room Angel says she stayed in — the oak tree right outside, branches that scraped the window at night. It doesn't look like the kind of place where awful things have happened. Tom and Wendy Walters, slim, innocuous in the smattering of photos on display, are unremarkable if a bit rumpled and dull about the eyes. They don't look like the kind of people who torture children.

But if I've learned one thing in my work and life, it's that bad things happen everywhere, and almost no one ever looks like the demon inside. Markham was movie-star handsome. The Boston Boogeyman looked like Mister Rogers, kind and graying about the temples, soft-spoken.

Forest bathing. I walk first, then jog, mindful of my step, picking my way through the trees. Yes, this is it, my last night out here. If I don't find the cellar, I'm going to have to let this go. Angel — she might be lying, or delusional, or just confused. She thought all of those boys were the boy she called Valentine. Her hands were shaking. When she looked at me, I saw confusion, fear. I can't act on what she's given me; but I can look one more time. Just in case.

The plan was for you to stand on the porch, an apparition, the thing that lured him into the house. When he drew you, you were always in a simple red dress, your hair loose around your shoulders. So, that's what you wore, how you had your hair. Maybe you would wave to him, then you'd turn and walk through the door. Once he was inside, you would leave through the back and wait in the car, the engine running, my getaway driver.

We'd never speak of it. Afterward, we'd never see each other again.

I was ready. I had been training and studying. At the gym, I had a trainer who conducted a punishing workout — heavy lifting, brutal cardio, wrestling, mixed martial arts. On the dark web: how to assemble a kill bag. How to best a larger man in a fight. How to immobilize a victim. How to commit a murder and not leave a single trace of evidence. It's out there. Some of it's bullshit; some of it is the ranting of madmen.

But if you know your way around, you can find anything you need to know. My favorite was the site of a paramilitary guy, who meticulously laid out his training as a fighter, a survivor, an interrogator, a killer. I learned everything I needed to know from a US soldier turned mercenary. *The most important weapon you have is your mind. If you're not prepared to kill, you'll die. There's not a gun or a knife in the world that will save you.*

He gave his video tutorials in a balaclava.

Turned out that everything he said was bullshit. Fighting for your life, and the life of your friend, is a very different thing than killing in cold blood.

Of course, things didn't go as planned, Harper's words suddenly making sense. *It's not what you think. Not during, not after.*

Funny how when you're a kid, grown-ups seem like gods. Impossibly powerful, free from rules, the keepers of secrets. Then you go through a phase where they seem so old, so out of touch, where you dismiss them completely. Finally, you realize that at least a few of them knew what they were talking about. By that time, you're old, too, having gleaned wisdom of your own that no one hears.

I remember that night, Lara. But the memory is like a low-quality film reel, something that I watched on a small screen. I remember the leaden silence between us, the pale of your face, how your expression was taut with fear and anger. When I caught your eye, I saw that you hated me. Who could blame you? Look what I asked you to do.

I have mistreated you, Rain Winter. I could blame it on him. But I am not separate from the beast within, not entirely.

Just like tonight, I hid the car and shouldered that pack. I walked through the woods and you followed. Your breath was ragged. You were crying, and I ignored you.

Tonight, I walk and walk alone. It's a slog for some reason. Though I've walked far harder terrain much faster, a kind of fatigue has settled in. I keep looking around for Tess, but she's abandoned me — like all smart women. They keep their distance.

I reach the fork Angel described and veer left, note the time to clock fifteen minutes. I haven't been this way before, so — maybe.

There's a waxing gibbous moon, casting off a weary light from behind drifting clouds. I hear the occasional cry of the barred owl, that mournful: *Who looks for you?* But largely it's quiet except for the skittering of a squirrel who dances across my path and up into the branches above me.

The woods thin, and I come to a clearing. This is deeper onto the property than I've ventured and suddenly I'm mindful of how far I've come, how no one knows I'm here. How I've left my phone in the car — after all, the intruder doesn't often resort to calling the police. Besides, I don't trust that thing. I know how easy it is to track and watch someone, how vulnerable these devices are to spyware. Using it, I've created a clone of your phone, Lara. I know every text and phone call, every move you make unless — as you sometimes do — you turn off your location services, or the phone itself. So, naturally, I'm distrustful of my own device. If people only knew.

I kneel down and open my pack, retrieve the metal detector I've purchased online, and assemble it quickly. I tested it at home. It's such a cheap piece of made-in-China garbage, I couldn't believe it would actually work. But it seems to. It's as light as a drinking straw, emits a low clicking noise when I turn it on.

I walk the clearing. The perimeter, then zigzag across. It isn't until I've almost given up that the light turns red, and the device starts to beep. I look down and see a wooden door in the ground, with a metal latch and padlock. I stare at it a moment.

Huh. Well, how about that? Angel was telling the truth. From my pack, I retrieve a set of bolt cutters. I could try to pick the lock, but the night is growing long, and I have a niggling sense of unease.

I cut the bolt, with effort.

It's not easy, any of this. The amassing of tools, the research, the recon, the stalking, the physical act of taking a life. You really have to commit.

The lock falls with a clatter, landing loudly on the wood. When I swing the door open, the smell hits me like a fist, knocking me back.

Oh, god.

"What the hell are you doing on my property?"

The voice causes me to spin and I'm standing face-to-face with Tom Walters.

He's thin and hunched, a kind of strange young-old to his drawn face. Straw for hair, cut badly, clothes ill-fitting. His face clenched in menace. In his hand a mallet of sorts, something that looks like it would hurt a lot if he managed to hit me with it. Which he won't.

"What's down there, Mr. Walters?" I say, opting for the direct approach. I square myself off against him, size him up. I estimate that I have about fifty pounds on him.

His expression broadens into surprise. Maybe he expected me to react with fear or retreat. "What the fuck — who are you?"

"Who's down there?" I repeat.

My pack. In a moment of carelessness, I've left it on the far side of the clearing, open after removing the bolt cutters.

He advances, and I hold my ground, bring my left foot forward ready to fight. I almost laugh when I think of all the men, nearly twice his size, that I've bested inside the ring and without. He'll swing high I bet, looking for strength from the shoulder. I see his shoulder twitch, a telegraph. I prepare to block. Instead he roots.

"You're trespassing. And I've called the police," he says. He glances behind me at the open door. "Best get out of here."

"I doubt you've called the police," I say. I advance a step; he takes a step back. I intend to relieve him of that mallet.

But the blow, when it comes, comes from behind.

The knock to the back of my head is brutal — the world tilts and my ears start to ring. The pain, it takes a second, but my nerve endings start a siren. I spin to see a woman I recognize as Wendy Walters standing behind me, holding a shovel, which she's lifted, followed through like a baseball bat swing.

I'm stunned, too stunned to defend myself as Tom Walters moves in with his hammer to deliver a devastating hit to the knee. I hear myself roar. And then the push.

I stumble back into the abyss of that hole, falling and falling, knocking stairs on the way down. Pain and fear delayed, just a horrible twisting disorientation, the knocking of my head, my hip, my knee.

The last thing I'm aware of is the door closing above me with a clang.

THIRTY-EIGHT

"Wear this."

Hank pushed a rubbery mask at her, covered with feathers.

"Why?" she asked, her voice wobbly.

"Just put it on."

She obeyed. It stank like chemicals, the plastic rubbing against her skin.

"Pull up your hood, and let's go."

After a certain point, the whole thing had taken on the unreality of a nightmare. It was so far out of the realm of anything she had done or would have thought to do. Her life since Kreskey, it hadn't been easy. But she was on a traditional path — therapy, school, internships, Greg. She knew what she wanted to do, where she was headed. Kreskey, and that awful, life-altering day — those things behind her, the fears and memories locked up tight.

Then Hank. He opened up something in her. Maybe it was always there.

They walked and walked, she following him, watching him through the eye holes of the mask. It made her feel invisible somehow, like she almost wasn't there.

The house rose in front of them, ugly and small. She nearly turned around then, chucked off the mask and started running. *You owe me this much, Lara.* It was the idea of that that kept her from bolting. She owed him. She did.

"Take off your coat," he told her. "And the mask."

He took both from her.

"When you see him, walk inside and out the back door. Wait in the car with the engine running."

When he backed away from her, she thought she saw something flash in his eyes, which she could see through his mask, a hawk, ferruginous feathers, sharp yellow beak. Was it regret, sorrow? That's when he stepped on a weak board on the porch, his foot falling through with a crack.

He swore a blue streak and when she tried to help him up, he pushed her away. It wasn't him, not the man she'd given her body to, not the boy who used to give her piggyback rides. It was the other one. She hated him.

She was shaking, a quavering that started

at her core and moved through her body like a virus. Her stomach was an acid roil of nerves. He freed himself and went into the house. He didn't seem scared — at all. He was a robot again, his focus and intent only on the task at hand.

She stood there — how long?

The night was silent and so cold. All stars obscured by cloud cover, and the tops of trees. She paced the porch, avoiding the weak board. Hope ballooned — maybe he wouldn't come. She wouldn't let Hank talk her into this again. In fact, fuck it, she was going to call Detective Harper and tell him what they'd tried to do. She'd tell her father. Maybe not Greg — who was never going to forgive her anyway. But he didn't need to know that she continued to sink lower and lower for this guy.

She was thinking about Greg, how alone she felt, how furious he'd be, how terrified, if he knew where she was, how wrong it all was — when she felt eyes on her, that tingling of the skin. Gaze detection.

A jolt of fear moved through her body when she saw that someone had emerged from the shadows, a bulky darkness leaking from the black all around, his face as white and round as a moon. Kreskey.

She backed away as he advanced, reaching out a hand to her, and she choked back a scream. Inside the door, Hank handed over her coat, her mask.

"Now go."

She moved quickly, blindly, through the house, down the hall, to the kitchen, feeling her way. As she left, she saw the living room — a tarp laid out. Tools. Rope. What was he going to do, exactly? She didn't need to know, kept moving.

The back door swung open, and the night lay out before her. She could run to the car. She could even leave him there, drive to the police station they'd passed on the way in, stop all of this before it began.

But she didn't.

She stopped in the door frame, the cold outside a wall, her hot, ragged breath in clouds. She stood a moment, listening to the silent night, and thought about the hollow of the tree that had hidden her. The sound of her friend screaming.

Then she turned around and went back inside.

What does it mean to be strong? To be brave?

When she was young, she thought she knew the answers to those questions. It was easy — you didn't back down from a fight,

492

you defended your friends. You got up on-stage to deliver your speech about recycling even though your stomach was queasy, and your voice shook at first. You didn't cry when you fell off your bike.

Later, it came to mean something different.

You didn't leave the room when your mother was living the last hour of her life, even though she didn't know you were there, even though you wanted to get out on the street and run away, as far as you could get, wailing with all your pain and sadness.

You endured hours of mind-altering pain so that you could have a natural childbirth. You gave over your body to your child. You gave up parts of yourself, of your life, to be a good mother, a good wife. You faced down the demons of your past, so you could be whole — so that you could counsel your daughter to live right.

Now, not even an hour after leaving Greg and Lily, Rain watched Hank park his car, and take that pack from his trunk. She wasn't sure if what she was doing was strong, or brave, or just plain stupid — reckless.

She almost called out to him.

Stop, she wanted to say. *I know what you've*

been doing. It has to end here tonight.

But she stood, silent in the night, miles from home, from where she should be.

Where was he going? Was it braver to follow him? Or to go back to her family and leave Hank to do whatever it was he was off to do? She could call the police. Or Agent Brower. Or Chris. But then again, she couldn't do that, could she?

Was it braver to keep a secret? Or to tell it, no matter what the cost to Hank, to Rain, to her family. Or she could go home and say nothing, as she'd done before.

She waited until he disappeared and then, she went after him.

THIRTY-NINE

In the hero's journey, there are always extraordinary trials, enemies to fight, crushing failures. The path is fraught with peril, from without and within. There are dark nights of the soul, where despair closes its black claws around you and you think that you can't, that you shouldn't, go on. And sometimes you just fuck up.

Do you know what I mean, Rain? Have you ever made a mistake so huge, suffered a failure so abysmal, that you think you might not be able to find your way back?

I am kind of in that place right now.

Get up, loser.

He's raging, filling me with the strength, with the power I need. Unfortunately, the body we're both in has taken a terrible fall.

I'm afraid to move, my arm and leg are twisted, my shoulder on fire, my hip, my head feels like it might not be on right. I breathe, try to extract myself from this unnatural position. The smell. The utter pitch-black. The leaden silence. Shit. Maybe I'm dead.

I used to think that as I floated in the Gulf of Mexico with my mother. That hot sun, the bathwater warm of the ocean, the smell of salt and sand and sunscreen. The jewel-green water lifted my body and I floated effortlessly. My mother sang, soft ballads by Joan Baez and Joni Mitchell, Norah Jones. Her voice was sweet and melodic, mingling with the calling of the gulls. What did we know about death? Maybe Kreskey killed me that day, and my soul moved to Florida with my mother.

With effort, I push myself to sitting.

"You have really fucked this up," Tess says. "Does anyone even know you're here?"

I can't even see her; she's just a disembodied voice. I pull my shirt up over my nose to block out the odor. My phone, my flashlight, all my tools are in that pack.

You never leave the fucking pack out of arm's reach. What is this, amateur hour?

I can move everything — fingers and toes. There's pain — head, shoulder, hip, leg. Knee badly twisted. But there isn't that crazy pain from a break, everything is intact. Everything moves. I can only chalk it up to my vigorous fighting and exercise routine, muscles strong and flexible. Bend and bounce or break and shatter.

"Hello?"

A frightened whisper coming from my right.

"Hello?" I answer.

"Who's there?"

"Billy?" I venture. "Billy Martin? Is that you?"

A sniffle. "Yes."

I get on all fours and crawl toward the voice. "I'm here to help."

Which is ridiculous because we're both trapped down here, thanks to my utter ineptitude.

"Do you have a light?"

"No," he says. "Don't you?"

"Is there anyone else down here?"

I come to the bars of a cage. There's not a single pinprick of light. I'm completely blind. I put my hands on the bars and feel a set of bony fingers. I cover them with mine. The kid absolutely reeks; I try not to retch.

"There were others," he whispers. "But it's been quiet for a while. Do you have any food? Any water?"

In my pack, yes. Protein bars. A bottle filled with water. "No," I say. "I'm sorry."

"How are you going to get us out of here?" His voice is a desperate croak. "Did you — fall in?"

"Don't worry," I tell him, deeply worried myself. "We'll figure it out."

I handed you your coat, Rain, and your mask, and I let you go. I knew you'd wait in the car — that you wouldn't leave me or go to the police. Because I knew you — your heart, your mind, or thought I did. I knew when I left that house, you'd be waiting for me with the engine running, just like we planned.

I was ready. He was in charge — and I wanted him to be. That part of me that didn't care what he did, or who he hurt, who wasn't afraid and who didn't have nightmares.

I watched you walk down the hall, small, slim — not much bigger than you had been when we were kids. I want you to know that I was — that I am — sorry. For how I treated you, for what I made you do. It was wrong.

Then I heard Kreskey, shuffling through the leaves outside, the groan of the stairs as he climbed onto the porch. All the blood drained from my body, my throat went dry. He moved so slowly, huffing with effort, then pushed the door open. He stood a moment, the night filling the corners of the doorway. Christ, he was more vile, uglier than he had ever been.

He was the boogeyman.

The monster in the closet.

I wasn't prepared for the rush of emotion, the dry suck of pure terror. The knife in my hand was too heavy; my arm filled with sand.

He regarded me. All the time I'd been watching him, he presented like a zombie. But when he looked at me, his eyes were bright and alert. His hands clenched in fists.

I felt my insides loosen. I was frozen. The beast inside me was gone and it was just me in my skin, a beaten, traumatized boy grown into a weak and fearful man.

"You," Kreskey said. He knew me, his mouth twisting into a hideous smile that revealed gray and crooked teeth. "You came back to me, you little bitch."

It took me a second to realize that he wasn't talking to me.

He was talking to you.

You came to stand beside me. I felt your cool small fingers wrap around mine.

You took the knife from my hand.

And, then, before I could stop you, you were running for him, a great warrior's cry exploding from your open mouth.

■ ■ ■ ■

I feel my way up the narrow staircase, and come quickly to the locked door, which I foolishly try to ram with my good shoulder, causing myself so much agony that I nearly black out. I almost take another tumble down the stairs. The door won't budge.

"So, Billy," I say, slinking against the wall, back down the steps. "How did you wind up in this mess?"

I've asked this question of countless traumatized children. It's not as flip as it sounds, though maybe a little. It's more a light way to get a young person to think about the journey. To think about the journey from the perspective of a person who had at least some control over the way things went. Responsibility. Not guilt. Not blame. Responsibility is the *ability* to *respond* better to our current situation, to consider ourselves the actor in what comes next — not just a victim of what happened to us.

"So, Hank," says Tess from the emptiness in front of him. "How did you wind up in this mess?"

Fair enough.

"My dad died," Billy whispers. I know

what he looks like from the pictures I saw. But now, he's not even a shadow. We are two voices in the black. "And my mom got married again."

"That's rough," I say. Acknowledge how hard it is, but don't encourage wallowing. Whether we survive trauma is all about how we narrate the past, the future. "How were things with your stepdad?" As if I have to ask.

"I hated him," he says. "He hit me."

"Did you tell your mom?"

"He hit her, too."

"And what about your father. Was he a violent man, as well?"

"Sometimes," says Billy. "But I knew he loved me. He was just — I don't know — he just got sad sometimes."

Depression. Violence. Abuse. How many of us grow up this way? A lot, with approximately 3.5 million claims of abuse or neglect investigated annually. Neglect is by far the most common maltreatment. Then physical abuse, then sexual. Some children are what we call polyvictimized, suffering more than one maltreatment. Four in five abusers are parents or stepparents. That's a lot of damaged people walking around. Not to mention the abuse that begat the abuse.

"So how did you handle the situation with

your stepfather?"

There's a familiar pause here. Most victims of childhood trauma are not asked what their role might have been. Again, not about blame. We don't blame the child victim. Just giving them a new way to frame the situation.

"What do you think you could have done differently, Hank?" asks Tess, snarkily.

Not left the pack out of reach, for one.

Not let my guard down.

"Did you do anything right?" asks Tess.

Maybe one thing. There is one person who knows where I am tonight, I'm pretty sure.

"I tried to fight him," Billy tells me. "When I realized I couldn't beat him, and that my mom wasn't going to stop him, I ran away."

"Was there someone you could have called? A family member. A teacher."

"My stepdad told me that they'd take me away," he says. "That I'd never see my mom again."

I'm guessing Tom Walters found him at the bus station, offered him a place to sleep and something to eat. He was probably kind, warm — an irresistible lure to a boy like Billy.

I wait a moment, let his words hover. Meanwhile, my own wheels are turning. I think my only option is to wait for Tom or Wendy to return, as they must.

"I guess that's what happened to me anyway," he says softly.

"Let's see if we can work together and find a way out of this, get you back with your mom and find some help for your family."

"That's what Tom said," Billy answers, sounding frightened. "He said he'd call my mom, offer her a place to stay."

"And that was a lie," I say.

"Yes."

"Well, Billy," I tell him. All we have at first, therapists, is our words. It takes time to earn trust, especially with young people who have been gravely injured by people or life, or both. "I'm not lying. I want to help."

It sounds really weak, especially given our current circumstances.

"Okay," he says after a pause.

There's a crash overhead then, and another. I leap from my place at the bottom of the stairs and hide against the cold cinder block of the staircase. My only plan is to trip whoever comes down first, use the dark to my advantage. Billy starts to weep.

"You are so fucked," offers Tess. "What a mess."

Another crash, then another. Then a heavy thud; the outer door opens slowly, someone grunting on the other side. Finally, a face appears above me like a moon.

I don't believe my eyes. I'm dreaming.

Or, this time, I've lost my mind completely.

FORTY

The locked box opened, that was the best way that Rain could describe it. It wasn't just the fear and sorrow, the shame she felt about the day she lost her best friends, that she hid instead of helped. It was the rage.

At the sight of Kreskey in that doorway, his words, something burst inside her and the world was colored red. Hank was frozen; limbs stiff, his face white, jaw slack with terror. Though Hank towered over her, was nearly double her weight, Rain could see he would be useless.

She grabbed the knife.

The weight of it in her hand, the gleam of that blade. It felt good.

And before she was even aware of herself, she was running.

In her mind there was a horrible film reel — standing on the bridge with Tess, Wolf issuing that guttural sound, his teeth in her flesh, Tess's terrified scream of pain, Kres-

505

key's blow, her own mind-numbing shock and pain, Hank's warrior yell. She was back there. But this time, she wasn't cowering in the hollow of a tree while he took her friends. This time, she was armed, she was strong. This time she ran to him, screaming with all her power, knife raised.

She could save them, save all of them. And they would all escape, grow up healthy and whole, raise their children together, watch each other grow old. They would have normal lives of proms and weddings, baby showers, moms' nights out. They'd cheer each other through the good days and carry each through the bad. Friends. They'd be friends forever.

She wasn't present that night in the Kreskey house, she wasn't herself.

Afterward, she'd claim — to Hank, to herself — that she didn't fully remember what happened. That night, too, she'd lock inside. Another box. Another nightmare.

But the truth was, she took that hunting knife of Hank's and ran without hesitation to drive it straight into Kreskey's heart.

He never had a second to react; she hit her mark and used all her weight to drive it in, knock him down onto the tarp beneath him, and fall on top of him. He issued a great gasp, opened his mouth to release a river of blood. She looked him straight in the eye, the stench of him nearly overwhelming her; she watched his light go out, his eyes go glassy and still, felt the final shudder of his body. And then she screamed again, releasing all the horror, all the terror she'd carried, all the nightmares she'd had, all the things about herself and her childhood that she lost to him.

Hank pulled her off, and wrapped her up in his arms, and rocked and rocked her until she stopped screaming, weeping, until she was just whimpering.

"Itsokayitsokayitsokay," he kept saying. "Imsosorrysosorrysosorry."

She clung to him, his arms strong and safe, and he held her, weeping himself. She turned away from Kreskey, buried her face in the rough of Hank's jacket.

That's how Detective Harper found them.

"Holy shit," he said, coming through the door, startling them both. Rain and Hank both froze, the three of them locked in a triangle of shock.

Detective Harper's face was slack a moment; he put a hand to his head. "Oh, my god," he breathed.

Hank and Rain clung to each other. She couldn't stop sobbing, but Hank was silent and stiff.

The air was electric with all the horrible implications of what could happen next, Kreskey slowly bleeding out on the floor.

"Okay," Harper said finally. "Let's get this cleaned up and get the hell out of here."

With Detective Harper's help, they stripped to their underwear and burned everything they were wearing in the fireplace in his living room. Rain shook uncontrollably, crawling into pink sweatpants and T-shirt that read Sexy Lady. Hank got a pair of jeans and football jersey.

"Now," Harper told them while everything burned, "this is done. You never speak of it to anyone. You forget it ever happened. No one will ever come looking for you. And if you ever have the urge to confess — to your shrink, to your priest, remember that you'll be frying me, as well as yourselves and anyone who ever loved you, for a man who destroyed your lives, killed your friend and would likely do it again if the opportunity arose."

Rain and Hank sat on Harper's couch stunned, speechless, nodding.

"Don't see each other for a while," he went on. "Maybe never. Easier for you both to move on that way, you know. Like war. Don't talk about it. Try to forget it.

"Can you drive?" he asked Hank, who

nodded, still mute.

"Good," he said. "Get out of here. And when the reporters come knocking? Don't answer. Whatever you do, don't talk to the press."

They rode in silence back to the city. When he stopped in front of her dorm, she climbed out and never looked back at him. She heard him roll down the window and say her name, but she didn't answer.

After Rain killed Kreskey, there was nothing. No regret. No nightmares. In fact, fewer nightmares than she'd had before. Rain felt, if anything, free. She'd freed the version of herself that Kreskey kept in his imagination. There was a giddy lightness, a raw sense of personal power. She'd faced down the boogeyman — and won.

Kreskey's murder hit the news the next day, and the wave of calls from reporters, the storm of photographers waiting in front of her dorm on Eleventh Street was massive. She hid in her room, exhausted on every level, Gillian coming and going for her — food, materials from her teachers. Greg didn't even call; she knew she'd lost him forever. Finally, Rain just went home. Her father sent a car, and she moved back into her old room.

On the third day of hiding out, Greg came

back to her. If he suspected what they'd done, he never said so. And she spared him the truth, spared herself his reaction. If she told him, she made him complicit. If he judged her, she'd have no choice but to judge herself.

He forgave her for Hank, for being unfaithful. He wanted to protect her, came clean about some failings of his own. She wasn't angry; in fact, she was glad he wasn't as perfect as he seemed.

"I think we are — us together — bigger than our screwups," he said. He sat on one of the rockers on her father's porch. "I hope we are."

"We are," said Rain.

When she made love to him that night, she thought of Hank, how he held her next to the corpse of the man who'd killed their friend. She pushed the gloom of her past away, forced herself into the light with the man she chose for her future.

The media storm passed quickly and the Kreskey investigation grew cold. Suspicion never once turned to Hank and Rain, not even for a moment. *This town takes care of its own business,* said Harper that night. Kreskey's body was buried in a pauper's grave, she didn't know where.

Eventually, she returned to school, to life.

"How is this sitting with you?" asked her shrink at the time. Dr. Coppola had a swanky office uptown; the bills went straight to her father.

"Not as I would have expected," said Rain.

The truth was, she'd started to wonder about her own internal coldness. She'd killed someone, murdered him in cold blood. This was a psychically damaging event, under any circumstances. Why did she feel so little?

"Oh?"

Rain never felt like this doctor was much older than she was. Her first doctor, Maggie Cooper, was comforting and motherly. But she felt like under other circumstances Dr. Coppola and she might be at a bar or a coffee shop, just chatting. Svelte and stylish, with a black tangle of curls, tortoiseshell glasses, he had a habit of reflexively pushing the hair from his eyes, which made him seem boyish and sweet.

"I feel freed," she said. "Released from his grip."

He nodded, even, gaze kind and warm.

She couldn't tell him everything, of course. "The death of someone who harmed us can be a kind of catharsis. It reveals the impermanence of all things — even pain."

"He was a person, someone who was

damaged and ill," she said. "Shouldn't I feel — something else?"

"Was he that to you? A person, someone who deserved your compassion?"

"No."

"What was he, then?"

"Someone evil who killed my friend, and damaged irreparably my other friend. Someone who stole my childhood. Who still had a version of me captured in his imagination. Those pictures he drew, and the people who bought them — whoever they are. It has haunted me."

He nodded, listening, handing over that eternal box of tissues to dry tears she didn't even realize she'd been crying.

"And now he's gone. Why wouldn't you feel freed? You're okay, Rain. Let it all go now."

And what would you say if I told you that I killed him with my own hands, that I drove a knife into his heart without hesitation? And that I don't have an iota of remorse. What does that make me, Doctor?

That might be a different conversation, one she had no intention of ever having. With anyone.

In the woods, Rain found Hank's pack first, knowing instantly that something had gone wrong. He'd never leave that pack out in the open. She knelt down beside it. She always thought of it as the kill bag — inside she found rope, a hammer, that same type of hunting knife, duct tape, a tarp folded into a tiny square.

She zipped it closed and hefted it onto her back.

Hank was nowhere to be seen, the night still, the air grown frigid. Her hands were stiff with cold, her face tingling, her jacket too light.

Instinctively, she checked the phone. It was a scroll of texts.

Gillian: He's calling me. I didn't answer. What am I supposed to do here?

Greg: I thought you'd be home by now. Lily's fussing a little in her sleep. What should I do if she wakes up?

Gillian: He just texted. This is not right, my friend. Loop me in here. What's going on?

Greg: She settled. I'm going to bed, I guess. Wake me up when you get home.

Greg: Rain. Wherever you are, you should come home.

A line from one of her mother's books came back to her: *Once a woman has a husband and child, her time, her heart, her desires never quite belong to her again. A blessing some days, a burden others, like all the other gifts that life brings.*

He was right, of course. She should go home. This was madness.

She checked the camera app; Lily was sleeping, peaceful. Greg was still on the couch, snoring, phone on his belly. The sight of her living room, pretty, softly lit, television flickering, filled her with longing, and with a sudden clarity.

Her life, everyone's life was split by these series of moments, these choices. Fight or flight. Go with Hank or call the police. Leave him in the house that night or go back and fight Kreskey with him. She'd made the choices as best she could. Some under duress, some out of guilt and fear, some out of anger. Right or wrong, they were all true. She had another choice now — keep following Hank into the darkness. Or turn around and go home to the people who needed her most.

She put the pack down, turned back the way she came. Whatever Hank was doing out in the woods, he was on his own.

That's when she heard voices. She kept walking, back toward the car. It was the other sound that stopped her cold. The sound of metal on flesh, a cry of pain, the hard slamming of doors. Then arguing.

But she wasn't just a mother, and a wife.

She was a journalist, a writer, a person with more questions than answers, with a complicated past. Maybe even with the latent desire to self-destruct, to race toward danger. She paused, listening.

Footsteps coming her way, urgent, swift.

She slipped off the path and into the trees, crouched down. More arguing voices — heated, the tingle of panic. A man and a woman, voices swelling and deflating as they approached, then passed her.

"There's someone else out here."

"There's no one else."

"I saw someone."

They walked right past the pack, which was just another shadow in a field of shadows. She waited, trying to control her breath, her shoulders hiked with tension, the night closing in around her.

And when they were gone, she grabbed the pack and ran back in the direction from which they'd come, away from Greg and Lily, toward — she had no idea what.

FORTY-ONE

How long did she jog along that path? Finally, she came to a clearing, the moon casting the open area in silver, an icy sheen clinging to the grass. Her breath came in clouds as she stood listening. Nothing. Silence.

Then.

An odd, arrhythmic thumping drew Rain's attention toward the edge of the clearing, the pack heavy on her back. Then it was quiet again, except for the sad calling of an owl. *Who looks for you? Who looks for you?* Rain kept looking back, around her. The trees seemed to have eyes; she felt watched, afraid.

The sound again, another hard thump. He was out here; she could feel him. Hank.

What binds you two together? Greg wanted to know. *Why can't you give him up?*

Of course, he knew the answer. They both did.

There was a final thump, resonant and loud, echoing off the trees — and then nothing. She kept moving, searching for the origin of the sound. She nearly tripped over the doors in the earth, some kind of cellar. Oh, god. Her heart lurched; there were voices within. Doors locked with a thick, heavy padlock. What good could come of a locked cellar in the middle of nowhere?

She dug through the bag and found a large hammer, a small sledge actually, heavy and hard. Using all her strength and both hands, she brought it down over and over again on the lock. The lock itself never broke, but the latch holding the doors together fell apart with her last blow, wood splintering. She sat, breathless a moment, then swung the doors open. She was nearly knocked over with the stench, swallowing back a roil of nausea.

Oh, god. What was down here?

She took out the flashlight and shone it down into the dark hole.

What she saw — it revealed itself in flashes. Three children, thin and filthy, two curled and cowering in the corners of makeshift cells. One looking up into the light, his face white, cheekbones pushing against flesh, bony shoulders.

And Hank.

It took her back to the woods with Tess, to the hollow of that tree, where she sat frozen inside. Though it was the dead of summer, she'd turned to ice. She wanted to go back there, to that empty place where the world just stopped and turned to frost.

The Winter girl safely encased in ice, a princess under glass like Kreskey's Snow White.

But no. She wasn't that girl anymore. She needed to help her friend and the other children down there. For Tess, for the kids that she and Hank were once, for the daughter she had waiting for her at home.

"Lara." Hank's voice was soft with surprise. "It's you."

There was a moment when she remembered everything about who he was — how he giggled like a girl, picked the pepperoni off his pizza — even though he insisted they order it on. How Batman was his favorite superhero, because he was a real, flawed man who built himself into something better. How he tried to kiss her when they were ten and she laughed at him, and he laughed, too. How he gave her a red crystal heart for her birthday, but that she'd lost it. Or thought she had. How she always believed that he and Tess would wind up together. And she would leave them and the place

518

they grew up together to travel the world, coming home for holidays to visit their kids. And how somewhere, somehow, she wished there was a universe where it was true.

Hank said something she couldn't hear. She was so stunned by what she saw before, the rush of memory playing before her eyes.

But then his expression hardened, turned cold, and he thundered up the stairs. She didn't have time to do anything but cower.

"Hank," she said, as he was almost on top of her. "Please."

But then he was racing past her, tackling a man who stood behind her with shovel raised. She heard their bodies connect with an ugly thud, hard release of breath, and then they were tumbling on the ground, roaring.

Rain grabbed the hammer.

FORTY-TWO

Bright moonlight, towering shadows of trees all around them, the sky a void above.

Rain stood, breath ragged, hammer poised.

The struggle between the two men on the ground was a tangle of limbs, a dervish. Hank delivered a blow to the middle of the other man. Then the stranger drove his elbow into Hank's ribs, eliciting a cry of pain.

She was hypnotized, thinking that violence between people was never as you imagined it. The sound of flesh on flesh, it was soft. Blows were awkward, the sounds guttural and strange. Something kept her from diving in, from helping Hank. Where? How? What if she hit him by accident? She stood, feeling like the helpless woman in the movies, the one she always wanted to scream at: Don't just stand there! Do something!

Then someone tackled her from behind

and the ground rose up in an unforgiving wave, knocking the hammer from her hand. Shock. The terrible grappling of the mind. What just happened?

She tasted dirt, an impossibly heavy weight pinning her to the ground. All her breath left her. A blow, another one, the pain rocketing up her spine, into her arms. Another to her ribs. She was paralyzed. She saw stars, the world spinning and tilting. She tried to turn, to face her assailant, but she couldn't move.

She felt herself freeze, go cold inside. It was too much, all of it. The things she'd seen and experienced. Kreskey in the woods. Hank and all his craziness. The night they went back. Markham. The Boston Boogeyman. There were too many monsters. And she was not strong enough to stop them all, and she was no closer to understanding why the world was what it was.

And then she thought about Lily, her daughter, sleeping peacefully waiting for her mama. Her child. The one thing she was sure she'd done right. How much Lily needed Rain, how much Rain needed Lily. Motherhood, it was a touchstone, or could be. The place you went to give meaning to all the madness outside your door.

A red-hot burst of adrenaline rocketed

through her, and Rain spun powerfully to fend off a woman she had never seen, someone wild-eyed, mousy, with a tangle of unruly blond hair.

Her elbow connected with the stranger's jaw. Hard. The other woman was surprisingly tiny, with sticks for arms — how could she be so heavy?

As the woman surged forward, Rain used her legs to knock her back, delivering a powerful shove to her middle. The other woman — who the hell was she? — stumbled, her body a comical arc, arms reaching. Then, backing over a fallen log, she fell. The other woman's head hit the ground with a terrible thud, and then she was still.

Rain tumbled away, scrambling after the hammer, adrenaline pulsing, breath frantic.

When she felt the weight of it in her hand, she was back there again in that house with Kreskey, the knife clutched in her grasp. She *ran* that day, all her rage and sadness, an engine. She had no regrets. No remorse, even now. She could do it again. Detective Harper's words bounced around her brain. *Some people are better off dead.* With effort, she pulled herself to her feet.

She lifted the hammer and the strange woman cowered, skinny arm up to hold her off.

"Please," she whimpered. She couldn't have been older than Rain, her clothing ragged and ill-fitting, "Please."

Another voice, this time Sandy's: *We fight violence with more violence and only more violence follows. We dig our grave deeper and deeper — there's no end.*

How, she thought, *how did I get here?*

She let the hammer lower, rage, sadness flooding through her system. The moment was ugly, twisted. Those children down there — three, each in a cage, curled into corners. She could hear voices now, calling out. It was a horror show. Why was the world so full of darkness?

Lara, Tess and Hank, all destroyed in different ways by Kreskey, who was destroyed by his own parents. And who knew what his own parents had suffered?

She wanted, truly *wanted,* to kill this woman on the ground in front of her — though she wasn't even sure who she was, what she had to do with the children. The woman moved to get up, and Rain lifted the hammer again, moved in quickly.

"Don't move," she warned.

She didn't even recognize the sound of her own voice.

How many evil people were there in the world? How could they ever find them all?

"Lara." No one had called her that in years. "Don't."

She felt him before she saw him standing behind her. The heat of his body; she knew it. She turned to find that Hank had come to his feet. The other man lay bleeding on the ground, groaning. Hank, too, was bleeding from the mouth, holding his shoulder.

His eyes — they were haunted, exhausted. The woman on the ground crawled away, still weeping. Rain watched her go — revulsion, anger, fear doing battle in her center. The hammer was still clutched in her hand. Who were these people? How had they all wound up here?

"It's done," Hank said, reaching out a hand.

He took the weapon from her and pulled her close. She sank into him, her old friend, and held on tight.

FORTY-THREE

"It's over." His voice was just a rasp. They could have been back there on the floor of Kreskey's house, his corpse bleeding out beside them.

It's over. She wasn't sure what he meant.

Would it ever be over? For them? For those children? But then the trees came alive, figures moving out from the black space between the thick trunks.

The field came alive with light and sound, with voices shouting. Hank pulled her to her knees, put his hands behind his own head and Rain did the same. There was an unreality to the scene as Agent Brower came to stand before them, gun drawn.

Hank looked up at her, over at Rain.

"We're not going anywhere," he said. "Just go take care of the kids. There are kids — who need help."

The young agent regarded them both, her gaze stern, bemused. But she holstered her weapon, snapping the clasp closed, then marched past them with a shake of her head.

"What's going to happen here?" Rain asked, dropping her hands, sinking down onto her heels. How was she going to explain this to her husband?

"Honestly, I have no idea."

The night was long, endless. It seemed to stretch and pull.

Three children — a boy and two girls — were retrieved from that cellar.

She watched them carried out of the hole on stretchers. Alive. All of them alive — weak with malnourishment and dehydration, in various states of injury, with long, twisting roads ahead of them. But alive.

Just like her and Hank so many years ago — but not Tess. They were all too late for her.

The spotlights all around them, the towering trees, the stars. It could be a dream, one of those nightmares that take pieces from your life and make them strange, recognizable but only distantly. If she woke up in her bed, next to her husband, she wouldn't be surprised. Rain closed her eyes and wished she would, that this would be like so many of her terrible dreams that faded in the light of the life she'd built.

But no. This was real.

Cool metal beneath her, some strange beeping, the crackle and hiss of a police scanner. Rain and Hank sat on the back of an ambulance, shoulder to shoulder. They'd been treated for their various cuts and bruises by a team of young and efficient EMT workers.

"What are you doing here?" Hank asked when they were alone.

It was the way it always was with old friends. Years had passed, but the energy between them was the same. They knew each other, were familiar in the way of family — they'd seen all the layers of each other, even those they'd managed to hide from others. Time and circumstance had never turned them into strangers. Enemies at one point. Antagonists. But not strangers.

"I followed you," she said simply.

He shook his head, mystified. "Why?"

"I have no idea," she answered honestly. "I was on my way to your house. I had questions, things I needed to talk about. But when I got there you were leaving. I followed."

"Where's your family?"

"Home," she said. "Sleeping, I hope."

"Well," he said awkwardly. He released a breath and looked off into the sky. "Thanks for coming. It's — good to see you."

She almost laughed at the banality of the statement, as if she'd dropped by to say hello and they'd had some tea. But then, he'd always been so stiff, awkward, no idea what to say. In the gaze he had on her, she saw her oldest friend. And yet he was so different. Older. Softer around the eyes, the first gray in his hair, the first wrinkles around his mouth.

She took the crystal heart from her pocket and opened her hand. They both looked at it, every facet of their history glittering in its deep red.

"Does this make us even?" she asked. "Finally."

He smiled lightly but didn't look at her. "I suppose it does."

"How did you know I'd go there and find this?" she asked.

"I know you, Lara," he said quietly. "I've always known you."

Agent Brower marched toward them, ponytail swinging. She was looking a little worse for wear — hair a bit wild, strands pulled from their tie, wisping around her pale face, shirt wilted, a corner of it untucked, flack vest crooked.

"How did you know these children were here?" she asked Hank.

"A patient I have, a girl named Angel," he said. "She claimed that there was a boy here, held captive. But she's troubled, so no one believed her."

The agent's expression was unreadable.

"But you did?" she asked. "You believed her?"

"I did."

"Did you think — I don't know — about calling *the police*? Instead of coming out here unsupported in the dead of night. You could have been killed. Both of you."

He ran it down for her, patiently — how Angel's claims had been investigated and dismissed, how he'd called a child advocate he knew, the detective working the case of a missing boy matching Billy Martin's description, how the detective couldn't come back here again without a warrant that he couldn't get without more evidence.

She watched him, pale, mouth open slightly. When he was done, she just stared a moment, brow furrowed, eyes stern and angry. Rain was about to tell him to stop talking, that he needed a lawyer, that they probably both did.

"You saved those kids," Agent Brower said finally. Her voice was soft. "They're *alive* because of you."

"That's what I do," he said, rubbing at his

eyes with thumb and forefinger, weary. "I try to save kids. Not usually like this, though."

Agent Brower nodded slowly, folded her arms around her middle.

"And bring justice when you can't?"

The agent looked back and forth between Hank and Rain, something doing battle on her face. How much did she know? Or was instinct, suspicion all she had? Rain suspected the latter. She averted her eyes, up to the sky.

"Do I need a lawyer?" Hank asked easily.

Agent Brower stared off at some point behind Rain and Hank, declined to answer.

"And you, Ms. Winter? How did you find yourself here? The last time we spoke you told me that you hadn't seen Dr. Reams in years."

Rain mustered her journalist self.

"I was planning on interviewing him for my story, the one we discussed," she said. "He was leaving his place when I arrived. And I followed."

Agent Brower cocked her head, frowning. It sounded every bit as crazy as it was.

"Why would you do that?" asked the agent.

Rain dipped her head, avoiding the other woman's intense stare. "I'm — not sure."

"We have a history," Hank interjected. "A connection. It's hard to explain."

Agent Brower's gaze continued back and forth between them, scowling, as if they were a puzzle that she couldn't solve.

"Were you tailing me, Agent Brower?" asked Hank. By the slight smile on his face, Rain thought he already knew the answer.

Brower's scowl dissolved into a similarly cryptic smile. "I'm the one asking the questions, Doctor."

Rain realized she was holding her breath, her shoulders hiked high. How was this going to go? Was she going to watch Hank get arrested? Was *she* going to jail? She made so many promises to her husband, just hours ago. She had broken them all. Would he forgive her this time? Would she lose him?

"Well," Agent Brower said with a sigh. "Tonight, you're heroes. Without you, I don't know what would have happened here."

Heroes. Villains. The lines were so much grayer than anyone knew, the truth so layered.

Rain saw him then, her husband, half running toward her. She got up and ran to him, fell into his arms and started to cry for the first time. He held her tight.

"Where's Lily?" she asked through her tears.

"I called your father," he said. "He came right over. What happened here? Rain, what's going on?"

She tried to tell him, but the words wouldn't come. He just held her. She felt Hank's eyes on her, a heat on the back of her neck.

"What's *he* doing here?" Greg asked, voice growing cold.

"It's — so complicated," she whispered.

He pulled away and held her by the shoulders, locked her with that intense stare. He was everything, the foundation of the life she'd built, in spite of Kreskey, in spite of Hank. He was the right choice, the healthy choice, proof that she'd survived the things she'd suffered. But how could he forgive her again?

"Tell me everything, Rain," he said. "The whole story."

It started back in the woods, a million years ago. Three children, all victims of a terrible man, all destroyed by what they encountered, a young girl losing her life. And now here they were again, but this time three children were saved. A winding path, a shadowy one, that led them both here together.

Yes, it was a long story. One she knew that she could never fully tell to anyone, not even her husband, even now, as much as she wanted to. That it was this more than anything that bound her to Hank; the truth that only they knew.

FORTY-FOUR

He loves you, I can see that, Lara. What I
guess I didn't quite realize — or maybe I
just didn't want to see it — is that you love
him, too. I thought he was just the man you
chose because there was no place in a
normal life for the relationship we share, for
the person that I have become. But, no. It's
more than that. I see it — his tenderness
and strength, your admiration and love,
your desire to be a better person for him,
his desire to take care of you — in spite of
yourself.

"She was never going to love you," says
Tess. "You must have known that. Even all
those years ago."

She's right, of course. She always is.

It was your tenth birthday party and we
were playing hide-and-seek in your huge
backyard. There had been a piñata, and the
grass was littered with candy, a red balloon
had escaped the bouquet and was trapped

in the tree high above the ground. The day was warm, almost hot — and we'd had too much cake and soda. All the other party guests were gone. And it was just the three of us. Tess was "it." You and I hid behind the great oak, with Tess looking for us on the other side, far from where she needed to be.

I had a little velvet box in my pocket. My mother had helped me choose your gift. A red crystal heart. I thought it was an extravagant gesture of my love. It cost ten dollars, a fortune, and the deep red, the way it glinted, it seemed like a precious gem.

Maybe it was the sugar rush, or how pretty you were in your dress, or the way the sun was setting and everything was summer golden. We were so close, shoulder to shoulder, the way we sat just now. I leaned in and kissed you, too quick, too hard, as awkward as any ten-year-old boy. You tasted like frosting.

You stared at me a moment, confused, I could tell. Embarrassed. Feeling foolish, I handed you the box. You opened it and smiled.

"Where are you guys?" Tess called out, whiny. "I'm tired. I'm going inside."

She always did that, got bored with the games and left. Remember?

Then you laughed, not mean, not cruel. Just with surprise, and the funniness of it all. It was sweet, a kind of nervous giggle. And I laughed, too — partially to save face. But mainly because even then I could see how awkward and silly love was, how vulnerable we all are, how unsure. We laughed awhile. I loved you so much that it didn't even matter whether you loved me back or not. Still doesn't.

"Thank you," you said, looking at the heart. "It's pretty."

There was no other kiss.

"You guys! Where are you?"

"Here!" you yelled. And I could tell that you were eager to run away.

I lingered a moment, burning with embarrassment and disappointment.

Then finally I followed you inside, where we all collapsed on your big couch, and your parents let us watch television — which they never did. *Star Wars* on the DVD player, the old one — with Han Solo and Chewy, and young Princess Leia.

And, yeah, Tess was right.

I knew even then that we would never be together. And that we always would be. You left it, the box with the heart in it, under the tree when you went inside. I took it and shoved it in my pocket. Kept it, all these years, until I left it for you to find again.

Inside, that other side of me, he is quieter than he has ever been.

How can he be angry at you, Rain?

You saved us. After all this time, you came back for us.

"You're such a man-baby," Tess says. "It was never her job to save you."

No, it's never our job to save anyone. It can't be. At the end of the day, we must all save ourselves.

I watch as they roll Billy on his stretcher toward the ambulance, and I walk over to stand beside him. He's so tiny, just the slightest bump beneath the white sheets, his eyes wide with fear. As I draw close he reaches for my hand and I take it.

"Will you come with me?" he asks.

He's engaged, still looking for help. This is a very good sign; it bodes well for his recovery. I glance back at you, but you're with Greg. He is wiping tears from your eyes, and you are looking up at him as if he's the sun and the moon. There's an energy around you both, a swirl — you're a family, with a child — whole, growing, with a life ahead of you.

I know that I couldn't have given you any of that. I am not the man your husband is.

"Of course," I tell Billy. And he closes his eyes.

Agent Brower comes up behind me.

"Dr. Reams." Her voice is sharp, official.

I wonder if she's going to arrest me, and part of me thinks maybe she should.

The things I have done, they're wrong. They are as evil as any crime ever committed, as arrogant and psychopathic. I have allowed my pain to turn me, part of me, into a monster. If she takes out her cuffs, I'll offer her my wrists. I may not need to be jailed, but *he* certainly does.

We move away from Billy, who is being attended to by the EMTs.

"When I was a teenager," she says and stops. She holds my eyes.

"Five minutes ago," I joke.

She doesn't smile but looks down at the ground. I know what she is about to tell me. I've done my research on Agent Brower. I wondered what drove her and dug around until I found out.

"When I was a teenager outside Boston, my younger brother was abducted and murdered by the Boston Boogeyman."

Her voice is low.

"He and I — we had it pretty rough," she says. "We suffered — various abuses, physical, psychological. My mother — she wasn't well. My dad had a drug problem. My brother got addicted to meth, ran away a few times. One time, he didn't come back."

"I'm so sorry," I say. I see the tension in her shoulders, the color drained from her face.

"Horrible things happened to my brother," she says. "And it changed me. Changed the way I saw the world and the people in it."

I want to apologize again but opt for silence instead.

"When Smith went free," she goes on, "I thought I wouldn't survive it, the injustice of it. It made me sick inside. I think — that's why I went into law enforcement."

"I understand that," I answer. "It makes perfect sense. You wanted to fight on the side of right."

The paramedics are about to lift Billy into the waiting ambulance. He's watching me, and I nod to him. I won't break my promise.

"When the Boogeyman was killed," she goes on. "I was already at Quantico. I know what they say, that there's no true justice. That even when evil is punished, it doesn't undo the things that have been done. Only forgiveness can salve the wound."

"But?"

"I was glad that someone killed him," she

says. Her voice has grown softer. "I was glad that the world was free of him and that he'd never hurt anyone else. I was *relieved.*"

I let her words float, drop a comforting hand on her arm. She's small but muscular, an intense energy coming off her in waves.

"I know just how you feel, Agent Brower."

She pulls away from me gently, moves back. She nods toward the ambulance, acknowledging that I have to go with the boy.

"Sometimes the wrong thing is the right thing," she says.

I climb in beside Billy.

"Sometimes that's true," I say to her.

As the doors close, Agent Brower and I lock eyes past my reflection in the glass. Her face is grim, her eyes green and clear. Sometimes it is true. But not always. I want to tell her about the toll it takes to do the wrong thing for the right reasons. But that's a line I don't think I should cross. I watch her grow smaller and smaller until she disappears.

Three children. A boy and two girls. We saved them tonight, Lara. Billy reaches for my hand and I take it in mine.

What if Kreskey hadn't found you in the woods that day? What if he hadn't taken me and Tess? What if I had left when I had the chance, not gone back for her? What if "he," that raging beast inside me, had never been born?

Would we have been here tonight? Would three other children have been lost instead of us?

There are so many questions that have no answers. Acceptance of these mysteries is the only way to peace. I'm finding my way. I hope you are, too, Lara.

■ ■ ■ ■

SIX MONTHS LATER

■ ■ ■ ■

FORTY-FIVE

In the end, the hero finds his way home.

After the trials have been faced, the demons bested, the hero returns and is welcomed into the arms of his love. Sexist, of course. Facile, definitely. There are no happy endings really. We just choose where we stop telling the story.

But am I a hero? Or am I villain? Do I deserve a happy ending?

I don't know the answer to that. But as Beth cooks in my kitchen — a savory chicken marsala — and we drink from a bottle of wine I've opened, listening to a band she favors, The Civil Wars, a peace has settled over me. For the first time in my adult life, I feel a sense of home.

Beth. Her body is lush; her hair — these glorious dark locks that are silky and thick in my hands. Her laugh never fails to make me laugh. Her eyes are expansive as sky, filled with wisdom and kindness. My feelings for her — it is not like what I felt for you, Lara. It's not young, impulsive, not grasping and clinging. It's not a passion that consumes like a wildfire, burning everything else to the ground. No, this is a love that lets other things grow, that breathes life, gives room. It allows for expansion.

"Sounds to me like you're in grown-up love," says Tess from over by the window.

"I am."

"What's that?" Beth asks, turning from the stove to look at me.

"Nothing," I answer. "I was going to say — I am happy. Happy you're here."

Tess offers a little chuckle. "Well, good for you."

Today, she is as she was that morning. A skinny kid with thick glasses and pigtails. I see her less and less. Which is a shame. Because she has been with me so long. I miss her humor, her unflinching honesty, her unconditional love. "It's about time."

Beth turns, wipes her hands on the apron at her waist — a thing she does that I find pleasantly old-fashioned. "Me, too."

Her smile wavers a little.

"I'm nervous," she admits.

I find this surprising. Dr. Beth Reynolds is a clinical psychiatrist, a researcher, a writer who has published in major journals.

She is a speaker, a caring doctor with a searing intellect, deep intuition, a powerful aura of authority. I've not yet seen her nervous.

"Rain Winter — she's famous, first of all. Maybe more so, she's iconic in *your* life," says Beth.

"She's just a friend," I answer, though this is not quite the truth.

"One who shares the most complicated part of your past."

"But that's the past," I answer. "Isn't that what you always tell me? This is now."

"Right."

Beth is the only person who knows about *him.* She has spoken to him, calmed him. She has accepted him as part of who I am. She has worked with me to help him integrate — I need his strength, his power. He needs my calm, the things I've learned as an adult and a doctor. We are no longer split as we were. Not entirely. But two parts of the same whole. He is not a beast in a cage.

Beth even knows about Tess. There are significant pieces of my history that I have not, cannot, share with her. And she knows better than to pry, because she is, above all her other sterling qualities as woman and physician, very wise. But I have shared those two with her, because really — it's me, isn't it? And Beth is the first person I've wanted to share all the parts of myself with. Everything. Most things.

When the buzzer rings, I open the gate. Then, after you've made your way up the drive, I watch as you emerge from your car, gather your things.

Today, you'll conduct our final interview for your story, our story.

The parts of it we're willing and able to tell.

Agent Brower's case has gone cold. The utter lack of real evidence means that connecting me to the murders of Eugene Kreskey, the Boston Boogeyman and Steve Markham is impossible. Which, of course, I knew. Yes, it's true that I was somewhere in proximity to each murder — either I lived there or was visiting for a lecture. But that is merely circumstantial, nothing on which to build an investigation, let alone prosecute a case.

Our presence on the property of Tom and Wendy Walters leading to the discovery of Billy Martin, Michele Racine and Olivia Grady is strange to say the least. Still there's a clear chain of circumstance, accompanied by some unstable reasoning on both our parts, for how we both found ourselves there. And who can argue with the results?

Three children saved — because of the tip of a troubled young girl, the dedication of her doctor, and his friend — victims of violence themselves.

The disappearance of my pack — my kill bag, as it were — is somewhat unsettling. I have not located it. But it's gone; it's obvious that someone took it. It has been six months since that night. I have a niggling suspicion that the bag is going to turn up. And I have a pretty good idea who might have taken it.

Meanwhile, Lara, there won't be any more letters, or visits to your neighborhood. I won't be eavesdropping on your monitors. Often.

Just enough.

So that I can make sure you're safe.

We have spent hours together over the last few months, as you and Gillian have interviewed me for your serial radio show, which will begin airing next month. The buzz is tremendous. I think it's going to be a huge success for you.

We have talked about our shared horror, the loss of our dear friend, the shattering nature of trauma — yours and mine, my journey to wholeness (sort of). How I have worked to save children brutalized as we were. We have used my knowledge to analyze the type of serial killer — if it is in fact that — who acts as a vigilante, delivering a form of justice where there was none.

We've talked about the question at the heart of our story. If what happened to us had not happened, what would have become of Billy, Michele and Olivia? Was there a balance to the universe after all? A divine plan? Were we its instruments?

That your story has no end. That there's a mystery at its center that will go unsolved — Who is the Nightjar? Will he strike again? — matters not at all. This story is not about the ending, is it, Lara? It is not about who killed Kreskey, Markham and Smith. There are others, too, but I have kept that to myself.

It's about the players, their journey, how they begin, how they evolve, and the point at which their stories cease to be told. There is always another monster to be slain, another trial to be overcome. There is always another chapter.

I can't promise he'll behave. But I can say that he's as quiet as he's ever been.

So, let's just say, for now, we will end our story here.

You stand and collect yourself at the door, preparing yourself for our final interview.

When you step inside, you will meet the woman I plan to marry, in the home where she and I hope to raise children of our own. Or give a home to children who need one, a place where they will be nurtured and loved. Or maybe we'll do both. I am in close contact with Billy, Michele and Olivia. They are my patients, my work with them pro bono. They are all in good foster homes, their families in therapy. I am optimistic that they — all of them runaways who fell victim to Tom and Wendy Walters — will find their way home. And, if not, I won't leave them to face their demons alone.

"Hi," you say, bringing the cool air in the door with you.

We embrace in the foyer. It's always a little awkward.

The energy between us, Lara, isn't easy; we are not just old friends.

But our conversations now are pleasant enough. When the microphone turns off, we all laugh sometimes, talk about our lives, our work. I know Greg will be happy when these interviews draw to a close; he doesn't like or trust me — and who can blame him? But he respects you. He understands that we have shared an ugly past that binds us. Close to your friends, right? Closer to your enemies.

Lara, you and I are like comrades in arms. We've done and seen things that wouldn't make any sense off the battlefield. We've seen the very worst in each other. And the best. We've seen all the gloom this world has to offer us. But we know the light now, too.

You and Beth exchange warm greetings, even a hug. The way you smile at her, and she at you, I could tell the two of you would be friends — under other circumstances. She invites you to stay for dinner when we are done. But you beg off.

"My family is waiting for me," you say. "But thank you. Another time."

Unlikely.

We climb the stairs to my office and close the door. It's my favorite time of day in here, late afternoon. The light is golden, washing surfaces, glinting in your hair.

"I just have a few more questions," you say, setting up the digital recorder on the table between us. "We won't be long."

"Why are you doing this?" I ask.

I've been wanting to talk about it, but this is our first conversation without Gillian present. You look up at me, dropping the hand that hovered over the record button back into your lap. Your wedding ring picks up the light.

"Knowing what you know about me, about us, about what we did," I continue. "What compelled you to do this story? Weren't you afraid of where it might lead?"

You bow your head, twist at the ring on your finger.

"I've thought about this, too," you say.

I wait for you to go on. I have some theories of my own, not the least likely of which might be your desire to self-destruct. When I think of all the choices you've made since Kreskey — to cheat on Greg with me, to follow me back to Kreskey, to lure Tess's killer into the house, to kill him with your own hands — none of them have been acts of self-preservation. In fact, the last healthy thing you did was hide in the hollow of the tree. Part of me wonders if you *wanted* to confess, if you wanted to answer for your crime. It's not unusual, so attached are we to the story of good rewarded, and evil punished.

"It was almost as if there were two of me," you say. "The one who almost died that day, the one who did what we did. And the one who emerged after — Rain Winter, journalist, wife, mother. That other girl was locked inside, buried deep. And once I let her free —"

You pause, not sure how to go on.

"You integrated," I offer. "The frightened girl with the woman you've become."

You consider it a moment. Then give an affirming nod. "Yes."

"There are only three of us who know the whole truth," I say. Agent Brower has her suspicions about me, but no proof. And I suspect she's running an agenda of her own. It's her who I think has taken the kill bag. What she'll do with it, I have no idea. Maybe it's a way to keep me in line, a warning not to continue. Or maybe it's something else. I keep this fact to myself.

"And none of us will ever tell," you say. "Not I, not you, not Harper. We'll take our secret to the grave."

"So, you weren't looking for answers, or punishment."

"No," you whisper. "I already had more answers than I wanted. I was looking to control the telling of what happened to us, I think. To control, to own it, to choose where our story ends."

"I understand."

You reach across the table and I take your hand in mine, a joining, a pact sealed.

"That part of it, who we were then, what happened to us —" You pause, pull your hand away to dig something from your pocket. Then you place the crystal heart on the table between us, where it picks up the sun and casts red flecks on the ceiling.

"Our story ends right here, Hank."

Tess stands by the window and watches, smiling sadly. She is as she would have been, like Sandy, willowy and blonde with kind, smiley eyes. Then, as I watch her, she fades into the sunshine.

FORTY-SIX

She rose before 5 a.m., the sun not yet lighting the sky, kissed Greg on the cheek.

"Mmm," he said, reaching for her.

She slipped from his grasp, causing him
to moan and roll over. She checked on Lily,
who was still sound asleep — thank goodness for small favors — then laced up her
sneakers at the door, slipped out into the
near-morning coolness. She jogged down
her drive, up the middle of the road through
her sleeping neighborhood, then through
the gate to the park.

She did not look for hulking shadows or
strange cars. She did not imagine fires and
earthquakes turning her pretty neighborhood to ash. Or at least, when the thoughts
came, she let them pass into the cool morning air.

The day stretched ahead of her as she
picked up her pace, footfalls on concrete,
the sound of her breath. Another runner

passed in the opposite direction with a wave, yet another overtook her from behind and disappeared. She was slow, steady; speed was not an option. That was okay. Mommy-and-Me Yoga (which basically meant no one got to do any yoga) this morning. Picnic lunch with the park mommies, a bitch and kvetch session that was nonetheless kind of fun now that it wasn't the only thing she had on the schedule. Final edits on their story "The Nightjar" in the studio tonight, Mitzi to come in the afternoon, Greg to take over in the evening. Another full day, one after which she would collapse into an exhausted pile of herself.

Don't let this slow you down, kid.

"Are you happy?" Dad wanted to know when he came for dinner on Sunday. "Are you well?"

"I'm not sure I have time to think about it," she'd laughed.

"Good answer," he said.

"Is it?" Greg looked a little miffed. "Is it a good answer?"

But, yes, more or less. She was happy.

"It is a good answer," said her father. "You can figure it out when the rush is over. Trust me, time to think about whether you're happy or not is not all it's cracked up to be."

Five miles later, she was back in the kitchen, making breakfast, when Lily's voice sounded over the monitor.

"Mommy. Hungy."

"Coming, bunny," she called.

"I got her." Greg from upstairs.

The bustle of morning — coffee brewing, Lily laughing, Greg running around looking for the keys that were in his pocket the whole time. Her phone pinging from somewhere — where was it? Once, twice, three times. She'd find it in a minute.

"Don't be late," she reminded him. "Mitzi has to go by six."

"I won't be late."

And then at the door, a kiss. A real kiss, where she snaked her arms around his neck and he held her tight. Because — she was a wife, too. A mother. A journalist. A runner. Herself. A wife who made promises to her husband, and kept them.

Don't let this slow you down, kid.

Greg left, and Rain turned on the live radio feed on her phone, Gillian's voice low and soothing.

"Brian Tome, the man who was tried and acquitted for killing his ex-wife and two sons in their home, was found murdered today on his isolated property in Ocala, Florida. FBI officials say that they are investigating this in connection with other recent murders in which the victims were accused of crimes for which they were found innocent, or unfit to stand trial. This investigation, and the others, are ongoing.

"Special Agent Brower, in charge of the case, had this to say — 'We are treating this like we would treat any serial murder case. No one has the right to kill in cold blood.'

"Gillian Murray, reporting for National News Radio."

The world seemed to stop, a hush falling. What did this mean?

Outside, Rain strapped Lily into her car seat.

"Time for Mommy-and-Me Yoga!" she said brightly. Lily bounced in excited anticipation.

It wasn't Hank, she thought. He hadn't murdered that man in Ocala. He had promised her that he would never do anything like that again; that he had that other side of himself managed. She'd believed him; he was done. He had Beth now, a calming influence in his life. Someone who understood his complexities, who loved him anyway. Maybe that's what he needed all along. Someone who didn't need him to be one man or the other.

So then, what? Another vigilante? A copy-cat? One inspired by the other vigilante killings?

What evidence?

A postscript to their story?

A sizzle of fear. Had she lost control of the narrative?

As she drove, Henry called.

"You heard, I guess," he said over the speakerphone.

"I did."

"Any theories?"

"No," she said. "Not one."

She'd spent a lot of time talking with Henry in recent weeks — trying to understand the dark web, murderabilia and the people who collect it, Kreskey's online fan club, and the one that had sprung up around the man people were calling the Nightjar.

"A journalist without a theory," he said. "I've never met one."

"Journalists don't have theories," she reminded him. "They follow the facts. The facts — that's the story. That and only that."

"Well," said Henry, cagey. "I do have one bit of info."

"Oh?"

"I heard that they found the kill bag at the scene."

Something tightened in her middle. Hank's missing bag. It had disappeared that night. Just gone. A big pack filled with tools, weapons, rope, tarps, duct tape. They'd both wondered when it might turn up.

She glanced in the rearview mirror at Lily, who was thumbing through a board book.

"And?"

"Supposedly they found something that connects it to the Markham murder. A knife that's similar to the weapon they suspect was used on Markham."

The jangle of alarm rattled her.

"Interesting." She kept her voice level, pulled into the parking lot.

Emmy was in front of the studio with Sage, waiting. She sent up a wave to Rain. Her other life, her other self. Mommy. Friend. Wife. It was waiting for her.

"Keep me in the loop?" said Rain. She lifted a hand to Emmy, held up a finger. *Just a second. I'll be right there.*

"Will do," said Henry and ended the call.

She dialed Hank, who picked up on the first ring.

"Don't worry about it," he said by way of greeting.

She didn't want to say anything else on the phone. After all, they were always watching. "You heard."

"Agent Brower called me," he said. She waited a beat. "For my help, my insights on this new development."

"Oh."

"It's fine," he said, his voice low and steady. "Really."

"How can you be sure?"

"I'm sure."

"It wasn't —" She knew she didn't have to finish the sentence.

"No," he said quickly. "God no. That's all done."

She'd have to take his word for it. What else could she do?

Her mind was on spin cycle. How did this fit into their story?

"Who, then, Hank?"

"I have some theories, one I've been working on with Agent Brower."

She waited.

"My guess is that we're dealing with a person in law enforcement or the military," he said, voice low. "I suspect that our perpetrator has been wronged or has lost a loved one. Our vigilante has lost faith in the system, even though he might be working within it."

She let the words settle.

The missing kill bag. There was only one person who could have taken it. The pieces fell into place. But why leave the bag? Was it a warning to her and to Hank? If they suspected Agent Brower had continued where Hank had stopped, they'd need to keep it to themselves and out of the story. Mutually assured destruction.

"How does Agent Brower feel about this profile?" she asked.

There was a heavy silence. "She's taking it under consideration.

"The bag they found was clean," he went on, intuiting her concern. "No DNA evidence. Just the knife that may or may not be the Markham murder weapon. It potentially links the crimes, but it doesn't bring them any closer to the perpetrator."

Rain watched Lily in the rearview mirror. She wasn't sure how to feel, how to weave this into their story — their story, hers and Hank's. Someone else was out there, delivering a certain brand of justice. That stranger inside her took a kind of dark pleasure in the thought.

She sat suspended — between her life in the light and her life in the dark, the past, the future. Emmy waved again, beckoning her.

"Hey, I was going to call you," he said into the silence.

"Oh?"

"I asked Beth to marry me."

Another impossibly complicated swell of emotion. Happy. Sad. A twist of regret. She still thought about what they shared that week. Sometimes. Sometimes she woke from dreams that shamed her.

"Congratulations, Hank," she said, putting a smile in her voice. "I'm so happy for you both."

"You assume she said yes."

"Didn't she?"

"She did," he said. "I don't know why. But she did."

She could hear how happy he was, and she felt the squeeze on her heart release.

Rain went around to the back seat, unstrapped Lily from her seat and lifted her, gathered up her things. Hank was still on speakerphone.

"Do you ever think about how things might have been different?" he asked. "If we'd made different choices."

She laughed, lightly, a little sad.

"I don't have time to think about things like that," she said, which was, of course, a lie. "When you and Beth have kids, you won't either. No more navel-gazing, Doctor. Just move forward, for you, but mostly for them. I gotta go. Mommy-and-Me Yoga."

He had a funny laugh, warm, smart,

knowing. He sounded far away.

"Goodbye, Lara."

Rain ended the call.

She jogged to Emmy, Lily in her arms, and together they walked through the door, setting off chimes. It was dim and peaceful inside, soft flute music, light incense.

They all spread out their mats, sporting their brightly colored yoga wear. All shapes and ages, mommies with time and money enough to be here.

"Welcome," said the lithe yoga teacher. She was a little too young, a little too hot to be teaching a mommy-and-me class, wasn't she?

The toddlers immediately descended into chaos, trying out their voices, greeting each other with laughter, waddling around. Which was fine — it was a safe space with everything soft, no hard corners, nothing sharp or unstable, everyone present, gentle and patient.

"I invite you to leave everything you brought with you — any stress, any worries, your list of things you have to do right after this — outside this room," said the teacher with a lovely smile. "Just be here, now — for yourself, for your little ones. And take the biggest breath you've taken all day."

Yes, thought Rain — she'd leave behind

the world with all its brutal edges, and hard consequences, all its confounding shades of gray, the chaos of the past, the uncertainty of the future. Just for a while. Lily ran back to Rain and tumbled into her folded lap.

And for just a little while, Rain would indeed let it all slow her down.

ACKNOWLEDGMENTS

Writers are hobbits. We settle into our space and spend the majority of our days dream weaving — if we're lucky. But we don't work alone. No novel makes it out into the world without a team.

My husband, Jeffrey, and our daughter, Ocean Rae, supply endless love, patience, kindness, and a life filled with light and laughter. I wouldn't be the person that I am or the writer that I am without them.

My agent Amy Berkower and her assistant Abigail Barce of Writers House keep the business of being a writer well in hand. I am grateful to them for their intelligence and guidance.

The sterling team at Park Row Books — my smart-as-a-whip editor Erika Imranyi, my partner-in-crime publicist Meredith Barnes, the elegant, in-charge Shara Alexander and powerhouse Margaret Marbury — well, a writer couldn't ask for more or better. My heartfelt gratitude goes to each of them, and to everyone from the brilliant art department, to eagle-eyed copy editor Jennifer Stimson, to the intrepid sales force.

I am blessed by a vast network of family and friends. My parents, Joe and Virginia Miscione, and my brother, Joey, are tireless floggers — spreading the word and facing books out in stores around the country. Erin Mitchell is early reader, voice of reason and champion. Susana Weymouth, Lorna Taylor and the board members of Tampa Bay Businesses for Culture and the Arts offer endless support in my local community, and bolster our burgeoning arts scene with all their efforts. And for all those faces I see again and again at my events locally and around the country, who buy books, who spread the word — family, friends, faithful readers — thank you. You probably don't know how much it means to a writer to have that kind of love and support. I'll tell you — a LOT!

I've cited this book before and it continues to be a touchstone for me in my writing; Donald Kalsched's *The Inner World of Trauma: Archetypal Defenses of the Personal Spirit* changed the way I thought about mental illness and the way I write about it. And *Essentials of Abnormal Psychology* by

V. Mark Durand and David H. Barlow is a resource I refer to again and again.

ABOUT THE AUTHOR

Lisa Unger is a *New York Times* and international bestselling, award-winning author. Her books are published in 26 languages worldwide, have sold millions of copies, and have been named "Best of the Year" or top picks by the *Today* show, *Good Morning America, Entertainment Weekly* and the *Sun-Sentinel,* among others. Her essays have appeared in the *New York Times,* the *Wall Street Journal,* NPR and *Travel + Leisure* magazine. Lisa lives in the Tampa Bay area of Florida with her husband, daughter, and labradoodle.